T0060604

Emma, Mr. Knightley and Chili-Slaw Dogs

Jane Austen Takes the South

Book #2

Mary Jane Hathaway

NEW YORK NASHVILLE LONDON TORONTO SYDNEY NEW DELHI

Howard Books
A Division of Simon & Schuster, Inc.
1230 Avenue of the Americas
New York, NY 10020

First Howard Books trade paperback edition July 2014.

Interior design by Jaime Putorti
Cover design by Peachpie Design Studio
Front cover dress photograph © Trevillion
Background images by Shutterstock

Manufactured in the United States of America

10 9 8 7 6 5 4 3 2 1

Library of Congress Cataloging-in-Publication Data
Hathaway, Mary Jane.
Emma, Mr. Knightley and chili-slaw dogs / Mary Jane Hathaway.
pages cm —(Jane Austen takes the South ; Book #2)
(ebook) 1. Women journalists—Fiction. 2. Caregivers—Family relationships—Fiction.
3. Dating (Social customs)—Fiction. I. Title.
PS3608.A8644E44 2014
813'.6—dc23 2013048430

ISBN 978-1-4767-7752-8
ISBN 978-1-4767-7700-9 (ebook)

For my children: Isabel, Ana, Jacob, Samuel, Edward and Elias.

Were I to fall in love, indeed, it would be a different thing; but I have never been in love; it is not my way, or my nature; and I do not think I ever shall.

—EMMA

Chapter One

Utter disaster on a cake platter.

Caroline Ashley stood back and surveyed her creation. The fabulous triple-layer fudge cake with light-as-air espresso-flavored chocolate frosting did not look like the photo in the magazine. It didn't look much like a cake at all. Leaning to the left and shedding gritty brown frosting in ultraslow motion, this cake wasn't quite what her mother had requested for her Wednesday bridge group.

The recipe looked downright simple. Mix together, bake, frost. How hard could it be? Caroline blinked the sweat out of her eyes and stared around the sweltering kitchen, groaning at the sight. Flour, mixing bowls smeared with batter and butter-cube wrappers dotted the workspace. A purist would never have upgraded from the original Civil War–era fixtures, but her mama was not a purist. The long marble counters, custom Mississippi-oak cabinets and a heated flagstone floor were all top-of-the-line. The hammered-copper sink was original, but it was obscured by dirty dishes more often than not.

Their cook, Angie, loved to create her masterpiece desserts in here, although Mama had been giving her more and more time off. All the fancy kitchen equipment was going to waste on Caroline's watch. She was trying, and failing, to be a personal chef. Not that it was a role she'd ever wanted.

Lifting the cake platter, she carried it to the freezer, sliding it in between the bags of sweet peas and a carton of vanilla ice cream. In only an hour the bridge group would show up, and there wasn't time to make another. She could pray the cake would miraculously right itself and set into something more like the picture. Or she could run away from home.

"Something smells good." Caroline whirled at the sound of the voice, even though she knew the speaker before she saw him. Brooks Elliot, her friend since before she'd learned to ride a two-wheeler down the long driveway, had a habit of showing up at all the best—and the worst—times. At his side stood a golden retriever, mouth lolling open, tongue half-out in a big doggy smile. Brooks looked cool, calm and collected in a perfectly tailored deep blue suit. His spotless white shirt and pale blue silk tie completed the picture of effortless style. It was unbelievably irritating.

He cocked his head. "Hiding something?"

Caroline rolled her eyes. "Not from you, Professor." She liked to use his title in a chirpy little voice that got on his nerves. Opening the freezer door, they surveyed the cake-that-was-not-a-cake together. "Although I don't trust Absalom within five feet of anything edible." She reached down to scratch behind the dog's ears, loving how the retriever's whole body wagged against her leg.

"Hmmm." Brooks pretended to be choosing his next statement carefully, but as her oldest friend, he knew he never had to watch his words. "Not so sure you need to take precautions."

"Hilarious. You're making fun of my cake, but I saw this dog eat through the leg of your grandpa's best rocker."

"Hey, we don't bring up the past. Right, Ab?" Brooks reached down and ruffled the dog's fur. Those two were thick as thieves. Better not get on the bad side of one, or you'd be on the bad side of the other.

It felt wonderful to stand inches from the frosty freezer. She wanted to crawl inside and never come out. But there was a bridge party to entertain. She closed the door and shrugged. The strands of hair sticking to the back of her neck reminded her she still needed to shower, and the reflection in the stainless steel door didn't argue. Blond hair escaped from her ponytail in several different directions. Her cheeks flushed pink, green-blue eyes just smudges. Behind her was a wavery image as familiar as her own. A head taller than she was, with sandy-blond hair and dark brows, Brooks was the kind of man that made women check his hand for a ring. When they'd first met, she'd been too young to think of him that way and preferred dreaming of boy bands and the quarterback at her high school. But as the years passed, she couldn't help noticing how the rest of the female population reacted to him. Every year it was more and more obvious that he was the catch of the tiny town of Thorny Hollow, and beyond.

She met his gaze in the reflection and grinned when he winked at her. Brooks, the consummate flirt. They were related, sort of, by marriage, and he always occupied that hazy area between cousin and guy friend. Whatever he was, catch or not, he was never less than a perfect gentleman.

"I'm sure it will be just fine after it sets." She spun to face him, tugging on the strings of her red gingham apron, which seemed to have tied themselves into a knot.

Brooks gently turned her around and brushed away her hands, loosening the apron strings. Absalom wedged his furry body between them, his tail thumping against the back of her legs in a steady rhythm of happiness. "How's the book?" Brooks asked.

Oh, that. "Coming right along."

"I think you should call it *The Never-Ending Story*." His expression in the refrigerator-door reflection was completely serious.

"Hardy har har." It was just a little bit funny, she had to admit. Her idea of the great American novel had morphed into a *Gone with the Wind* remake, which had become a historical saga spanning the Russian Revolution. Why? Because she was bored. It was not a great reason to write a book and it showed. She'd been working on it for two years and it wasn't even close to being finished.

"You know, just because your mama asks for a chocolate cake doesn't mean you have to make one."

She stared up at the high, arched ceiling, biting back words. It was easy for Brooks to give advice on family matters when he lived a happily independent life, or as independent as that of a good Southern son could be. He was still expected to come home for weddings and holidays and weekends regularly. But being a journalism professor at Midlands came with respect, a nice house and a decent distance from his cranky-pants father. No such luck for her.

"Bravard's Bakery makes a great triple-layer cake. You could have asked me to pick one up on the way through town. You know

I'm here almost every weekend. Absalom's so used to the drive, we're going to switch places next time. He'll drive and I'll stick my head out the window and yell at passing cars."

She snorted at the image but regretted the ungenerous thoughts of a moment ago. Brooks lived a few hours away in Spartainville, but that didn't mean he was immune to the call of the needy parent. "Your grandma moved in to keep your father company, but she wants to get out of that old house every now and then, too. Your mom passed away so quickly, I don't think he had a chance to come to terms with what happened. I think he's just lonely without her."

"I'm not sure why. Maybe he misses the constant bickering. You know, I don't really mind hanging at the old homestead every weekend, but with our grandmother off on another cruise, Manning needs to step up once in a while."

"They're still in the honeymoon phase." Brooks's brother and her cousin were happily ignoring the entire family now that they had subjected the town to an over-the-top Southern-style wedding. Ten bridesmaids in rainbow-hued gowns, ten groomsmen in matching bow ties, a catered reception featuring every Southern delicacy known to mankind and a live band playing in an old barn for a dance that went on until dawn? It was enough wedding to last Caroline all year. Maybe more. Nobody could get married simply out here. That was just one more reason she'd never dreamed of every girl's "special day." Too much fuss, too much money spent on nothing real and everyone else had to play along just to make the bride happy.

Brooks sighed. "It's been a year. Since you take full credit for getting them together, it's up to you to tell them it's time to rejoin the real world. Hard as it is to believe, I do have a life in Spartainville."

"Did you finally find a girlfriend?" She knew even before she turned around that he would say no. Brooks just wasn't the type to marry. In fact, he didn't really date. He'd never said much about it, but she knew his growing up as a child of an unhappy couple made him less than eager to enter into his own romantic union.

"You'll be the first to know." He lifted the apron strap over her head and hung it on the peg near the back door. "Why are you cooking on a hot day like this, anyway?"

"Because my mama asked, and I always feel like I need to prove myself in the kitchen."

His mouth twitched. "Finley, a brilliant journalist can't be expected to bake triple-layer cakes. It wouldn't be fair to the rest of the world if you were that perfect."

She shot him a look. He would never give up that silly nickname. Caroline Ashley had nothing in common with Finley Peter Dunne, great American political humorist and newspaperman of the turn of the century. But Brooks had called her Finley ever since he saw some little sketch she'd made about their high school principal, and that was that.

Brilliant journalist. He was just being kind, but she smiled as the words reverberated in her head. Coming from Brooks, it meant a lot. Graduating with highest honors and landing the job of a lifetime after her internship at the *Washington Post* still gave her a glow of pride. It was the best thing she'd ever done.

The smile faded from her lips. It was the only thing, really.

"I'd trade all that supposed brilliance for a decent approximation of that magazine picture," she said.

"And a chili-slaw dog."

"You know me so well." Absalom's head went up at the mention of a chili-slaw dog. The only other creature who loved them more than Caroline was the golden retriever sniffing around the large kitchen, hoping for edibles dropped by the careless cook.

"When you have a big wedding like Manning and Debbie Mae, you'll have to have one long table of chili-slaw dogs instead of the cheese straws and hush puppies."

"I'm not jumping on the marriage train. I feel like Pleasant Crump most days, but finding a husband isn't the answer." Crump was famous in these parts for being the last living Confederate soldier until he passed away in the 1950s.

"That's a bit dramatic."

"Maybe to you. As a man, you can take all the time you want, but women are groomed for the big white day from the moment the doctor slaps our little bottoms in the delivery room." She wiped her forehead with a kitchen towel and watched Absalom vacuum up all the cake crumbs from the floor. "And anyway, I've seen what happens in a Thorny Hollow wedding, and even if I wanted chili-slaw dogs, I wouldn't get to have them. The bride never gets her way. It's all run by the old ladies, every single detail."

"Probably right."

"Speaking of old ladies, if I don't get showered and spiffed up, Mama is going to have a breakdown when the bridge group gets a look at me."

"And I've got to get home. Come on, Ab." Brooks patted his leg and the golden retriever reluctantly withdrew his nose from under the cabinets. The dog looked up at Caroline with hope in his bright black eyes and she shook her head.

"Chocolate isn't good for dogs, buddy."

"I don't think that chocolate is the real gastronomical danger here." Brooks cut his eyes to the freezer and bolted out the back door, with Absalom hot on his heels. The kitchen towel she tossed at him thumped harmlessly against the leaded, diamond-pattern window of the antique kitchen door as it swung closed.

Caroline stood for a moment, listening to the two of them cross the old wooden wraparound porch and head for the car. Brooks had been driving back to Thorny Hollow almost every weekend to fix windows or oil squeaky hinges or even weed the flower beds. That a full-time caretaker lived in a carriage house a short distance from the main house didn't seem to matter at all to Brooks's father. His marriage had been notoriously acrimonious, but he seemed unmoored without Nancy.

Grabbing a clean towel and trotting upstairs to the bathroom, Caroline sighed. Almost three years ago her daddy had passed away, leaving her mama in absolute shock. Lonely, lost and refusing to leave her room. When Mama asked Caroline to come home, she hadn't hesitated. She walked away from the job she loved and the years she'd put into her career because that's just what good daughters did. It killed her to leave it all behind, but she'd done it.

Rejoining the workforce was going to be harder than simply packing a few boxes, if she was honest with herself. She'd been writing freelance articles and doing online news services, but it wasn't the same as joining the hustle and bustle of a big city and a powerful company. She'd lost her groove, her confidence. She might not be completely happy here, but she knew this town and she knew how to stand around in pearls at a party. Taking care of her mom had turned into taking the easy way out.

The ornately framed bathroom mirror showed a clearer version of the stainless-steel-fridge reflection, but this one mercilessly highlighted her shiny forehead and sweaty hair. Poor Brooks. He didn't seem to mind the hot mess he'd seen, but a tiny part of her wished he had walked in before the cake, not after. At least she wouldn't have been drenched in sweat.

She put a hand under the dribbling showerhead and tested the water, knowing it took at least four minutes for the water heater to kick in for this part of the house. Her mother had recently redone her private bath in marble and heated stone tile, junking the claw-foot tub and built-in antique vanities despite Caroline's protests. But this bathroom still had the original fixtures. Caroline ran a finger along the curved, cool edge of the claw-foot tub before her, smiling at the pink porcelain. She'd hated this tub when she was younger, wishing she had a sparkling-new shower stall and gleaming fixtures like Debbie Mae's. The eighties had been the age of glass and chrome, of Robert Palmer video vixens with slicked-back hair and bright red lips. It was not the era of pink claw-foot tubs and copper fixtures and itty-bitty pink, octagonal tiles covering one enormous wall.

But her daddy had refused to change a thing about their home, saying it was unnecessary. Just like the tiny gap between her front teeth. He'd said it was the way she'd been made and it was beautiful. The thought of him sent a sharp pain through her. She acknowledged it with a quick prayer of thanksgiving. Gratitude helped the loss, somehow. She was grateful for him, for his quiet humor and stubborn personality. Wishing him here didn't help one bit, but she still did. Their little family just wasn't the same without him, especially her mama.

If only her mama hadn't given up everything when she married. If only she had kept her job, maybe working on the side while raising a family. But that wasn't done. Not back then, and not around Thorny Hollow. Now her husband was gone and Mama had no reason even to get out of bed. No matter how much she loved them both, Caroline felt a chill at the thought of marriage. They'd been happy, so happy, but what happens when the person who is your everything dies? What then?

Caroline stuck her hand into the cold spray of water. No, she wasn't ready for any kind of serious commitment. She wanted to have a good job and be professionally fulfilled before she vowed a lifetime of love to another person.

All of this was far away from the pressures of the moment. She hauled in a breath and let it out slowly. It didn't make any sense to worry about how her husband would treat her professional life because she didn't have a single prospect for either at the moment. The tepid water shifted to warm and she shrugged off her clothes. Stepping carefully into the old tub and drawing the curtain closed, she tried not to focus on the problems ahead. Mainly, that her mother was minutes away from welcoming ten of Thorny Hollow's finest bridge players and there was no cake.

I'm not jumping on the marriage train. Brooks felt a smile cross his face. He completely understood that decision. His parents had spent four decades alternating between utter devotion and fighting over which of them got to file for divorce first. Until-death-do-we-part sounds so romantic unless you've fallen out of love and into something close to hate. It had been terrifying as a child. As an adult, it was merely annoying. The constant drama was exhausting.

Caroline would set her own course, he was sure. As much as her mother might wish for her to stay in Thorny Hollow forever, she was going to leave sooner or later.

A miracle of modern machinery, the air conditioner shifted its output from warm to tolerably cool. Absalom let out a short bark as the windows rolled back up, then sat back against the seat, ready for the trip home. The best dog in the whole world, Absalom didn't mind the drive from Spartainville at all and loved to chase the squirrels in the country. But it would be nice not to pack his food up every Friday and Sunday evening.

Backing into the main drive, Brooks glanced up at the stately Ashley home. "I just can't imagine Caroline living the rest of her life in that big ol' house, Ab. If she's afraid of getting shuttled down the aisle, there were other ways to cut the apron strings than by getting married."

He needed to help her find one before she wasted another three years at the mercy of her mother, making light conversation and bad cakes.

The large living room buzzed with the soft, cultured voices of Thorny Hollow's finest female citizens. The air-conditioning was barely keeping up with the humidity, and the contrasting perfumes made Caroline's head swim. Bright sunlight glanced off the antique brass sconces and reflected onto the high ceiling, throwing the intricately carved medallion into a spotlight. Women moved through the room, greeting one another or avoiding one another, depending on past squabbles. To Caroline, it seemed the opposing currents of guests in single-strand pearls and high heels created a powerful whirlpool, and she was the center of the vortex.

She glanced at the cut-crystal punch bowl, ice floating gently on the surface of the light pink lemonade, and wished she could drink it by the pitcher. A cool shower had helped a bit with her baking-induced hyperthermia, but she felt parched. She didn't even like pink lemonade. It reminded her of every boring party she'd attended in this very living room in the past twenty-five years. But it didn't matter how thirsty she was, these parties had a rhythm, and it wasn't time for iced lemonade.

These ladies were of the generation in which you didn't leave the house without heels and full makeup. A relaxed spring bridge party wasn't anything like it sounded to an outsider. It was serious business in Thorny Hollow.

"Hello, Caroline." Mrs. Gray was at her elbow, five feet of perfectly coiffed Southern womanhood. She smiled the sort of smile that gives smiles a bad name. Her gaze flickered over Caroline's outfit, coming to rest at her throat. She blinked at the multicolored strand of pearls and green-hued gemstones, her nose wrinkling infinitesimally at the unorthodox display. Her own lengthy strand of unblemished white pearls swooped in graceful lines down the bright orange linen of her dress front. "I hear Brooks Elliot stopped by today."

"Yes, he was on his way home." Caroline felt off-kilter. That's what happens when you daydream at a bridge party. Someone sneaks up behind you, like a shark zeroing in on the trail of blood in the water.

"Marian Birdsong said she invited him to her dinner party tonight but he declined. It's curious that he would have stopped here but he's too busy for a nice home-cooked dinner at Marian's." Mrs. Gray's tiny teeth made another brief appearance.

Not curious at all. Marian Birdsong was determined to marry by her twenty-fifth birthday and had approximately eight months left to snag a husband. The entire town knew her deadline, and good, honest men fled at the sight of her. "I think he needed to help his father with some repairs."

Mrs. Gray threw back her head and let out a trill of laughter. "Repairs? The Elliots have their own handyman!" She patted Caroline on the arm and blinked up at her in a kindly way. "I didn't mean to betray his little white lie. Forget I ever said anything. I'm sure he'll bring her to meet you very soon, whoever she is."

Before Caroline could muster a response, Mrs. Gray turned to a knotted group of women. They parted and absorbed her within seconds. Caroline could feel her pulse thumping in her temple. The very idea of Brooks's lying to her was laughable. First of all, he wasn't afraid of telling anyone the truth. Secondly, she'd be the last person on earth he'd lie to because . . . She nibbled at her lip, trying to pin down the reason for her certainty. Because they were friends, and friends were honest with each other.

"Why, Miss Ashley, I declare you are prettier and prettier every day!" She'd been caught unfocused again. Their longtime neighbor Mrs. Reynolds squeezed Caroline's upper arms as she spoke, her wrinkled hands surprisingly strong. The woman's hair was the shade of a blackbird's wing, which would have been striking if Mrs. Reynolds hadn't been close to eighty. Still, her pale blue eyes were bright with warmth.

"Thank you," Caroline said, and meant it. There were worse

things than being fawned over by old women. To them, she was charming and pretty and smart. The vision of the ruined cake flitted through her mind and she almost groaned. She was smart until they saw she couldn't bake worth a darn.

"When are you getting married? You need to hurry or I won't be able to attend."

"Are you moving?" Mrs. Reynolds's son had a successful law practice in Memphis, but somehow Caroline couldn't see Mrs. Reynolds in Memphis. She was Thorny Hollow through and through.

"No, dear." She leaned closer, dropping her voice. "But I'm getting older, you know."

Caroline wanted to laugh, but wasn't sure if she should. Apparently, the ever-present marriage harangue had a new twist: *hurry and get married before I die*. "I'm sure we've got plenty of time. And Mama isn't ready for me to move out."

Mrs. Reynolds dropped her hands from Caroline's arms and shot a glance across the room. "She'll have to let you go sometime. It's not right for you to pass your best years in this old place."

"I'm perfectly happy here." Caroline was happy, truly. A little bored, maybe. But a few personal projects and some close friendships got her pretty close to contentment. If she never had to cook, life would be perfect.

"My granddaughter is moving here next week. You remember Lauren? She's just finished her master's program. She graduated at the top of her class and has her hands full of job offers. You two should go to lunch sometime."

"That would be lovely." Caroline had heard a bit too much about Lauren Fairfield over the years, and it was mostly how Lauren amazed everyone with her brilliance. Caroline shook off the niggle of jealousy. How insecure was she to be irritated with Mrs. Reynolds's grandmotherly bragging? "Have her call me as soon as she gets to town."

"Caroline dear, could you bring me my pillow?" Mama's green eyes shrewdly cataloged Mrs. Reynolds's every movement as if she could tell they were discussing weddings and moving and Caroline's present happiness. Mama beckoned Caroline to her side, as if she could hear the conversation from across the room and didn't approve. Smoothing her light plum silk dress over her knees, she gave a tight smile.

They looked so much alike, mother and daughter. Caroline knew exactly how her lids would sag as she aged, how her pert jawline would develop a bit of softness, and how the slight curls in her hair would become nearly unmanageable coils in time. It was comforting to look at her mother and know no surprises were in store for herself.

"Yes, ma'am." Caroline retrieved the small, embroidered pillow from the wingback armchair and brought it to the couch. The red velvet settee was a family heirloom but hideously uncomfortable. Without a little lumbar support, Mrs. Ashley would complain for days afterward. Of course, she complained a lot about almost everything, but Caroline did her best to nip it in the bud.

"It's about time to serve the punch, don't you think?" Her mother tucked the little pillow behind her back and tugged a lace handkerchief from her sleeve. Patting a small line above each brow, she heaved a sigh that spoke of deep suffering and unrelenting pain. Caroline would have suggested she go and rest if she wasn't well, but the truth was that her mother was perfectly well. She just enjoyed the drama.

"Of course, Mama." Thank goodness. Then the bridge party

would begin in earnest. Caroline wouldn't think of what would happen after, of the ladies waiting patiently for a bite of the lumpy, gritty mess in the freezer.

As she neared the punch bowl, a movement caught her eye. Brooks stood just outside the living room, wiggling his fingers at her, crooked smile wider than usual. Absalom's big head was peeking around the corner of the doorframe, mouth wide-open in a lolling grin. She cocked her head, hand poised over the punch ladle.

He waved her toward the kitchen. "Finley, get over here," he whispered.

"I'll be right back," she murmured to no one in particular. Scooting into the hallway, she practically ran into his chest.

"Whoa, there." He laughed and cupped her bare shoulders in his hands. Absalom nudged her leg with a wet nose.

"Your dog just kissed the back of my knee. What are you doing here? Are you rescuing me from the crazy-lady guild? Because it won't work. They'll track us down in minutes."

His eyes traveled from her sleeveless, green-blue, patterned silk top to the large green bow at her waist to the bright blue of her above-the-knee skirt. His gaze reached her kitten-heeled sandals with a matching green bow at each toe, took in her perfectly pedicured feet and traveled back up to her glossy, blow-dried hair. She felt like the Christmas tree in a grade-school play; all she needed was a giant gold star on the top of her head. From his expression, he was comparing her to the sweaty, panicked mess of an hour ago . . . and trying desperately not to laugh at her party getup. His dimples were deep indents, even though his lips were pressed firmly together. He finally let out a low whistle. "Tempting, but, no. I just wanted to tell you there was something in the kitchen for you."

"Is it a teleporter? Because I'm going to need one when my mother sees that sorry excuse for a dessert." Caroline suddenly felt tired, as if she'd run a marathon. The party hadn't even really started yet and she was ready to call it quits. Dodging questions about her single status and fending off snide comments over Brooks was just the beginning.

He grabbed her hand and tugged her down the hallway, with Absalom trotting behind them. "If I had one, it'd be all yours."

On the kitchen counter was a small paper bag and a bright pink cake box printed with a delicate trim of forget-me-nots, the signature design of Bravard's Bakery. Caroline turned to him, eyes going wide. "You didn't."

"I did. And a little something from Shorty's. Did you have any lunch? I figured you were too busy creating the Franken-cake."

"I was saving space for the pink lemonade." Between the heat and the anxiety and the cake flop, she was running on empty. Her breakfast bagel seemed years ago.

He snorted. "Which you hate."

"Well, desperate times and all that." Caroline bypassed the cardboard box, which she knew would contain a perfectly delicious triple-layer chocolate cake, and grabbed for the bag. "I can smell a chili-slaw dog."

"Did I surprise you?"

"Totally. And I never thought that would happen."

"There's a first time for everything." Brooks grinned, his smile lighting the room. "I would hate to hear that you'd died of hunger halfway through the bridge party." He stuffed his hands in his pockets and rocked back on his heels, looking immensely pleased with himself. Absalom wagged his tail so hard it looked a if he were going to lift off.

She lifted out the small paper container and inhaled the scent of a grilled-to-order hot dog topped with thick chili and sweet, creamy slaw. The bright smear of mustard on the toasted bun was Shorty's trademark. She tore off a bit of the bun and tossed it to Absalom, who caught it neatly in his mouth and swallowed it whole. "I can never repay you for this one."

"I wasn't thinking of payment." He paused, as if thinking about whether to say any more. "I don't like to see you trapped here."

Caroline swallowed, her smile fading away. "I'm not trapped. I just don't like parties."

"Okay." He held up his hands in a don't-shoot gesture. "I might have used the wrong word. I know you're working on free-lance projects and the never-ending book, but it might be time to get out into the world again."

Caroline took another bite to keep from having to answer. She saw the hesitation on his face, the worry in his eyes. He didn't want her to be angry with him, but she felt irritation rise up in her chest. She was trying so hard to balance duty against her own ambition; did she really need a lecture on getting ahead?

But that wasn't exactly fair. He wasn't saying she had to be famous or wealthy. Brooks only wanted her to be fulfilled, and he knew being a hostess for her mama wasn't going to cut it.

She sighed. "You're right."

His relief was almost palpable. "I'm not trying to boss you around."

"I know." That was all she could think to say. She could make no promises at the moment as she hid in the kitchen, holding a slopping chili-slaw dog.

"Come on, Ab. Let's let her eat in peace. You've already had yours." Brooks opened the kitchen door and paused. "If you're really that grateful, here is one thing you could do for me. My dad's supposed to go to a party next weekend. My grandmother isn't back from her cruise yet and he won't go alone. He's guilted me into going and I need a date."

Caroline froze, mouth full of chili and slaw. "Who?" The word came out sounding like *moo*.

"Well, you, of course." An expression flitted over his face that she didn't quite catch, but the next moment he was smiling. "Who did you think?"

She swallowed and waved a hand. "No, I mean, whose party?"

"Oh. The Werlins are having a housewarming party."

"They moved?" Where had she been? Under a rock? The Werlin estate was one of the most beautiful in Thorny Hollow.

"No, they had some renovation work done on their house and want to celebrate." Brooks shrugged. "I would normally pass on something like this, but our families are old friends." He grabbed for Absalom's collar as he tried to sneak back into the kitchen. "Come on. Just one evening won't kill you. What else have you got planned?"

Nothing, obviously. "If I'd known this was the price of a chili-slaw dog . . . ," she muttered under her breath. She would have added a smile, but Brooks knew her so well it wasn't needed. Too bad his grandmother was still in Jamaica. Everyone had a good time when Blanche Elliot was at a party. "I'll only agree if you drive a car and not that old motorcycle. Remember when you picked me up for Debbie Mae's rehearsal dinner? I have helmet hair in all the pictures."

"It's not an old motorcycle; it's a classic Triumph 6T Thunderbird. Marlon Brando had one." Brooks looked honestly confused by her request. "You looked fine. Bring a brush if the helmet bothers you."

She waved the chili dog in the air. "It's not just the hair. I was wearing a dress! I had to keep my knees clamped against your hips the whole time to keep my skirt from blowing over my head."

"I thought you were scared." He shrugged. "I suppose I could bring the car, but someone always parks behind me at those big parties, no matter how much trouble I take to find a good spot. Then it's impossible to leave when I want, how I want."

"Maybe Mrs. Werlin will let you park out in a field somewhere." Caroline thought they would likely get boxed in by late arrivals, but she couldn't bear the idea of riding over on the back of his clunker Brando-mobile.

"I better get back home. Don't overdose on pink lemonade."

"Never." She grimaced. The two were gone in the next second, the kitchen door thudding closed. Caroline took another bite, chewing thoughtfully. Mrs. Gray's ugly insinuations echoed in her head. He didn't seem like a man who was hiding his personal life. Then again, maybe he didn't think she could handle whatever developments his personal life had taken. They were friends, just as they'd always been, right? Nothing had changed since she'd moved home.

A small voice in the back of her head whispered the truth. When she worked at the *Post*, they had enjoyed long, complicated phone calls that covered politics, philosophy and the state of journalism in America. But now? She looked down at the remains of the chili-slaw dog in her hand. Now their world had shrunk to complaining about the heat, conspiring to provide suitable desserts and juggling familial duties.

Or maybe it was only her world that had shrunk. Maybe Brooks was still discussing politics, philosophy and journalism . . . but not with the girl hiding in the bright yellow kitchen with a smear of chili on her upper lip.

The thought made her heart drop in her chest. He'd remained loyal even though she'd lost her spark, her wit, her Caroline-ness. It seemed as if her life were becoming one long round of parties. This certainly wasn't what she had envisioned when she'd come home three years ago.

Indistinct murmurs from the living room reminded her that time was of the essence. She quickly took a few swallows of iced tea. It was time to branch out, try new things. Working on the never-ending novel wasn't what she wanted to do with her life.

She checked the front of her dress for any telltale splotches of chili, slaw or mustard.

Brooks was right. The image of his face flashed through her mind. He'd been afraid to say anything. She hated that he felt there was something they couldn't talk about, but apparently, her self-imposed exile was a sticky topic. He must have thought she'd get upset at being told to head back to the real world. And she had, just a bit. She had let things go too far, for too long. It was time to ease her way out of the family home. She was a grown woman and needed to act like one. Faking Baking 101 and serving pink lemonade wasn't her God-given purpose in life. Of course, she wasn't even going to think about telling her mama that right now. She had a bridge party to host.

What did she say? Just what she ought,

of course. A lady always does.

—EMMA

CHAPTER THREE

It's been forever. I almost wondered if you'd forgotten about me." Caroline wasn't trying to sound pathetic, but she'd missed Debbie Mae's quirky sense of humor. She'd also missed their shopping trips. For the first time in over a year, they were hitting the small boutiques, scouring the racks for the perfect dress.

"Oh, honey." Her cousin reached over and gave her a quick hug, her flowery perfume as familiar as an old family photo. The rack of bright summer dresses rattled between them. "I never forgot you, not for one little second."

"Brooks told me newlyweds are just that way so we thought we'd give you some space." Caroline extracted a peony-pink dress with a thin organza sash at the Empire waist.

"Ha! Like Brooks knows anything about newlyweds. Blanche probably told him that. I just love that old lady."

Old lady wasn't the right term for Blanche Elliot. She was seventy-eight years young and was on her tenth cruise for single seniors. She didn't bother to watch her waist, indulging in chocolate and pie whenever she wanted because she went out dancing three times a week. The words *old lady* and *Blanche* didn't fit in the same room.

"She's always asking me whether Brooks has a girlfriend. Has he said anything to you?" asked Debbie Mae.

Caroline froze, one hand holding out a bright yellow sheath dress. "No. Why would she ask?" Had he met someone and Caroline was the very last to know?

Debbie Mae brushed back a stray curl and shrugged. "Not sure, but I think Blanche is afraid he's never going to settle down."

Caroline frowned. "Why do people call it *settling down* when it's a man and *finding the right one* when it's a woman? Like the man has been leading an adventure and the woman has spent all her time searching for a good mate."

Debbie Mae held up an elegant, pale blue, strapless dress that was embroidered with gold thread. "I have no idea. She probably thinks he should get married before he's too old."

Caroline paused, considering her cousin, searching for the right words. "Too old? What does that even mean? You're making it sound as if he's half-dead."

"Hey, don't shoot the messenger. I'm sure she just wants him to be happy!" Debbie Mae said, blue eyes wide, as if it were the most obvious thing in the world.

"But, Debbie Mae"—Caroline hung up the bright yellow dress and met her cousin's gaze—"he *is* happy. Why is married any better than unmarried? His parents spent years shouting at each other, and now his father is lost without the woman he couldn't even stand. I don't think that's exactly the perfect advertisement for entering into the married state."

The boutique's sound system blared out the final bass beats of the techno song, and the momentary silence was deafening. The next song started with a high-pitched note liked a siren.

"I understand what Blanche means." Debbie Mae held up a hand. "Wait, let me explain. You know *Emma*, the Jane Austen book?"

Caroline nodded. "I never read it, but I saw the ads for that PBS miniseries. Loved the clothes. In fact . . ." Her voice trailed off as she pulled out another gown, palest lilac, draping in soft folds to the floor. "This looks like it should be in their costume department."

Debbie Mae snorted. "Not with spaghetti straps. A Regency woman would be considered a woman of ill repute in that."

"Ill repute?" Caroline pretended to consider it. "Well, I could live with that, I suppose, for a color this gorgeous."

"My point"—Debbie Mae waved a hand—"was about Mr. Knightley. He was a happy bachelor, but when he fell in love with Emma, everything changed."

Caroline let out a short laugh, shaking her head. "Did you just hear what you said? He was a happy man and then everything changed? You're really not convincing me here."

Her cousin laid a flowered, sleeveless button-up over one arm and giggled. "You know what I mean." Her smile faded and her eyes grew serious. "I was happy before I met Manning. But I don't think I really knew what intense love could be like before him. It's so different, it's hard to describe."

Caroline flipped the metal hangers to the end and scoured for another possibility. "Eros."

"Okay, right." Debbie Mae nodded. "But I don't know if all that can be crammed into one little Greek word."

"I'm sure it can't. I meant to say that's the difference. Eros, agape and . . ." Caroline snapped her fingers.

"Phileo," Debbie Mae supplied. "Romantic love, friendship, brotherly love. Anyway, I mean that until you experience it, it's really hard to say whether you want to spend your life without it."

"So, what does this have to do with Mr. Knightley and Brooks?"

"He's got great friends and a brother, but he's missing out on a big area. I just would hate for him to discover it too late. Knightley had Emma as a friend, but when they fell in love, they were fulfilled, completed."

"Don't let Brooks hear you call him incomplete."

Debbie Mae didn't laugh. "He's just not the type of guy to stay single forever, no matter what he says."

Caroline chewed her lip, flipping dresses on the rack, unseeing. Would he regret having spent so much time with friends when he could have experienced the powerful, all-consuming passion of an erotic love? She didn't want Brooks to miss out, but the thought of his being swallowed up by a *grande passion* made her feel more than a bit anxious. A vision passed before her, of Brooks and a tall, elegant woman, looking complete. The shadowy figure of this woman flashed in and out of focus, long dark hair changing to a bright blond pixie cut and finally to waves of gentle auburn curls.

"Is that what Manning says?"

Debbie Mae snagged a yellow scarf from the display shelf and draped it over her dresses, eyeing it for clashing hues. "Actually, he told me to stop hounding Brooks. He seems to have this odd idea that Brooks knows exactly what he's doing."

"Maybe you should invite him to your house to watch *Emma*. That might bring the point home." Her little joke was lost on her cousin.

"Great idea!" Debbie Mae wrapped the scarf around her neck.

"We should throw an Austen party. Blanche can help! She knows everything about parties! We'll dress up in Regency clothes and eat pickled partridge eggs or whatever they ate." Her face was alight with enthusiasm.

Caroline felt her brows rise to her hairline. What on earth had she started? "Let's go try these on and then we can talk specifics."

Maybe Debbie Mae would forget all about it when she focused on summer dresses. Shoe shopping was next, and surely that would make her forget about the crazy plan.

Forty-five minutes later, Caroline slipped her sunglasses down from her hair and pushed open the glass door of the boutique, walking into the sweltering Mississippi heat. The lilac-colored, floor-length dress was carefully hung inside a garment bag.

"Oh, and we can learn some of those old dances!" Debbie Mae clutched several plastic bags and bounced alongside Caroline, her glee apparent even in her steps. Debbie Mae had refused to let go of her brilliant idea, quoting lines from the movie at Caroline over the top of the changing-room walls.

Caroline snorted. "Really, Brooks is never going to agree to that. I can see a movie night, but a costume party with square dancing? Never going to happen, I can tell you."

Debbie Mae's face fell, small frown lines appearing at the sides of her mouth. "It's not square dancing. It's graceful and elegant. I thought you'd help out. If you don't want to be part of it . . ."

"It's not that I don't want to help." Caroline paused under the shade of a magnolia, a bead of sweat making its way down the curve of her spine. Her feet were aching in her new silver, strappy sandals, but the wrought-iron-and-wooden bench looked ten degrees hotter than the air. "And I'm glad you guys have started being more sociable. I know Brooks missed you, and I sure missed you, but maybe this isn't the best way to spend time together."

To Caroline's surprise, Debbie Mae's large blue eyes misted with tears. "I'm sorry we haven't been in touch very much."

"Hey"—Caroline reached out, touching her hand—"it's fine. I didn't mean to make you feel bad about it. But a year is a long time without even a coffee date." Debbie Mae nodded. "I'm up to my neck with my mama's parties right now. But tell you what—let's plan that party for Christmas or New Year's Day." Caroline hoped that a few months might shake loose that idea once and for all.

Debbie Mae turned and sank onto the bench, her bags clutched to her chest. Such grief was in her expression that Caroline sank down next to her. Something was very wrong. Caroline's heart twisted in her chest. Was Debbie Mae sick? Was Manning dying?

"I just didn't know how to tell you." Debbie Mae's voice broke on the last word and her chin dropped to her chest.

"Debbie Mae," Caroline said, hearing the panic in her own voice. "You can always tell me anything. I promise I won't be mad."

Debbie Mae laughed, a sad, little choking sound that was as far from a laugh as could be. "I know. It's just so hard to find the words. We tried right away and we were so excited to find out we were pregnant. I started creating the cutest little cards to announce it." She took a shuddering breath. "It's a good thing I couldn't decide between the baby-giraffe theme and the daddy-penguin theme."

Caroline held her hand, her throat tightening in response to the utter devastation on Debbie Mae's face. Her mind flashed back to those months after the wedding, when her cousin seemed distant, silent.

"The second time, we decided to wait a little longer." Debbie Mae paused, looking up into the tree branches above them, her face dappled with bright sunlight. Her eyes glittered with unshed tears.

The second time? Caroline's stomach clenched. She had missed so much, assuming Debbie Mae was caught up in the bliss of a new husband. Instead she was drowning under a tidal wave of grief.

"When that one ended, I needed to take a break." She looked down at her hands, one clutching Caroline's as if for dear life. "We waited until February, and I didn't even get excited when the little stick turned blue this time."

It was May and there had been no happy announcement. Obviously there would be no happy announcement. Caroline leaned forward, folding Debbie Mae's shaking shoulders into a fierce hug. They held on to each other in the sweltering morning sunlight, on a public bench in the swanky downtown shopping area, mourning.

Debbie Mae finally leaned back, wiping her face, trying to keep her mascara from smearing. Caroline dug a tissue from her purse and handed it over silently.

"I'm sorry I didn't tell you. I just knew it would be like this, and I couldn't face any more tears." Debbie Mae laughed, shaking her head. "As if this is any better."

Caroline rubbed Debbie Mae's back, feeling her thin shoulder bones through her pale yellow linen shirt. She'd thought Debbie Mae was watching her weight, maybe running more. Now she could see the weight loss was grief and tragedy showing through.

"We've decided to put it all on hold. I can't take another . . ."

Debbie Mae's voice trailed off and Caroline wondered what her cousin was going to say. *Disappointment* didn't seem the right kind of word for a loss so deep. "And I know people will say that it's so much easier to lose a baby at that stage, before you're even showing, before you tell everybody." Debbie Mae's brows drew together in anger. "But it's not easier for us. I was so mad at God, I couldn't even sit in church. I would just fume the whole time. I'm not saying our loss is any bigger or any more awful than what other people are facing. But I don't even know if they were boys or girls."

Caroline nodded, feeling the yawning chasm of the unknown that would never be filled. Never knowing the gender meant you might not give the child a name. If no one knew about the baby, you certainly wouldn't be able to have a public ceremony to mourn and show respect for the short life. It would be forever unfinished, no healing closure available. And multiplied by three, the burden was unimaginable.

"I feel like a failure as a woman." Debbie Mae watched the shoppers pass on the sidewalk, happy chatter filling the air around them. "You always hear what a 'real woman' is. You know, 'real women have curves' and 'real women make biscuits from scratch' and 'real women run marathons.' I thought 'real women have babies.' Or maybe I didn't even think it. Maybe I just believed it without even considering whether it was true."

Caroline smiled a little at the marathon comment. She liked to run, but she didn't think she could ever do a marathon. Or biscuits from scratch. But of course, she had just assumed about the babies. Like Debbie Mae.

"When it didn't look like that was going to happen for us, I felt like someone had canceled my woman card." Debbie Mae looked up, face stricken. "Really, what do I do now? I had it all planned out. College, good job, marriage, and babies. Just like that."

Caroline wondered for the first time what Debbie Mae thought of her. She'd gone to college, gotten the good job, and then come home. No marriage. No babies. Probably, like most people, her cousin's false perceptions were applied most heavily to herself, not those around her. Caroline rubbed Debbie Mae's arm, at a loss for words.

Caroline had always felt like a woman, even when she'd been making cake flops for bridge meetings. Her disappointments hadn't touched her faith, hadn't made her question whether she was loved by God. She just couldn't imagine the depths of the grief Debbie Mae was feeling, a grief so deep that it had consumed the whole of the last year.

"Right now, I just want to focus on something else. I missed my friends." Debbie Mae, her lips tilting up in a hopeful expression, looked at Caroline. "If they can forgive me for being so quiet."

"Oh, honey." It wasn't the most articulate sentence, but Caroline hoped her hug said it all. "I'm so sorry."

"I am, too." Debbie Mae straightened up, brushing back her hair. "Now, I want this to be a summer to have fun, recuperate and reconnect. I think your idea about a Regency party is so incredible!"

Caroline opened her mouth to remind her that *she* wasn't the one who'd come up with it, and that she didn't actually like the idea all that much, but decided it didn't really matter. If Debbie Mae wanted an Austen party, Debbie Mae was going to get an Austen party.

"I'm still not sure if Brooks is going to want to show up in tails and dance around your patio."

"Well, we'll just have to work on him." Debbie Mae stood up, shouldering her purse. "Come on, we've got shoe shopping to do. And after lunch, we'll strategize."

Caroline followed along, outwardly remarking on the chances of their finding Regency shoes without resorting to an online store. Inside, her heart was trembling with the knowledge her best friend had been enduring a life-changing trauma. And she hadn't even known.

She'd been so caught up in her own problems with her mother, her own loneliness, wishing everyone would come visit her. Perhaps if she hadn't been so focused on her own troubles, she would have seen Debbie Mae struggling. She'd been a bad friend, and nothing was worse in Caroline's book than someone who let down her friends.

Before they entered the next shop, she'd decided this Austen party was going to put all other parties to shame. If she had to drag Brooks there and force him to dance, she would do it. Debbie Mae deserved a little happiness, and if they all had to dress up like something in a BBC miniseries to make it happen, then that would be a small price to pay.

Indeed I will. You have shown that you can dance, and you know we are not really so much brother and sister as to make it at all improper.

—EMMA

Brother and sister! No, indeed.

—MR. KNIGHTLEY

Chapter Four

Brooks hesitated, standing on the tidy welcome mat, the heat of the sun blazing against his back. The familiar green rockers at either end of the long porch were gone. The two matching sets had been bought from the local carpenter when Caroline's grandparents were just a young couple, and it was strange to see the cleanly painted planks where they would have been. Probably being refurbished.

The Japanese honeysuckle was clambering over the side of the porch and winding up one fat, square pillar. He made a mental note to offer to trim it if the gardener didn't. Left alone it would work its way under the eaves and twist wrist-thick stems around the gutters, crushing the delicate woodwork.

His gaze took in the overgrown hydrangea visible near the opposite edge of the porch and he frowned. It wasn't like Mrs. Ashley to let the vegetation run wild. The Ashley home was one of the few truly historic homes in Thorny Hollow, and Caroline's mother usually made sure the grounds and the veranda were immaculately maintained.

He stood, fist raised to the door. How many years had he been dragged to parties, his parents bickering in the front seat? His father would drink too many bourbons and everyone was miserable by the end of the night. Brooks hated facing another party, especially when he should have been doing the party rounds at home, in Spartainville.

Academics loved a party just as much as genteel Southerners, and he always had to participate in the endless rounds of get-togethers. Otherwise, he would end up getting shut out of the ivory tower, out in the cold of the real world. Academia wasn't all about the pursuit of knowledge, and they all knew it. If only his father could understand that. Maybe when Blanche came back, they could all sit down together and talk it out.

Brooks straightened his tie and tried to muster some enthusiasm. It had been a hard week and he'd love nothing more than to make some popcorn and watch a ball game. But he'd promised he'd be there. Maybe Caroline wouldn't be ready. Maybe she'd make him sit in the parlor, next to the long rows of floor-to-ceiling bookshelves while she took an hour or two getting dressed. The term had been rough, and although it was almost over, the worst was yet to come. Finals made everyone nutty. He needed a break. Maybe by the time she emerged, they'd decide it was too late to go and end up staying in, debating politics and planning the summer late into the night.

Not likely, but he could dream. He knocked on the glossy

black door, the heavy oak swallowing the sound completely. He heard the faintest sound of footsteps, and Caroline opened it not two seconds later.

Caroline peered behind Brooks, noting the empty car. "Where's your dad?"

"He's not feeling up to it. So we get to be the Elliot family ambassadors." Brooks felt his lips turn up in a smile, even though seconds before he'd knocked on Caroline's door, he'd been dreading the prospect of this party. He took a slow breath. This wasn't the way he wanted to spend a Saturday evening and he was sure Caroline felt the same, but it seemed the curse of the Southerner to attend every party out of polite obligation.

"Is he sick?" She got the little frown line between her brows that meant concern and sometimes confusion. Today it was just concern.

"Tired, I think." Brooks had driven all the way to Thorny Hollow for a party he didn't want to attend only because his father asked. Thirty minutes before they left, his father had decided to stay home and watch TV. The bait and switch really pushed Brooks's buttons.

"I hope he's all right. Maybe we should pick him up some tea or something from the Piggly Wiggly on the way home."

Brooks leaned against the doorframe and waited while she rooted through her tiny purse. He'd seen Caroline's dress before, but he'd forgotten how pretty it was, with cream-colored roses on pale turquoise. The fabric was soft and flowing, and the design of the dress accentuated every curve. He allowed himself one admiring survey before forcing his gaze above the shoulders. Her wavy blond hair was twisted up into something carelessly beautiful and she smelled delicious, like violets and vanilla.

"My phone . . . was just . . . here." She frowned and dug further, as if the bag were miles wide.

"You can use mine, if we need one."

"I know, but Mama might want to call me and I'd better answer if she does." Caroline brushed back her blond hair and started removing objects from the small purse. He watched a small hairbrush, a silver tube of lipstick, keys and assorted doodads emerge until the little table by the front door was cluttered.

"She doesn't like you to go out." It wasn't a question.

"Aha!" She held up the small, red phone triumphantly. "She just worries a bit when I'm out." The pile on the table disappeared back into the purse, one item at a time.

"How did she manage when you were at Midlands? Or at the *Post*?" He spoke gently, not wanting to cause an argument. But Caroline's mama had her on a short leash.

Just yesterday Caroline had called him at the crack of dawn to go running. It was the last on his list of most favorite exercises, but somehow she'd pried him out of bed. They'd gone for a long loop around the kudzu-covered neighborhood, well before the rest of the world had risen. When they'd returned, Mrs. Ashley had complained about how long it had taken, as if she'd made plans herself to jog with Caroline at six in the morning on a Saturday.

"It was different then. Daddy was alive and they kept each other company." She snapped the purse closed and looked up at him, green-blue eyes as clear as the sea. "It was such a shock for her when he passed. I can understand how she gets anxious when I'm out of sight."

Brooks didn't answer. A strange feeling was in his chest, as if an ice cube were slipping down into his stomach, melting all the way. Out of sight? The leash was shorter than he thought. He'd assumed Caroline got out at least a few times a week, if only for a run.

"She doesn't mind if I go somewhere with you, though. We're practically related."

"We're not hardly related," he choked out, laughing.

"We are, sort of. Your brother married my cousin."

"Finley, that makes us not at all related."

She cocked her head, lips twitching. "All right, but we look it. Your cream linen suit"—she waved a hand—"with that mint-green, patterned tie next to my dress? It's just like we planned it."

"If anything we look like one of those couples that buy everything in his-and-hers pairs." He didn't even know why he was arguing. He could tell she wasn't serious.

"Ha! No one would ever think we're a couple." She pulled the door closed. "I'm too young for you. I would never survive the rigors of being an academic's wife. All those little parties, all that ivory-tower political maneuvering, aren't my style. I'm too blunt. Anyway, if you ever got married—which you won't—the woman would be . . ." Her voice trailed off and she paused at the top step as if she'd forgotten something.

"Would be what? Ninety? Toothless? A mail-order bride?"

She laughed, but it sounded slightly forced. "I was going to say she would be successful, worldly, know everything there was to know about ambition. She'd help you climb the ladder one impressive social coup at a time." She hesitated just a fraction of a second. "At the very least, she'd be someone with a job." Her words were light, but the tone betrayed her. A hint of sadness followed the last word.

He tucked her hand into the crook of his arm and they walked down the wide front steps of the Ashley house. "Wrong. The personal ad clearly states I'm looking for an unemployed, undervalued and completely unschooled woman to be my future bride.

That way, she'll see my meager salary as a college professor as quite impressive."

She snorted. "You might have to add a few items to that list in order to reach 'quite impressive.'"

Opening the car door, he shook his head. "Even if I was in the market for a wife—a phrase I really hate, by the way—you're right about us. You know too much. See, there's no mystery, no romance, no excitement. I'm just Brooks to you. I think a mail-order bride is my only hope."

He could hear her giggling as he crossed in front of the car. Sliding into the driver's seat, he noticed that the small cockpit of the car already smelled wonderful, like some favorite candy from his childhood that he couldn't quite place.

The bright sunlight glanced off the inside of the console. He slipped on his sunglasses and backed out of the circular drive. The long, narrow road to the main street was filled with dips and bumps. He should find someone to fill it in for them before the rainy season started. A good, hard downpour and that Mississippi clay washed toward the lowest point, which was the pasture to the north, leaving the driveway rutted and uneven.

Again, the light waft of something he half remembered. "Have you been baking again?"

"Me? Never unless I have to. But Mama loved that cake from Bravard's and now she wants me to make it all the time."

He grinned, wondering how she was going to hide all those cake boxes. "You'll have to explain someday."

She blew out a breath. "I know. But it's nice to have her approval for just a little bit."

He shot her a glance, startled. What kind of mother wouldn't approve of Caroline? She'd succeeded in everything she'd ever tried. The sadness in her statement was just one more point for Caroline's getting out of the house regularly, and not just for a run.

"Have you talked to Manning lately?"

"Not much. He calls, but doesn't really seem like he wants to talk. Just sort of . . ." Brooks thought for a moment. "Checking in."

She nodded, as if it made sense. It didn't make much sense to him, but there it was. He missed his brother, missed their long talks while fishing and the Saturday afternoons spent watching baseball. Now that the season had started, he noticed his absence even more. Shouting at the TV as the Braves struggled through a tough game wasn't as fun without Manning.

"Maybe you should go down there and have lunch."

"If he's busy, he's busy. I don't want him to have to drop everything to grab a burger with me." Brooks could hear the tone in his voice and hated it. Manning's focus on his newly wedded bliss had stung him where it hurt: right in the brotherly love department.

"Sometimes we need someone to tell us when to slow down and take a break." Caroline paused. "Or when to speed up and get a real job." One side of her mouth went up but it wasn't a real smile.

Brooks felt his stomach drop. "I didn't mean to say you weren't working hard or—"

"I know." She waved a hand. "You said what I needed to hear. I've been so jealous of people like Lauren Fairfield but wasn't doing anything about it."

"Mrs. Reynolds's granddaughter?"

"That's the one. She's editing a book on Southern mansions. Got a big, fancy publishing job and is heading up one of those glossy coffee-table photography books that weighs thirty pounds."

He glanced at her, surprised to see the slight frown between her brows. "And you're jealous of her?"

"How can I not be? I've been hearing about her my whole life. Lauren this, Lauren that." She flapped a hand. "*Lauren* graduated from Yale summa cum laude and *Lauren* was offered six jobs right out of college and *Lauren* learned Spanish by hiking in the Andes." Caroline hauled in a breath.

"I've never met her, but I wouldn't cross her off before you even set eyes on the girl." Caroline was generally an open, friendly person, but she did get a little jealous now and then.

She let out a harrumph and crossed her arms. "Mama said Lauren will be at this party, so after tonight, you'll be able to tell me how impressed you are with her."

Brooks kept his eyes on the road. Something was bothering Caroline, and if he waited long enough, it would all come rushing out. Usually sooner rather than later.

She adjusted her skirt a little, letting the silk fall against her tanned knees. "Mrs. Gray mentioned you had been invited to Marian's for dinner."

"Mmmm." So he had. Several times.

"And?" She was looking straight at him now, those green-blue eyes narrowed.

"And what?" He slowed the car and let it idle, pausing at the entrance to the main road. There wasn't any traffic to speak of on a late Sunday afternoon, just a few slow-moving vehicles in the distance. The heat waves shimmering on the blacktop made the cars seem as if they were moving underwater.

"Why didn't you go?"

He felt his brows go up and searched for words. He didn't want to be unkind. Nothing was more irritating than a woman who was desperate to marry just because it was on her schedule of tasks to accomplish. He didn't want to be on someone's to-do list.

"I was busy." And he'd continue to be busy until he was too

old to be considered a candidate for Marian's desperate bachelor-go-round.

He moved to shift, but her touch on his arm halted him mid-motion. "Doing what?"

"Why all the questions, Finley? My dad wanted me to help him fix the storm windows, remember?" He shook his head, feeling as if the logic were falling out of the conversation.

"Can you take off your sunglasses?" Her voice was soft and her hand hadn't left his arm. "I can't see your eyes. It's hard to talk to you when I can't see your eyes."

Brooks glanced in the rearview mirror and frowned. They'd talked a thousand times before—with sunglasses, in deep shade on a hot day, in the rain, while running the last of five painful miles at sunrise. She'd never needed to see his eyes before. He slipped the glasses off and half turned his body toward her. "Better?"

"Much." Her lips tugged up a bit although her eyes were still somber. "We're friends, right?"

If he knew where the conversation was headed, he'd feel better about answering, but as it was, he only had one answer: "Always."

"If you wanted to go to dinner at Marian's, you'd tell me? If you skipped it because you had a date, you'd tell me? Or if you were plain sick of my annoying self and wanted to hang out on the couch watching football, you'd tell me?" She actually looked nervous, as if she wasn't quite sure what he'd answer.

He let out a long breath and ran a hand over his face. "So, Mrs. Gray said that Marian said that I'd refused to have dinner with her because I had a date." He wanted to roll his eyes but tried to approach the problem calmly. Small-town gossips had nothing better to do than stir up trouble.

"Something like that." Bright spots of pink bloomed over her cheekbones. It was ridiculous, but here they were, dissecting the latest round of hearsay.

"And why do you care?"

"Excuse me?" Her voice went two octaves higher than normal and her hand dropped from his arm.

"Really. Why do you care what Mrs. Gray thinks? You've never cared about what other people thought before."

"Well, it was just . . ." Her voice trailed off. "She made it sound like you were lying to spare my feelings. And I don't want you to ever lie for me." She leaned forward, bright blond hair shining in the sunlight, her face tight with emotion. "If it's something I need to hear, don't be afraid, especially if you think I can't handle it. If no else will say it, please be the brave one."

He stared into her eyes, noting the flecks of gold in the deep green-blue, her features as familiar as his own. "I've never lied to you."

Caroline relaxed against the seat, inhaling deeply. "Good."

"So, when do you want to hear it?"

Her head popped up from the seat back. "What?"

"All the things you need to hear." He flashed a grin and put his shades back on before pulling onto the main road. He had a whole list of subjects, starting with the absurd amount of time she spent locked in that old house.

"About Marian?"

He choked back a laugh. "You're obsessed with her. Afraid she's going to snap up all the most eligible bachelors?"

"She can have them all." Rubbing her temple, Caroline smiled crookedly. "Bless her heart. She's three gallons of crazy in a two-gallon bucket and no one has time for the mess. I don't know why Mrs. Gray threw me with that comment at the bridge party. Silly, isn't it?"

"Absolutely. But anytime you want me to use my oldest-friend superpowers, let me know. I have a lot of advice for you."

"I'm afraid to hear it." She stared out at the houses, each carefully rimmed with white wooden fences or ironwork posts. "I can guess what you'll say, anyway."

"That saves me the effort, then."

"You want me to tell my mother I'm not her party planner."

"Or her chef. Or her companion. Or her watchdog." He checked the rearview mirror before sliding into the far lane.

"I know. And I'm sure it will get better with time." But she didn't sound convinced. He glanced at her, afraid to speak what they both knew: Caroline's mother was becoming completely dependent on her daughter. No amount of waiting was going to help the situation. Three years had gone by and she had gotten more possessive, not less.

"You're right." Caroline straightened up, forcing her lips into a bright smile. "I've been thinking of starting something new."

"Another book?"

"Well, I never finished the last one." She shrugged. "Fiction isn't my forte. I've been thinking of an essay for the *Atlantic* on the rise of disaster memoirs."

"I-lived-through-the-greatest-plane-crash-in-history type?"

"Right. There was that book about the girl lost on Mount Hood and she had to bury her dead fiancé in a snowbank with his shoes as markers. The advance was half a million, which is a lot of money when we already know how it all ends. It's definitely a trend in memoirs right now." She beamed at him and he forced his gaze back to the road. He'd forgotten how happy she looked when she got an idea for a story.

"I could be wrong, but I think the *Economist* just had a story like that a few months ago."

"Oh." She visible slumped. "I feel so out of the loop."

"You can keep up with all of this stuff online. Even my grandmother keeps up with what's happening in the world." He kept his tone gentle, but if Caroline wanted to get a piece printed in a national magazine, she had to know what'd already been done.

"Right, but that's Blanche. She said she was starting a seniors Internet-dating site, too." Caroline's lips tilted up.

"You know what I mean."

Her smile faded. "I know. I just get so caught up in . . ."

"Bridge parties." He turned off the main road and slowed, shifting down as they entered the long, tree-lined drive leading to the Werlin mansion. The early-evening sun illuminated every leaf and tussock of grass with a golden glow.

"Right. And it's my own fault."

Her voice was so defeated that he let the car slow to a complete stop and shifted to neutral. "Listen. It was one idea, a good one. But somebody already got there before you. How many times has that happened?"

Her lips tilted up just a fraction. "About a million."

"Exactly. I think you're out of practice. You've gotten soft. You get a good idea, it's shot down, you want to slink back under the porch and lick your wounds."

She snorted. "Don't hold back or anything."

"You want me to be honest? Well, here's the truth. You used to be a lot tougher, because you had to be." He remembered the year she worked at the *Post*. She was darn near frightening. If she thought she had a story, she chased it down without giving up. The girl next to him was as beautiful, as smart and as generous, but she'd lost her confidence.

She was quiet for a few moments. He hoped he hadn't said too much. People always asked for the truth, but not many truly wanted to hear it. His chest constricted a bit, wondering if he'd hurt her. That wasn't what he'd intended at all.

"You're right. And it was just one idea." She turned to him, new resolve in her gaze. "I'm crawling back out from under the porch, okay?"

"Perfect." He shifted into gear and let the car move smoothly forward. The long paved drive was sheltered on either side by enormous pine trees, their branches arching toward the darkening sky. The pillars of the Werlin home gleamed in the distance. The sunset behind them tinted the white paint the palest pink. Brooks felt pride rise within his chest. He didn't own this house and his family was unconnected to it. But it was a testament to Southern grace and power, an immutable sign that these people, in this place, held deep respect for their history.

As they drove nearer, the plantation home came into full view. Twenty-six columns supported the double-galleried porch above. Two stories rose above that, with the ten-foot-high, paned windows reflecting back the bright sunset. The deep green of the lawn spread out on either side, and the smaller outbuildings that housed the cotton gin and the sugarcane press stood at a respectful distance from the main house.

"I haven't been to the Werlins' since that New Year's Eve party." She cocked her head. "Whatever happened to your date, that reporter from Natchez?"

"Sandy? Oh, I see her around." He tried to make it sound as if they had some sort of friendship, but truthfully, he actively avoided the woman.

"She asked me if you'd inherit Badewood or if your brother would get it."

He threw her a look and was glad the tree-lined drive was a straight shot.

She shrugged, as if she knew what he was silently asking. "I figured you'd use your own best judgment. I don't blame her. A girl can be distracted by the idea of having a third-floor ballroom all to herself."

He supposed so, but it had still taken him by surprise. "Somehow between my invitation and the day of the Werlins' party, she'd done a little investigative work. Whenever she looked at me, I could see that Ionic portico reflected in her eyes."

Caroline raised a hand to her mouth, unsuccessfully trying to stifle her giggles. "Poor you."

"Yes, poor me." He made the saddest face he could manage but couldn't hold it for long. He'd been disappointed, true. Sandy kept asking him where he'd bought his car, his watch, even his suit, as if she were prepping for a turn on *The Price Is Right*. Offensive then, amusing now.

"Looks the same." He motioned to Werlins' home, happy to see the bright new paint but nothing else of note on the Greek Revival–style mansion. Adding wings or changing the face of such a historic house was an offense punishable by social shaming.

"Remember the old Muro place?" Caroline seemed to read his mind. "That businessman from Florida that tore out all the bright red brickwork?"

"And then covered the timber framing in pink stucco." The man claimed he'd been blacklisted because he was from out of town, as if Miami were Memphis. No, it was the crime he'd committed on that beautiful old house.

She slid out of the car and they stood together in the grass, taking in the bright spring evening. The frogs from Yellow Creek were in full song, peepers and bullfrogs giving their best in the hope of attracting a mate. Deep green Kentucky bluegrass covered the expansive front lawn, and Brooks could see the swell of manicured acres rising in the distance, dotted here and there with giant oak. He would never leave his teaching position at Midlands College, but moments like this made an emotion rise in his chest that was akin to the deepest longing. This was his town, his people, his heritage.

He turned to Caroline, taking her hand and tucking it in his elbow. "Too bad the party is inside. It would have been a wonderful night for a garden party."

She stood still, as if she hadn't heard him. "I know I should want to travel the world, to have a demitasse of espresso at the Eiffel Tower or lie on the white sands of Bora Bora. Maybe even move to Rome and get an Italian boyfriend who drives a Fiat." Glancing at him, she smiled. "But I don't know if anything will come close to Thorny Hollow."

He wanted to agree, say that was just what he'd been thinking, but somehow the words stuck in his throat. This place truly was close to heaven on earth, but he wanted more for her. A lifetime of garden parties, no matter how perfect, was not what she was born for.

He struggled to put this into words, but every phrase that occurred to him seemed as if he were lecturing her on how to live her life. "Then let's not waste a minute of it."

A bit of reality might help. The particularly grating relationships of a small town might be a better tool of persuasion than any nagging he could do. There was nothing like a long-held feud or a dose of small-minded bigotry to convince her to expand her horizons.

Men of sense, whatever you may choose,

do not want silly wives.

—MR. KNIGHTLEY

CHAPTER FIVE

Caroline inhaled the smell of freshly mown grass and felt a sense of well-being spread through her, from the top of her head to her toes. This very moment, life was as perfect as it could possibly be. The setting sun lit up the Werlin house like a spotlight. Every detail of the historic old home seemed to shimmer. The combed-gravel circular driveway was shadowed by enormous cedar trees.

"Looks like Manning and Debbie Mae are here." She pointed to the sleek silver coupe at the far end of the drive. "This past weekend was the first time I'd seen her in forever. She kept saying we would get together for coffee, but it never happened."

"Same here. Manning says his caseload has been crazy this year, but things change when you get married."

Caroline brushed her hair back and lifted her chin. Obviously, that wasn't the whole story, but she couldn't share their losses without asking Debbie Mae for permission.

He went on, "There couldn't have been a sudden spate of property-development disputes in our little county. Nor could Debbie's fourth-graders need twice as much lesson planning as last year."

"Maybe it's not just about being married. That sounds so . . ." She waved a hand, searching for the right word.

"Disloyal?" Brooks dropped the keys in his pants pocket and shrugged. "But it's human nature, Finley. I know how you feel. I haven't seen Manning since the last reenactment, at the Battle of Champion Hill." Brooks said that as if she'd remember exactly which month it was held. Although she teased him about what she'd once called his "little obsession," she knew it wasn't just marking Civil War history for him; it was family time. Blanche raised funds for battlegrounds, and the boys were both die-hard Civil War buffs.

"Does he come visit you at Midlands much?"

"Not since the wedding. He keeps saying he will, but you know the rest." Brooks grinned. "It's love. I'm not holding a grudge. She's perfect for him. Thoughtful, smart, funny. I'm glad they found each other."

Caroline almost missed a step, catching the toe of her sandal in the soft blue-green grass. "You mean, you're glad I fixed them up. Without me none of that would have happened." She paused, her gaze fixed on a distant point. "When they first started dating, I sort of regretted it. She was with him all the time. Now I remind myself he could have ended up with someone we both hated."

"Hmm? I would have made an effort to get along with any woman he decided was the one he wanted to spend the rest of his life with."

She fell into step beside Brooks, noting how he walked more slowly so she could keep up with his long legs. "You think so?

What if he'd chosen some fake-tan, big-haired bimbo for a wife? I worked hard to bring those two together. He needed someone who shared a lot of his interests, especially that nutty reenactment stuff you guys do. You know that Debbie Mae even bought some old tin cookware so she could join you? She'll be cooking for the camp."

"Really." His tone wasn't overly enthusiastic, and she wondered if he'd wanted to keep the reenactments as sacred brotherly bonding time. If she were Debbie Mae, she'd let them have it. Swatting mosquitoes, eating off tin plates and washing her hair in a creek wasn't her idea of a great time. History or no, sometimes a girl just had to lay down some ground rules. Sleeping on a real mattress was one of them.

"She's also planning a big party sometime this summer. I think she missed us."

His lips tilted a bit. "She does have a knack for entertaining. Her Super Bowl parties are the bomb. As for Manning, I don't think he would have married just any girl. You know, whatever the commercials say, men don't want an airhead for a wife."

Caroline rolled her eyes at him. "Please don't tell me you're trying to insist that men will choose brains over beauty? I think we both know that's not true."

He stopped, leaning back, taking her in from the top of her perfect blond hair to the delicately painted toenails. "Women put the greatest burden on themselves to be beautiful. I'm not saying you should all stop brushing your teeth or shaving your legs, but women could always put more time into being interesting than being beautiful."

Her mouth dropped open a little bit and a small puff of air escaped, as if he'd socked her in the stomach. "Even if the entire female population swore off highlights and manicures, men would still choose the most beautiful woman in the group. It's just the way men are. No amount of women's lib will change that fact."

"How can you, an educated woman, say something so sexist?" His eyes went wide. "What about gender equality? What about enlightenment? What about"—he gestured mutely at the space between them—"friendship?"

"All very good things. But no match for basic biology." She sighed. "I wish I were wrong, but I'm not."

"Fine. If we're going to start pointing fingers, women are just as shallow. They'll choose the tallest man in the room, the one with the deepest voice and the biggest muscles. It doesn't matter if he can't string two words together, he'll have women falling all over him."

"Ha!" She started toward the house, leaving him to follow in her wake. "We may go for a quick look, but there's a difference between momentary distraction and enduring boring chitchat for the rest of your adult life. True attraction has to survive a twenty-minute conversation."

He'd caught up with her, his long legs keeping pace with hers as she stalked toward the wide, sweeping veranda steps. "Wait a minute." He held out a small spray of forget-me-nots and tucked them into the back of her hair. His lips tugged up as he looked her over. "Pretty."

"You stole flowers and want to plant the evidence on me?" Her tone was arch, but she couldn't help smiling a bit. Every girl liked to be called pretty, which reminded her of the conversation currently derailed by a well-timed compliment. "Hold on, are you trying to make a point?"

"No point. The color brings out the blue in your eyes."

Caroline rolled her eyes at him and headed toward the steps.

"You know what the real kicker is? For men, it's not looks or brains. If all else is equal, women might choose the smarter man, but they'll always choose the richer one."

She whirled on him. "Patently false. I know plenty of women who have married down, even though women are statistically the ones who should be making conservative financial decisions."

Brooks stepped forward, glaring down at her, the evening light glancing off his hair and casting his features into half shadow. She could smell his cologne, not his everyday aftershave but the darker, muskier one he wore for parties. Even in high heels she had to tip her head back to meet his eyes. Their gazes locked and she stuck her fists on her hips, waiting for a nice little debate to begin. He never passed up an opportunity to argue with her, even standing on the front lawn outside a party they should be attending.

She watched his lips start to twitch as if he'd thought of something amusing. She refused to blink. Of course he knew that women came out on the short end of the stick for pay scale and retirement packages. It was a fact. But if he thought he could say women always checked the bank statements before committing, he was dead wrong.

"Finley, name one." His voice was a low drawl as if he'd checkmated her in a game of gender-equality chess.

"Well, there was . . ." She felt her face start to burn. There were plenty of examples, but she couldn't think of any of them right now, standing on the front lawn of the Werlin estate while music poured out the open door.

He shook his head, a quirk to his lip signaling his refusal to laugh. "Quite a list there." He stuffed his hands in his pockets in that way he had, the way that said he was tallying up a point on his mental scoreboard.

"My limited knowledge isn't the final word on the subject.

How about we make this party a test? We'll observe and make careful notes on interactions. But it has to be a clear case of beauty over brains. Nothing in between. We both have to agree the person, male or female, is . . ." She frowned, thinking.

"Not as bright as they are attractive, and not as attractive as they are rich?"

She nodded. It felt ungenerous to state it so baldly, but that was the reality. So many people spent hours at the gym and on their beauty regimes, but would never pick up a decent book.

"I don't like the idea of searching out examples of bad behavior just to win a bet." Of course he wouldn't. Brooks was a firm believer in keeping one's nose in one's own business. "But it won't hurt to simply observe, I suppose."

"Exactly. We're not tricking anyone into anything. Now, let's get this party started before we miss all the fun and end up crawdad fishing at the creek."

He snorted. "You've never been crawdad fishing in your life."

"True. But I could always start."

Brooks couldn't help smiling back when Caroline flashed that brilliant smile. She could make the driest party seem like a bit of a sneaky adventure.

The chances of him winning the bet were good. It was a flimsy societal myth that men were brainless oglers. In reality men avoided being trapped in an intellectually unequal relationship just as much as women. He would have plenty of examples to state his case, he was sure of it.

Caroline's eyes were narrowed, as if she were determined to march into this party and prove her point. Well, they'd just see, wouldn't they?

"Brooks, dear!" Mrs. Werlin was already crossing the ballroom, hands outstretched, as soon as they were ushered through the foyer. Her round face was creased in a wide smile, and her pale blue eyes were wide with enthusiasm. Her midnight-blue gown was elegant and timeless, like her historic home. He liked Mrs. Werlin for her commitment to preserving the region's history, but he loved her for her personality. He wasn't quite sure what she saw in Mr. Werlin, who was several decades older than she was and had all the magnetism of wet cardboard, but love had its own rules. "I thought Blanche would be back by now. She's been gone for weeks!"

"She decided to take the extended cruise. Something about a ship full of hotties." Brooks smiled, knowing Mrs. Werlin was perfectly clear on what Blanche was doing in the bright blue waters of the Caribbean Sea, no matter what story his father had told this time around.

"Oh, my." Mrs. Werlin shook her head but looked more delighted than dismayed. "And, Caroline, how lovely. I stopped by the other day to see your mother, but she was not well enough to visit."

"The weather sometimes gives her a bit of a headache." A faint pinkness bloomed on Caroline's cheeks, and Brooks knew how awkward it was to use the same excuse time after time. Mrs. Ashley had debilitating headaches when it suited her. Otherwise, she was quite healthy.

"Give her my best." Mrs. Werlin gave them both a flyby kiss and waved toward the middle of the room. "So many old friends have come to celebrate the completion of our new home. Thank you for coming tonight."

"We're happy to be here," Caroline said. "I hope we didn't miss the tour."

"Not at all. We're going to begin in the atrium in a few minutes. The leaded glasswork was preserved beyond anything we imagined. Brooks, you should give our contractor's name to your father. He mentioned Badewood needed some repairs on that gorgeous portico."

"I will. And I thought I saw Manning's car out front."

"He was talking to Colonel Bradley about next month's field maneuvers." Mrs. Werlin frowned, as if the words she'd heard hadn't made much sense. "Something about how the Bahala Rifles regiment kept several goats for milk and he thought it would be more authentic to bring a few along for the weekend. Your sister-in-law reminded them her role as company cook did not extend to milking goats."

Caroline laughed. "Perhaps the men could perform that task and give Debbie Mae the milk for cooking."

"I can't see Manning milking a goat," Brooks said. Manning was a Civil War enthusiast, not a farmer.

"Hey, you two." As if on cue, Manning appeared and gave Brooks a brotherly punch to the shoulder. "Where's Dad?"

"He didn't feel up to it." Brooks resisted rubbing the throbbing spot and wished he could lob a punch right back. Manning was younger, but Brooks had always been the better athlete. An old-fashioned headlock would even things out.

Manning raised his eyebrows. "He hasn't been feeling up to a lot."

"That's too bad. You give him our love, hear?" Mrs. Werlin patted Manning on the arm and turned to speak to a young man hovering at the edge of their small group.

"How have you been, Manning?" Caroline gave him a quick hug.

The guests in the room seemed to be shifting around them as more attendees arrived. Manning saw a lot of familiar faces and old acquaintances. "Gooder'n grits," he said, laughing. "Debbie

Mae's got me training for a triathlon. We're doing the Gator Bait in August."

"Glad to hear it! I dragged your brother out for a sunrise run yesterday and he still hasn't stopped complaining."

Brooks snorted. "I stopped complaining within a few hours."

"I want you to meet someone, if I can catch his eye." Manning waved toward a cluster of well-dressed women. From the center of the group, a young man disentangled himself. He smiled his way out of their reach and crossed the room, bright teeth flashing in the light. A pin-striped, three-piece suit paired with an outrageously patterned tie made Brooks think of entertainers and politicians. He felt immediate remorse for the unkind comparison and fixed his face into a friendly expression. Maybe the guy couldn't help having perfectly straight teeth and overly styled hair. Well, he could probably help the hair.

"I'd like you to meet Franklin Keene. He and Debbie Mae went to grade school together. He came up from Oxford to celebrate the completion of the renovations," Manning said.

"Pleasure to meet you." Frank reached out and grasped Caroline's hand, flashing that toothpaste smile. She said nothing, and for a moment Brooks wondered if she might be fighting back an impulse to laugh.

But when she spoke, her voice was a bit breathless: "Caroline Ashley."

Frank was still holding her hand and his smile grew wider, if possible. Brooks swore he could see every tooth in the man's mouth.

"This is my brother, Brooks," Manning continued as if he hadn't noticed Caroline and Frank were having a moment.

Frank withdrew his hand, slowly lifting his gaze to acknowledge the other person in the group. "Lucky man. A brother like Manning and a date like Caroline." The words included Manning, but they all knew who was being complimented. Brooks felt his jaw tense. This kid was getting on his nerves.

He shook Frank's hand, resisting the petty urge to grind his knuckles a little bit. "You and Debbie Mae are good friends?"

"I moved away from Thorny Hollow in sixth grade when my father was transferred to Nashville, but this place has always been like a second home to me." Frank motioned around the expansive ballroom.

"Mrs. Werlin is his aunt," Manning clarified.

"I don't remember you." Caroline put a finger to her chin and gave Frank a long look. "Unless . . . you were that skinny kid that always rode the green bicycle around the end of our driveway. You had glasses and hair that . . ." She made a movement above her head that seemed to indicate either a severe cowlick or intentionally dramatic styling.

Frank laughed and leaned forward. "You *do* remember me. I was uglier than homemade sin. Let me tell you that skinny little kid was so in love with you that he tried to tattoo your initials onto his own arm with a ballpoint pen."

Her eyes went wide and she raised a hand to cover her mouth, laughing. "You weren't! You didn't!"

"Miss Caroline Ashley, I assure you I was and I did. My daddy whupped me for it. I was so in love with you, I'd ride my bike to the end of your driveway every day in the summertime, waiting to see if you'd be coming to Mr. Hardy's store for a Coke. I'd pretend the chain had slipped if anyone drove by. I never could figure out a pattern to your comings and goings. Most days I went home without a glimpse of you and a near dose of heatstroke."

"I'm sorry I was mean." Her brows drew together. "I'm pretty certain I was. At least, I remember telling you to go dunk your head."

He laughed, all those teeth on display again. Brooks was beginning to hate the sound of Frank's geniality. "I probably deserved it. I just wouldn't leave you alone."

"Well, I promise not to repeat my bad manners. I'll be good." She looked up at him from under her lashes and Brooks almost choked. She was flirting!

"I'm not sure I can return that promise." His eyes went half-closed and he was inches away from her. Brooks cleared his throat, hoping to remind them other people were in the room.

"I think the tour is about to start." Brooks took Caroline's elbow and tried to steer her toward the atrium, but her feet were planted.

"I didn't hear any announcement."

Brooks looked at Manning, who shrugged. "I'll go find Debbie Mae." Manning was gone in the next moment.

Brooks took a deep breath. There wasn't any reason to be so annoyed. This guy was clearly a schmoozer and a charmer, but not seriously dangerous. Surely Caroline saw through him from the first moment and was just being kind. Brooks glanced at her as Frank launched into another story from his childhood spent chasing the dream of Caroline Ashley. Her face was flushed and her bright green-blue eyes reflected the faceted-crystal chandeliers above. She laughed, a sound that was as familiar to Brooks as his own heartbeat, and laid a hand on Frank's arm. For a moment, he saw her as a woman, not as the girl he'd always known. Gone was the kid who preferred cherry Popsicles to green ones and who painted her bedroom walls pitch black without permission and who started her own tiny newspaper as a high school senior.

Brooks felt something stir in his chest, like an animal being roused from sleep. It wasn't a pleasant feeling, and he pushed it away, refusing to surrender to petty jealousy. Caroline should go out more often. He'd just said so himself not even an hour ago.

He forced his expression into something he hoped would pass for relaxed, but it probably landed somewhere near sullen. It was natural to feel a bit left out when your friends started a new relationship. When Manning started dating Debbie Mae, months stretched between his trips to Midlands College to visit. Now Brooks hardly saw him unless there was a reenactment, and apparently Debbie Mae would be there from now on, too.

It was just exactly the same situation. Brooks said this a few times to himself as Caroline beamed up at toothy, perfect-hair Frank. Brooks said the words, but the truth was quite different, and deep down, he knew it. He hadn't been jealous of Manning's new girlfriend. He hadn't even minded the brotherly excursions' being curtailed for the new wife.

Franklin Keene had landed firmly on Brooks's bad side, and there was no way he could make friends with the man. It didn't matter how interesting he turned out to be or how many stories he told of his childhood in Thorny Hollow. They would never be friends; the reason had nothing to do with Frank's style and everything to do with the woman standing between them.

Why not seize the pleasure at once?–

How often is happiness destroyed by

preparation, foolish preparation!

—FRANK CHURCHILL

CHAPTER SIX

Caroline realized that this was the best thing that had happened to her in months. A party on a perfect summer evening combined with a brand-new and interesting man had coated her entire life with the stardust of satisfaction. Of course, all was rosy before you got to know a person, but so far, Franklin Keene was about as perfect as a man could get. She tried not to stare, but he was breathtaking in his effortless elegance. Obviously cultured, Southern and handsome, all he needed to do was to say he spent his days doing something impressive, such as researching cancer cures.

"Well?" Frank was smiling down at her, deep brown eyes intense.

She blinked, scrambling to recall his last few words. He'd been telling some story about meeting her grandfather and she'd lost the thread of the conversation. She opened her mouth to apologize but Brooks cut in.

"She's a freelance journalist working on the Great American Novel."

She turned to frown at him but Frank was already speaking. "Fascinating! I've been dealing with quite a few freelance writers lately. You might know some of them. Scott Drexler? Terry Lewis?"

"No, I'm afraid I've been very bad about keeping up my professional contacts lately." Her face felt hot but she kept the smile fixed to her face, hoping he wouldn't interpret her words to mean "living in my mom's house and eating ice cream out of the carton," which was the truth of it.

"I understand. It's become such a trial for writers. So much of it is marketing. That's why I have an entire team devoted to keeping them happy, although the days of Thoreau's cabin in the woods are over. Tell me you at least go on Twitter once in a while."

She blinked, wondering why on earth writers would need to be on Twitter. With 140 characters, they could impart much. "I leave tweeting to the haiku masters."

Frank laughed, a lovely, warm sound that made a shiver zigzag from the top of her head to her toes. "There, that would have been perfect. More of that and you'll have a platform in no time. To make your marketing effective, I advise aiming for at least five thousand followers."

Brooks made a noise that sounded suspiciously like a groan covered by a cough. Well, he could dismiss the idea all he wanted, but maybe Frank had a point. If she wanted to get back into more steady work, she needed to build her connections. "Do you work in public relations, then?"

"Me?" Frank looked shocked, brown eyes wide under that unruly wave of hair. "No. I work in publishing. Cutting-edge. We buy foreign rights and get them ready for American distribution. Strictly digital, no paper copies."

"So, you hire translators?" Caroline felt her cheeks growing hot. She couldn't quite grasp what Frank did, exactly. A journalism degree covered a hundred separate categories and she desperately searched her memory for anything related to foreign rights.

He cocked his head and smiled, as if she'd said something charming. "Not quite that. Our publishing house is pretty specific and only acquires rights to manga books."

"Those comics that start at the back page?" Caroline remembered Debbie Mae reading those when they were in high school. One whole series was about a girl who found out on her sixteenth birthday her real father was a bird and she could fly. The absurdly large eyes and short skirts made her wonder if it was secretly targeted toward teen boys. She'd never bothered to open it since reading a comic version of any book seemed a travesty of literature.

"Right. We hire young, fresh writing voices to help spruce up the dialogue. We have in-house translators, but they're not writers." He leaned forward a bit and deep brown eyes locked on hers. "You'd be perfect for our team."

It had been a long time since she'd been part of anyone's team. Caroline felt herself warm to the idea, even as it took shape in her mind: a group of young, hip professionals gathered around a conference table throwing ideas at each other with rapid-fire genius, and herself there in the middle of it all.

"You've never read anything she's written," Brooks spoke into the moment, his voice dry.

"I can remedy that." She smiled tightly, refusing to look at Brooks. "Let me know when and how. I'd like to know more about your company."

Frank pulled out a card and handed it over. "I can tell you right now, this is going to be epic." He said the last word without any hint of embarrassment.

"Caroline Ashley and Brooks Elliot," a voice exclaimed right behind Caroline's left shoulder. She turned, almost bumping into Mrs. Reynolds. She was holding a large champagne glass and clutching the elbow of a strikingly beautiful woman. "I want to introduce my granddaughter Lauren Fairfield. She's working on a book about our little town."

"Oh, Nana, I wish it was just our town. We're gathering photos and history of the whole area of Thorny Hollow." The girl smiled ruefully, one bare shoulder lifting, the delicate strap of her cream-colored summer dress slipping an inch or two. Her skin wasn't tanned by the sun, but she had a natural color that paired perfectly with the fabric. "But my boss knows I have family here and agreed to let me spend a bit more time on this lovely area."

Caroline forced her face into a pleasant expression and worked at hiding her surprise. Of course, Lauren wasn't just brilliant, a high-powered editor, and preparing a coffee-table book on their hometown history. She was beautiful. Not an ordinary beautiful, no, but enormous gray eyes rimmed with dark lashes, set over sculpted cheekbones. A rippling sheet of dark, glossy hair hung in waves on either side of her face. Not just beauty, but elegance and sophistication. She smiled and Caroline wanted to roll her eyes at the sight. Lauren's matching dimples framed an impossibly sweet smile and white, straight teeth. It was the icing on her jealousy cake.

Caroline said, "I think you visited my mother last week. I was running an errand and I missed you, but she was pleased to hear about your book. You spent some time looking at the flatware and the old kitchen fixtures, I think." She meant it to be an opening for

Lauren to talk about her area of expertise, but the woman frowned at Caroline, as if struggling to remember the visit at all.

"Oh, right. The little place down from the rural highway exit?" Lauren's voice was soft, even a bit musical.

Little place? It had ten rooms and three stories of antebellum beauty. Caroline swallowed back a retort and nodded.

"I'm afraid I didn't find exactly what we needed, but we know this area has a very rich history and we're not giving up." Lauren turned to Brooks and asked, "Are you related to the Elliots of Badewood?"

Brooks seemed pleased that she had recognized his estate by the mere mention of his name. "It's my family home."

"It would be wonderful to visit Badewood. I'm particularly interested in the outbuildings."

"We'd be happy to have you." His slow smile was genuine and Caroline wondered how he could be so happy with the idea of a photographer tramping around the place. Maybe it would be a different matter if Lauren were an ugly toad. If Caroline thought she could get away with it, she'd use his attention as a point in her favor, but Caroline had to admit that Lauren was everything Mrs. Reynolds had said she would be. And more. She couldn't blame Brooks for giving her more than a passing glance.

The two rambled on a bit about Badewood and the local historic buildings, but Caroline had the distinct impression that Lauren was practically reading from a script. Maybe she was nervous, or intimidated.

"Miss Fairfield, I've heard that your publisher is close to being swallowed up by a larger imprint. Is that true?" Frank's question seemed straightforward, if a bit awkward, but Lauren's reaction was swift. Her cheeks deepened in a blush and she blinked several times, as if struggling to find words.

"Mr. Keene, I'm sure that I know very little about the financial state of the company." Her words were stiff, clipped. She turned to Mrs. Reynolds. "Nana, let's get closer to the atrium before the tour starts. We don't want to be left behind."

The group murmured their good-byes and waited in silence while Lauren moved away, her dark hair swinging in a silky curtain around her shoulders.

"She seems a little defensive," Caroline mused. It was surprising that Frank could elicit a response with one sentence.

"Everyone in traditional publishing is. With the digital market, we're on the cutting edge. Anytime we have to partner at all with them, it's like using the Pony Express. Absolute waste of time and energy." Frank's lip curled as he spoke, his eyes following Lauren across the room. "I'm glad I don't have to work with that sort of backward attitude."

"Perhaps a partnership would be the wisest course," Brooks said in that calm, slow way he had when he completely disagreed with someone but was too polite to say so.

Frank considered Brooks's words for a moment and shrugged. "I'd better go apologize, then. I'd hate to burn any bridges. You can never tell when you'll need to ally yourself with a bloated, tyrannical publishing company."

Reaching out, Frank touched Caroline's elbow. "Call me and we can go to lunch. I'm based in Spartainville for the next few months."

She nodded, feeling a rising sense of purpose for the first time in a long while. "I will."

He was gone a moment later, back into the swirling group of guests making their way toward the atrium. She watched him go, his dark hair and tailored clothes standing out, even though the room was filled with elegantly attired guests. He turned just before he rejoined his friends, catching her eye. A wide smile crossed his face and Caroline felt her cheeks go hot.

"Don't tell me you're actually going to call him?"

Whirling, she frowned up at Brooks. "Why the sudden negativity? You wanted me to get back into the loop. Well, a small press could be just the thing."

"Right. Because working on a manga comic would be totally epic."

She raised her chin. "You're being petty and it doesn't become you."

"I don't care if it becomes me. I think brains are more important than looks, remember?"

Her mouth dropped open in shock. "You're implying that I gave Frank attention because he's handsome?"

"You can't deny that he's preoccupied with his appearance."

Manning hurried to their group, breathless. "I think we've got about two minutes before the tour. Debbie Mae is stuck over with Mrs. Kropp, and she says if you two leave without seeing her, she'll hunt you down." He called over his shoulder, already on his way past them. "Don't think she doesn't mean it, because she does."

Caroline snorted. "Mrs. Kropp is a black hole of Southern sweetness. Once you've wandered into her orbit, she'll keep you trapped there forever."

They were slowly making their way through to the atrium, as fellow guests murmured around them, holding glasses and small bone-china plates piled with half-eaten canapés. "I've never seen a shinier suit outside of Nashville," Brooks said. "He looks like one of those people that scout for models in the local mall on Saturday afternoons."

"That's harsh. I expected more from you." Caroline's jaw

went tight. "About the slang, he's probably surrounded by college kids and is more flexible in his word choices. You know, the days of those author and editor teams like James Thurber and Harold Ross are gone. An author can have dozens of editors over the years, and they're all going to be about age twenty-five. *You* can afford to stagnate in academia as a revered professor, but the rest of us are fighting the inevitable slide into obsolescence."

"'Stagnate'?" The calm in his face warned her she was pushing his buttons, but Caroline didn't care.

"I'm sure when you were younger and working toward tenure, you had to be up on all the current news. But now you're comfortable and secure. You're looking down your nose at him because he's trying to stay relevant."

Brooks stood still, eyes narrowed. Caroline knew she was being a little unfair, but Brooks was out of line. Frank seemed no worse and no better than most of the people in the room.

"I guess time will tell whether I'm just a dull and lifeless academic, too comfortable to rouse myself from the reveries of my youth." Brooks paused. "But I can tell you that if I'm right, and Frank is part snake-oil salesman, part publishing hack, then you'd best be staying far away."

They stood there, gazes locked in anger for the second time that evening. Caroline wouldn't back down. He had an annoying habit of bossing her around, and she was perfectly capable of making decisions for herself. Just when she felt her resolve begin to wither, his eyes flickered past her and his expression shifted to a neutral smile.

"Dr. Stroud, how nice to see you here. This is Caroline Ashley." Brooks put a hand on the small of her back while reaching past her to extend his other hand to an elderly man with the brightest blue eyes Caroline had ever seen. A white, three-piece linen suit was perfect for the late-spring heat, but with the man's white hair grown long to his collar, he looked a bit like Mark Twain.

"I think Caroline and I have met once before. At a party quite like this one, I believe." He turned to her and leaned forward, whispering conspiratorially, "Your friend Shelby Roswell and I discussed the many methods in which a Civil War soldier could lose a limb. When you made a graceful exit, I realized how inexcusably rude I'd been. I'm glad to have the opportunity to offer my apologies for my shocking behavior."

Caroline gasped, laughing. "I remember you! When you mentioned necrotic tissue, I was forced to retreat to the pink-lemonade table."

"I hope all is forgiven. I hear Miss Roswell has moved to Jackson?"

"She took a position at Millsaps right after she got married." Shelby's wedding was one of the most romantic Caroline had ever attended and it still gave her a flush of happiness when she looked at the photos.

"Ransom Fielding is a lucky man." Dr. Stroud paused. "But I have to admit I wasn't quite sure whether they were friend or foe the times I saw them together."

Nodding, Caroline couldn't hold back another laugh. "Well, from what I heard, they were enemies who decided it was better to end their little war and become something much better."

"They make a very formidable team, those two historians." He rubbed his chin, the rasp of his whiskers clear to Caroline's ears. "I miss him at our field maneuvers, although I hear he's coming in September for the one hundred fiftieth celebration at the Chickamauga National Military Park. If I have to drive to Georgia to see him, I guess that's what I'll do."

"It's a big year for reenactments. I wish I had more time, but between teaching at Midlands and spending weekends down here . . ." Brooks's voice trailed off and he shrugged.

"No excuses. We're a dwindling band of old-timers with long memories. Brooks, you must come to Iuka next month." Dr. Stroud leveled a sharp gaze under heavy brows. "It's not accurate if every able-bodied man walks off the field after the skirmish, is it? I'm not asking for a dramatic rendition of their pain and suffering, either. Since the surgical tent is right on the battlefield, I uncork the chloroform and the soldier just pretends to fade away into sleep. I suppose, if they wanted more excitement, they could be one of those few men who struggled during the first stage of anesthesia."

"What would you do? Thump them on the noggin?" Brooks looked to be relishing the idea of playacting a medical reaction.

"Chloroform didn't cause as many complications, but it took longer than ether. So, I suppose we could bring out the ether vial, instead." Dr. Stroud rubbed his chin thoughtfully. "But no one would be fooled, as ether smells terrible and usually caused coughing and vomiting."

"Let's skip the ether," Brooks said, grimacing.

"Is there any attendee who might expect the real thing?" Caroline couldn't refrain from asking the question. It was a reenactment. Surely no one expected real ether in the fake surgery tent.

"Absolutely. We like to make it as realistic as possible. That's the fun." Dr. Stroud beamed, those bright blue eyes lit from within. "I do wish the men would be more eager to adequately represent a few of the forty-five thousand amputee veterans the war produced. Apparently, it's not as heroic as losing one's life on the field. During the last battle, I had to persuade quite a few men that there was no dishonor in losing a limb in my care."

"You can count on me and my limbs." Brooks held out both arms, as if offering himself at that very moment. His large hands curled into fists, thick veins stark against his tan skin. Caroline fought the sensation of rising nausea at the thought of anyone's pretending to remove Brooks's well-muscled arms. He spent his days teaching, but he was athletic and fit. Of course, it was all just make-believe, but it still filled her with horror.

"I knew I could." Dr. Stroud inclined his head. "Miss Ashley, I hope to see you there. We'll keep you far from the gruesome realities of the War Between the States, perhaps in dinner preparations. We can't allow you to farb your way through, but we can try our best to find something to suit your talents."

She could only smile, hoping against hope she wouldn't ever have to spend the weekend in the baking-hot sun, dressed in multilayered petticoats and a bonnet. Or worse, restraining perfectly healthy men as they playacted an amputation. She knew these men, heard the stories. These were not bored professionals on a weekend jaunt. They were serious historians, sometimes spending tens of thousands a year and sewing their own clothes.

As Dr. Stroud walked away, she leaned close and whispered, "'Farb'?"

"Farbs do everything the easy way and just pretend they're in the war."

She shot him a look.

He shrugged. "Right, we're all *pretending*, but some pretending is of a higher quality than others."

She stowed the term in the back of her mind, hoping she'd never have to use it. She'd like to keep the pretending at a minimum, no matter the quality. Brooks had griped about getting the "anchor" position last time, and she'd made the mistake of asking. In the early spring, a man would risk frostbite if he slept alone with the threadbare Confederate-issue blanket. Brooks had explained that on the coldest nights the soldiers spooned together for warmth, and the men on the end of the rows only got warm on one side, half the time. When the commander yelled for the men to flip, the anchor could thaw out his frozen side on his bunkmate . . . until the next call to turn. Caroline had almost rolled her eyes out of her head at the description, but Brooks was a die-hard reenactor. No amount of mockery would change that.

She glanced at him, feeling her mouth tilt up at the man she knew better than any other man in the world. A universe of contradictions, a wealth of knowledge, and the gentleness of a friend. She could see how women found him attractive.

Dr. Stroud joined an older woman with a pinched-looking expression and crimped blond hair. She met Caroline's eyes for just a moment, then turned away, muttering out of the corner of her mouth. Caroline wondered if Dr. Stroud's wife was jealous of all the time he spent on reenactments. Or maybe it was the time he spent talking to other history buffs. Caroline never remembered her parents straying far from each other at a party. They might join smaller groups, but they were still just feet away, glancing over, smiling or giving those looks that long-married couples give each other and that no one else can decipher. Caroline felt a pain near her ribs and wondered if her mother would ever go to another party. She used to enjoy them, especially the garden parties in the spring and the Christmas festivities. But since Caroline's daddy had passed away, her mama hadn't been to a single one. As Caroline and Brooks moved toward the large, arched doorway of the glass-enclosed atrium, she tried to push her sadness aside and focus on the tour.

"Finley, as I was saying . . . ," Brooks began, his voice pitched low. He'd leaned closer and his breath shifted the hair that hung near her cheek, as if he were running a finger across her skin.

She put up a hand to halt what would undoubtedly be a long speech on the merits of a more traditional writing career. Or at least something that didn't involve Franklin Keene. "You've already made up your mind not to like him, but I'm glad there's somebody interesting around here for once. Thorny Hollow is made up of nosy old ladies and desperately single young women." Staring straight ahead as the guests shuffled toward the entrance, she could hear Mrs. Werlin directing people to one side or another as they entered. "Anyway, Frank seems perfectly normal, and just because he wears a suit in a style you don't like doesn't mean he's running a scheme."

"It's not the suit." Brooks's words came out on a groan of aggravation. He dropped his voice again as they stood shoulder to shoulder with the other guests. "And it's not his age or his stupid hair. He seems to ferret out what you want him to say and then makes sure you hear it. He's shifty."

Caroline bit her tongue and tried her best not to respond. She gazed around the enormous, glass-domed atrium. The evening light sparkled against the newly restored leaded panes, and potted citrus trees stretched toward the ceiling. The air was thick with the rich scent of hibiscus and orchids. She could see Frank across the room, talking to Lauren Fairfield and Mrs. Reynolds. She couldn't quite catch a glimpse of Lauren's expression unless she craned her neck, but Mrs. Reynolds was smiling and chatting animatedly. "I appreciate the heads-up but I don't intend to give him my bank account number. I'm interested in joining the workforce. I would think you'd be happy about that."

Out of the corner of her eye, she could see Brooks shaking his head. "So now I'm the bad guy for saying you need to get out of the house. Flipping burgers is a job, too. I don't see you running for the striped hat and matching apron."

With every new body in the room, they shifted a few more feet along the rounded wall of the greenhouse, nodding and exchanging smiles with guests. She moved a little farther from a woman with a prodigious beehive hairdo and perfume so strong it made Caroline's eyes water. They stood directly under a mandarin-orange tree and she focused on the glossy leaves and neon-colored fruit.

She didn't want to fight with Brooks. He was being strangely unreasonable and she couldn't even guess at the reason why. She would just wait patiently for Mrs. Werlin to begin the tour of the reconstruction. Ten seconds passed in acute silence and she felt Brooks at her shoulder, his brooding presence like a small thundercloud ready to crackle with lightning.

It was impossible to stand so close together, seething with unsaid words. She turned her head a fraction of an inch. "I appreciate the advice, I really do, and if I was in any position to lose my professional reputation, then I would be grateful for the warning. As it is, I'm not risking anything except my mother's approval. When she hears I'm thinking of looking for employment, she won't be happy."

It was the first time she'd stated the situation so plainly, and she felt the relief of being honest at the same time she saw the anger slide from his face. He nodded, as if finally understanding her position. "I know."

She turned her attention back to the center of the room, determined to enjoy the rest of the party. Historically accurate renovations took tens of thousands of dollars and whole teams of advisers. It was a thrill to witness the Werlins' mansion restored to its antebellum beauty.

If she could just reconcile her dreams with all the expectations around her, then life would be perfect. Caroline straightened her back and breathed deeply, the scent of tropical foliage and rich soil filling her with optimism. The time for change was now. Brooks might argue and complain, but surely he could see that this was a wonderful opportunity. It could be the first step out of her present life, the one that was dictated by bridge-club meetings and failed chocolate cakes.

She will never submit to anything requiring industry and patience, and a subjection of the fancy to the understanding.

—MR. KNIGHTLEY

CHAPTER SEVEN

Mrs. Werlin's voice carried through the atrium as though she were holding a microphone. "Two centuries ago, a pioneer brought cedar saplings in a cigar box from China. Today, those trees stand healthy and strong, greeting every visitor to this house."

The space had amazing acoustics, despite being filled with all sorts of shrubs and trees, including the one currently poking an especially sharp branch into Brooks's shoulder, even as he hunched awkwardly to avoid one of the tree's lower limbs. He shifted closer to Caroline, wishing he were about four inches shorter than his full six feet. He tried to focus on the presentation, rather than his awkward position.

Mrs. Werlin continued, "Twenty-nine acres of manicured gardens include a fountain and award-winning azaleas. Along with our goal of updating the heating system, we included a major renovation of the outbuildings. The carriage house, barn, cottage and schoolhouse were repaired and repainted in keeping with the original paint colors."

Schoolhouse. Brooks felt his lips twitch. The Elliot mansion also had a schoolhouse. Though just a one-room, pine-floored room with a potbellied woodstove that leaked smoke from a crack in its pipe, he used to spend a lot of time there when he was young. One summer he'd pried up a few floorboards and found Indian-head pennies and clay marbles that had been lost by children a hundred years previously. By the time he'd grown out of playing school, Caroline had taken up the game. On certain summer days he could peek in and see his neighbor friend teaching her imaginary class while waving a battered yardstick. The floor would be littered with little pieces of broken chalk, and she would be in the middle of sending some invisible troublemaker to the naughty stool in the corner.

His gaze wandered to the curve of her cheek and he almost let out a laugh to see the blush of pink. She remembered, just as he did. He leaned close, keeping his voice just a murmur. "Maybe if you're good, Mrs. Werlin will let you be the teacher."

Caroline turned her head just a fraction and wrinkled her nose, before returning her attention to the speech. He felt laughter rising up in his chest and fought the urge to give her a little poke in the side. She was so much fun to tease.

"The decision to add a large home theater was a difficult one for us, but it made perfect sense as we thought about it more." Mrs. Werlin cast a loving glance at her husband, who nodded, unsmiling.

Caroline whispered out of the corner of her mouth, "Home theater?"

"I guess so." Brooks was a little surprised they had added something so out of character in the historic home.

"The pool was enlarged to Olympic size, and the wraparound deck can now accommodate several hundred people. The new hot tub can hold thirty guests at once," Mrs. Werlin said.

Caroline turned her head, catching his eye. Her expression was a mix of confusion and curiosity. He understood her unspoken question: What would they need with a deck that size? The guests in this room numbered barely a hundred, and it was unlikely the majority of them would be taking a soak in the new hot tub.

Caroline seemed to notice for the first time that he was crouched forward under the citrus-tree branch and tugged on his sleeve. "Here," she whispered, "switch places with me. I'm shorter."

"Our home has been a landmark in the Thorny Hollow area for close to two centuries and we're delighted to be announcing a new chapter." Mrs. Werlin moved toward a small easel in the middle of the atrium, her hand hovering over the white cloth that concealed a placard.

Brooks stepped to the right and Caroline slipped behind him, ducking under his arm. She put a hand on the back of his suit coat and smiled up at him. He loved how the tiny gap between her front teeth added to her smile. "See? Now we fit perfectly."

He grinned back at her, noting the way her hair just brushed the gnarled branch. Turning his attention back to Mrs. Werlin, he watched her pause, silent. Then with a flourish, she lifted the white cloth from the square board, and as it floated up, his eyes seemed to lose focus for a moment.

The sound in the room was as if all the air had been sucked out in one loud whoosh. Caroline's fingers clenched into a fist, pulling the fabric of his jacket tight. That tiny movement, unseen by anyone else in the room, matched his own dismay. A hard lump of despair settled in his gut as he read the words on the shiny brass plaque.

CEDAR POINT HOTEL AND RESTAURANT, engraved in a fancy font, beamed out at the room in an unequivocal fashion. This renovation had undeniably been for one purpose only: turning one of the most beautiful antebellum estates of Thorny Hollow into a commercial enterprise.

"We're excited to open to the public immediately, including weddings and graduation parties." Mrs. Werlin nodded as if the idea of hundreds of rowdy high school students tromping through her house were a perfectly wonderful prospect.

The room slowly came back to life and guests began to clap, although not with any sort of enthusiasm.

Caroline was still clutching the back of Brooks's coat. He turned, catching her eye. The glint of unshed tears sparkled on her lashes. His throat constricted at the sight. "They must not have had any other option," he whispered in her ear.

"I never liked that woman." Her tone was furious.

"Now, now. She's always been nice enough."

"Nice doesn't cut it." Caroline lifted her eyes to his and blinked back tears. "How could they?"

He shook his head. Every owner of a truly historic Southern mansion had to make this decision, at some time. "Finley, these old places don't support themselves. You can't let them fall into ruins, either."

"It was nowhere near ruins. It was *fine*." She leaned into his shoulder and took a shuddering breath. "It's awful. I can't bear it."

He leaned close, whispering, "Mr. Codd down on Market Street told me that it cost twenty thousand to paint his house the last time, and they'd painted just four years ago. We're lucky to have mostly brick, but these enormous wooden places take so much more than you can imagine."

"No, what I can't imagine is turning a home into a restaurant, overrun by kids from New Jersey on spring break. It's criminal, Brooks. It's just not right." Her voice was filled with anguish.

Brooks said nothing, feeling the weight of dismay in his chest. His father was tight-lipped about finances, no matter how Brooks offered to help out with any taxes or the costs of the perpetual renovations that occur with a building centuries old. Perhaps Badewood was teetering on the edge of financial ruin as well. He didn't know.

"Why can't everything stay the way it's always been?" She seemed to be talking to herself and not requiring a response.

"Change is inevitable." It was painful to admit, but nothing good lasted forever. He wasn't a fatalist; he was a realist.

Caroline's sunny nature seemed to set her up for disappointment, time after time after time. At moments like this, he wished that he could simply wipe away the pain of ruined expectations. He wrapped an arm around her and tried to focus on the rest of Mrs. Werlin's speech, but his thoughts were on the woman next to him.

Caroline fought to control the ache that was creeping up her throat. She would not cry, she would not cry! It would still be here, in all its splendor, just in a different fashion. More visitors, more people to enjoy the beauty of the place. That's what she told herself, over and over.

But she grieved for the Werlin place. Thirty-person hot tub, indeed. It was ruined. It wasn't the stately antebellum home she'd always admired. It was now Cedar Point Hotel and Restaurant, and it made her heart feel as if it were being squeezed in a steel trap. Mrs. Werlin proudly led the group out the far door of the atrium, and Caroline wondered if it would be rude to skip the rest of the tour.

"There you are." Debbie Mae grabbed Caroline's hands and gave her a huge kiss. Debbie Mae's knee-length, mint-green dress and matching heels were offset by a few strands of perfect pearls. All that was par for the party course, but she had swept up her dark red hair into a complicated hairstyle that reminded Caroline of Regency heroines. Tiny, pearl-studded pins dotted the elaborate hairstyle. The effect was breathtaking. Just like Debbie Mae, her outfit was impossible to ignore. "Can you believe it? Manning told me something was up with that enormous pool. I guess he was right."

Caroline struggled to speak past the lump in her throat. "He certainly was." She'd been excited to see Debbie Mae, but now all she wanted to do was run home and crawl into her soft bed. Pulling the covers over her head and never coming out had never seemed more like such a good idea than at this moment.

"Pretty." Debbie Mae touched the flowers in Caroline's hair and smiled. "I love forget-me-nots. They're so hard to find. Did you order these?"

Brooks coughed into his hand and Caroline shot him a look. "No, I just . . ." She wasn't sure what to say. *Found* wasn't quite the right word.

"Brooks, stay here. I want to introduce you to a friend of mine." Debbie Mae scanned the crowd for her friend.

Caroline tried not to sigh out loud. Of course Debbie Mae was on a mission to keep Brooks from ending up an old bachelor, but introducing him to every woman under forty wasn't going to work. He wasn't the type to ask for anyone's number. Unless the woman was very, very special. Caroline couldn't help trying to pick out which friend Debbie Mae had in mind.

She motioned to a young woman on the far end of the greenhouse. "There she is. We met at the party the firm threw last month in Oxford. Her grandfather lives in Thorny Hollow, running the gas station on Sixth Street. Small world, right?"

Caroline raised her eyebrows but said nothing. Brooks wasn't a snob. He was probably the most open-minded man she knew. But the woman making her way toward them couldn't have been more than nineteen. A fitted red dress, matching high heels and an updo featuring lots of glossy curls might have been overkill on someone else, but she had a quiet confidence that pulled it all together.

Smiling shyly, the dark-haired girl paused a few feet from Debbie Mae. Large brown eyes framed by thick lashes made Caroline think of a doe. "This is Lexi Martinez. She's a very talented artist and she designed the new logo for Manning's firm."

Debbie Mae finished the introductions and went on, "She's been accepted to Ole Miss so we'll only have her around for the summer, then off she'll go to change the world."

"Wonderful to meet you, Lexi. What's your favorite medium?" Brooks asked.

"I've been working with computer graphics for a few years but I really love to sketch. Pen and ink, mostly." Even her voice was soft and pretty. She glanced at Debbie Mae, as if making sure she'd said the right thing.

Caroline felt a twinge of sympathy. It seemed the confidence only covered the dress. Having an actual conversation was a bit harder. She couldn't imagine standing in this atrium filled with the area's oldest and wealthiest families when your father ran a gas station on Sixth Street.

"You'll be majoring in art, then?" Caroline could remember exactly how it had felt to leave her friends and family for college.

That summer stretched endlessly in her memory, full of promise and thrilling fear.

Lexi shook her head, one dark curl on each side sweeping against her sharp cheekbones. "No, I think I'll major in accounting. It's safer."

Caroline felt her eyes go wide. How awful to know your passion lay in art, but you had to be an accountant to pay the bills. "You'll minor in art, at least?"

"I don't think so. I need to get through school as quickly as possible."

"It's a shame you can't make a living right now from your art. In fact"—Caroline swiveled around, searching for Frank in the atrium—"we were just talking to someone who works in a publishing company, with those manga comics."

"Really?" Lexi lit up as if someone had shone a spotlight on her. She peered around, eyes sparkling.

"But he wasn't hiring artists, really," Brooks cut in, his tone measured.

"He made it sound as if his company was growing by leaps and bounds." Caroline ignored the warning note in his voice. "I just think it's a shame you're going to major in accounting when you'd rather make a living in art."

"We all make some sort of compromise, I suppose." Debbie Mae shrugged lightly.

"Did you?" Caroline wasn't trying to provoke an argument, but she was fairly sure that Debbie Mae had always wanted to be a teacher.

Her cousin's cheeks went pink. "Not really, I suppose. There was a time I wanted to get a doctorate in education, but by the time I got my master's in teaching, it seemed like overkill. I'm happy teaching fourth-graders."

Caroline said nothing, her point made. She thought she glimpsed Frank's profile and a flash of Lauren's silky black hair, but the next moment they were gone. "Lexi, give me your number, and when I talk to Frank, I'll ask him about any jobs in the art department."

"That would be great." Lexi rummaged in her small black purse for a pen. "I'd love to talk to him."

As she scribbled her number on a slip of paper and handed it over, Caroline could feel Brooks at her shoulder, disapproving. In the few minutes that followed, he didn't say a word. The shock of Mrs. Werlin's announcement was wearing off, and Caroline was filled with resolve. She wouldn't allow a young girl to throw away her dreams because of sheer pessimism. Someone had told Lexi to put her dreams in a box and bury them deep. Well, Lexi was going to get the chance to be an artist, if Caroline could help it. If everyone compromised on his or her passion, then only thirty-person hot tubs and a world full of accountants would be left.

Upon my word, Emma, to hear you abusing the reason you have, is almost enough to make me think so, too. Better be without sense than misapply it as you do.

—MR. KNIGHTLEY

Chapter Eight

Brooks stayed silent, watching Caroline encourage Lexi to abandon accounting to pursue her dreams, but he'd be sure to bring up this little conversation in the car. Caroline had no business telling a kid to focus on something that wouldn't pay the rent. Lexi might even be the first person in her family to go to college. Majoring in art wouldn't do anybody any good, unless she was prepared for the lean years. And if her father owned that little gas station on Sixth Street, then she didn't have a built-in financial cushion. Accounting would give her the space to support her artistic dreams, but Caroline was acting as if it would be the death of all Lexi held dear.

He let out a slow breath. Caroline was compassionate and loved to encourage others, which he loved about her, but sometimes her advice wasn't particularly realistic. Her wealthy background colored her reality with possibilities, where others had none. Lexi Martinez deserved a clear picture of what a major in art would entail, especially financially. *Starving artist* was a popular phrase for a reason.

As soon as Lexi moved toward another group, he opened his mouth to remind Caroline of it. "I don't believe that's the best course—"

Debbie Mae interrupted with a whisper. "Did you two see Lauren Fairfield? I remember her when she was in sixth grade and spent the summer here. Boy, has she changed or what?"

Caroline frowned. "I don't think I've ever met her."

"Of course you have! Remember the pool party for my twelfth birthday? She was the one who wore jean cutoff shorts and a T-shirt instead of a swimsuit. We all thought she was hiding some kind of skin rash."

"Wait, the girl with the big teeth?" Caroline's eyes widened in recognition. "But she had crazy hair, all wiry like she'd been electrocuted."

"Straighteners, I'm sure." Debbie Mae nodded. "But talk about a transformation. I think her parents were in the middle of a really bitter divorce and she had to stay with her grandma for a while."

"That age is rough, but to be shipped off to your grandmother's house and stay in a little place like Thorny Hollow . . ." Caroline's voice trailed off.

Brooks could tell she was lost in thought and said, "I'm sure you all took her mind off her troubles." As if anything could truly help an emotional crisis such as divorce in the family, but still. Friends and sunshine were good medicine. His own parents' constant bickering faded away when he spent time with his brother, fishing for catfish in the creek, even when it was so shallow there was hardly a minnow.

"I'm not so sure about that." Caroline chewed her lip. "I left her alone because I thought she was weird."

He wanted to say it didn't matter, not to worry. But it did matter, especially to some young kid who was forced to spend the summer in a town where she knew no one. Caroline was gracious and kind, but she didn't waste a lot of time on people who she figured wouldn't return her friendship. That summer probably didn't stand out as the happiest time in Lauren's memory, and the fact that Caroline didn't even remember her said that she had been completely oblivious of anyone except herself.

She went on, "Funny, every time Mrs. Reynolds has bragged on her, I've wanted to plug my ears. It seemed so over the top. Every tiny achievement was shouted to the high heavens. But now I can see how she'd be proud of her, going through such a rough time and not carrying it around like a shield."

"I think she enjoyed meeting our Brooks," Debbie Mae said. She winked at him, her blue eyes sparkling with mischief.

"And I equaled her in that enjoyment." He pretended not to understand her pointed comment. "I admire anyone who can take the love for her home and bring it to the attention of the world. We need more people like Lauren Fairfield."

"Perhaps her love for Thorny Hollow has taken on some particular interest tonight." Debbie Mae was giggling now, her hand covering her mouth. They were nearly at the far end of the atrium. The wall was broken up into six pairs of elegant French doors, opening onto an enormous deck that wrapped its way around the back of the mansion. Brooks moved slightly ahead to hold the door.

"Oh, you don't think that Brooks is interested in her? He was just being polite." Caroline shot Debbie Mae a glance. "And acting like a man. Men can't resist a beautiful woman."

He stopped, his hand on the edge of the doorframe. "Oh, are we playing matchmaker or just bashing men? You can't have it both ways. It's bad enough that Mrs. Gray is setting me up with Marion Birdsong, but now you're accusing me of ogling any available females within a ten-mile radius."

Debbie Mae gave him a pat as she stepped through the door. "Not at all. I just know a good prospect when I see one."

"Do you mean Brooks or Lauren?" Caroline followed her through, brows drawn down. He smelled the vanilla-violet scent and inhaled, wondering for the tenth time why it seemed so familiar.

"Both. I think they'd be perfect together. Just the right height, matching temperaments, and both value our town's history." Debbie Mae scanned the crowd. "There, she's just a few feet from that Frank guy."

Brooks snorted and raised an eyebrow at Caroline. That "Frank guy" was as annoying as all get-out, and if it meant he had to miss out on more of Lauren's company just to avoid him, then so be it. And valuing a town's history seemed a bit of a stretch for picking out a marriage partner. "She would never date someone like me, even if I asked her out. And I can assure you I have no intention of doing that." For some reason it hadn't even crossed his mind. Probably that equally natural and equally powerful urge to avoid marriage at all costs. He'd had enough of watching his parents bicker through several decades.

Debbie Mae rolled her eyes at him. "Well, you don't have a big head about being a professor, that's for sure. But it's a little-known truth that women just love the nerdy men."

"I'll pretend I didn't hear you call me nerdy. And I have to differ on what women love. Caroline and I were just discussing how women always go for the richest guy around."

"I said no such thing!" Caroline whirled, hands on hips. "Don't believe him, Debbie Mae. We were on opposite sides of that discussion."

Debbie Mae shrugged. "There's a little truth in that, I think. And if anyone would know, it'd be Brooks. He's probably had half the female population of this state chase him just because of Badewood."

"Not quite half." He kept his tone light, but it got old, real fast. Being attractive because your family owned the largest estate in the area wasn't anything to brag about.

"You'd much rather be admired for your brain." Caroline shot him a sly glance. She knew exactly what made him feel good because she was just the same.

He let her comment pass with a smile. In truth academia was uglier and more like junior high than most people could ever imagine. He was lucky that his department was relatively normal, but he'd seen pettiness that would make first-graders seem mature. "So, am I your new project? Have you got a list that has 'finding Brooks a wife' right at the top?"

"Maybe we should make that list. What do you say, Caroline?" Debbie Mae ticked off her fingers one by one. "Redecorate living room. Plant perennials. Find Brooks a wife."

Caroline crossed her arms over her chest and gazed out at the group of guests milling around the cedarwood deck. It was definitely large enough to hold a wedding party. White-gloved waiters trotted around with heavily laden trays of champagne and cold drinks.

Brooks hadn't thought of finding her something else to drink after she had finished her first glass of punch. He felt heat creep up his neck in embarrassment. Some date he was, failing to fulfill his "hunter-gatherer" party role.

"I would never." She turned, giving him a grin. "You'd be stuck following your wife around and would never get to come hang out with us. Married men don't get to keep their women friends, especially not the single ones. I'd be all alone at every party, hemmed in by Mrs. Reynolds and Mrs. Kropp and listening to Dr. Stroud describe amputation techniques."

"You're denying me the joy of holy matrimony out of sheer selfishness?"

"Absolutely." She linked an arm through his and pulled him toward the middle of the deck, where Mrs. Werlin was unveiling the raised barbecue pits. "I don't want you to marry anybody, no matter how much they love this town." Her tone was teasing and she laughed up at him, green-blue eyes reflecting the flickers of the outdoor torches.

Brooks opened his mouth to respond, but found nothing to say. He couldn't imagine choosing a wife over a friend like Caroline. A loud, forced sort of laugh floated over the crowd and he watched Caroline turn her head in response. He loved the long curve of her neck, the elegant arch of her brow. There wasn't a more beautiful woman at the party, but Caroline didn't know it. Her utter lack of ego made her all the more attractive.

"Fine, let's forget about the elusive wife for a moment and talk about that party I'm having." Debbie Mae nudged Caroline, as if reminding her to say her piece.

"Whatever party this is, you'll have to wait until after finals. I'm booked solid."

Caroline bit her lip. "So, that's a yes? We just tell you when and you'll be there?"

"Sure. You two can paint your toenails while Manning and I work on that old Civil War cannon he bought."

Debbie Mae smiled. "Excellent. That's not what we had in mind but we'll talk specifics later."

Another loud laugh caught Brooks's ear. It was Frank, at the edge of a group, working another assembly of pretty, sophisticated young women. Flashes of jewelry, the swirl of fabric, the gleam of wide, white smiles, surrounded him like sacrificial offerings to a god. The guests on the deck seemed to turn their attention in his general direction, falling under his spell.

"He's got such a great sense of humor," Caroline observed. She seemed captivated by the scene, her body leaning forward, as if wishing she, too, were part of the inner circle of Frank's adoring tribe.

Brooks grimaced at the feeling of ice melting slowly in his gut. Caroline might not want him to marry, but that didn't mean she wouldn't make that choice for herself. A vision flashed before his eyes: Caroline and Frank, walking arm in arm through the atrium, guests of honor, laughing in unison, a beautiful couple that everyone would admire. This would be the perfect place for a wedding because they had met here. The vision shifted and Caroline was wearing a simple, elegant gown of white silk. Her blond hair was piled carelessly in wavy curls, strings of pearls at her throat. The dream Caroline turned to Frank, eyes bright with newlywed joy as she stood on tiptoe and pressed her lips to his.

Brooks swallowed, surprised at the wave of jealousy. If she was happy, he would be happy. A friend would never stand in the way of another's happiness. Then why was he sick at the thought of it?

The answer was creeping at the edges of his heart but he pushed it away. Sucking in a deep breath, he argued some logic into his foggy brain. He was having an off night, nothing more. His father was struggling with his grief, and Brooks didn't know how to help. Coming home on the weekends wasn't making it better. Brooks was just there, doing nothing. He tried to talk to his father but he wanted to spend his time alone, in the library, sitting in his favorite chair by the window that overlooked the gardens.

Debbie Mae was chattering in the background and Brooks let himself relax into the sound. He needed some rest, maybe a bit of fishing. Everything would make sense in the morning.

He said those words, again and again, to himself, but a hard rock of unease did not budge. All he had to do was glance at Caroline and all his explanations crumbled away. . . . Something had changed, probably the moment she flashed her brightest smile for that smooth-talking creep. The way Frank had touched her arm made Brooks's blood pressure climb. He wanted to order her to steer clear of him, but she was a grown-up and could make her own decisions. Friends didn't tell each other whom to talk to or whom to be friends with, unless they had a good reason. And he didn't. Not one that he could easily define at that moment. He could hope it would all be clear in the daylight, but he was afraid that it would only seem more confusing. As for not working so hard, deep down he knew that no amount of vacation would fix what was happening in his heart.

Yes. But what shall I say?

Dear Miss Woodhouse, do advise me.

—MISS SMITH

CHAPTER NINE

Caroline closed the last page of Lexi's enormous sketchbook and held it on her lap. The images swam before her eyes. Unique, vibrant and touching, the art was stunning. "I know we barely met the other evening at the party, but you've really stayed in my mind. I'm glad you called."

Lexi's cheeks turned pink and she brushed her dark, curly hair back from her forehead. "It's real nice to get away from the gas station once in a while. My day is normally all about frying up the gizzards and wings, then stocking the fruit pies before the lunch crowd hits. Every now and then I have to shoo someone out of the bathroom when they take too long, but mostly it's just cleaning up the soda machine and making sure people don't park at the pump."

"How did you find time to do all this work?" Caroline gestured to the sketchbook. "You must never sleep."

"Oh, it gets quiet right around ten in the morning." Lexi glanced at her nails, scratching off the sparkly blue polish from one thumb. "At least I have the summer to spend on my art. I'm not even going to bring my supplies when I leave for Ole Miss. It would be too tempting to spend all my time sketching instead of studying."

Caroline felt her eyes go wide. "Don't you think that's a little drastic? You can't study all the time, you know."

"But, don't you think it's better to focus?" Lexi's brown eyes were shadowed with doubt. "I just figured it was the right thing to do."

"You mean that you're not going to draw, at all, *ever*?" Caroline sat back, stunned.

"It sounds awful, I admit it." Lexi dropped her head in her hands. "But my dad worked so hard and saved for years for me to go to college. I can't disappoint him by not giving it everything I've got."

Caroline shook her head, feeling as if she were missing a step in the logic of the conversation. "I don't see how denying your true self will make studying go any better."

"My true self?" Lexi stared up at the leaves shaking in the light breeze. "I—I never quite thought of it that way."

"You told me yourself that you were an artist! Isn't it your calling, your God-given purpose?"

Lexi frowned, brows coming together. "Finding your calling sounds like something rich people worry about." She glanced at Caroline and shrugged. "Sorry. I'm not trying to be rude."

"No worries. I can see how you've been brought up to focus on being useful or having a trade that will support your family." Caroline grasped Lexi's hand. "Lexi, true artists are so hard to find. I don't want to see you give up your gift because you're supposed to earn a living wage."

"But what do you think I should do?" Lexi's brown eyes were wide, confusion in every line of her face.

"You need to follow your heart. God's given you a gift and you shouldn't squander it in accounting classes."

"I've already registered. I've accepted the scholarships. I don't know how to back out now."

"I don't want to tell you what to do, but if you're not sure, then you need to think about this plan. You don't want to wake up forty years from now hating your life because you compromised on your art."

"Do you think I might?" Lexi blinked back tears. "It's just me and my dad. I don't have anyone who cares enough to give me advice. The guidance counselor at school gave me fast-food applications instead of college applications."

Caroline winced. Lexi had made it this far on her own wits and talent. She needed someone to guide her, someone who had been through college and knew the value of a degree.

"I'm sure there's a way to make it work. The first step is to talk with your father. Let him know how you really feel."

"Oh." Lexi stared at the sidewalk, tapping the toes of one foot, her bright red toenails like berries against her tan skin. "I guess I should."

"Wonderful! I'm so glad you're taking your talent seriously. And I talked to Frank Keene the other day, the one who owns that small publishing house. We're going to lunch on Monday. Do you want me to ask him if there's an opening for someone like you? I'd be more than happy to do that."

"Really? I can't imagine earning money with my art. I mean, even earning enough to pay the bills would be wonderful."

"Why not? You're amazing! You've got to fight for your gift, Lexi." Caroline gripped Lexi's hand, willing the young girl to see the truth.

Lexi took a shuddering breath and straightened up. "You're so right. I'm going to tell my father tonight that I want to defer going to college."

Caroline felt a weight lift from her shoulders. "Perfect. And call me right away to tell me how it went."

Lexi nodded, her face pale but determined. Caroline knew it would be hard to change tracks, but it was better than changing course years from now. She felt as if she had done some real good, helped in a tangible way for the first time since she'd returned home.

Caroline picked up the paperback book for the tenth time that day and read a few lines. *Real, long-standing regard brought the Westons and Mr. Knightley; and by Mr. Elton, a young man living alone without liking it, the privilege of exchanging any vacant evening of his own blank solitude for the elegancies and society of Mr. Woodhouse's drawing-room, and the smiles of his lovely daughter, was in no danger of being thrown away.*

It made no sense. She read the line again. She'd only made it to page fifteen and she was already lost. There were commas where there should not have been commas, sentences that went on for paragraphs, and odd words that she knew meant something more than the vague meaning she had for them. Sighing with frustration, Caroline closed the book and flipped open her laptop. She couldn't force her way through that book, but she could definitely look for costumes. A simple Web search brought up hundreds of Austen sites, dedicated to reenactments and the various film and stage versions of the books. The attention to detail reminded her of the Civil War groups, except for a complete lack of guts and gore, for which she was extremely thankful. It seemed that Jane Austen had inspired the best of everyone: gentility, a love of beauty, and good manners.

An hour later, there was a tap at her bedroom door. She looked up, surprised at how fast the time had flown as she'd devoured page after page of Austen ephemera. "Come in," she called, guessing it was Brooks before he came through the doorway, Absalom trotting behind him.

"Working?" He took in the papers, covered with scribbled notes, spread out around her.

"Not really. Just helping Debbie Mae with that Austen party she's throwing." Caroline pointed to a picture on the screen, Colin Firth in a deep blue morning coat, his curly hair tousled. "You're going to wear something like this."

"There's no way on God's green earth that I'm dressing up like Mr. Darcy." Brooks stretched out on Caroline's bed, hanging his tan suede wing tips off the edge and crossing his ankles. He laced his fingers behind his head and looked infuriatingly cool and relaxed.

"Not Mr. Darcy. That's the guy from *Pride and Prejudice*. You're supposed to come as Mr. Knightley." Absalom rushed to give Caroline a quick lick and receive a week's worth of scratches. He sniffed the carved claw-foot of her desk and she shooed him away. She loved the dog, but if he took so much as a nibble of her great-grandmother's Victorian, drop-front secretary, there would be trouble.

Brooks snapped his fingers. The golden retriever hung his head in a reasonably good imitation of canine depression and shuffled off to settle on the carpet beside Brooks.

"Whoever. I'll come to the party but I'm not playing dress-up." His usual combination of khakis, button-up, blue oxford shirt and a subdued tie signaled he'd just driven down from Spartainville. He still looked like a college professor, clean-shaven and tie on straight, but that stubborn expression was all Brooks.

Caroline flipped to another page on the Etsy site and pointed to a green velvet morning coat. "See how handsome this is? You always complain about tuxes. This is as far from a tux as you can get."

"No."

One word, calmly spoken, and Caroline felt her blood pressure rise. "Why can't you just play along?"

"Explain to me again why you're throwing this party?" He narrowed his eyes at her. "Because Frank will come and be adorably wonderful in his Mr. Darcy suit and you two can dance the night away?"

Caroline's mouth dropped open but no words occurred to her for a moment. She couldn't exactly say why she was determined to throw this party until Debbie Mae felt that she could share her pain with the rest of their friends. But somehow Caroline had to make it happen. "Yes, I invited Frank, and *he* very graciously agreed to do everything he could to make his role as authentic as possible."

"Whoo-hoo for Frank." Brooks dropped his head back on the bed and stared at the ceiling. The lines around his mouth had gone tight. His blue eyes studied the ornate medallion in the high ceiling as if it carried a secret message.

She let out a huff of air and went back to scrolling through the Internet pages, unseeing. Her laptop was at a slightly awkward angle on the drop-down shelf, which was meant for a single piece of writing paper and a fountain pen. Her mother complained that the entire bedroom set was dark, depressing and outlandishly dramatic, but Caroline loved the look of the scrolling and the dropped finials. The high, arched headboard sported a crest topped with a detailed carved head. Although her mother pointed out that no one knew the identity of the boy with the feather in his cap and wondered how Caroline could sleep with it hanging over her at night, she loved to gaze at the serene face, imagining the wood-carver and the subject, hundreds of years ago.

Plus, it was built like a tank. Brooks had flopped onto her bed and it hadn't made as much as a squeak. Sure, the matching high-boy and dresser tended to have a sticky drawer or two, especially in the humid summer months, but it spoke of the best kind of history to her.

She shifted, trying to focus on the screen. The chair was getting harder by the minute, and her shorts felt sweaty and wrinkled from sitting for the last hour staring at Regency costumes. It was true, Brooks didn't have to come. But Debbie Mae wanted him to see the movie, and if Debbie Mae wanted it, Caroline was going to do her best to get him there. She had no idea what bait to use, and apparently appealing to a dormant love of Regency fashion wasn't going to work.

"Listen, I know you love a good party," Brooks said. He rubbed a hand over his face and sat up, planting his shoes firmly on the Oriental carpet. Absalom raised his head, apparently wondering if the visit was over already.

Brooks held up a hand at her snort of laughter. "I mean, a really good party. Not a bridge club meeting and pink-lemonade party. And I'm sorry you don't get to go out more."

It was true; she missed having a good time that didn't include chatting with her mother's odd friends. She shrugged. It was what it was.

"It's a strange stage. We grow up, move away, then come home to help our parents. I'm going to be in the same boat pretty soon." She glanced up, frowning, and waited for him to continue. "I've been thinking about this for a while, but I've decided to move back here for the summer."

"Is your dad worse? Blanche is back now, isn't she? Does he need full-time care?"

He shook his head. "She's back now, but I can't expect her to be making sure he eats and sleeps. I don't think he needs a caregiver; he's just lonely. And sad. But he definitely needs enough supervision that I'm down here every weekend. So I might as well just stay for the summer as soon as classes are finished and finals are turned in."

"What about your house? You can't just leave it empty." Especially in a college town. There would be summer squatters in the garden shed about two minutes after he left the area.

"I have a friend who needs a place for the summer. I'm going to let her stay there. She can keep an eye on the place and water the grass when needed."

"She?" It shouldn't have mattered, but Mrs. Gray's ugly little comments were lodged somewhere in the dark recesses of Caroline's mind. A woman would suddenly take up residence in Brooks's house and Caroline had never even met her? A tall, gorgeous woman appeared in her mind's eye, and she looked an awful lot like Lauren Fairfield, with large gray eyes and a perfect smile.

"Yes, Finley, it's a she. You're as bad as my mother was."

Her face went hot, not from being called his mother, but from being outed as a jealous friend. It didn't matter what he did with his house. It was no concern of hers. He was a grown man and he had grown-up friendships with other people, many of whom happened to be women. Now one of those grown-up women would be living in Brooks's house, touching his dishes, using his bathroom, maybe even sleeping in his bed. She shouldn't care. But for some reason, she did.

"As I said, I'll be here for the summer." He looked at his

hands, as if unsure what to say next. "We can run in the mornings, if you want. I won't ask you to spend weekends at the reenactments because I know your threshold for grits is too low to measure, but maybe we could take a few trips, get out of town."

The thought of Brooks's being around all summer was like finding out they'd skipped half the year and ended up right at Christmas. She felt a huge smile crease her face and she popped up from her chair, launching herself at him. "You're probably doing this as an act of mercy to atone for some horrible past sin, but I don't really care!"

Her arms were around his neck and she could feel him laughing into her hair. The warmth of his palms went through her cotton T-shirt and right into her skin, filling her with a glow that was like stepping into the sun. When he was gone, how she missed his warmth, his smell, his laugh!

He pulled back, his blue eyes lit from within by a familiar joy. "You're just counting all the chili-slaw dogs I'll bring you."

"Absolutely not! It hardly even crossed my mind." Although, at this moment it seemed like a pretty fine idea. Her arms were still around his neck. She dropped one hand to his tie, absentmindedly fiddling with the knot. "Honestly, I feel like I don't have anyone to talk to when you're gone."

"Surely not. You've got loads of friends." His voice was rough.

Her gaze still on his tie, she frowned. "Not really. I can't think of a single person to call when I'd like to go out to lunch. You have to admit, that's pretty sad." She bit her bottom lip. "I'm not saying I've not got a short list of people I could call in a time of trouble; I'm saying the list of people I could call for a no-stress social occasion is a complete blank. Debbie Mae has such a busy schedule, I just wait for her to call me. It will be so nice to have someone to hang out with."

He said nothing for a moment. "And what about that list of people to call when you're in trouble?"

She met his gaze and smiled. "You're pretty much it . . . Hope you don't mind being my go-to guy for everything."

Something flashed behind his eyes, an emotion she couldn't quite catch. He seemed to be choosing his words carefully. Before he could speak, she leaned forward and inhaled, her nose inches from his jaw. "Hey, is that a new cologne?"

He cleared his throat. "I . . . can't remember. Maybe."

Leaning back, she shot him a look. "Can't remember? The man who hasn't changed his brand of breakfast cereal in twenty years? The man who's had his hair cut at the same barbershop every six weeks since the age of twelve?"

"Okay, maybe it's something I picked up recently. I thought it smelled good." He took a deep breath. "You don't like it?"

She leaned closer, eyes squeezed shut. He smelled like Brooks: a combination of soap, guy and those hot, little spearmint candies he liked to chew. She wasn't quite sure about the cologne. It wasn't him. She was so used to the Brooks she knew, the guy who never changed, steady as a rock. Her nose bumped his jaw as she tried to decide, but another sniff left her feeling just as confused. The thought occurred to her that he was trying something new for someone special, maybe even Lauren.

Caroline sat back, dropping her hand from his tie. "Did you have someone in mind when you bought this?"

He opened his eyes as if he'd been about to drop off to sleep. "Why?"

She crossed her arms over her chest. "Did Manning tell you Lauren will be at the party? I'm sure she'll make a gorgeous Regency woman, with that tall, willowy figure." An even worse idea occurred to her. "Or maybe you don't have to go to the party to see her. Maybe you've seen her around Thorny Hollow since we all met at the Werlins'."

His chest was rising and falling as if he were angry, but he let out a short laugh. "Haven't seen her."

"But you'd like to."

He shrugged, running a hand through his hair. It wasn't something he usually did and Caroline felt a thrill of alarm run down her spine. Just talking about Lauren unnerved him. "As much as anyone, I suppose."

"More than me, I'm sure." She'd tried to like the woman. Once she got past Mrs. Reynolds's incessant boasting of Lauren's many accomplishments, she'd thought they could be friends. But Lauren was cool, quiet. It had nothing to do with Lauren's describing Caroline's home as "that little place down from the highway exit." At least, that's what Caroline told herself.

Brooks answered, as if he hadn't really heard her, "It's true she's coming to Badewood tomorrow to look around. She wants to take some pictures of the ballroom and the greenhouses." He paused. "Would you like to come, too?"

Caroline stood up and went to the laptop, fiddling with the screen for a moment. Of course she wanted to go hang out with Brooks. She loved every inch of Badewood, almost as much as she loved her own home. When they were kids, they'd run a dirt path through the adjoining pasture between their houses that was visible to this day. But she didn't want to be there while Lauren took her photos, amazing Brooks with her knowledge of antebellum mansions and porticos and Greek Revival architecture.

"No, you two have fun. I'd just be in the way." She clicked through a few screens, trying to find her place in the Regency costumes again.

He let out a sigh. "Finley, you wouldn't be in the way. You're so at home there, it's almost like your house, too."

"Oh, I don't think so." She looked up, laughing. "My own house is enough for me. Just think how much of a mess I'd make if I tried baking triple-layer cakes in your kitchen, too."

He said nothing for a moment, then stood. "I'd better get on home for dinner."

Absalom jumped to his feet in excitement. Caroline had to smile at an eighty-pound dog doing the whole-body wag. "You don't want to stay? I think there's lasagna in the fridge. Don't worry, Angie made it."

Brooks's lips tilted up. "I'm not worried. And I'd stay but my dad's refused to eat anything but boiled chicken breasts for weeks. I'm going to try and tempt him with some simple pasta."

Weeks? Caroline's heart clenched in her chest. She complained about her mother's hovering but she was eating well enough and seemed healthy, if a little obsessed with keeping track of her only child. Brooks was dealing with parental issues in a whole other realm of seriousness.

"I'll walk you downstairs." She minimized the page. "I need to get some iced tea before I melt into a puddle, anyway. What I wouldn't give for AC up here."

They walked through the narrow hallway and onto the landing, Absalom's nails ticking against the pine-plank flooring. The sound of voices drifted up the wide staircase as they neared the first floor.

"Your mother has company."

Caroline frowned, trying to identify the speaker. "If it's Mrs.

Reynolds, you're on your own." Caroline could take only so much inane chatter, especially when it revolved around Lauren and her brilliance.

He stepped onto the landing. "Sounds like a man. Expecting anyone?"

She shook her head and wondered if Frank had popped by. It wasn't likely, since he lived in Spartainville and would have called. Or maybe not. He seemed a spontaneous sort of guy. She smoothed down her wrinkled shorts, adjusting the pretty blue, polka-dot scarf she was using as a belt. The red-striped T-shirt had seemed bright and cheerful earlier but now seemed immature, even a little silly. It was too early for the Fourth of July and she looked as if she should be twirling a baton in a Main Street parade.

"You look fine," Brooks said.

She rolled her eyes at him and started down the stairs. "Right, to *you.* The problem with men is that I could have lipstick on my teeth, crazy bed head and be wearing three shades of green, and you'd think everything was *fine*."

"Are you saying I'm unobservant?"

"No, I'm saying your focus is elsewhere." She'd reached the last step and the man's voice was much clearer. Definitely a male, Southern, and able to entertain her mother. The low laughter echoed from the living room.

Brooks stopped her with a touch on the arm, tugging her around to face him. "Elsewhere?"

She huffed out a breath. "As long as there's a baseball game on or food around, guys just don't pay attention to women."

He blinked, as if he'd been prepared for some other answer.

"Everybody needs a little baseball once in a while. We can't sit around and talk Regency costumes all day."

Shrugging, she walked as quietly as possible to the double doors that led to the living room. The heavy maple doors were pulled together, with only a gap between them. Odd, since her mother detested the sound of the cast-iron rollers as one hauled the four-foot-wide doors into the wall. She kept them perpetually open, letting the housekeeper dust the tall, paneled doors once a week. Caroline crept forward, peering into the gap.

Nobody, who has not been in the interior of a family, can say what the difficulties of any individual of that family may be.

—EMMA

CHAPTER TEN

"Don't you think you should knock?" Brooks whispered. His dimples were showing, as if he were trying hard not to laugh.

"Shhhh! I just want to see who it is before I—"

"Caroline? Is that you?" her mother called.

She shot Brooks a look and tapped on the door. "Knock, knock!"

The door slid back on its track with a metallic squeal, revealing a middle-aged man. His smile was wide but a tightness was around his pale eyes. "You must be Caroline! So wonderful to finally meet you!" He gripped her hand and pumped it for several seconds.

She nodded, trying not to flinch at the cold dampness of his palm. "And this is my friend Brooks Elliot."

"Aha! Your mother said you were entertaining up in your bedroom, and I can see why she wouldn't want you disturbed. Young love, how sweet it is!" He smoothed a lock of hair back from his forehead and smiled again.

Caroline wasn't socially naïve. She could spot a backhanded compliment at fifty yards and had a practiced smile that didn't betray her irritation. But this man's crude implication left her speechless. She said nothing, at a loss as to which part of his sentence to attack first.

Brooks cleared his throat. "Are you from the area, sir?"

Absalom let out a soft whine and nudged Brooks's leg.

Caroline knew, without turning her head, that Brooks was barely hanging on to his self-control. The calm fury in his voice made her eyes go wide.

"Yes, indeed. Marshall Jackson is the name. My people have lived near Thorny Hollow for centuries."

"He's been living in Oxford for quite some time and just returned to the area." Caroline's mother offered that up from her usual place on the couch. Her hair was curled, lipstick applied, and eyelids brushed with metallic blue. Caroline tried not to gape at the garish makeup. Her mother believed subtlety was the best course of action at all times, but not today. She looked like an aging movie star, posed in her starched dress, tiny waist displayed to good advantage while leaning back against the silk cushions.

"Jackson? Are you related to Norman Jackson who runs the hardware store?"

"Hardware store?" Marshall let out a chuckle that was about five seconds too long, mouth open far enough that Caroline could see he was missing a molar. "No, siree. No merchants here. We're tradesmen, through and through. Carpenters, furniture makers. A long line of men who know a piece of fine furniture when we see one, which is why I have an antiques shop. I connect the best people with the items they've always needed to make their homes shine. A mutual friend told me your mother might be interested in bringing her home up to the next level."

"How wonderful." Caroline tried not to grimace. The *next level*? Was the house in disrepair? But she thought she could stand the man if he knew the value of a Victorian highboy.

Marshall sighed. "Not really. Most of what my forebears spent their time on is worthless now. These old pieces just don't hold the value in today's market. Take this Empire settee." He motioned to a low sofa near the corner of the living room. Caroline had always loved how the rich mahogany wood contrasted with the pale mint-colored silk of the cushions. "All that carving is too dramatic for today's discerning homeowner. Honestly, eagle heads and furry feet have no place in a modern Southern house."

"But I thought the acanthus leaves signified the cyclical nature of life. And the hairy paw feet are carved like lion's paws." Caroline cocked her head. "Overall, I think it makes a strong statement for a Southern mansion that survived the Civil War."

Brooks glanced at her and looked to be choking back a laugh. She knew what he was thinking. Why on earth was she familiar with acanthus leaves and lion's paws? But give a girl enough time in an old house with nothing better to do and she'll either start a novel or study the furniture. In her case, it had been both.

"Well, I hate to break it to you, my dear"—Marshall smoothed his hair again, a gesture that Caroline was beginning to recognize as a sort of conversational pause—"but antiques are my specialty, and these just aren't hardly worth the wood they're made from. Now, if this set was a Federal table and chairs? Then you'd be sittin' pretty." He leaned forward, smile widening, waiting for them to chuckle at his pun.

Caroline caught a whiff of stale cigarette smoke and onions. "I see." It was all she could muster. She glanced at her mother, surprised that she was entertaining a man who talked about the value of furniture in broad daylight. Nice folks such as the Ashleys just didn't stand around discussing the resale possibilities of family heirlooms. For some reason Marshall Jackson was not only forgiven, but encouraged.

"I should go," Brooks said quietly, touching Caroline's arm.

Absalom shifted, not sure whether to snuffle Caroline or stay where he was.

"But you just got here." She hated the desperate sound to her voice.

Her mother spoke up from her place on the couch. "That is our Brooks. He never stops for long, but he'll be back soon." Her tone was affectionate.

Brooks nodded agreement. "It's true. I'm drawn to this place like a magnet. But my father will be wondering where I am."

"Okay, I'm going to meet Frank for lunch on Monday but I'll see you . . ." Not tomorrow afternoon because Lauren would be there, impressing him with her knowledge of old mansions. She wished he would stay just a bit longer. Caroline tried to catch his eye but he resolutely ignored the message she was beaming into his head. He left, not bothering to slide the door closed behind him.

Being left with Marshall and her mother was not in her top ten list of great ways to spend the afternoon. Not even the top fifty. She had an Austen party to plan and Brooks was slipping out the door with hardly a backward glance. Absalom turned and gave her a lingering look, as if worried whether she'd survive the afternoon with these two. It was definitely more support than she got from his owner.

Men. She let out a sigh and went to sit next to her mother, struggling to refocus on Marshall's monologue.

"And everyone loves those Carolina ladder-back rockers, but a little company in Houston is turning out porch furniture that shows true craftsmanship."

Caroline grimaced. She didn't care what company it was, but surely her great-grandparents' rockers were better than anything new. "Didn't you just send them to be refurbished, Mama?"

Her mother shifted against the cushions. "Yes, well, I'm not even sure they can be saved."

Caroline sat up with a gasp. "Saved? But they were perfect!"

Marshall chuckled. "They might have looked perfect, but those old things were riddled with termites."

"Impossible. I sat in one a few weeks ago." Brooks had come by and they'd sipped tea on the porch, listening to the peepers in the creek. The idea that the rockers were falling apart was alarming.

"I can't imagine you would be able to spot the problems, not being trained in the mysteries of antique wood." He shrugged his shoulders and his thick fingers fiddled with his tie, as if it were too tight. "But we'll do our best to save them."

Caroline stared at him, her mind working overtime. Was her family home being eaten away by termites? Her gaze raked the high ceilings, searching for cracks and stains. It looked immaculate, but looks could be deceiving. Perhaps beneath the perfection of this historic home, it was rotten from beam to basement. Marshall seemed an irritating sort of guy who dismissed anything that wasn't completely modern, but maybe he knew the signs of rot and she didn't. The thought sent horror coursing through her.

Brooks was glad he'd walked to Caroline's place. He was so angry his jaw felt wired shut and he could hear his own pulse pounding in his ears. Getting in a few good jabs to Marshall's soft middle would have helped his mood, but walking with Absalom through the tall grass back to Badewood was probably better in the long run.

After a few minutes of deep breathing and forcing Marshall out of his thoughts, Brooks felt his emotions slip back into something closer to their usually sedate rhythms. Fury wasn't a feeling he enjoyed. Everything about that man set his teeth on edge.

He stopped under a weeping willow at the edge of the creek and gazed toward Badewood. Absalom let out a deep bark of happiness, chasing butterflies from their roosts and splashing through the shallow creek water in search of frogs. Badewood rose proud and stately in the distance, the afternoon sun bathing it in golden light. The trim and roofline gleamed whitely, while even at this distance the long windows sparkled. This was the perfect spot for a panoramic shot. Lauren would want to see this tomorrow. Perhaps they could walk out after lunch; Absalom always needed a good walk around then.

He imagined standing under the willow, showing Lauren how Badewood sat like a perfect jewel in the crown of Thorny Hollow. In his mind's eye, Lauren's face softened and her hair lightened until it was Caroline at his side. He rubbed his forehead, feeling a deep sense of unease settle in his gut.

To be completely honest, his emotions had been a mess even before Marshall had opened his mouth. The last week of classes, he'd thought the feelings would fade away, settle back into the way things had been. He'd tried to pretend everything was fine, he was the same old Brooks and she was pesky little Caroline. Pretending hadn't helped a bit.

Maybe because he'd been spending so much time back home, he couldn't seem to admire Badewood without thinking of Caroline. She was wrapped up in everything he loved about the place. When he saw the carriage house, he thought of the summer they'd spent hours playing with a batch of new kittens. When he looked at the rose gardens to the south, he thought of how she'd learned the names of all the roses one year. Even the portico gave him pause, since she'd called Badewood "toothy" in comparison to the admittedly more graceful lines of her own home. Of course she was part of this place, but now the memories came with a rougher edge, as if they were rubbing against a sore spot.

So he'd pretended all was the same. Same old Brooks, same old Caroline. And then she'd thrown herself into his arms. He closed his eyes, unable to keep the memory from washing over him again. She'd been saying something about not having friends, and all he could think of was how wonderful she smelled, how soft her skin was, how he wanted to press a kiss against the curve of her neck. Even now, standing on the bank of the lazy, little creek, his heart started to thud in his chest. His eyes snapped open. This was wrong. She didn't feel the same way, clearly, and it smacked of a sick desperation to stand around reviewing every detail of their time together. She wasn't interested, end of story.

He took another breath, letting it out slowly. Absalom ran toward him, mouth open, tongue lolling, the picture of happiness. The dog paused to shake, water droplets flying in all directions. Brooks stretched the muscles in his shoulders, hoping to ease some of the tension. A bright, early-summer afternoon beckoned and it would do him a world of good if he could just place all those complicated feelings back into a tidy space inside.

He called for Absalom and jumped the creek, striding toward Badewood. He had enough on his plate without feeding the infatuation. It would pass. He was under a lot of stress and his psyche had latched on to Caroline as a diversion. Nothing more. Snatching up a dead branch, he swung at the feathery seed heads of the tall grass, letting out his frustration with vicious accuracy.

Ten minutes later they wandered around the northern side of the house. The scent of jasmine was heavy in the warm air, struggling through the thick ivy that covered half the brickwork. Absalom was a little drier, but definitely needed a bath after running around the soft Mississippi-clay banks. He'd better change before attempting the task, knowing how the retriever loved to soak them both.

Badewood faced east, to catch the rising of the sun, but his preferred room was in the part of the house reserved for servants. His childhood bedroom had lit up like the sun every morning at daybreak. He'd never been a morning person, and now that he was old enough to choose, he found the darkest room at the back of the house.

Manning once teased him about moving to the old servants' quarters, asking if he acted out of guilt. But being a wealthy Southern man didn't weigh on his conscience as much as being born into an educated family. So many folks never got the chance to go any further than high school, and plenty in his classes at Midlands were the first in their family to go to college. He loved his town, its history, his home. But of all the wonderful things he'd been born into, not earning an ounce of it, his family's tradition of higher learning was the best of them all. Without the chance at an education, life was an uphill climb.

He opened the screen door and stepped onto the enclosed porch. A round dining table stood waiting for guests. The family's cook, Ruth, had replaced its spring tablecloth with the summer one. The bright diamond pattern reminded him of the care his mother had taken in choosing the nicest oilcloths. It had been one of the last household tasks she completed before her stomach trouble had turned out to be terminal cancer.

The porch ceiling fans hummed softly, stirring the warm air away from the light blue planks above his head. His mother had insisted on "haint blue," driving to every paint supply store in Thorny Hollow until she found the exact shade. Sometimes he wondered how the house could still stand without her. It was his father's family home, but she had taken to it as if it were her birthright, not his. From the kitchen-cabinet knobs to the flagstone path to the Robert E. Lee portrait in the front entrance, the care she'd invested in Badewood was everywhere he looked.

The long stone hallway from the back porch to the kitchen echoed with every one of his footsteps. Ruth would be working on dinner, even though his father had refused to eat a proper meal for weeks.

Sure enough, the clatter of cookware grew clearer as he neared the doorway. Fifty years ago, the kitchen was housed a few hundred feet behind the main house, in its own redbrick building. His mother didn't think it was necessary to keep the servants running back and forth to the main house so she had the equipment moved to Badewood proper. His ancestors would be horrified to know the cook wandered the main floor as if she owned the place, the carriage house was filled with dusty horse tack that was slowly rotting to nothing and their great-great-great-grandson was living in a maid's bedroom. But times changed and Badewood changed with them.

He poked his head through the narrow entry to the kitchen and blinked. Ruth's face was shining with sweat as she frowned into an enormous pot, apron spattered with sauce. She looked as if she'd been working on a feast for hundreds of people. His grandmother stood next to her, the same frustrated expression on her face. Her skin still glowed with a Caribbean tan, and beaded bracelets jingled as she stirred the pot. The front half of her hair was braided in tiny rows and decorated with brightly colored beads, her scalp glowing pink between the braids. She was wearing a pink T-shirt that read JAMAICA DAYS on the back and lime-green Bermuda shorts with embroidered flamingos all over them. Striped ankle socks peeked out of her orthopedic shoes. The overall effect was dizzying.

"Grandma, what on earth are you all up to in here?"

"Brooks, honey! Come taste this. Ruthy and I are makin' susumba and saltfish."

Ruth frowned over her shoulder. "I'm not so sure what Blanche is making. I'm just following her directions. Looks like poison to me."

Blanche tutted. "Now, then. We haven't even added all the ingredients. We've got the gully beans and the saltfish cooking and we just need to add the hot Scotch-bonnet powder and the—"

"Where did you find all of this stuff?" Brooks held up a jar of something that looked like small green olives floating in syrup.

"I ordered it. Isn't the Internet amazing? You can buy anything and have it delivered right to your house!" Blanche beamed at him, as if she'd discovered Internet shopping before anyone else on the planet. The back of her permed white hair was suffering from the humid kitchen heat and she looked a bit as if she'd been electrocuted.

Ruth took a turn stirring the pot and sniffed, her dark face wrinkled in concentration. "I've eaten a lot of strange food in my life. When my boy came back from Afghanistan, he brought me some Persian-carrot-and-rose jam. He put it on toast with orange-blossom syrup. I ate that up and it wasn't so bad. But this . . ." She leaned over the pot, her nose wrinkling at the smell of the steam rising from the food. "This might be where I draw the line."

"Now, Ruthy. I never pegged you for a timid woman. We're

havin' an adventure here! Plus, I ate this in Kingston and it was delicious. I said to myself, 'I'm-a gonna get home and Ruthy will help me whip some up.'" Blanche shot a look at Ruth and sniffed. "If I'd have known you were so shy about tryin' a new recipe, I wouldn't have bothered to order all of these spices. I even got boiled bananas to go with it."

Absalom took a cautious sniff and seemed to decide there wasn't anything edible. He trotted to his favorite spot under the old oak kitchen table and stretched out. Brooks perched on a stool and surveyed the boxes and jars of ingredients. It certainly smelled interesting, but there was no way his father would eat any of this food. For forty years he'd expected pork chops on Tuesday and meat loaf on Friday, mashed potatoes and gravy on the side. "Is there another dish for the less adventurous?"

"You, too?" Blanche planted her fists on her ample hips. "Well, I'll be eatin' all this soup myself, I suppose."

"Not for me, for your son-in-law. I hate to remind you that he hasn't been particularly open to new dishes around here." Brooks glanced at Ruthy and she nodded. She'd tried a spaghetti dish that she'd seen on the Cooking Channel and his father wouldn't take a single bite. It was Italian food, and he'd declared it "too foreign."

To Brooks's surprise, Blanche sighed and sat herself down on the old kitchen step stool. "I know. That man is just determined to waste away."

"It's been over a year and he doesn't seem like he's getting any better." Brooks didn't want to have a discussion about sensitive family topics while standing around the kitchen, but Blanche had to see that his father wasn't anywhere close to reclaiming his normal routine. "I know it's hard. It seems like just yesterday she was here." He stared at his shoes for a moment. "But curling up into a ball isn't the answer."

"I miss her, too," Blanche said softly, drawing a finger under her eye. "She was my baby girl and I miss her crazy laugh and those awful slippers she wore and the way she walked around the house brushing her teeth."

Brooks snorted. He'd forgotten about the awful slippers: cheetah-print corduroy with rubber soles that squeaked on the pine floors. The sound drove everyone in the family nuts but she said they kept her feet warm, so they all lived with the squeaking and knew exactly where she was at all times.

"She was a character, your Nancy." Ruthy shook her head sadly and gave the pot a few slow stirs. "Took after her mama."

"I'm not sure if that's a nice thing to say or not." Blanche considered for a moment. "People say someone's a character when they're fun to be around. But they also tend to say that when they can't stand the person."

Ruth snorted. "I can stand you, no worry. But I never thought I'd see an old white lady with cornrows. You didn't even put on a hat and now you got a sunburn on your head."

"Everybody was gettin' them done! That singles cruise I took to Alaska was all whale watching and binoculars. I wore a raincoat for two weeks. Never again. Jamaicans really know how to have a good time." Blanche shook a finger at Ruth. "Next time, you're coming with me!"

Ruth shot Blanche a look. "And how do you suggest I persuade my husband to let me go on a singles cruise?"

Blanche frowned. "True. That will take some consideration on our part."

Brooks tried not to laugh out loud. When he was a teenager, his grandmother had been embarrassing and weird. Now he appreciated her commitment to wringing the joy from every moment. Especially now, when there was so little joy at Badewood. "I wish Dad would find a hobby or maybe take one of those vacations. He needs to get out."

"Find a hobby? He lost his wife of forty years. No hobby can replace her." Blanche shrugged.

Brooks paused, not sure how to say what was so obvious to anyone who had ever met his parents. "They never seemed very . . . happy. And I just assumed that he would try to move on after a while."

"Well, there's happy and then there's married." Blanche stared up at the pressed-tin ceiling, as if watching a movie. "Your grandfather and I used to bicker like that. But as we got older, we realized there wasn't time for nit-pickin'. I'm glad we had a few peaceful years at the end. I remember him that way, not the fights we had in the beginning. We got married so young, we hardly knew each other."

Maybe Brooks's parents would have figured that out if his mother had lived long enough. But surely forty years was long enough to work out some compromises. Or at least be able to hold a conversation that didn't end in dredging up old hurts.

"My Barry and I have never shared a cross word. But then, we're best friends." Ruth shook some pepper into the pot and took another sniff of the roiling steam.

"Never?"

"Nope." Ruth turned and gave Brooks a look. "I know what you're thinking. It's as clear as the nose on your face. You think I'm saying that because it's polite, that no one wants to hear about a couple's troubles. Well, let me tell you that living through a rough marriage is a lot braver than staying married to your best friend. And Barry's my other half. We finish each other's sentences, he knows the way I like my coffee, he always leaves the window cracked just a bit at night because I like to hear the frogs and the crickets."

Brooks nodded, a strange feeling spreading through his chest. Love and war went together, right? Two people committed for life, and eventually they rubbed each other raw. No personalities fit perfectly, but they threaded through each other like hands clasping.

"But then some days I look at him and feel like I've married a stranger. He always surprises me. But it's a stranger I really like so I never pay it any mind." Ruth pursed her lips, the ladle raised in one hand. "Funny how he knows me so much better than I do him. He's never once told me I surprised him. I guess I'm an open book for my Barry."

Blanche nodded. "I miss someone knowing me better than I know myself. It's a comfort to think a person can be known through and through and not scare off her husband."

Brooks stuck his hands in his pockets and examined his shoes. It would be nice to be known fully and still loved, but what if it was one or the other? What if by the time someone got to know you, the person didn't love you anymore? And when could you be sure the person really knew you? Two years? Four? It was probably better to pull back while the going was good, rather than to risk losing a marriage on the gamble of someone's still liking the real you, the forty-years-of-marriage you. Yes, definitely better to leave good things alone. Things such as friendship.

"You look like someone ran over your dog." Blanche nudged him with her elbow.

"I do?" He straightened up. All this marriage talk was giving him a headache. Or maybe it was the fumes from the crazy Jamaican soup. "I'm hungry is all. When will this strange brew be ready for tasting?"

Ruth moved to the fridge, withdrawing mayo and cold cuts. "Honey, it's probably not a question of time. I'm not sure anything will make this soup ready. How about I fix you a sandwich so's you don't starve to death?" She started to assemble the sandwich on the oak countertop but he waved her away with a smile. He was a little past the age of having the cook make him a snack. Ruth was more than a cook, anyway. She made sure the house ran smoothly, from answering the phone and scheduling private tours, all the way down to making sure the houseplants were watered.

"O ye of little faith, just wait and see." Blanche stuck her nose in the air and went back to reading the recipe out loud. The terms didn't make a bit of sense to him and he wondered if she'd even measured the ingredients, or if they'd all been thrown in the pot willy-nilly.

"Is Caroline coming tomorrow to show Lauren around?" Ruth asked.

"No. She's busy planning some party." And planning her lunch date with Frank. He hated the idea of them spending time together. He told himself it was because something about Frank set off his warning bells, something that reminded him of a bad amateur magician, but he knew it was more than that. He almost asked why Ruth thought Caroline would be showing anyone around Badewood but decided to let it go.

"What kind of party? Another bridge function? Poor girl. She's turned into her mama's event planner."

"No, it's something about Jane Austen." Brooks took the bread from the bread bin and laid out a few slices. On second thought, he took out another two. Maybe if he brought a sandwich up to his father, he'd eat.

"A western?" Blanche frowned over at him, clearly mishearing.

"No, *Austen*. Like *Pride and Prejudice*. Long dresses, men in top hats."

"Oh, that sounds wonderful! I think that's just what we

need!" She plopped the ladle into the soup, completely forgetting about the saltfish.

Brooks sighed. "Grandma, how is an Austen party what we really need?"

"It's romantic and fun and we'll learn lots of dances." Her eyes went out of focus as she gazed into the distance.

"I'm not sure about the dancing part." He swiped mustard on the white bread and grabbed for the bologna. He'd love a pastrami on rye, but this was Thorny Hollow and it was bologna on white or nothing.

"There has to be. You couldn't have an Austen party without it. In fact"—she paused, finger on her chin—"my friend Roger Simmons is real involved in the contra-dancing group that meet on Tuesdays. Maybe we can pay his band to play and he can teach us the reels."

Brooks worked in silence for a moment, ripping lettuce a bit too forcefully. This party was getting better and better. First Caroline was determined to make him come in a costume, now his grandmother was arranging the dancing lessons. Excellent.

"So, are we supposed to come as someone special, or just dress up?"

"We?" He waved a piece of lettuce in one hand. "There's no *we*!"

Ruth shot him a look. "That's not very hospitable."

He felt their combined disappointment and cringed. "Listen, I don't want to dress up. I don't want to dance. And I really, really don't want a crowd of witnesses in the event I actually get dragged into this fiasco."

"Hmm?" Blanche narrowed her eyes at him.

He sighed, turning back to the sandwiches. When he'd decided to move home for the summer, he'd had some idea of writing articles and maybe doing research on the maneuvers at Vicksburg. This wasn't what he'd planned.

"But you're going?"

Brooks felt his shoulders slump. He'd told Caroline no, but deep down he knew he was going. "Yes. And I'm supposed to go as Mr. Knightley."

Ruth chuckled, covering her mouth with her hand. She dropped the hand and forced a bland expression. "Sorry, don't mind me."

"I don't even know who that is, but I know it involves a morning coat and breeches." Just saying the words made his head throb. He looked over just in time to see Blanche giving Ruth a look, an "Isn't this wonderful" sort of look. "Is there something I should know?" He stacked both sandwiches on a plate and turned to the older women, arms crossed over his chest.

Blanche shook her head, eyes wide. "No, no, everything's fine. And who suggested you come as Mr. Knightley?"

"Caroline. She's already planned it all out." He didn't know where this was heading. "What's with the guy? Didn't he have a crazy wife in the attic and she burned down his house?"

Ruth snorted, shaking her head. "That was Mr. Rochester in *Jane Eyre*. Barry and I saw George C. Scott play him. Must have been, oh, 1970 or so. He was right handsome, even though he has that crooked beak for a nose."

"I didn't see that one." Brooks ran a hand over his face. He had zero interest in reading up on Mr. Knightley. His journalistic focus was magazines, not historical literature. "I'm going to go check my e-mail and see what Dad's up to. Let me know when the soup is done."

"Does that mean you're going to taste it?" Grandma perked up, her blue eyes wide with hope.

"Sure does." Brooks stacked the sandwiches on one plate, hoping she wouldn't guess he was going to tempt his father with one. "And I'll bring the Maalox just in case."

Absalom jumped up as Brooks moved toward the door but he held up a hand. "Sit. You're in no condition to be wandering the house. You'll get a bath when I get back." The look on the retriever's face was surprise, followed by a rapid retreat back under the table at the dreaded B-word.

Brooks left the kitchen by the same long hallway, but turned east to the front of the house. His father hardly moved from his study anymore. He sat in the darkened room and watched ESPN for hours, his recliner fully extended and an old gray blanket on his lap. It was depressing to witness, and even more depressing to spend any amount of time in the dank hole. It was time to get his dad out of the house. Even if he had to drag him out by his heels, enough was enough.

Of course, getting out wasn't always the best option, since he had somehow just agreed to go to a Regency costume party.

There are people, who the more you do for them, the less they will do for themselves.

—EMMA

Chapter Eleven

"I'm glad you had time to meet me for lunch." Frank's tone was offhand but he held Caroline's gaze a few seconds longer than necessary. He must have come straight from work because he was dressed as if he'd been in a meeting. The flashy party suit was gone, replaced with an obviously expensive tailored shirt and dark blue slacks. On anyone else it would have looked like an airline-pilot uniform or corporate gear, but Frank gave it an edginess. Maybe it was his shaggy haircut or the heavy-framed glasses that changed everything. She felt a blush begin at the base of her neck and spread upward.

"Not a problem. I was happy to get out of the house for a while." Out of the house and out of town. She hadn't been to Spartainville since her friend Shelby had moved away to Millsaps. Caroline smoothed her light pink skirt and hoped the matching jacket didn't make her look like Barbie. She loved pink, but maybe at some age a girl had to choose other colors. She wasn't sure what that age was, exactly.

Frank leaned across the small red Formica-topped table. "You're probably thinking I brought you to Peggy's because of the décor." He paused, motioning to the black-and-white photographs of Elvis and Tony Bennett and the checkerboard floors. "But they have the best food in town. If you're lucky enough to find the place, of course."

She smiled, remembering the long trip through the back streets of the town's seedier neighborhoods. She was reserving judgment on the diner, especially since her Coke came served in a glass with Rhett Butler's face on it.

The waitress returned and pulled her little notebook from a pocket, pen posed. "Y'all decided?" Her bright orange-red lipstick contrasted with the neon-green gum that appeared every time she worked her jaw. A brown plastic name tag with white capital letters spelled out JENNISE.

"I'd like the catfish and collard greens, please." Caroline's mama didn't like the smell of cooked fish so it wasn't something Angie made for them at home. She should take advantage of her freedom, at least culinarily.

Jennise turned to Frank without making a note and chewed a few times.

He took that as a sign to order. "Chicken fried steak and buttermilk biscuits."

"Not the usual, huh? Guess you're branchin' out." She shot a look at Caroline and walked away, tucking the still-blank notepad into her apron pocket.

Caroline started to laugh, expecting Frank to roll his eyes at the mysterious ways of small-town waitresses, but he held up a finger. "Listen! Isn't that Buddy Holly?"

She cocked her head. "I guess so. I'm not really familiar with that era."

"Come on." He slid out of his seat and held out a hand, grinning.

She laughed. "What, you can't expect me to . . . You're not . . ."

"Hurry up, before it's over." Grabbing her hand, he pulled her out of the booth and walked her backward to the jukebox. The diner was almost empty, with only an elderly gentleman at the counter. Holding both her hands, Frank pulled her close, then pushed her back, singing in an attractive alto. It was completely familiar but absurdly foreign at the same time. Had she ever listened to the words before? Some girl would make him cry and how that'd be the day, the day that he died.

She grinned, following Frank's movements as best she could. Her jacket was keeping her from reaching back over her shoulder to grab his hand when he turned her. She quickly slipped it off and draped it over a chair, leaving only her silk tank top. Now they could really dance, moving in perfect rhythm, faster and faster as she felt more comfortable. She couldn't help laughing, the joy of the moment breaking through her reservations.

When the song ended, she was breathless with laughter. Frank pulled her close and kissed her cheek. "That's the way to do it," he said.

"To do what?" She couldn't stop smiling. "I thought we were having lunch and then we ended up over here, jitterbugging."

"That was swing. I can teach you some other moves, but we better get some food first because it burns about five hundred calories an hour and I don't want you to waste away. Your mama would never forgive me."

Caroline snorted as they settled back in the booth. "I'm not in any danger of wasting away, believe me. I hardly ever get out to run anymore."

"When are you moving to Spartainville?"

His question took her by surprise. It was a leap from not getting out for a run to moving to another city. She blinked, searching for something to say.

"I'm sorry. I just assumed you were moving back here."

"I'm—I'm working on reestablishing my professional presence before I make any big decisions."

Frank laughed, a deep chuckle that made her lips turn up without her permission. "You're looking for a job."

"Well, if you want to put it that way, yes."

He sipped his Coke and said nothing. Caroline felt the seconds tick away. He must think she was a pretty sad example of educated Southern womanhood, stuck at home in the middle of nowhere. She wanted to defend herself, explain about her father's death and her mother's sudden hypochondria, but it seemed inadequate. It would probably only make her look weaker.

"Caroline, if you don't mind, I'd like to make this more than a social lunch." His face was serious, eyes dark.

"Okay." She wasn't sure what he meant but couldn't see the harm in hearing what he had to say.

"My company is growing so rapidly that we're short-staffed in all areas. We're handicapped. There are so many projects we can't accept because we can't produce the work in a reasonable amount of time." He looked down at his tan, manicured hands. "I'm desperate. I didn't want to make things complicated between us but I'd like to offer you a job at Vertical Pop."

Caroline felt her cheeks go hot. Complicated? He'd clearly implied that they were on a date, but that he needed to step back and be a professional for the sake of his company. She felt admiration rise up in her.

"And I'd like to consider your offer."

He laughed out loud, shaking his head. "You're wonderful, you know that?"

She shrugged, smiling. "If you say so. I'm unemployed, for sure."

"I think you'll be happy with us at Vertical Pop. We need people like you who're plugged into the entertainment scene."

Caroline frowned. She didn't see how she could possibly be considered plugged into any sort of scene when most of her time was spent in her own house. "Frank, you may have gotten the wrong impression. I'm not—"

"I'm sure I didn't." He waved a hand. "The way you dress, the way you talk. I can tell you're the type of writer we need. These manga books are massively popular but the translations they give us are horrible. We need someone to rework them, make them really appeal to the American audience. Everyone's doing video blogs, setting up Kickstarter campaigns and running counterculture online magazines. You'd be perfect at things like that."

She fiddled with her napkin. She knew nothing about what "everyone" was doing. Her journalism degree was losing value faster than a brand-new car after being driven off the lot. The longer she stayed out of circulation, the more obsolete she got. But this probably wasn't the time to explain all of that. Was she trying to talk him out of offering her a job? Who cared if he thought she spent her time watching *The Lizzie Bennet Diaries* and campaigning for new *Veronica Mars* episodes instead of making pink lemonade for old ladies? She could catch up. All she needed was a little time to get back in the groove.

"So, these translations come straight from the Japanese publisher?"

"Right." He rubbed his hands together. "It's complicated. We can get into that more when we've got you officially on board."

She nodded. There would be time, no hurry. "I'll start looking into those sites you mentioned, get myself more acquainted with the way the marketing works. I'll let you know if it seems like something that would benefit both of us."

"Don't take too long. This business changes every day. You can't afford to sit on my offer. We need someone like you. There might be a small investment needed on your part, just to help offset any training costs, but it won't be anything substantial."

Caroline paused. Investment? What was it exactly that made him think she would fit in well at his company? A suspicion was growing in the back of her mind that Frank was interested in someone who came from a wealthy family such as hers, someone who might be more of an investor than a team member.

She didn't know what to say next. He seemed to be waiting for some kind of response. Poking at her food for a moment, she suddenly remembered her promise to Lexi. "If you're really interested in finding bright, new talent, I met a young artist the other night, at the Werlins' party."

Frank nodded, looking over her shoulder in a slightly distracted way.

"She's heading off to college, but she'll be studying accounting because she can't afford to major in something that may not pay the bills."

"Sounds smart." He was still focused on something behind her.

"Does it? I really felt like it was such a sad way to start her career. I think she should at least minor in art. It's not like it was fifty years ago. Artists can actually support themselves doing what they love."

"Hmmm. You're right." His eyes flicked to her face, then back to whatever was near the front door.

She turned, scanning the restaurant. "Is there—" She broke off at the sight of Lauren Fairfield, who seemed to be in the middle of mouthing a word at Frank. She froze, then her expression settled into something pleasant. Her usual sleek hair was pulled back in a ponytail and curled at the ends. As tall and elegant as ever, her simple turquoise sheath dress was decorated with a patterned scarf tied at the end of her ponytail.

"I think that's Lauren Fairfield, isn't it?" Frank asked. "That woman who was so defensive about being an editor for that editorial dinosaur with one foot on the way to extinction?"

Caroline swallowed back a response. It might be better to be with a dinosaur on the way to extinction than be working with a start-up that would fold in a year from lack of investors. "It is. I wonder what she's doing over here. I thought she was touring homes in the Thorny Hollow area this week." She knew where Lauren had been a few days ago, certainly. She and Brooks had been wandering Badewood together.

"Really? Interesting. And don't look now, I think she's heading over." He said this through his teeth, a smile plastered to his face.

Caroline turned around, wishing Frank would stand up and greet Lauren like a gentleman. She didn't take to Lauren the way she should, but that didn't mean she wanted to be rude.

"Hello, there. It seems that Peggy's isn't the big secret it's made out to be." Lauren's smile was tight, eyes flicking back and forth between them.

"Apparently not. Soon we'll see whole tables of editors in business suits, right?"

Caroline cringed inwardly. These two weren't able to get past their professional differences, but they had a lot in common otherwise. Thorny Hollow was a small county and

Southern to the core. In a place where they counted cousins once removed and six times down, these two definitely qualified as hometown folk. They should treat each other better than strangers.

Lauren's lips curved up in a slight smile. "Maybe only one or two at a time." She turned to Caroline, giving her a once-over. "Is this a business luncheon, or should I pretend I didn't see you here?"

Caroline felt her brows rise up in surprise. "No pretending needed, and you're welcome to join us." But if her mama hadn't raised her right, she might point out that Lauren's blatant curiosity was distinctly *un*invited.

"No, thank you. I'm just picking up a quick lunch before I get back to proofing the photos from Saturday. Brooks was such a gracious host when he showed me around Badewood. I was surprised that you weren't there to help." Lauren's large gray eyes narrowed the tiniest amount.

Caroline took a moment to respond, unsure of why she'd be giving tours of Brooks's family home. Maybe Lauren thought the Ashley home was a sort of annex to Badewood? The idea was laughable, but Caroline tried to ignore the wave of irritation that rose up in her at the idea. They were built in the same era, but in distinctly different styles. Plus, Badewood was a solid ten times larger than her own home.

"He's definitely the one to help you. I'm not sure I've ever had the entire tour, honestly," Caroline said. When you grew up in a home, you didn't need the tour. She took a breath and made an effort to be gracious. "When I saw him on Sunday, he mentioned it had been a great experience. He learned quite a lot from your visit."

"I'm glad. So sweet you spend Sundays together. My father always took his older sister to Sunday brunch every week as long as she was alive."

Caroline felt her jaw drop. Lauren had just called her an old maid, she was certain of it. So, was she some sort of modern-day Miss Havisham, locked away in her house wearing a tattered wedding gown and only one shoe, with a rotting wedding cake on the table? And Brooks wasn't like a younger brother. Or even an older brother, really. He was, once, but things had changed. She wasn't sure what he was now, but it wasn't a brotherly relationship. The realization came so clearly that she sat speechless for a few moments.

"We attend the same church," she choked out. It was all she could say, and to her horror, she felt her face turn hot in anger.

"How sweet. There's nothing like being with family in a charming Southern church on a summer morning." Lauren smiled kindly, as if Caroline were the epitome of sweetness. The blush must have confirmed her innocent nature, but her thoughts at the moment were far from sweet. They were downright deadly. She'd never liked Lauren, never felt as if she were having a conversation that wasn't riddled with nasty undercurrents. But she was decided now. Lauren wasn't worth the trouble of making friends.

Lauren brushed back her hair and sighed. "He's such a nice person and I would be interested, really, if he wasn't a bit of a . . . you know." She shrugged apologetically.

"Excuse me?" Caroline felt the blood drain from her face. It was one thing to field insults about being a homebody, but Lauren had wandered into all new territory.

"Well, a woman knows when a man is interested, doesn't she?

And don't get me wrong, he's very handsome and so educated and the way he knows every inch of his family's historic home is commendable. But . . ."

"But what?" Caroline couldn't imagine what Lauren was trying to say.

"I'm just not into the nerdy type." She rolled those gray eyes in a you-can't-blame-me expression. "I prefer the bad boys. Always have, always will."

Frank chuckled. "I think he's great. Definitely a geek, though. You charmed the socks off him at the Werlins' party. Don't feel bad about turning him down. I'm sure he's used to it."

Caroline swiveled to look at Frank, surprise washing through her. She felt slow and stupid. She'd wondered if Brooks would be attracted to Lauren simply because she was so polished, educated and beautiful. But although she thought she knew him better than anyone else, she had overlooked what was obvious to the rest of the world: Brooks *was* interested in Lauren.

"He asked me to come to that Jane Austen party you all are putting together. I just don't know if I have the time," Lauren said.

"He did?" Of course he did. If she wouldn't go out on a date with him, she might still attend another party where he could see her again. Caroline couldn't blame Brooks for trying.

"I love a good cosplay. It seems the anime crowd has one every month or so. I have lots of gear. I think I can whip up an Austen character in no time."

"And who will you be?" Lauren put a finger to her chin and squinted at him. "You should go as Willoughby, I think."

Caroline searched her memory and came up with nothing substantial. "Who's that?"

Lauren smiled. "A very bad boy. He shows up in *Sense and*

Sensibility, leaving a trail of broken hearts across the countryside."

He laughed outright. "That's a role I can commit to, for sure. I'll be sad if you can't make the time to attend. All work and no play, as they say. On the other hand, I'd hate to see the big book get behind schedule."

"We're weeks ahead of the deadline." Lauren's face had gone tight and she pulled her elbows in to her sides, as if she meant the exact opposite of what she said.

"Can't wait to see the final product," Frank said.

"Well, I'll make sure you'll be the first."

Something about her tone made Caroline think of secret codes and pig latin. She glanced at Frank and saw a flash of laughter in his eyes. For a moment, she was absolutely sure he and Lauren were having a silent conversation right under her nose. But in the next second, it was gone and Caroline wasn't sure if she had seen anything there at all.

"I'll let you two finish your lunch. I'm sure we'll see each other around Thorny Hollow." Lauren smiled and walked away, her long ponytail swishing against her back.

"I can't stand that woman," Frank muttered, reaching for his Coke.

"Because of your disagreement on traditional versus independent publishing? I don't see why you two are on opposite sides, honestly. You're not competing in the same market at all. Coffee-table books and manga? Should be enough room for everybody."

"I'm sure we could have a civil conversation if she wasn't such a snob. It's everything about her. She's cold, like she grew up in New York City instead of Mississippi." He shrugged. "Let's forget about her. We were having such a good time before she showed up."

Caroline forced a smile. It was terrible to talk about a person the moment her back was turned. She understood what he meant, but a certain unease spread through her as she watched his face. Frank had the ability to make her laugh, to be spontaneous in a way she never usually was. But another side of him didn't sit well with her, no matter how hard she tried to excuse his behavior.

He had been in love with Emma, and jealous of Frank Churchill, from about the same period, one sentiment having probably enlightened him as to the other.

—EMMA

Chapter Twelve

Brooks settled himself at the small wooden table and felt a wave of contentment. This is what it should be like every Monday afternoon: classes over, his little brother in town and a triple shot steaming before him. The Daily Grind bustled with students and the late-afternoon sun streamed through the window, setting every nick and dent in the old wood into bas-relief. The quintessential campus coffee bar, it had Wi-Fi, Fair Trade coffee and rickety chairs circa 1980 with Naugahyde seats.

Manning was at the counter, talking to the tall, skinny kid who took the food orders. The kid shrugged, pointing at the menu. Brooks smiled to himself.

Seconds later Manning was at the table, plopping into the chair. "I don't get it. If you can make fries, you can make hush puppies."

"I think they just dump frozen fries into the fryer. Hate to get in the way of your national campaign to reclaim Southern food in public places, but hush puppies require a bit of preparation."

Manning leaned back, crossing his arms over his chest. "It's not like I'm asking them to outlaw junk food, or to call them Freedom Fries. I just want an even representation of our culture."

"Starting with fried food?"

"We have to choose our battles." Manning grinned and jerked a thumb at the counter. "He said his name is Tater. I can't be mad at a kid named Tater."

"Agreed. Poor guy, he got the short end of the naming stick, for sure."

Manning frowned. "Really? I think it's way better than Joe or Thomas or . . ."

"Or Manning?"

"Well, no, because that's a family name. But I don't think it's so bad."

"Are we gonna have a Tater Elliot in the family sometime soon?"

Manning didn't laugh. He sat forward, wrapping his hands around his mug.

"Hey, don't take it so seriously. I was just yanking your chain." Brooks gave him a light punch to the shoulder, the brotherly equivalent of a hug.

"I'm glad you were free this afternoon." Manning looked up, eyes serious.

Brooks would always find time for his brother, no matter the day or time. Something in Manning's expression set off alarm bells. "It's been a long time since we've just sat down and had some coffee." It wasn't supposed to be an accusation but it came out abruptly.

Manning glanced up, nodding. "I know, and I'm sorry for that."

"I didn't mean—"

"It's okay. I let things go." Manning stared at his hands, as if searching for words. "We've had a tough year and it seemed easier to batten down the hatches than to come out looking for help."

Brooks waited, surprised. Manning and Debbie Mae had seemed so happy. Maybe their marriage wasn't going as well as everyone thought.

"We wanted to have kids right away, but it's not looking like that will happen." Manning's face was tight with grief.

Brooks took a moment to process his words. "Have you been to any specialists? Infertility is so common; you should be able to find a doctor to help."

"No, we're fertile." Manning's mouth quirked. "I bet you didn't think you were going to discuss your brother's fertility over coffee, did you?"

Brooks waved a hand. He wasn't squeamish and he wasn't a jock. Modern men could have a discussion about conception without batting an eye. "I don't understand. If you're fertile, then—" He realized the other alternative. Able to conceive but not carry to birth.

Manning nodded, eyes cast down again. "We've been through the wringer three times now and Debbie Mae is ready to take a break. She says she just can't handle the heartbreak anymore."

Brooks wanted to say there would be time, they could try again later, that maybe the fourth time was the charm, but he knew better than to speak up. The last year had been emotionally savage and Manning didn't need platitudes.

Manning took a drink of coffee and let out a long breath. New wrinkles between his brows, hair a little grayer at the temples. Brooks hadn't noticed these changes. Of course, he hadn't seen Manning much the last year or so.

"Tell me what I can do to help," Brooks said.

Manning smiled, but his eyes remained shadowed with sadness. "This, what you're doing right now. Not giving me the what for because I've been in a cave since this all started. And you can let me borrow your regimental jacket when we go out to Vicksburg."

"Ha! This has all been a ploy for sympathy. I sewed that jacket myself. I left it out in the weather for six months straight until it was perfectly aged. Besides, it won't fit you. I'm bigger through the shoulders."

"It'll look authentic. Tubbs said he's lost another fifteen pounds and he'll look nicely malnourished." Manning patted his gut with both hands. "Debbie Mae cooks too well for me to pull off the starving rebel, but in that jacket it will hang real nice. I'll look just like a well-fed man gone off to war who's shrinking away to nothing."

Brooks laughed but the smile faded from his face. He knew Manning was just trying to lighten the mood. "If I thought that a jacket from the Tenth Mississippi Regiment, Company H, Rankin Rifles, would help, I'd hand it over in a heartbeat."

"And if I thought it would help, I'd take it." Manning took a sip of coffee. "When we went to the luminaria ceremony this year at the Antietam National Battlefield, she cried through the whole thing. Twenty thousand candles commemorating fallen soldiers is a tough sight to behold, but she took it personally. Debbie Mae has really been carrying the burden. It's been hard for both of us, but she had appointments and the tests and then at the end . . ." He shook his head.

"You feel helpless."

"Right. And it's my job as a man to protect her, to keep her from harm." His jaw went tight. "I know we're supposed to be modern, educated men, but deep down we all just want to keep our wives and children safe."

Brooks felt a heaviness settle in his chest. Children. Plural. They had suffered such loss and he hadn't even known. He wanted to apologize, to say how he'd failed Manning for not asking, for not visiting. But inserting his own guilt into the conversation seemed wrong.

"Anyway, she's decided we need to focus on other things. She definitely seems happier, although there are days . . ." Manning stared into his mug, lines tight around his mouth. "I told her she needed to go see Caroline. They're best friends and she didn't even visit her at all this year."

"I know Caroline missed her."

"It'll be good for both of them. Caroline needs to get out of that house before her mother locks her in the attic."

Brooks laughed. "I was just telling her the same thing. Of course now she has this idea that we're all going to dress up in Regency costumes for some Austen-themed party."

"I think that was Debbie Mae's idea, actually. She saw that PBS special and got it into her head that it would make a great summer shebang."

Brooks sat back, considering for a moment how Caroline hadn't defended herself, how she could easily have told him it was all her cousin's idea. Instead Caroline did her best to convince him to come. He felt a pain in his ribs, part admiration for her loyalty and part sheer dread at the realization he was bound to this party now in a way he hadn't been before.

"I thought it was pretty crazy, but the more she smiled as she was planning, the more I figured it doesn't matter if we're all coming as elephants and bicycling dogs. It makes her happy and I'm doing whatever I can to help her pull it off."

"I'll be there. Caroline's been shopping Etsy for costumes. Promise me you'll be wearing something equally silly."

"I think I'm supposed to be a Mr. Martin, a farmer. So maybe I don't have to wear the fancy suit."

"If you wear normal clothes and get to carry a pitchfork, I'm switching roles."

Manning laughed, holding up both hands. "Ask her if there's someone else you can be. There must be hordes of villagers. How about some ancient, one-eyed cripple that begs in the town square? That would be fun."

"And a cripple wouldn't have to dance, either." Brooks made a mental note to push for another role. He didn't care if he looked like a bum.

"I think Caroline invited that Frank guy from the Werlins' party. He'll be perfect for it. They can take turns dancing with him and we can sit in the corner and plan for Mobile Bay."

Brooks cringed. It was bad enough knowing they'd gone to lunch. The image flashed before him of Frank squiring Caroline around a dance floor, delicate music accompanying their every move.

The sun beat down through the glass and Brooks could feel the early-summer heat on the back of his neck. He stood to adjust the blinds and caught a flash of color. A smooth cheek, a few careless blond curls, the angle of her shoulders.

He jumped up, stepped to the door and opened it just as she walked by. "Caroline?"

"Oh!" She stepped sideways, hand on her heart. "Brooks! You scared me to death." She laughed and he felt himself laugh in response, although he didn't know why. Seeing her there, on the street, was like finding something precious out of the blue. Or maybe something he'd lost a long time ago and forgotten about.

"Come on in and have some coffee." He held open the door and she stepped through. As she passed, the light scent of her perfume made his smile even wider. He'd missed her and it was only Monday.

Manning stood up and gave her a hug. "I'll order for you. What will you have?"

"Single vanilla latte, decaf," Brooks answered, and pulled out a chair for her.

His brother shot him a look and went to the counter.

"What are you doing here? I didn't know you were headed down this way." He noticed for the first time she was wearing a pink suit and a simple strand of pearls.

"I was meeting a friend for lunch." She scooped her curls into a simple ponytail. Tugging a pen from her purse, she maneuvered and twisted the hair around in several swift movements until it was a softly made bun. Tendrils framed her face and she glanced up at him, smiling. "I went to your office but you were out. So I left a note and was heading for Nick's Big Bookstore on Thirteenth."

He nodded. She loved that place. Especially the historical fiction section on the third floor. "If you stay here too long, someone might snag your favorite beanbag."

"Probably. I'll sacrifice." She gazed around. "It's been so long since I've been in here. It really brings back memories. Shelby and I used to come here, before she moved."

"Does she come home at all?"

"Every now and then, but this summer she and Ransom are coming to stay in Flea Bite Creek for a while. He's probably more concerned with the one hundred and fiftieth reenactments this year than visiting her parents, but he's a good sport about it."

"We're not in the same company, but I remember him at the Battle of Boonville. He was die-hard, head-to-toe and never stepped out of the role. When tourists came up to take his picture, he kept giving the name of a real rebel soldier." Brooks grinned. "Folks never questioned whether Gideon Johnson Pillow was really his name. The only time I saw him break character was when he was talking to the African-American guys who made up the Corps d'Afrique. One of them had his great-great-granddaddy's Medal of Honor and Ransom had to go get his camera from Shelby so he could take a picture."

Caroline leaned forward. "Now explain to me why this is perfectly normal and dressing up in Regency gear is not."

He blinked. "Finley, because the Civil War is history."

"So is Regency England." She laughed, eyes bright. "Just because we're not firing cannons or riding horses doesn't mean it won't be fun."

Manning arrived, setting her latte on the table. "Hey, maybe we should bring that new cannon. Although, I still haven't got it to the firing stage yet."

"No, you should bring the Parrott thirty-pounder. Not as impressive, but at least it's functional."

"Now, you two. We're not firing any artillery. Can you imagine what a disaster a wild shot would be around all those people? It's too dangerous!" Caroline said.

"Wild shot? They're extremely accurate up to a mile. No one is going to get hurt. And if we want to be really historically accurate, we can stage a little battle. Not sure which, but I'm sure they were in some kind of war at that time. England was always in a war with somebody," Manning said.

"I don't think the Napoleonic Wars count since it wasn't on English soil. We're not turning this into a battlefield. There will be music and dancing and fine food and gracious conversation." She ticked them off on her fingers, one by one.

"Oh, great idea." Brooks brightened. "We can borrow the smoothbore Napoleon. It's Southern made, but no one will know that."

"I wish they hadn't cleaned it." Manning shuddered. "It was a perfectly acceptable oxidized patina, but some misguided soul thought he should shine it up. Now it's as shiny as a new penny."

"I'll carry my cavalry revolver. The musket has the bayonet and doesn't look as dressy."

"The Colt 1860 Army?" Manning leaned forward. "I've been looking and looking but no one will part with one for any price. I wouldn't care if I had to come in a hat and tails if I get to carry a Colt .44."

"Listen to me!" Caroline held out both hands, one to each brother. "This is Debbie Mae's party. If she wants cannons, she'll tell you to bring cannons. If she wants everyone to bring their rusty old service revolvers, she'll tell us. As far as I know, this is a weapons-free dance."

"Rusty?" Brooks sat back as if he'd been slapped. "It's not one of the cheaper brass replicas. It's the original steel frame with engraving on the cylinder, although it's a Navy scene on an Army gun and nobody can explain why. Anyway, I've got the attached shoulder stock but I can just use the holster. It's not anything close to rusty."

She let out a sigh. "I'm sure it's pretty. But can we just forget what *we* want and pull together for Debbie Mae?"

Manning was silent, nodding his head.

Brooks realized Caroline didn't want to have a Regency party any more than he did. His chest tightened. She put the needs of her friends above her own, no matter how silly and inconsequential they seemed, and worked to bring everyone else in on the plan. He, on the other hand, thought simply showing up was a big contribution. A wave of shame went through him at the comparison. Caroline had always been the kinder person, and the more thoughtful, of the two of them. "You're right. No firearms. No cannons. We'll be there and we'll be as Regency as possible."

"Thank you," Caroline said, laying a hand on his. He could tell a weight had lifted from her shoulders.

Brooks opened his mouth to respond but a car at the corner caught his eye. The familiar bright red Miata paused at the busy intersection to let foot traffic pass, and he could see Lauren at the wheel. She leaned over to kiss her passenger. A hand slipped behind Lauren's head, fingers threading through her dark hair. After several seconds she leaned back and the passenger door opened. Frank jumped out, shutting the door and jogging to the other side of the street.

"Isn't that Frank Keene?" Brooks pointed across the street.

Caroline half stood, shading her eyes with her hand. "Sure is. We had lunch a few hours ago at this kooky little café on the east side of town. He taught me to swing dance and it was so much fun." She watched Frank jog down the sidewalk. "He must really be in a hurry. I think he mentioned he had a meeting."

"You had lunch with him again? Why?"

She glanced at Brooks, surprised. "Because he asked me."

"How come you've never come down to have lunch with me?"

"Because you've never asked!" She laughed, watching Frank until he was out of sight.

"Lauren dropped him at the corner and—"

She sat down, shooting Brooks a glance. "No, must have been someone else. They can't stand each other. She showed up at the same café when we were eating and they near about had a fight over nothing."

Brooks glanced at Manning, hoping he'd seen the kiss. Manning looked back and forth between them as if he were watching a tennis match.

"I'm pretty sure I saw them—"

"I don't think we'd want to put those two in the same car. There might be trouble." Caroline grinned at Brooks, green-blue eyes crinkling at the corners. After pausing, as if choosing her words carefully, she said, "He was pretty clear about how much he dislikes her uppity attitude."

Something about that just seemed wrong. Frank was too quick to label others, and Brooks didn't appreciate hearing Frank's words come out of Caroline's mouth. "I don't think she's uppity at all. I think she's confident and ambitious. Neither of those things are bad," Brooks said. "Just because she knows what she wants doesn't mean she's a snob. I admire a woman who has high expectations of herself and others."

Caroline stared down at her napkin, twisting it between her fingers. She went quiet. Brooks suddenly wondered if Lauren's success made Caroline feel inadequate. He wanted to reassure her, but Lauren had worked hard to have the job she did. Nothing he could say would diminish that.

He took a slow sip of coffee. "You came all the way to Spartainville for lunch?"

She nodded. "He came all the way to Thorny Hollow for dinner last week. I didn't mind returning the favor. It was nice to get out. The café might be real retro, or just weird, I'm not sure.

The short-order cook kept playing 'Dixie' on the jukebox, and they had a big poster of Jefferson Davis."

"Did they have hush puppies?" Manning asked.

"Don't mind him." Brooks paused, wondering if he should push the issue. "I really think I saw Lauren drop him at the corner. It even seemed . . . it seemed like she leaned over and gave him a kiss."

Caroline's eyes went wide and she stared at Brooks for a full three seconds. Then she burst out laughing. "Oh, Brooks, that's impossible! Gave him a kiss?" She laughed until tears came to her eyes. "At your age, eyesight is the first thing to go. Maybe you should schedule a checkup."

Manning let out a low whistle and pretended to examine the poster of a Scottish castle on the wall.

Brooks sat back, setting his jaw. He wouldn't try again. He knew what he'd seen. For some reason, Frank was determined to pretend that he and Lauren were enemies. What that meant for Caroline, Brooks couldn't even guess. From the sinking feeling in his gut, it couldn't be good.

"Look," she said, leaning forward and putting a hand on his. "I know you want to protect me just like an older brother, but I can take care of myself. I promise I'm not jumping into anything. Plus, Frank wouldn't be kissing Lauren in the middle of traffic if he was . . ."

"What? Swing dancing in a little café with you?"

"I'll be right back. I need to . . . get some napkins." Manning bolted from the table.

Caroline's face went pink. "I'm surprised at you. I always figured you for the kind of guy that accepted a person without judgment. But you've made up your mind to dislike him and I don't know why."

Brooks clamped his lips together. It didn't matter what he said now. Caroline was convinced Frank was a good guy, and Brooks was sure Frank was not. Brooks hadn't liked him the first time they'd met and now he positively loathed him.

She let go of his hand and they were both silent for a moment. "Do you have any more classes today?"

"No, no, but I forgot I have something to take care of." He stood up as Manning came back to the table. "I'll see you at Pegasus Pizza at six. And you're welcome to join us, Caroline."

"I have to get back." She looked at her coffee. "I'll just finish this."

"I'll keep you company." Manning sat down, glancing at Brooks. "Go do your thing. I'll catch up with you later."

"Drive safely." Brooks put his half-full cup of tepid coffee in the rubber bin for used dishes and headed for the door. His stomach was in a knot and he felt a dull throb in his right temple. He'd always loved Caroline's company. He preferred her over just about anybody else. But right now, sitting across from her was like having a knife stuck in his chest.

Pushing open the Daily Grind's heavy glass door, he headed back to his office. He sucked in a deep breath of the warm afternoon air and tried to relax the tension in his neck. *I know you want to protect me just like an older brother.* It felt as if someone were kicking him in the gut every time he let his mind replay her words.

He walked against the light, half-hearing the beep of a car creeping through the intersection. *You've made up your mind to dislike him and I don't know why.*

He knew why. Not that he could tell her. It was clear as day to him that he was firmly stuck in the "friend zone" with Caroline. That had always been the way he'd wanted it, but now everything had changed. His feelings had changed and hers had not.

He swallowed hard and swung open the door to Allen Hall, seeking the comfort of his academic cave. He could do nothing but try to put it out of his mind. He'd be her friend, always. As long as he didn't catch Frank anywhere near her, he would probably keep from doing anything stupid. He didn't want to ruin their friendship, and he certainly didn't want to doom it over some slimeball such as Frank. He could only pray she saw through the charming exterior before it was too late.

Seldom, very seldom, does complete truth belong to any human disclosure; seldom can it happen that something is not a little disguised or a little mistaken.

—EMMA

Chapter Thirteen

Another weekend, another party. That was the way it went in Thorny Hollow. Not that Caroline minded at all, as long as she wasn't the one serving punch. She enjoyed the chatter, the visiting, the guests mingling and gossiping. And it was all so much better that Brooks was coming home for the summer. Just a little while longer and she wouldn't have to suffer through the dull, boring weekdays without any real conversation. Her mother was up in her room all the time, and Caroline had nothing to do but work on freelance articles. A girl could do only so much writing before she needed a bit of human interaction. Of course, Caroline didn't want to spend the whole day chatting, either. Work came first. Not only was she determined to get her career back off the ground, but she vowed never to turn out like her mama. She wished for the thousandth time that her mama had put less of her energy into her marriage and more into some kind of career. Caroline loved her daddy and was thankful for her happy childhood home life, but now that he was gone, her mama had nothing.

Caroline surveyed her outfit in the mirror, frowning a bit over the length of the skirt. Or lack of length. It was a little short, but nothing too shocking. Frank should be there. He'd seemed . . . interested. She wasn't quite sure what she felt. Definite interest. Maybe more.

The doorbell rang and she could hear Angie letting in Brooks. One last smooth with the brush and she figured she was set. And now for the heels. Pulling them from the box, she stared at the three-inch stilettos. There was no way she could make it down the stairs. She'd have to put them on right before she met Brooks in the living room.

Minutes later, Caroline teetered into the room, willing herself upright. Brooks turned from the shelf, where he'd been examining her set of clothbound, first-edition George Eliots, a small book resting open in one palm.

His eyes followed her progress across the room and she felt the heavy weight of his gaze. She had taken extra time to shave her legs and rubbed them thoroughly with a deep moisturizer. Her early-summer tan was a perfect complement to her long legs, and with a skirt that barely reached above her knees, no one could miss them. Her face felt hot and she angrily brushed back her hair. "Let me just get my purse and we can go." She snagged it from the low table, making sure to bend at the knees so her skirt didn't ride up in the back.

Brooks cleared his throat. She turned to see if he was reshelving the book, but, no, he was in exactly the same position as before.

"Are you coming?" She frowned at him, noting the way his jacket draped his wide shoulders just so and the perfect tailoring in his cuffed pants. The man had style and she was just pretending. It was so obvious, it was humiliating.

"Finley, those heels are a bit high for a garden party, don't you think?"

"No, I don't. And it's an engagement party. Held in a garden. It's supposed to be fun and flirty and romantic." She smoothed her hair and pretended to be waiting, but inside all her previous resolution was melting away. "Well, maybe they're a little bit high. I'll be careful."

He raised an eyebrow, that book still open in his hand, and said nothing.

She tapped a foot, hands on hips, gaze fixed on the front door as if she could force him toward it by sheer stubbornness. The seconds ticked on, until she finally dropped her purse on the small table with a resounding clunk. She stalked toward him, stepping ever so carefully over the edge of the area rug so she didn't break an ankle, and stopped directly across from his handsome self.

"Fine! Do you want to know why I'm wearing these heels?" She hated the defensive tone in her voice but his quiet disapproval was galling.

"Sure." The word came out slowly and deeply, as if nothing she could say was going to convince him that she didn't look ridiculous.

"I saw Lauren standing with Frank at the Werlins'." His brows drew down at her words but she went on, "He's pretty tall. About your height, maybe a little taller. And she was wearing these high heels and looked him right in the eye." She crossed her arms over her chest, sure that she'd made her point. Now she was just a few inches shorter than he was, and it felt great to barely lift her eyes to meet his gaze.

"So?" His one-word responses were getting on her nerves,

along with that guarded expression that meant he was thinking a lot of things he wasn't permitting himself to say.

"So, I'm tired of being short. I'm tired of"—she kicked off the heels and walked forward, bare feet padding against the carpet, and practically pressed her face into his chest in an exaggerated example of her shortness—"tired of having to crane my neck to look men in the eye. Right now, I can barely see your expression. It's a total handicap."

In fact, all she could really see was his tie, knotted just so, the way he always did it. And the line of his jaw, freshly shaved. A pulse was jumping in his throat and his chest rose and fell as if he were trying to keep his temper. In fact, he looked just the way he did when they'd talked about Lauren that day up in her bedroom.

"You think I'm being petty, but Lauren Fairfax commands a certain respect, and maybe it's the fact she's not a foot shorter than every man in the room." Caroline stared up at him, daring him to disagree. She inhaled lightly, enjoying the familiar scent of his cologne. She'd never asked what it was called, but she could have picked it out of a hundred others. He wasn't even bothering to meet her eyes, but rather was staring out into the room. He'd moved his arms out to the sides as she'd walked into him, and she turned her head just in time to see the open book in his palm begin to fall.

It landed with a soft thud against the Oriental carpet and she ducked to retrieve it. "You'll break the binding like that." She pressed it closed and inspected it for any damage. "It would be nice, however silly you think it looks, to be a little taller for the evening."

He turned toward the bookshelf, his back to her, saying nothing. He held out one hand and she gave him the Eliot to shelve.

His voice was rough. "'Our words have wings, but fly not where we would.'"

Caroline stepped back into her heels. "I always thought she stole that line from Homer. He was all about the 'winged words' in the *Odyssey*, and then Eliot comes along with that line and everyone falls all over it."

Brooks seemed to be examining the shelf again. "I thought you liked George Eliot."

"I do. I think she was brilliant. But what does that line mean, anyway? Is it about influence? Writing? Distance?" She shrugged, wishing he would step away from the books and turn around.

"Maybe it means that sometimes what we say doesn't come across the way we mean it to." He finally turned, his lips turned up a bit at the corners. "I always liked 'nothing is so good as it seems beforehand.' I think that's the perfect Eliot quote for the moment we head off to a garden party."

"I never took you for the brooding type, but you're getting that way in your old age. You surprise me." She gave him a playful punch on the arm and grimaced at the crack of her knuckles against solid muscle.

He laughed out loud, but it sounded forced. "It happens, remember? You don't know everything about me. Let's go get this party over with. We're still keeping track of who is chatting up whom?"

"Well, of course. I can't wait to prove that men only look at beauty and women go for brains."

He sighed and held the door for her. "If only that were so."

The drive over seemed to take seconds, even though it was close to fifteen miles out. Sloping green hills passed them in a blur and

Brooks nodded every so often as Caroline talked. He loved to hear her talk, but he couldn't focus enough to join in on her discussion of the current trend of linking humorous commercials to more serious literary articles in order to boost page views. Something he would usually have jumped into, on one side or the other, was leaving him completely uninterested. Instead, he watched her, noted the way her hands moved like extra punctuation to her words.

She was so beautiful. So full of brightness and hope and all the best things in the world. She had no idea that a little skirt and high heels didn't make a difference. She could be wearing a potato sack, have her hair in a ponytail and be barefoot, and she'd attract every man in the room like a moth to flame. He felt a creeping sense of dread and wondered if Frank would make a move when he saw her. Frank seemed the type of man whose affections could easily be swayed by the length of a skirt.

They turned down the long drive to Mont Liewan, one of the best-kept secrets of the area. Mr. and Mrs. Anderson did a lot of entertaining and didn't even mind a few tourists' showing up to snap photos, but they didn't go out of their way to advertise their presence. A neoclassical-style antebellum mansion, it was planted at the top of a small hill, surrounded by ancient elms hung with Spanish moss. The perfectly trimmed yew hedges curved from the front walk around each wing of the house, as if inviting guests deeper into the property. He parked to the east, at the end of a line of vehicles. The midafternoon sun was strong and the humidity hit like a warm blanket as Brooks opened the car door. The sound of a live jazz band carried all the way to the drive.

Brooks helped Caroline out of the car, averting his eyes as she adjusted her skirt. She was frowning as she gripped his elbow, wobbling toward the front door. "I hope they don't have gravel all over the garden. Or grass. Don't they have flagstone paths? I can't remember."

"I haven't been here in a year or so, but I think James redid the path in limestone." James Anderson always had a project. He owned his own kiln and was a professionally trained painter, although he'd spent years working as a civil engineer, commuting to Oxford. Between him and his wife, Gail, a never-ending string of accomplishments stretched from half marathons to midlife doctoral studies to neighborhood fund-raisers for local kids. Brooks wasn't a fan of garden parties in general or engagement parties in particular, but he knew this would be the most enjoyable party of the season, if only because of the hosts. They were humble and friendly, seemingly happy to be married to each other for close to three decades. Brooks wondered if that was why their daughter was able to walk into marriage in her twenties.

Caroline smiled as they neared the house. "They remind me of my parents. I mean, if Mama had kept her job and Daddy had been an artist." She laughed, looking over at him. He was surprised to see they were almost eye to eye. Even after the conversation in her living room, it still took him a second to focus. She went on, "That sounds silly. They're completely different, of course. But something about them is the same."

He nodded. "I can see it. I think it's friendship."

She wobbled a little and paused to glance back at an offending pebble in the path. "Friendship?"

"They like to be together. Even when they're working on their own projects, they enjoy being together." Brooks saw it clearly because he'd grown up with just the opposite. His parents hated being in the same room together. They pretended the other didn't exist, unless they were fighting, and then Brooks wished they'd go back to pretending.

Caroline cocked her head, the afternoon sunlight making her blond hair seem even brighter. "I think you're right. My parents were friends, but I never thought of them that way. . . . Maybe that's why she's having such a hard time. It was like losing her best friend."

They reached the front door and stood there for a moment, looking over the decorations on the porch. Sheer ribbon with little, white polka dots wound around the small posts of the railing. Delicate sprays of pale pink rosebuds and magnolia blossoms hung in blown-glass vases suspended near the door.

He covered her hand with his, reading the expression on her face as clearly as he felt it in his own heart. It felt odd to look on such a joyful celebration as an impending marriage while living in the rubble of one that had ended.

"I always wonder why people never regret loving someone." She glanced at him, her face somber. "I mean, if you ask them after it's over whether they wish they'd never met the person, they always insist they're glad it all happened. They wouldn't exchange all those years of happiness no matter how miserable they are in the end."

"The happiness must outweigh the bad, I suppose."

"But"—she turned and looked at him, words tumbling over each other—"I don't understand it. If you know it's going to be that awful to lose them, why not just avoid it altogether? Of course, we're assuming that the marriage lasts and the best-case scenario is one of you dies."

Brooks snorted. "You're a true romantic."

"Wouldn't it be better to try and avoid it, to get some life experience, some other good memories to hold on to? I think my mama would be handling this all so much better if she'd kept her job and hadn't gotten married so young. She wouldn't have poured her entire heart into my daddy. She would have something left to live for now that he's gone, some kind of accomplishment."

Caroline seemed almost angry. Brooks wondered if she was hurt that *she* wasn't enough to bring her mother back from the edge of grief. He spoke cautiously, trying to explain what was taking shape in his mind, conscious that he was speaking to the person who had made him realize it in the first place. "I don't think a job would have kept her from loving him less. You either love, all the way, or you don't. Maybe when she fell in love, she had other plans. But you don't tell your heart to wait a bit, you have something else to do but hold that idea for a few years. You love, completely, and everything else is secondary. At least, that's what happens with the best kind of love."

He swallowed, wondering if his words were going further than was wise. He searched for a way to change the topic, but the only thing he could think of was her, Caroline. Everything seemed to come back to her. "Like friendship, really. You wouldn't want a friend who loved you half the time, who only cared once in a while, who cheered you on and taught you things you needed to know and remembered your birthday only half the time."

She stared at him, her green-blue eyes startlingly clear. "Or even three-fourths of the time." Her voice was soft. "You're saying it's all or nothing?" She seemed almost sad, as if she was coming to a decision that caused her pain. "I know I'm not ready to take this kind of step"—she waved her hand at the rosebuds and magnolias and ribbon—"but I still think if I work hard at my job, then . . . if something happened . . . my heart wouldn't break as much. That may be silly, but it's the only way I can see myself getting married."

He wanted to say it didn't work that way, but he was no expert. He stared at her hand on his arm. They had never before talked about marriage or heartbreak or true love. Was it because both their parents had become widowers? But that had happened over a year ago. Now it was different. In some mysterious way, they had been thrown together, emotions raw, over and over again. He didn't know if he was going to survive the summer with his heart intact.

The door swung open and he started, feeling almost guilty for standing on the porch for so long without knocking.

"Well, there you two are!" Mrs. Anderson waved them in. Her pale green dress was complemented by a cream-colored orchid pinned near her shoulder. "I was wondering where you'd got to. Come on through and join the party." She reached out to hug Caroline first, then Brooks, hardly pausing as she talked.

"I hear good music," Brooks said, struggling to rejoin the world of jazz bands and garden parties.

"You betcha. Franklin Keene put us in touch with them. Such a nice boy, I'm so happy he's been around more this summer. We've hardly gotten to see him since he moved away in grade school." Mrs. Anderson swept ahead of them, down the wide-open hallway toward the back of the home.

So Frank was here, just as Caroline had said he'd be. Brooks forced himself to keep walking. He wanted to grab Caroline's hand and turn around, head right back outside, put her in the car and drive away. He didn't want to see her laugh and make witty conversation with Frank. He didn't want to stand there with a smile and a glass of pink lemonade in his hand while Caroline and Frank flirted, eye to eye, thanks to those ridiculous heels.

A memory flashed through his mind, of how she'd kicked off her shoes and stalked toward him, just a little while ago. She'd been making a point about height when she pressed her nose into his chest, but all he'd felt was how his heart had jumped into his throat. No matter how he fought it, his feelings for her wouldn't stay firmly in the friend zone. Whenever he thought he had them under control, all she had to do was get close, and he remembered much too clearly. Add in Frank and his over-the-top flirting and Brooks was in no doubt that he was in serious romantic trouble. And the stakes were much higher than the usual broken heart. A friendship hung in the balance, and he would do anything in his power to keep from being the one who destroyed it.

The garden was packed with guests. They went to congratulate the happy couple and stopped by the punch table. Brooks handed Caroline a glass and she sighed. She could have counted her years in tumblers of pink lemonade and it would have stretched on beyond the average life span. Caroline peered through the crowd, searching for Frank. He was there, standing in the middle of the grass, surrounded by women. She felt herself smile just to see him. He should have had a sign over his head, a big neon arrow pointing out the funniest guy at the party.

"Caroline, I didn't know you were coming." Lexi crossed the path toward them, winding her way between small groups of partyers, her dark eyes shining with happiness. Her dress was a bright purple, with splashes of blue. She looked like a work of art, her outfit fitting for a painter.

"Sure, we've known the Andersons forever." Not quite forever, but longer than Caroline could remember. She wondered what Lexi was doing here but didn't know how to ask. Caroline was sure the Andersons didn't hang out near the Martinez gas station.

"I just met them a few weeks ago. Mr. Anderson teaches an art class at the senior center on Sunday afternoons. I volunteered to help clean brushes and wipe down the tables after the seniors left."

"That's a good project. Funny how he always finds time to be an artist, even though he's an engineer by day," Brooks said in an offhand way. Caroline knew that he was trying to say that Lexi would be able to paint in her off time so she didn't have to worry about majoring in accounting.

"I wonder which one he likes better," Caroline said.

"Maybe he likes them both and one pays the bills." Brooks didn't look at Caroline as he said this, but she knew he was talking to her, and not Lexi. Lexi had already made her choice, and Caroline didn't think the girl knew what she was setting herself up for by heading off to college and giving up her art.

"Wouldn't it be great if he didn't have to split his life into parts? Maybe he could just do what he loved and pay the bills at the same time. Like a history professor." Caroline couldn't help the irritation in her voice. She didn't want to argue about Lexi. Frank was charming a whole group of women with some story and she was standing here debating with Brooks.

"I . . . I think he's happy with both," Lexi joined in, looking a bit lost. Caroline didn't blame her. She was a sweet girl but she didn't seem to catch a lot of conversational nuances. Add in that Caroline knew Brooks well enough to hear what he was saying underneath his words, and Lexi was probably thinking the two were arguing over nothing.

Caroline turned her head just in time to see Lauren join them on the other side of Brooks. Caroline frowned, thinking how odd it was that Lauren didn't stand next to Lexi and greet them both. It was as if Lauren was cozying up to Brooks. Or maybe she was imagining things.

"Hi, everybody." Lauren made the simplest statements seem a little bit sultry. Her low-cut wrap dress clung to every curve and she flipped her dark hair back over one shoulder. "Brooks, you're looking quite handsome."

He smiled and thanked her, but Caroline swore he gazed a little too long at Lauren's getup. And he had complained about Caroline's shoes. The nerve.

Lexi held out her hand. "I'm Lexi. We met at the Werlins' party but you probably don't remember me." Her voice was a little breathless and her cheeks were pink. "I heard about the book you're doing on Thorny Hollow, and I wanted to say my daddy's gas station was the first general store in the area, back in 1910."

"Gas station?" Lauren repeated. "The one down on Sixth Street?"

"Right. We have pictures of the first owners, the Kirchels." Lexi paused, as if waiting for Lauren to offer to take a tour. "Um, it's not much but we're definitely part of the town history."

"Absolutely, you are." Lauren's smile was kind, even though her words cleared up any misconception Lexi might have had over being in the book. "But we're focusing on the historic homes. And the gas station probably doesn't fit into that group."

"Oh, but it does," Lexi said, her eyes wide. "See, the gas station attendants have always lived at the station. So, we have a little room near the back. They built an indoor bathroom on about forty years ago."

Lauren's lips turned down by the faintest of degrees, as if she were grimacing. "I'm still not sure that would fit, but I'll ask my boss and see what he says."

Lexi beamed. "That would be amazing to be in the book. I just love this town and I know it would mean so much to my daddy, too."

Caroline could see Frank waving to her over Lexi's shoulder and grinned. "I'll be right back," Caroline said to Brooks, excusing herself from the conversation. She took a few steps and realized it was a whole lot easier walking around holding on to

Brooks's elbow than strutting down the path by herself, but she pasted on a smile and tried not to trip.

"I've been waiting for you to come over here," Frank called out when she was still a few feet away. The music was louder here, the clarinet hitting several high notes that made her ears ring. The circle of women widened just enough for her to squeeze in, and she had the impression they didn't appreciate one more female in the group.

"You can't have been waiting that long, I just got here," she said, laughing. Caroline decided the problem of walking in the heels was definitely a fair trade for seeing eye to eye with Frank. He was handsome, no doubt about it, but she loved that she didn't feel like a little kid next to him.

"There's something different about you," he said, a finger on his chin. He looked her up and down. "Twirl."

"Excuse me?"

He moved his finger in a circle. "Twirl."

She hesitated, feeling the heat rising to her cheeks. Suddenly, her skirt seemed even shorter. Caroline took a step back, raised her arms and moved in a slow circle, feeling awkward. She laughed, covering her discomfort. As she made the full turn, she caught a glimpse of Brooks across the lawn. His face was serious, almost angry. She wondered what Lexi was saying that made him look so irritated. It couldn't be Lauren, she had her hand tucked into his elbow, right where Caroline had been moments before. They looked nice together, like a couple. Her chest tightened and she quickly refocused on Frank, refusing to be jealous of Lauren any more than she already was.

"Aha. It's this little pin you have in your hair," he said, reaching up and touching the sparkly barrette she'd clipped on to keep some of her curls out of her face.

Her face went hot. "I've worn it before."

"But did I notice it before?" His voice was low, husky. A dark-haired girl to his right let out a huff of air and rolled her eyes. Caroline would have laughed if she wasn't so caught up in Frank's flirting.

"I'm . . . not sure."

"Oops, looks like I set off an alarm." Frank was looking over her shoulder and Caroline turned to see Brooks making his way toward them. Lauren hung on his arm, still talking, but Brooks didn't seem to be listening.

"Alarm?" Caroline hated that she kept repeating Frank but didn't seem able to catch up.

"He must have you wired. If anyone triggers the electronic nexus, he gets a signal that it's time to intervene," Frank said, leaning close and whispering in her ear.

The idea of Brooks's setting her up with a security system made her giggle.

"And he's bringing that woman. I wonder if she'll have anything more to say than the usual spiel about her fantastic book project." Something in Frank's tone made the smile slip from Caroline's face. She suffered through a lot of boring conversation and she was no fan of Lauren Fairfield's, but Frank didn't even seem to try to tolerate her. "You know, I'm going to let you guys hang out without listening to us argue. I'll catch up with you later."

And then Frank was gone, slipping through the crowd. Caroline frowned after him. For someone who'd seemed so glad to see her, he hadn't spent a lot of time in her presence.

She turned and tried to smile as Brooks and Lauren arrived, joining their conversation with half an ear. In a few minutes, the newly engaged couple would probably make some sort of announcement. Then the caterers would bring out the food, probably family favorites of Mr. Anderson's. Then there would be more dancing. But for Caroline, the joy of the party had faded from a few hours before. She'd been excited to see Frank, to stand tall in her heels and flirt with him in the middle of a beautiful Southern garden. But he didn't seem to want to be with her. He would rather avoid Lauren than spend another minute with Caroline.

Brooks glanced over at her and raised an eyebrow. Caroline shrugged and took a sip of pink lemonade. She shouldn't care whether Frank was interested in her because she was going to focus on her career, not a relationship, but somewhere deep down, she couldn't help feeling a twinge of disappointment.

We think so very differently on this point, Mr. Knightley, that there can be no use in canvassing it. We shall only be making each other more angry.

—EMMA

CHAPTER FOURTEEN

A light knock sounded in the living room and Caroline bolted from the couch. It was a week to the day since the garden party, but it had seemed much longer. Her mother was retreating to her room more and more often, spending hours at a time locked away. Caroline felt as if she lived alone most of the time.

"You're a sight for sore eyes! I wondered if the thought of more garden parties had made you change your mind about moving back." Caroline swung the door open wider and grinned to see Brooks standing there, holding a pink cake box. Absalom wiggled beside him, wagging his tail furiously. She'd actually expected them yesterday, but Brooks must have been busy. He couldn't come running back home the minute classes were out.

"No, it was a fairly run-of-the-mill torture session. Except for watching you wander around in those heels, it was boring, boring, boring."

"Well, I'm glad I was entertaining. What do you have there?"

"My little celebration for being done with the term. I knew you'd be happy to see this." He held up the cake box, the pale blue forget-me-nots printed on the lid announcing this was no normal offering of baked goods.

"I would never refuse anything from Bravard's. Come on in." She waved him inside and tucked her knitting under one arm. She reached down to give Absalom a nice, long welcome. Brooks sidled into the living room and put the Bravard's box on the side table. He stuffed his hands in his pockets as if he were out for a stroll. Absalom licked every inch of skin he could reach, and when she was tired of dodging his frantic greeting, she stood up.

"Are those . . . knitting needles?" He cocked his head, dimples showing.

"Knitting is all the rage right now." She waved her project, bright pink loops dangling crazily. "I'm trying to get good enough to make some mittens for Christmas. A pair for everyone. Better choose your color before all the good ones are taken."

"Mmm-hmmm. I can't say I've ever minded the cold."

"Smarty-pants. Are you meeting someone?" She gave Brooks the once-over, loving every line of his well-dressed self. Nicely pressed tan suit, check. Freshly shaved, check. Smelling delicious, check and double check.

"You look so nice." She picked up the box and playfully flipped his tie on her way past. "And this is new."

"Ever-changing tie fashion is a thorn in my side," he said, smoothing it down.

"My daddy wore ties from the 1960s all the way until the week he died. You don't have to be a slave to fashion." She tried to keep her voice steady but it wavered just a bit. She had so many good memories but it was still hard to talk about the little quirks and habits that made her daddy dear to her. "Come on in the kitchen. And no need to be afraid of food poisoning, I was just making iced tea."

He hadn't answered her question, and Mrs. Gray's ugly comments flashed through her mind. For just a moment she wondered if he had a date but wasn't telling her. Brooks wasn't a man to keep secrets; it's not what a gentleman did. If he loved a woman, he'd be proud to share it with the world. He was an open book.

He leaned against the wall and smiled tightly. "This feels like undergraduate days all over again, when I packed the car and came home every summer."

"Your woman friend is all moved in?"

He snorted. "*Woman friend*. That just sounds awful. But, yes, we moved most of her things in yesterday. She didn't have much since she's a visiting professor from China."

Caroline imagined a graceful, long-haired beauty who could cook a five-course meal of Asian delicacies. She glanced at his face, noting the line of his mouth and the wrinkle between his brows. She knew just what he was feeling. Trapped. Obligated. Doomed to a summer in Thorny Hollow.

She started to ask about his plans, but stopped. He probably didn't have much on the schedule except watching over his dad. Something inside wished he could be happier about spending the summer with her, but could see how giving up his life in Spartainville for a countrified summer filled him with dread.

Opening a plastic container of dog biscuits, she fed a few to Absalom. If they were going to have a treat, he should, too. She flipped open the cake box and grinned at the sight of a mud pie. Leaning forward, she inhaled deeply. "You're my hero."

His lips tilted up just a bit. "Always at your service."

She retrieved two china plates and a silver pie server. "You have to help me eat this. If you leave me alone with all this chocolate, I might eat myself into a coma."

"Don't have to ask twice. I could smell it all the way here." He was looking more relaxed by the minute. Caroline glanced at him, wondering how to say what was on her mind.

She handed him a slice of the thick chocolate pie and he accepted it wordlessly. She took a bite, savoring the smooth chocolate. She wanted to roll her eyes and groan, but that would have been unseemly. She settled for a demure word that didn't come close to what she was thinking. "Nice."

He laughed, the sound bouncing off the kitchen walls. "Understatement of the year. I saw your face. I think you need to sit down before you pass out."

She plopped into one of the antique wood-and-cane chairs. "You know me so well." Absalom came to sit under her feet, watching her movements in the hope of a tasty crumb. She took another bite, enjoying every second of the experience. It occurred to her that she never brought Brooks gifts. He was always bringing her cakes and chili-slaw dogs and mud pies. She chewed slowly, thinking.

"What's wrong? You find a shell?"

She shook her head. Peanut shells happened, but not in this slice. "I'm just wondering why you're the generous one and I just sit around receiving your gifts like the queen of England."

His brows went up and he shrugged. "Don't they say not to look a gift horse in the mouth?"

She snorted. "That saying means you're not supposed to find out how much your gift costs or you'll be sorry, right? I mean that you're the giver and I'm . . ." She paused. "Like a kid, getting presents every time her old uncle visits."

"Old uncle? You want me to take the pie back? Because I can, you know." His words were light but he looked uncomfortable.

"No!" She put the plate on the counter and came toward him. "I just feel like you're the real adult and I'm just some sort of wannabe adult."

His eyes locked on hers, the lines of his mouth gone tight. He swallowed. "I don't think you're a wannabe adult."

"Well, that's what I feel like. It's hard when the rest of the world views success as a good job and I'm unemployed at home." She knew she was pouting, but it was hard to stop. "I had lunch with Lexi Martinez, that girl from the Werlins' party. And I realized that if I could do everything over, I might do it all differently."

"As in?"

"I went to college because that's what I was supposed to do. I got a good job because that's what I was supposed to do. Maybe I should have skipped college and just . . ." She waved her hands, lost for words, frustration spilling out. "Just traveled the world. Explored the country. Gotten drunk every New Year's Eve like the rest of the population instead of having half a glass of champagne because a full glass would have given me a headache the next day."

Brooks set his plate on the counter and held up both hands. "Wait, wait, I'm lost. You said you had lunch with Lexi Martinez and now you're having some sort of midlife crisis?"

"That's just it!" She couldn't help how her voice went up an octave and a half. "Midlife crises are for old people! I'm twenty-seven and I feel like I took the wrong path somewhere. I need to turn around before it's too late."

He put his hands on her shoulders. "Okay, take a deep breath and tell me again how this all started."

She laughed, a crazy sound that was closer to crying than laughing. Absalom lifted his head and let out a soft whine. "Lexi is an artist who is going to college to study *accounting*. I'm sick of women being pushed into jobs just because someone told them they should be cautious and logical. God doesn't want us to waste our talents. I don't want to see her make the same mistakes I made."

"But, Finley, it's a totally different scenario. Lexi needs some sort of trade that will pay the bills. Accounting will give her the breathing space to create her art, when she's ready. I didn't say anything at the party, but I donated the scholarship money that she won through the Thorny Hollow High School Honor Society. I think she's making the right choice."

Caroline stepped back, away from the warmth of his hands. "You—you set her up for a life of accounting?"

"I didn't know what she'd choose. But it's a scholarship for needy kids who will major in the applied sciences. Our town needs more careers that will support the economy here. You can't imagine what's happening, how kids are leaving school with useless degrees and twenty thousand in debt. They struggle to pay it off and end up worse than they started."

She crossed her arms over her chest. "I told her to skip college and focus on her art."

His mouth fell open. "You didn't."

"I did and I'm not ashamed of it. I think she's telling her father in the next few days that she's going to refuse that scholarship. She needs to believe in herself and her unique God-given gift."

Brooks stepped toward her, eyes dark with fury. "Refuse the scholarship? Are you crazy? Her father runs a *gas station*, Caroline! This is her one chance to go to school and have a life that's a little better than her parents had."

"Maybe it's her one chance to follow her dream! Did you think of that?"

"If you want to talk about what God wants, let's ask ourselves if God would want Lexi to throw away a chance to support herself and her family." Absalom shuffled over and stood between them, leaning first against Brooks and then against Caroline.

"But she won't be *happy*. I don't want her to wake up at my age and realize she's spent the majority of her life serving pink lemonade."

Brooks let out a bark of laughter. He looked as if he was doing everything he could to keep his temper. "No, Caroline, she won't be waking up and realizing that, because she's not you. She's not coddled and dressed up and introduced all over the county." He pointed to the pile of knotted yarn on the counter. "She won't be living at home, picking up projects and never finishing them. She'll be stocking cigarettes and pumping gas because someone told her to follow her *dream*."

"You're saying this as if you know the future. Well, I hate to break it to you, but just because you're a professor, it doesn't mean you have all the answers."

"Believe me, I know that." His voice was low, the anger resonating deep in every syllable. Absalom lifted his head, worried eyes looking from one to the other.

"All that time I spent on Etsy searching for Regency costumes taught me something. We don't live in a world where artists struggle just to eat. There are markets for everything now. I saw someone selling bottle-cap necklaces for fifty dollars!"

"And some junk art for sale on the Internet prompted you to tell a young girl to skip college."

"See, right there! You say 'junk art' because it's not something you would make or buy. But other people do and will. She could put up her art and sell it, right now, without ever leaving her house."

"What a ridiculous plan." His anger radiated outward like heat waves. "As if college is all about the degree. It's about learning to live independently, to get along with other people, to see life beyond your own little town. You convince her to turn down this scholarship to sell her drawings on eBay and she may just never leave. She may be stuck in Thorny Hollow forever."

Caroline felt the words reverberate in her head. *Forever.* He sounded like the ultimate failure would be to live here. Like her. Absalom nudged her hand, giving a few tentative licks, as if to say he still loved her, no matter what. "The world has changed, Brooks. We don't have to spend four years learning something we don't enjoy, just to survive. And it's not all about eBay anymore. Artists have options."

"And who's going to help her set all this up? You? As far as I know, you're not particularly skilled at selling on the Internet."

Her face went hot. She had no idea how a person went about starting an online business. But how hard could it be? "Of course I'll be helping her, but Frank might have work for her, too."

Brooks went quiet, eyes narrowing. "Frank said he'd give Lexi Martinez a job?"

"We talked about it." It was not too much of an exaggeration. She'd started to talk to him about it and they would have figured out something concrete if Lauren hadn't shown up.

"I guess you and Frank can take responsibility for this train wreck of a plan, then." Brooks looked as if he was struggling to find words, but then just shrugged. "I have to go. Absalom, come."

The next moment they were gone and Caroline was staring at the empty doorway in the bright yellow kitchen.

"Well!" She grabbed her pie and thumped back in her chair. "If that doesn't beat all." Taking a bite, she chewed furiously, willing her heart rate to slow. She was so angry she couldn't even taste the dark chocolate.

Setting the plate on the counter, she paced the kitchen. It would work. It had to work. She would show Brooks that he wasn't always right about everything.

Footsteps came down the hallway and she knew it was him before he appeared in the doorway.

"I'm so glad you came back!" She felt utter relief slide through her. He was a man of faith and honor, and she couldn't imagine life without Brooks's friendship. His quiet presence was the pillar, the anchor, the compass, for her existence. "It's such a silly thing to argue about."

His face was tight with fury. "No, Caroline, it's not. I just came back to say that even if you and Frank take responsibility for this fiasco, it can never make up for what you've taken from Lexi. If she chooses to give up her education and it doesn't work out, no amount of cake baking or mitten knitting will fix it. She's not some project for you to start and then discard when it doesn't work out quite the way you want. She's a human being."

She stood there, speechless, throat squeezed closed. Then he was gone again, the kitchen echoing with his words.

Pleasure in seeing dancing!—not I, indeed—I never look at it—I do not know who does. Fine dancing, I believe, like virtue, must be its own reward. Those who are standing by are usually thinking of something very different.

—MR. KNIGHTLEY

CHAPTER FIFTEEN

"I'm not sure why I need to be involved in this part of the planning." Brooks slouched in his seat, legs outstretched and ankles crossed. Absalom sniffed the old barn in ever widening circles. Dust motes swirled in a shaft of sunlight and Brooks tried not to inhale too deeply. He looked up at the rafters and watched the swallows and pigeons sidestepping their way across the thin beams. The place was filled with ancient smells of horse and straw and stale beer from some other parties. It was hard to imagine how this place would be transformed into a space for a Jane Austen–themed party.

"Because you're stuck in that room too much of the time. It's not healthy." Blanche wiped a sheen of sweat from her forehead.

The cornrows were gone but she was still a bit tan. Her sunflower-yellow shirt clashed mightily with a bright red pair of capri pants, a black fanny pack the only concession to her age. "I told Manning I'd handle hiring the band, and I need your help."

"I've got a deadline." He had been working on an article for *Newsweek*. If he was truly honest with himself, he'd been doing more brooding than writing. When his grandmother told him to get down to the old Wrigley barn off the highway, he didn't have any choice about the matter.

"You'll make it. You always do. My friends will be here any moment so let's go check out the stage." She trotted across the wide plank floor to the front of the barn. Brooks followed, stepping over clumps of what he hoped was dried mud. A small stage had been built sometime in the last few decades, and aside from the dust, it seemed sturdy enough.

"Can't you just see it?" Blanche clasped her hands together and looked out into the middle of the space. "Couples in their finest party clothes, courting the way couples have courted for hundreds of years."

"How? With exposed cleavage and blatant mentions of wealth?"

She turned and glared. "No. *Dancing*. And not that writhing and grinding you young kids do now."

Brooks snorted. He wasn't young and he certainly wasn't writhing and grinding. To his grandmother, anybody under fifty was in the prime of life.

"You see, when the dance begins and the couples face off, the scene for romance is set." She swept her arm across the barn. "Men on one side, women on the other. It's like waving a red flag at a bull. Excitement, anticipation, danger!"

Danger of having one's toes smashed, maybe. Brooks squinted, trying to envision the scene.

"The music leads and the bodies follow. You're giving up control, meeting your partner again and again, weaving through the obstacles just to find them. And at the end, the sweetest moment, the union of hearts." She looked dreamily across the space.

He coughed. "Until you get partnered with Frenchy D'Auberg and he pinches your bottom. Not so romantic then."

She cocked an eyebrow. "For you or me? I wouldn't mind a little pinching. I'm a lonely old lady. When your grandfather was alive, we had such a thriving—"

"Oh, no." Brooks pretended to plug his ears. "Remember I'm one of those innocent young people."

"Ha! I said *young*, not *innocent*." She paused. "How come you never bring anyone home to meet me?"

"Never found anybody I really liked, Grandma." He stuffed his hands in his pockets. Truthfully, the girl he really liked already lived here, and bringing her home wasn't an option.

"I just want you to know that whatever kind of lifestyle you live, I'll still love you."

He rolled his eyes. "So, because I'm not living with a woman, I'm gay?"

"Well, there must be some reason. A handsome boy like you must have loads of girls chasing him."

"Right. Loads."

"What about that nice—"

"Before we go down the whole list of candidates, let me just say that being a nerdy professor and the heir to Badewood isn't as attractive as you think."

"Why ever not?"

"It's hard to explain, but sometimes I think it would be better to be poor and homeless. Then I'd know if a woman loved me for who I am, and not for my house."

She paused, as if choosing her words wisely. Her bright orange lipstick feathered into the wrinkles when she pursed her lips. "If that's your fear, then you'd better choose someone who has a home as nice as ours."

He laughed, a sharp sound that echoed in the enormous cavern of the barn. "There's nothing like Badewood around here. The only people who aren't awed by the old place are the ones who've practically grown up in it with me, like—"

She waited for the rest of his sentence. "Yes? Like?"

Like Caroline, obviously. Every thought led right back to her, every time, like some kind of cursed boomerang. "Let's move on to some other topic. Finding Brooks a wife seems to be at the top of everyone's list lately. I'm almost glad we're having this crazy party. Maybe it will take some of the heat off me."

"If you think God wants you to stay single, that's perfectly fine with me."

Brooks sighed. "There's a lot of talk about what God wants, isn't there? Always speculation, never facts."

She stopped on her way across the stage. "What does that mean? We're supposed to ferret out God's will for our lives."

"Okay, true, but I also hear a lot of speculation on what God wants everyone else to do."

"Is this a sensitive topic? You look ready to have a duck fit."

He shrugged. Kicking the toe of his old running shoe into the dust of the stage, he felt irritable, exhausted, twitchy.

"Your grandma has had quite a few more experiences than you have." She smiled at him. "Just letting you know that, in case you'd ever like to bounce anything off my many years of living."

"There's nothing you can do about it."

"Maybe. But sometimes it helps to share the burden." She walked to him, her white hair frizzed around her head, eyes bright.

She barely reached his chest but she never seemed small. Larger-than-life, louder than doubts.

He thought of Manning and Debbie Mae. They had suffered for a whole year without leaning on anyone else. But sharing his unrequited love wasn't something he was really aching to do.

A dove took flight from one of the rafters and they both turned to watch it circle the barn. It flew overhead and dropped its load with a splat, right on his shoulder. He grimaced.

"Now I'm afraid you're dyin' of a terrible disease. Bird poop should register more emotion than that." His grandma was searching through her small fanny pack for some tissues.

It should, but it didn't because it was just one more irritation in a week filled with irritations. He hated being at war with Caroline. Hated it more than anything he'd ever hated before. The dull ache never lessened.

His grandma wiped off the mess as best she could, saying something about how a summer at home would make him happier. He wasn't listening. He felt so tired, so weary of holding on with an iron grip to something he knew was slipping away.

"You can't make someone love you," he said.

Her hand stilled for a moment, the dirty tissue between her fingers. "True."

"Even if you love them so much you'd do anything, anything, for them." The truth of his words sank in. Speaking about it wasn't helping. It felt worse, like probing an open wound.

"Even if," she said, nodding.

"Sometimes they pick another person to love when you've been right in front of them the whole time."

"It does happen." Her voice was soft.

"And then there's nothing left but to keep going as you were, pretending you never felt anything more than . . ."

"Friendship?" Her eyes met his and there was the faintest glimmer of tears.

"But I don't think I can have even that, anymore." His throat constricted at the thought. They hadn't spoken since the argument over Lexi's scholarship.

"Why not?"

"I wish I was a better man, but seeing her with someone else makes me crazy. Especially since the guy is a jerk."

"Maybe it will run its course and you'll have your chance."

He laughed, the bitterness in his voice loud to his own ears. "Grandma, don't you see? If she didn't choose me the first time around, she won't choose me the second time."

A sudden breeze blew open the barn door, clouds of dust gusting into the air. She patted his arm. "Sometimes a girl's got to kiss a few frogs before she finds her prince."

The thought of Caroline kissing Frank dragged a groan out of him. "Thanks, Grandma. Just what I needed."

"Like you've never kissed anybody?"

"Well, of course I have, but—"

"Then you don't have any right to begrudge her a few kisses on her way to finding out you're the best man for her." Blanche flashed a big smile, as if everything were all fixed.

He nodded, more to end the conversation than anything else. He didn't know if he could stand watching Caroline date someone like Frank. He didn't know if he could watch her date anyone. The usual hugging and kissing and public displays of affection were annoying, but when you were in love with one of the participants, it was torture.

He was a tough guy. He'd lived through the tenure process, after all. Gossip, backbiting and close-quarters verbal sniping didn't make him blink. He'd handled that slow burn of dislike for

Frank. But the idea of Caroline being touched by Frank made him skip from calm logic to blowing an emotional fuse.

He had to get a grip on his emotions. The argument over Lexi was probably the biggest disagreement they'd ever had, and he had a terrible suspicion that his jealousy had played the biggest part in it.

Brooks cocked his head at the sound of a truck motor. "Must be the band."

He helped his grandmother down from the stage and she went to the door, waving excitedly. Three African-American men and an elderly woman exited the 1980s extended-cab truck. The pale blue paint had oxidized around the hood and one headlight was cracked. Absalom took an immediate interest in the tires, sniffing his way along in a full circuit.

"So this is where the party will be, huh? We can work with this."

"Brooks, this is Gideon West, our fiddler," Grandma said. "John Asbury plays the banjo."

The first man tipped an old straw hat and gave a long, slow smile. The second nodded, holding up his instrument.

"Rufus Warren here plays the concertina and Jennie Purdy is our caller."

Rufus held out a hand to Brooks and gripped hard. Brooks wondered if concertina players had bigger finger muscles than regular folks.

Jennie whispered something so softly he leaned down to hear. Her shoulders were stooped and one thick-soled shoe was higher than the other to make up for the unequal lengths of her legs. "I'm glad we're getting some new blood in here. All these old men can't dance the jigs no more."

Brooks blinked. "A jig? I'm not a dancer, ma'am. I'm just here to help out."

"It's not hard. Six/eight time. You can count to six, can't you?"

"Even in my sleep, I reckon."

"Good. Nobody comes to the dance and sits in the corner. It's real bad manners." Her brows lowered until they almost blocked her sight.

Brooks sensed a whole lot of dancing in his near future. "I'm not sure how everyone can come in without knowing any of the dances and have it all work out. Don't we all have to practice?"

"No, sir. We start with a melody, plain and simple. Show 'em, Gideon."

The older man smiled that slow smile again, tucked the fiddle under his chin and played a clear, lilting tune. While he was playing, Jennie spoke over him. "He keeps a-going on it. Then we gots to have some rhythm." She pointed to Rufus, who unclasped what looked like a miniature accordion and joined in, lending a powerful rhythm to the same tune.

John waited a few bars, then jumped in, the frantic strumming of the banjo actually pulling the instruments together. Jennie shuffled her feet a bit, weaving to the beat. "This one is 'Trippin' up the Stairs.' It's my favorite." She held out her hand and Brooks took it, not sure what she meant for him to do.

"We be the top set and be walking through the hall." She moved gracefully forward, singing phrases such as "circle left" and "hey for four." Her feet moved faster than he could catch and he felt clumsy and awkward.

"You have a sweetheart?" she asked as the band played on.

"I—I don't . . . I'm not sure . . . ," he stammered, trying not to step on her toes. Injuring the elderly dance caller was not on his list of things to do.

"I's understandin' that as a yes." She smiled at him. "You let me know when she's your partner. I'll call you some gypsies and a few court'sy turns."

"'Gypsies'?"

She held out her thin arms, nodding for him to copy her. He held out his arms and they circled each other. "Look me in the eye. I know I'm a short one, but it's all in the eyes."

He tried his best to stare into her eyes, willing himself not to grin. If Manning could see him now, he'd fall over laughing.

"And the turn." She took his left in hers, then motioned for him to put an arm around her waist, gripping her right hand. "Now we turn real slow."

"Slow is good." The music was fast, but the moves weren't as frantic as the notes. He had to be more than a foot taller than Jennie and looked over her head to see his grandma smiling hugely.

Jennie waved her hand and the players finished the last bar. "And we bow to each other."

"Jennie, I'm so glad you all can help us out." Blanche rushed forward, hands outstretched. "These young folk don't know how to woo a woman. This will be the loveliest dance we've had in years."

The two women held hands for a moment, nodding at each other. Blanche was a plotter and usually finagled her own way, no matter what the obstacles were. The usual constraints of time, place and manner didn't apply to her. Now there seemed to be two of her. Brooks wondered if the universe could withstand two little old ladies bound and determined to wreak romantic havoc on Thorny Hollow.

"I hear you, Miss Blanche. My granddaughter Stephanie never takes those silly plugs out of her ears long enough to hear the real music we got. These reels come straight down from my great-great-grandpappy, but she more interested in some kid with diamonds stuck in his teeth." Jennie shook her head. "The music don't have a bit of tune, either. Just noise."

"You've got to bring her. Tell her to wear something long, like she's from a hundred years ago."

Jennie shrugged. "I'll do my best. Most of the time she wears shorts that don't hardly cover her hind end. Lord have mercy, I despair over these children."

Brooks couldn't imagine this modern teenager putting on a Regency costume and coming to dance with a bunch of Thorny Hollow professionals. But stranger things had happened. This moment in time, for instance.

"Well, I better get Brooks home so he can finish his project. We'll spit-polish this old place and have it all decorated. I can't thank you enough for giving us your time."

"It's our pleasure, ma'am." Gideon looked around the old barn. "We're aiming to revive our music and bring the young people back to the traditions of this place."

Brooks followed them out, feeling a lifting in his chest for the first time in over a week. The combination of tradition, music and folks with long memories made him haul in a deep breath. There were still treasures in the world and moments to savor. An image of Caroline's sweet smile flashed through his mind and he struggled to push it away. He would survive the summer if he concentrated on one thing at a time, and right now, the contra dance was that one thing.

The other problems in his life would just have to take a ticket and stand in line. One disaster at a time was his new theory.

With all dear Emma's little faults, she is an excellent creature . . . where Emma errs once, she is in the right a hundred times.

—MRS. WESTON

Chapter Sixteen

"I think we need to upload the pictures to a zip file." Caroline stood over Lexi's shoulder and pointed to an area on the screen. What had been a mildly uncomfortable work position at the laptop on her old desk was now causing backaches. The space was never meant for two people cramped together, staring at a glowing screen.

"I didn't understand a word you just said." Lexi was laughing but her words had a serious undertone.

Caroline sighed. She wondered how Brooks and Blanche were getting along with scoping out the dance site in that old barn. She'd said she was too busy to go, promising to help with the decorating tomorrow, but now she'd wished she'd gone with them, even though Brooks had made it perfectly clear he thought she was ruining Lexi's life. Walking around in the dust and heat with an angry Brooks might have been preferable to what she was doing now. She and Lexi had been at it for hours. First they had to find the websites and sign up to be a vendor. Lexi didn't have a credit card or bank account, so Caroline had put in one of hers. The forms had been irritatingly long, but they'd finally finished the sign-ups. Then they had taken pictures of all Lexi's art for two hours. Finally, the walk-through directions suggested they put the pictures up in a bundle, but Caroline didn't even know if her Internet connection could handle that kind of file transfer. She wasn't low-tech, but getting the pictures onto the site was proving more than Caroline could handle on an empty stomach.

"Let's break for lunch. I'm sure it will make more sense after we have some food in us."

"Excellent." Lexi stretched and yawned. "And when this takes off, my dad will have to see that I'm right."

"How did it go when you told him?"

Lexi stood up and followed Caroline to the hallway. "I haven't told him yet."

She stopped. "Not yet?"

Lexi looked uncomfortable. "Well, I thought I might wait a short while. Since it's just him and me, I don't want to be fighting with him until I have to. I have all summer. And classes don't start until September."

Caroline nodded. "I suppose you're right, but don't put it off too long." She led Lexi down the long hallway to the front stairs.

As they got closer to the kitchen, Caroline could smell fresh-baked corn bread. "Bless Angie's heart. I thought I was going to have to make myself a sandwich." She smiled at Lexi, but the girl didn't respond. Of course, she was used to grabbing lunch and making do.

"I'm spoiled and I know it," Caroline said. "I like to walk into the kitchen and be served a hot meal, three times a day. I don't know if anybody has it better than I do."

"About half the population, probably." Lexi grinned. "My dad likes his food hot and on the table at six every evening. I sort of wish I'd been born a man so someone would serve me dinner for the rest of my life."

Caroline laughed, realizing Lexi was right. "My mother doesn't understand why I don't want to get married, but I have everything I need and no one wants me to cook for them."

Lexi paused on the landing of the stairs and shook her head. Her dark eyes were wide with surprise. "You're not looking to get married?"

"Not really." Caroline shrugged. "Like I said, I just don't see the benefits right now. I haven't even gotten my career off the ground." Or gotten it back off the ground, since she'd abandoned the corporate ladder midstep.

"That's just so weird to hear a girl say that. I mean, everybody wants to get married."

"Well, not me, not right now." Caroline tried to sound cheery, but Lexi was reminding her of how very different they were. Sure, some girls had gone through college on the husband hunt, but most of Caroline's friends were focused on a career path. It just wasn't about getting a man anymore. There were better ways to happiness. Her mother had a degree in mathematics, and Caroline remembered, clearly, the few times her mother had wistfully wondered what it would have been like to be a career woman. Caroline shook off the deep sadness and tried to focus on the next step, which was lunch. One thing at a time. They'd have a fresh start right after they got something to eat.

Lexi followed her down the stairs to the kitchen. A pot of homemade chicken soup and dumplings sat on the stove. A pan of corn bread was cooling on a pad on the granite counter. Lexi plopped into a chair and inhaled the tantalizing kitchen scents. "Is it like this all the time? I could so get used to this."

"Not all the time." Caroline smiled a little. If only Lexi had seen the Frankencake, she wouldn't be so jealous of the sunny-yellow kitchen with the industrial-grade appliances. An image of the cake was followed immediately by a vision of Brooks. It came so quickly she didn't have time to push it back. His sandy-blond hair a little too long, brushed back from his forehead. Those deep dimples that appeared when he was trying not to smile. The way in the sunlight the stubble on his jaw looked like sand. The way he had to stoop down to hug her.

"Are you okay?" Lexi's voice cut into Caroline's thoughts.

"Sure." She blindly reached for the buffet where the china was kept. Blinking furiously, she swallowed back the ache in her throat. It was silly to fight over Lexi's scholarship. She made her own decisions, no matter how much they wanted to influence her. In the end, she was a grown woman making her own choices.

"I think my whole house could fit in this kitchen."

Caroline turned, hand still on the cabinet knob. "Come on, maybe just your bedroom."

Lexi shook her head. "No, we live in a studio at the back of the gas station. There's a screen divider between my bed and where my dad sleeps. I decorated the back so it has all my art projects where I can see them, but it's . . . probably just about the size of your kitchen."

Caroline turned back to the cabinet, feeling dread build inside. The kitchen was maybe fifteen feet by fifteen feet. It was big, sure. But the size of someone's house? The idea shook her to the core. Brooks's words came back to her louder than ever. *No, Caroline, she won't be waking up and realizing that, because she's not you.*

She pushed away the memory and reached into the cabinet for the china and stopped short. In the antique hutch were stacks of white china plates with a light green ivy pattern. She drew one out, barely believing her eyes.

"Oh, those are real pretty." Lexi pointed to the plate in Caroline's hand. "I saw those on special down at the Walmart Supercenter. They only came in a box of forty pieces so it was just too expensive for me and my dad."

"At the Walmart?" Caroline couldn't help repeating the words. Her voice had gone all whispery. She turned the plate over to see a Corelle marking on the back. She felt a pulse pounding in her head and she opened the next cabinet door. And the next. And the next. All the Ashley family china was gone, replaced by a Supercenter special. Her stomach clenched and she took a deep breath, trying to stay calm.

"And the bowls and salad plates, too!" Lexi came to lean over her shoulder. "You could throw a party with all of this."

Caroline nodded dumbly. A terrible idea had occurred to her and she could barely bring herself to open the slim drawers at the front of the buffet. Her fingers trembled as she gripped the brass handles and pulled. The drawers that held the silver were full but not of the familiar pieces she'd held at every meal. Stainless steel gleamed brightly back at her, and she shut the drawer with a smothered cry.

"Did you slam your finger? I've done that, it hurts like a son of a gun."

"I'm okay." Caroline turned and tried to smile. "Let me get you some chicken soup and dumplings. I need to go ask my mother something, if that's okay?"

"Sure, not a problem!" Lexi settled at the table.

Caroline filled the brand-new bowls with shaking hands,

grabbed a spoon without looking too closely at the impostor silverware, and dashed upstairs.

"Mama!" She knocked on the bedroom door and waited for a reply. She thought she could hear her mother talking, but the sound stopped and footsteps approached the door.

It swung open and her mother stood there, as if she'd been asleep, blinking at Caroline. Her blond hair was flat on one side and her eyes were puffy. The room behind her was a hurricane-style mess of clothes strewn across the floor. Drawers hung open, throw pillows were piled on the floor and a chair was covered in what looked like half her closet. She smelled faintly of whiskey. "What's wrong, honey?"

"Mama, the china is gone! And the silver!" Caroline's heart was pounding in her chest.

To her surprise, her mother just nodded. "Marshall said those plates were too old for that beautiful kitchen. He brought me that set with the ivy. It was real expensive but I think it's important to upgrade once in a while."

"Too old? They were antique Stubbs pearlware from 1850. Of course they were old! And the silver? What happened to the silver?"

"I bent one of those spoons one day, just trying to get some peanut butter. Really, they are just not made well. Marshall brought the new set and it's practically indestructible." Caroline's mother waved a finger as if she needed spoons to withstand a stress test before use.

"Daddy loved that silver." Caroline rubbed her face and tried to swallow back the tears. He used to tell her how the Cincinnati company had had to make the twisted stems just so or the balance would be off, and no one wanted an unbalanced spoon. He usually let out a chuckle at that part because the idea of balanced silverware wasn't something most people spent a lot of time on.

Her mother's face went dark. "He loved it but I never understood why. It's my family's silver. Why did he love it when it wasn't even his? And those old trunks and buckets and pots. They look horrible, all stained and catawampus."

Caroline sucked in a breath. "You mean the firkin bails, the ones that look like an old wooden bucket?"

"Right. Most of them had cracks and nicks and dents. Marshall took them off my hands and brought some really pretty stacking totes. They're see-through and fit right under the bed."

Caroline's mind went to the ancient camel-top trunks in the attic, the hand-hooked rug in the entryway, the pots that had hung over a fire before the kitchen had been wired for electricity. Most were tucked away, out of sight. She hadn't even realized they might have disappeared. Until now.

"I never knew you hated all of the antiques, Mama." Caroline sagged against the doorframe.

"Oh, I didn't care that much, but when Marshall reminded me that our house has a reputation to uphold, I had to agree. I can't have junk like that hanging all over."

Caroline shook her head, not even knowing where to start. Her home had been raided of all the things that connected it to her ancestors, and in their place were cheap, disposable reproductions. All in the name of upholding the family reputation. She took a long look at her mother for the first time in months.

Her eyes were bloodshot and her nose was red. This wasn't due to crying. This was a woman who had been drinking hard liquor. And it wasn't even noon. Caroline's heart sank to her shoes as she realized her mother had a problem with more than grief. Caroline's father's death had been sudden and terrible, but her mother had never faced it. She was drowning her grief in whiskey and hiding in her bedroom.

Caroline had never felt so alone in all her life. Her eyes filled with tears without her permission. All she wanted to do was to call Brooks and tell him the whole story. But she couldn't do that. They weren't speaking anymore.

And that hurt more than losing any of the rare family antiques that Marshall had carried off.

That is the case with us all, papa. One half of the world cannot understand the pleasures of the other.

—EMMA

Chapter Seventeen

Brooks brushed off a bit of lint from his pants and knocked on Caroline's front door. Spending the morning helping Manning cleaning out an old barn was bad enough, but having that pigeon poop on him sealed the deal. His day couldn't get any worse, so he might as well go see the person who probably wasn't speaking to him right now. He'd run home to change, including his shoes, and hoped he didn't smell like a barn. Brooks almost stepped back as Caroline swung open her front door and glared. Her expression was one he didn't usually see. Maybe one he hadn't ever seen before. It was the face of a woman who was ready to go toe-to-toe with someone she absolutely despised.

"Hey." So, it wasn't the smoothest beginning, but she'd thrown him off his stride.

Her face relaxed into a light frown. "Hey."

He shuffled his feet, wishing she'd invite him inside. Was their friendship so broken that they couldn't have a conversation past the threshold?

"I thought you were Marshall. I'm ready to drop-kick him into Louisiana."

A flood of relief went through him. So the fighting stance wasn't meant for him at all. "He still hanging around here?"

She waved him on into the house and shut the heavy door behind him. "Come in the kitchen. I'll show you."

Minutes later he gazed into the antique buffet, mouth open. "All the silver? And the china?"

"Every last bit. He didn't even really pay her. A few hundred dollars and . . . this stuff." Her voice was thick.

"Oh, Finley." He reached out instinctively and pulled her close. He'd come over to make peace with her, but that could wait. Under his hands she felt fragile. She dragged in a shaky breath.

"You know what I hate the most?" Her voice was muffled by the front of his shirt.

"What?"

"I look at those dishes and I see my daddy. I see birthdays and Christmases and that time I got a perfect score on my physics test and he made me waffles for dinner." She clutched Brooks tighter. "I see him carving the turkey at Thanksgiving and trying that awful casserole I made in high school with the pickles and raisins."

He choked back a laugh. "Pickles and raisins?"

She lifted her head, face streaked with tears. "Tammy Wiggins said it was the best thing she ever made. She thought it was pretty funny that I fell for the joke." A small smile appeared. "Daddy got about three bites into it and I think he just couldn't force down any more. But he never said anything."

Brooks put a hand to her cheek and wiped a tear away with his thumb. He was going to say something comforting and sensible. His gaze dropped to her lips, swollen with crying. He was suddenly, painfully aware of how tightly she was wrapped in his arms, how close they were from head to toe.

He took a step back, away from her, away from what he would have given anything to touch. But he didn't have any right to her, not that way.

Clearing his throat, he said, "Is anything else missing?"

She slumped into one of the kitchen chairs. "I haven't found it all yet." She reeled off a list of items that ranged from Civil War era to fifties kitsch.

"Looks like he's into American primitives, although that vintage Pyrex serving set could have been worth something."

"It's so depressing." She looked completely defeated.

He wanted with everything that was in him to hold her close and make it all better. But neither of those were options. One wasn't prudent and the other wasn't possible.

As if realizing he was there in the middle of the week, in the late afternoon, when they were not speaking to each other, she looked up. "Did you come here for something?" She blushed. "That didn't come out right. I mean, did you come here for something other than listening to my tale of woe?"

He smiled. "I know what you meant. And, yes, I'm here on a mission. I was right in the middle of working on a press release for the Civil War Trust and my phone kept going off. I wasn't going to answer it because Parker's Cross Roads is going to be made into a parking lot if they can't outbid a developer by next week, but . . ." He had thought it might be Caroline. "Anyway, Debbie Mae wants us to try on our costumes before the big dance."

Caroline's eyes widened. "Right now?"

"I'm not sure. She's been trying to call you but you weren't answering." He supposed she'd been taking stock of how much of the house had been raided. The idea gave him a fresh wave of fury mixed with a desire to find Marshall and wring his neck.

"Let me call her." She looked around for her phone, patting her pockets.

"Here." He dialed and held out his cell.

When she hung up, she said, "Well, I guess we're all meeting at Badewood. I'll go change."

"Do you need to tell your mother?" She'd seemed to be keeping Caroline on such a short leash, he couldn't imagine that she could leave without permission, even to Badewood.

Her eyes were shadowed and her mouth went tight. "She's . . . resting."

Something in her expression spoke of a whole other story, but she obviously didn't want to tell it. He felt as if the distance was growing between them every day, and he didn't know if it was his fault or hers.

Caroline stood up. "Are you ready, Mr. Knightley?" Her tone was unnaturally bright.

"Huh. Why couldn't I have a really good name like Jubal Early? Or Zebulon Baird Vance? Mr. Knightley sounds so . . ." He shrugged.

"Noble? Refined?"

"Sissified. And why don't we use his first name? Does anyone even know it?"

"We can ask Debbie Mae. She's the one who's in love with all things Austen. Frank is coming as Willoughby, so you won't be the only one in a morning coat. Plus, there's an Austen group in Oxford that has a yearly dinner with everyone in costume. They've promised to come, and there are at least fifty members. There will be lots of Darcys and Elizabeth Bennets. You could always be Sylvanus Cadwallader going as Mr. Knightley. A reporter in disguise, looking for a story."

"Have you been studying up on your Civil War? Cadwallader was an interesting guy. I could do that."

She poked him in the side as she walked past. "Just because I'm not completely obsessed with the war doesn't mean I don't know anything." Her words betrayed nothing, but he could feel the tension in her. The easy way they had with each other was gone.

He opened his mouth to give a retort, but something else occurred to him. "Finley, I'm glad we're talking. I wanted to . . ." He cleared his throat, not sure how to start.

"Wait. Is this about our little disagreement?" She stacked a few glasses in the old copper sink, not meeting his eyes. He could tell by the set of her shoulders that she didn't want to discuss it.

"Little?" He hoped that was the biggest argument they ever had, and the only one.

"I don't think we should talk about this. It'll only make us mad. Can we just call it a difference of opinion and leave it at that? We're not going to convince each other." She walked toward him, laying a hand on his arm. Her face was deadly serious, her lips a thin line. "I can't stand being at war with you."

His gaze dropped to her hand and he wondered if now was the time to speak. He wasn't prepared, hadn't thought of how to compose his feelings into something that made sense. His heart jumped into his throat. "It was a terrible week."

"I know!" She frowned, shaking her head. "You're my best friend and I kept reaching for the phone to complain about my day."

My best friend. He forced himself to breathe normally, thankful he hadn't said more.

"Let's not argue about Lexi, okay? We both want what's best for her. She'll make her own decisions in the end." Caroline was so close that he could see the golden flecks in her green-blue eyes. She smelled like vanilla and . . . he leaned forward, inhaling.

"Brooks?" she asked, but didn't move away.

"I just realized what you always remind me of."

"I'm afraid to hear it. My hygiene isn't the best when I don't get many visitors. Or maybe that's why I don't get many visitors." She made a face.

"Jordan almonds. You smell like Jordan almonds."

"Those pastel candy-covered almonds they serve at weddings?"

He nodded. "Must be your shampoo."

"I don't think so. But I'm glad it wasn't ginkgo fruit. Those trees smell like cat poo."

"No, definitely not cat poo."

"I'm going to change. I won't take long. Feel free to wander." She didn't bother to wait for his response but disappeared through the kitchen doorway.

Brooks let out a long breath and didn't move from the spot. He had come so close to ruining their friendship. If he thought last week was bad, he needed to remember that it could be a permanent situation. Caroline would never want to hurt him. If she felt being his friend, when he wanted more, was hurtful, then she would cut off all contact. Obviously she cared for him. But not that way. Maybe not ever.

Misery covered him like a blanket, dampening any joy he could have felt about putting aside their differences. Like a man caught between a cliff and an army behind him, he didn't know which fate to choose. Coming clean and losing her friendship, or suffering along in silence?

Then again, the battle at Parker's Cross Roads might apply to the present moment. He lifted his gaze to the pressed-tin ceiling. Like Nathan Bedford Forrest, outflanked by Federal soldiers, maybe he should "charge 'em both ways."

The noble thing, the right thing, would be to fight for their friendship until he couldn't take the pain any longer. When he reached his breaking point, he would act like the man he was and be honest with her. He had nothing to lose, after all.

Debbie Mae stood in the living room at Badewood and held up four large dry-cleaning bags. "Let's see. Caroline, this one is yours." She handed it over and Caroline was surprised by the lightness of the costume. It seemed there wasn't much except the bag and the hanger.

"Sweetie, this one is yours. Jacket, shirt, pants. You can use those hobnail boots you have for the reenactments."

Manning accepted his costume and shot a sly grin at Brooks.

"Here, Brooks. Yours was the hardest to find. True Regency from head to toe. As soon as you get into the shirt, we'll practice tying the cravat."

Caroline held her dress over her face to smother her laughter at the expression on his face. It was the look of a man being walked to the gallows. She'd never thought of how Brooks could have joined the reenactments as a colonel or a lieutenant but he'd preferred to wear the threadbare uniform of a conscripted soldier. She was almost positive they had relatives who had earned a high rank in the war.

Debbie Mae clapped her hands. "Off you go. Brooks, should we change in the bathroom on the first floor?"

"That's fine. There's enough room for both of us to be

throwing our clothes around," Caroline answered, not waiting for Brooks to bother showing them the way.

"Actually, the pipes are being torn out and redone." Brooks shrugged. "Always something in these places. Come on back and use my room. Manning and I will change in his old room."

They followed Brooks back along the narrow hallway, passing the kitchen, down another hallway and past the smaller rooms that were once servants' quarters. He started up a narrow staircase, a smooth groove worn in each step. "Watch the top step; it's got a bit of an overhang. It took me weeks to stop tripping on it."

"Why do you sleep back here again?" Debbie Mae wrinkled her nose. "Manning's old room is really lovely. What's wrong with yours?"

"Just the morning sun hitting my face at the crack of dawn."

"Did you try blackout curtains?" Caroline didn't mind the sun. It was like a natural alarm clock.

"Yes, but the crows gather in the elm right outside. There's no curtain that can block out that infernal cawing."

"I didn't know you weren't a morning person. Don't you and Caroline go running every morning?"

"Not every morning, no." He turned down a narrow hallway and opened a plain oak door. "Ignore the mess."

They trooped into the room and gazed around. An armoire stood sentry in the corner. Every wall held mahogany floor-to-ceiling bookcases, except for a space for an old painting and one area that held an antique rolltop desk. The desk faced a simple window with double-hung panes of glass. It was tidy, except for the stacks of books by the bed and a few papers on the bedside table. The bed wasn't particularly wide but was certainly long enough to accommodate a full-grown man.

"Cozy," Debbie Mae said, eyebrows raised. "You don't even have your own bathroom?"

"Sure, I do. It's right down the hall."

"No, I mean . . ." She opened the only other door in the room and gazed at Brooks's clothes in the deep-set closet. "An attached bathroom, like people have when they can live in any room in Badewood. I don't believe you have thirty-five rooms to choose from and you picked this one."

Caroline walked into the room, leaned over the desk and stared out at the view. "You can see for miles! Isn't that the creek?"

"Yup. I see some herons there every evening, looking for crawdads. I think your house is about there." He pointed over her shoulder, through the trees.

"I love this view. No wonder you moved out of the front of the house, crows or no crows." She could see him sitting here, writing articles for big New York magazines. Of course, he was only here for the summer and would leave again in a few short months. She shoved the thought away. She ran a finger along the inset panels of the desk, admiring the burl pattern. It was a bigger desk than her secretary, just right for a six-footer such as Brooks. She started to lift the top, wondering how his laptop fit inside and if he'd found a way to coil the cord out the back without cutting a hole.

Brooks reached over and stayed her hand. "No snooping, Finley."

"Ha! Snooping implies curiosity and I was only checking to see how—"

"Come on, you two. Let's get changed so we can see if we need to make any adjustments." Debbie Mae was already shooing Brooks from the room. He put up his hands in a "no contest" move. Just before closing the door behind him, he shook his finger at Caroline as if to remind her to keep her paws off his stuff. Like the educated, mature woman that she was, she stuck out her tongue. A flash of his grin and the door was pulled closed.

"Okay, let's see how this thing fits." Debbie Mae unzipped the dry-cleaning bag and pulled out the dress.

Caroline gasped, hand to her mouth. She was shocked that the dress wasn't plain white, with a little decorative piping, maybe a velvet doodad here or there. The dress was the palest blue silk, gathered right under the breasts and draping in long, soft folds. A sheer overlay covered the entire dress, and tiny, embroidered flowers dotted the netting. The neckline was scooped, not too low, and edged with froths of lace. The short sleeves were trimmed with deep blue velvet. The real jaw-dropper was the hem. Sprays of flowers inched up from the border, tiny forget-me-nots and lilies of the valley embroidered in a repeating pattern that was both delicate and stunning. "What is this? I thought we were going as peasant girls or something."

Debbie Mae blinked at her. "Peasant girls? I'm Harriet Smith, your simpleminded but very beautiful protégée. Manning is Mr. Martin, the farmer. She loves him, but Emma convinces her to refuse him and then tries to fix her up with all the eligible bachelors in town."

"Wait, so I'm the one who keeps you apart?" Caroline put a hand on her hip. "That's not even close to reality. Don't you remember how I fixed y'all up that summer—?"

"Of course I do," Debbie Mae said, laughing. "But if you're Emma, and I'm your best friend, and your best friend is in love with Mr. Martin the farmer, then Manning has to be the farmer. Right?"

Caroline stood there, trying her best not to look confused.

"Did you read the book like I told you?" Debbie Mae asked.

"I tried. I really did. But there were so many characters. I must have counted twenty characters in the first chapter. Did she need them all?" Caroline was teasing, but part of her honestly wondered if Jane Austen enjoyed throwing in characters the way some cooks tossed ingredients into a soup. It seemed so random and disjointed; Caroline couldn't imagine how all those plots and people would come together in the end. But millions of Austen fans couldn't be wrong, she supposed.

"True, the book can be a little much to wade through. Did you even watch that movie? You'll love it, and you're the perfect Emma. She dresses impeccably, has great style, and is effortlessly beautiful."

"I promise, I'll watch it before the party." Caroline flopped onto Brooks's bed, not caring if she disturbed the old patchwork quilt. The frame let out an alarming creak and she froze. Probably just old wood. Probably nothing to do with the Pop-Tarts she'd been eating every morning for breakfast. She made a mental note to run a little longer tomorrow.

"You better get acquainted with the Regency ideas or you're going to stick out like a sore thumb."

Caroline rolled to her side and propped her head in one hand. She could smell Brooks in this room, his soap and the scent that was only his. "So everybody's going to be so amazingly in character that I'll look like I was dropped there by aliens?"

"Maybe. Think of it like Brooks and Manning going to a battle. They don't even carry stuff in their pockets that is from the wrong era."

"Not even a wallet?"

"Especially not a wallet." Debbie Mae got a dreamy look on her face. "Manning asked me for a lock of my hair. He keeps it in an old locket, sewn in the hem of his jacket."

Caroline smiled. "That's so romantic. He loves you even when he's pretending to be someone else."

"I don't deny that it's why I decided to join him on the reenactments."

"I thought it was the goat-tending," Caroline smirked, remembering how Manning was determined to be as historically accurate as possible, right down to the company goat.

"It's not bad. I've learned a lot of history and met some nice folks. Seriously, maybe you should think about coming with us."

"No, thanks. I don't have anything to wear." She didn't have anything better to do, but Debbie Mae didn't know that.

"Please? I'd love the company. There aren't very many women there. I get tired of being stuck in the mess tent." Debbie Mae unzipped her own dress from the plastic covering, in pale green silk with soft velvet, cream roses dotting the neckline and the hem. Simple but elegant.

Caroline chewed her bottom lip. She felt the tug of old guilt and wondered if she'd feel better after the dance. She didn't want to get dragged all over the countryside every time Debbie Mae said she was lonely. Caroline traced the edge of a quilt patch with one finger, admiring the tiny hand-sewn stitches. It was just like Brooks to have some old thing on his bed instead of a goose-down comforter from Lands' End. She looked up at the painting over the head of the bed. A Confederate soldier stood looking down, his face covered. The top half of a white cross appeared in the bottom of the frame.

Debbie Mae followed Caroline's eyes. "That's a real Winslow Homer. It's called *Trooper Meditating beside a Grave*."

"How do you know all these things? Is it because you're a teacher?" Caroline was honestly awed by her cousin's store of knowledge, mostly because it wasn't Debbie Mae's hobby.

She rolled her eyes. "I teach fourth grade. Winslow Homer doesn't come up too much. Those two brothers talk a lot. You've probably noticed."

Caroline thought back to the meeting at the café. Manning hadn't talked much. And Brooks did talk, but she was usually running over him with some story of her own. She felt a sharp pain around her ribs. She was a selfish friend. Was it so hard to show a little interest in their hobbies? It was not as if she were swamped with projects. She could spend some time visiting a battleground if it made them happy.

"Help me get into this before the guys come back."

Caroline pulled herself upright and held the dress while Debbie Mae stripped off her striped T-shirt and red shorts. She slipped the dress over Debbie Mae's head. When the dress was on, Caroline stepped back to take it in. Debbie Mae looked beautiful, though it was truly strange to see her standing there like a woman out of Regency England.

"Maybe you're right. I should know more about the war than I do. As part of our heritage, I should be willing to do what I can to represent the women." Caroline paused. "As long as I don't get stuck in Dr. Stroud's amputation tent, I think it might be sort of fun."

Debbie Mae threw her arms around Caroline's neck. "Really? You won't regret it. I promise."

Caroline laughed, knowing Debbie Mae couldn't promise any such thing. Her cousin was making an effort to reconnect with her and she was glad about that. But maybe Caroline needed to show some support to Debbie Mae's husband, too. Manning had suffered the past year, along with his wife. It wouldn't kill Caroline to hang out at a battleground and watch the crazies for the day. Really, how bad could it be?

I know no man more likely than Mr. Knightley to do the sort of thing—to do anything really good-natured, useful, considerate, or benevolent. He is not a gallant man, but he is a very humane one—and for an act of unostentatious kindness, there is nobody whom I would fix on more than on Mr. Knightley.

—MRS. WESTON

CHAPTER EIGHTEEN

Caroline held up the dress carefully with one hand. Making her way back down the narrow staircase from Brooks's room was harder than she thought. The little slippers on her feet were soft, and she could feel the wood grain through the fabric. The mirror in the bathroom was much too small to see anything except her head and a few inches of the dress, so she and Debbie Mae had decided to troop back downstairs, to the large standing mirror in one of the sitting rooms. The men must be still struggling into their outfits. It made Caroline smile to think that, for once, men had a harder time getting ready than women.

Debbie Mae chattered the entire way, listing the places she'd had to call before she could find a caterer that would agree to make Regency food. Towering Jell-O molds, meat pies, mulled wine and all sorts of tiny sweets were on the menu. Caroline sent up a silent thank-you for the lack of pink lemonade.

Debbie Mae led her down another staircase. "I think Mr. Elliot is going to have to do something about those outbuildings. This looks nice enough, but I walked through the gardens and saw someone had broken into the old schoolhouse."

Caroline sucked in a breath. "What did they do?"

She shrugged. "I couldn't tell. It's not exactly fit for guests. Maybe they just snooped around a little. He should board them up."

"Don't some of the tours go back there? The sugarcane fields are all grass, but you can still see where the slave quarters were."

Debbie Mae nodded. "But nobody wants to look at that sort of thing anymore. It's bad publicity. Manning said someone told them they should be ashamed to preserve any of it, that taking a torch to it would be better. I think Mr. Elliot felt like they were calling him a racist."

"Ridiculous. Just because history isn't the way we like it doesn't mean we can change it." Caroline didn't want to carry the burden of being the heir to Badewood, but she certainly didn't think hiding the past would help anyone. "The school visits are worth the cost to keep up the buildings. I hope he doesn't do anything sudden."

Absalom appeared and followed them to the sitting room. They stopped, side by side. A floor-to-ceiling, gilt mirror reflected the image of two young Regency ladies. One with dark auburn hair, one with light blond curls. Debbie Mae reached out and grasped Caroline's hand. "Oh, Caroline!"

She nodded, not trusting herself to speak. The hairstyles were wrong and they didn't have gloves and Debbie Mae had painted nails, but it was almost perfect. Absalom stood behind them, wagging the back half of his body in happiness.

The sound of someone's clearing his throat made them both turn away from the sight of their reflections. Manning and Brooks stood there, side by side, looking nothing like brothers, more like distant cousins. "Hey, check it out." Manning spread his arms. "It's country mouse and city mouse."

One was roughly dressed, with a simple vest and old-fashioned trousers. His boots were held together with twine. Manning grinned and swept the hat from his head with a deep bow.

Brooks seemed frozen to the spot. Caroline smiled at him but he didn't respond, obviously uncomfortable in his costume. Breeches clung to his legs, tapering into tall riding boots. The deep blue morning coat fit perfectly, and the white waistcoat buttons didn't strain across his flat stomach. He put his hands on his hips, and not finding pockets, he just dropped them to the side, as if he didn't know what to do with them.

Debbie Mae rushed forward. "Sweetie, you are *adorable*." She turned Manning around, tugging at the back of his vest to see if it was too tight. "The butt on these trousers is a bit saggy, but that's probably more a problem with the man inside than the tailoring."

"Hey, now!" Manning protested with a laugh. He grabbed Debbie Mae and kissed her soundly on the mouth. She reached her arms around his neck and they grinned at each other, lost in their own little world.

Brooks coughed politely. "Should we leave you two alone?"

"Later, babe." Manning gave Debbie Mae a final squeeze and let her go. Caroline laughed at the pink in her cousin's cheeks. Maybe it never got old, being in love with the same person year after year. These two made it look downright easy.

Manning's phone chirped and he looked at the display. "Andrea is coming over with catering samples."

"Right, I totally forgot. I can't wait to taste the flummery."

"I'm not sure if I want to know what that is," Manning said.

"It's a sort of jelly, but made into a mold that is shaped like a castle or a tower or just a"—Debbie Mae wiggled one hand—"big wobbly thing. The ragout of veal will be a hit, I'm sure. And the Roman punch will have to be changed a little bit. It's usually lemon water and hot syrup with a lot of rum."

"Rum and hot syrup? Maybe we could just have beer," Manning suggested.

"No, no beer. I want the Roman punch, but we'll have to make it nonalcoholic. I'm not feeding thirsty guests a forty-proof drink and then sending them out into the night to drive home."

"Very wise. Also, I think there will be some minors, relatives of the band. Unless we're positioning an adult by the punch table, it's better if we don't have to monitor who gets which brew," Brooks said.

"True. Well, let's get working on that tie before she gets here." Debbie Mae took her phone from her purse and found a pictorial how-to. "Okay, 'Neckclothitania' is an original pamphlet someone put out to help men tie their cravats."

"Wait, say that again?" Manning had stretched out on the couch and was obviously already enjoying the idea of Brooks's getting fussed over.

"'Neckclothitania.' Don't interrupt." Debbie Mae gave him a look and went back to her phone. "So, there are a few you can try. Um, maybe Caroline can start slow and see if the basic knot would look nice."

"Me? Why me?" Caroline held up her hands. "I don't know a thing about tying ties."

"I've got to go clear off counter space and get out serving spoons. We're all going to taste the food when she brings it." Debbie Mae handed Caroline the phone and left before she could argue.

"I'll help." Manning got off the couch and was gone seconds later.

"Huh. What do you think? I bet they'll be making out in the kitchen while we struggle with the"—Caroline peered at the tiny screen—"the Mathematical Tie. Whatever that is."

"I can do it. Let me see." Brooks held out a hand.

"These directions are from the front. That makes no sense."

"Men had valets back then." His face was tight, as if he would have loved to be anywhere but there.

"Oh, true." She scrolled through a few photos and then shrugged, laying the phone on the table. "Nothing we can do but try."

He stood in front of her and she ran her fingers up around his collar, finding the long strips of fabric. She had to stand on tiptoe, missing the few inches of height her running shoes gave her. "You're so tall, lean a little closer."

Brooks shifted, bending down a bit. He said nothing, focusing his gaze somewhere over her left shoulder. His mouth was a thin line.

"You look very nice, you know. There's no reason to be upset."

His gaze shot to her face. "I'm not upset. Why do you think I'm upset?"

Caroline leaned to the side, tugging him with her while she frowned at the pictures on the phone screen. Standing straight, she crossed the strips, tucking one under the other. "You don't think I know you? I know everything about you, Professor Elliot."

His lips parted as if he were going to say something, then he simply shook his head. "If you say so."

She mumbled under her breath. "Two diagonal creases from under each ear to the knot, and a horizontal crease at the front, which reaches to each side." She folded the strips carefully, her bottom lip between her teeth. It was distracting to be so close to him while trying to perform cravat origami. The instructions flowed out of her head as soon as she read them. And he smelled good. Really good. She wanted to lean forward and stick her face into his shirt. How could Lauren refuse him? He was everything a woman could want. Smart, funny, honorable, handsome, educated. Sure, he had that little problem, the Civil War reenactment obsession, but he was a Southerner through and through. Lauren should be able to understand that.

"Now *you* look upset."

Caroline laughed, feeling her cheeks burn. "No, just irritated with myself. This should be simple. I'm just not concentrating."

He nodded. "Take all the time you need. I'll be right here . . . in my morning coat and hunting boots."

She snickered. "Sorry, I shouldn't laugh. If it helps, you look absolutely dashing. Debbie Mae couldn't ask for a better Regency hero."

"That's what I don't understand. Why doesn't she make Manning wear this getup? Why me?"

Caroline swept the last strip under the other and stood back to admire her creation. "It actually worked!" She cocked her head. "We should try another. Just to make sure we've got it covered. And to answer your question, I think it's all part of her plan to find you a wife."

"Ah. The women will come running when they see me in my fancy Mathematical neckcloth."

Caroline pulled the tie apart, letting the starched fabric run through her fingers. She knew he was being sarcastic, but she didn't have to guess what would happen at the dance. Women would fall over in a dead faint. Lauren would have to give him a second look because he certainly wasn't any kind of nerd in this outfit. He'd never before looked so handsome. She hadn't even read the book and she was half in love with Mr. Knightley.

"I wonder what it was really like back then. We think it's all fun and flirting, but there was probably a lot of ugly reality."

"Like the dancing."

She grinned and looked for another example to try. "Oh, here. The Ballroom Tie! We'll try that."

Wrapping the strips around his neck, she let her fingers rest for a moment against his jaw. "You feel hot. Are you too warm?" The weather was much cooler than it had been the day before, but he was wearing about four more layers than she was.

"I'm fine." His tone was short, as if he were thoroughly and completely bored. "I hope they don't make us wander the dance, asking women for their hand. I had enough rejection in junior high to last me a lifetime."

Caroline was quiet for a moment. "You'll be fine. Nobody is going to refuse to dance with you." She paused to check the pictures. "And we wrap it around again. Bring the ends under the arms and pinned in the back." She leaned forward, reaching under his coat with an end of the cloth in each hand.

"Wait, wait." Brooks backed up a step, then another.

"Don't worry, I won't stick you with a pin. I don't even have one." She still had her hands under his coat, flat against his rib cage. She could feel the hard ridges of muscle under his vest and shirt.

His jaw was tight but he nodded.

"I think . . ." She put both hands behind his back, feeling her fingers touch. "I think I might just be able to tie the ends. We wouldn't even need a pin." She was talking right into the front of his shirt, eye to eye with the cloth-covered buttons. She could feel his chest move with every breath, and his heart beat directly into her right ear. He did smell very good. She allowed herself one small moment to inhale deeply, to forget all the worry about Lauren, their arguments about Lexi, her mother's health, his father's depression and every other nagging problem in her life.

"There." She moved back and straightened his coat. "Now you're ready."

He nodded. "I am." Something flashed behind his eyes. "Caroline, I thought I could wait, but I need to tell you something."

Brooks had finally found someone who'd made him rethink his avoidance of marriage. And she could guess who it was. The look on his face said it all. There was nothing else it could be. She had been too close to him, probably making him feel uncomfortable. He needed to set boundaries, make sure he was clear about where they stood. Her cheeks flamed. "It's all right, you don't have to share anything you don't want to." She looked at the floor, feeling humiliation flash through her. "I was just teasing about knowing everything about you. Of course I don't. Of course you have interests and ideas and . . . friends that have nothing to do with me."

"That's just it. It does have to do with you." He hauled in a breath. "Remember when we argued about Lexi?"

She blinked, confused at the direction he'd taken, and nodded. Who could forget? She'd felt as if she'd lost his friendship forever.

"That week, I did a lot of thinking—" The doorbell sounded and he stopped.

"Debbie Mae will get it."

He nodded. His eyes were shadowed with anxiety and he rubbed his face. "Okay. What I was saying was after we had that fight, I had a lot of time to think. I realized that this friendship"—he motioned to the space between them—"is more important to me than almost anything else. I don't want to ruin it."

"Um, well. Good." His words should have made her feel relief, but instead dread crept over her. He was preparing her for something awful, something he felt she couldn't bear to hear. She was going to have to let him know that she could deal with Lauren. He didn't have to choose between them. She knew what happened when men had to choose between their friends and a woman they loved. They chose the woman.

"I want you to understand that because I think things are changing. Or will change. Between us." He looked at her, then, with a gaze so direct that Caroline felt a thrill of dread course through her. She didn't want to hear him. She wanted everything to go back to the way it was before he had come home, before Lauren had shown up in town, before everything had become so complicated.

The doorbell rang again.

"Maybe they're still kissing in the kitchen. They probably can't even hear the doorbell." Her voice trembled a bit at the end, but she lifted her chin. She would be brave. She would put herself last. If Brooks had finally found someone, then she would support him no matter how much she hated the thought of losing him. "And you're right about our friendship changing. It's natural. It's another stage in our lives, right? Falling in love with someone and getting married shouldn't keep us from being friends."

Brooks stared at her for a moment, then started to shake his head. "I—that wasn't quite what I meant. I mean, it was." He ran a hand through his hair, the way he never did unless he was at the end of his rope. The doorbell rang once more and he looked toward the door, exasperation written on his face. "Let me get it."

She nodded and he left the room, striding out like a man on a mission. She sank to the couch, clutching her hands together. She was shocked to feel them trembling. So, he found a girlfriend. It wasn't that bad. It didn't mean he would actually get married. The vision of Brooks in a tuxedo, standing at the altar in front of hundreds of guests, flashed through her mind. Her stomach twisted. Maybe she could be friends with the new girlfriend. Maybe they could all hang out together.

She almost laughed out loud at the ridiculousness of the idea. No woman would ever want to share Brooks. *She* didn't want to share him.

"Caroline?" Debbie Mae poked her head in. "I'm going to change. I don't want to get any food on my dress before the big night."

"Good idea." Caroline stood up, feeling weak at the knees. She followed Debbie Mae back up the stairs. Whatever Brooks had been planning to say about Lauren, he'd have to wait until later. Maybe by then he'd have decided he didn't need to drop whatever bomb he'd been holding. She would just have to show him that their friendship was solid, that nothing could crack the years they had behind them, that he didn't have to choose between Lauren and her. She could play nice. She wished she hadn't been so rude about Lauren before. He might think they could never get along. She could only hope he would forget all about it.

Seldom, very seldom, does complete truth belong to any human disclosure; seldom can it happen that something is not a little disguised or a little mistaken.

—EMMA

There is no charm equal to tenderness of heart.

—EMMA

CHAPTER NINETEEN

Only two more days until the dance. Brooks trudged up the path to Badewood, willing himself not to think on how awkward the evening could be. Or how wonderful. His mind seemed to be stuck in a continuous loop. One part of him hated the idea of ending up like his parents, bitter enemies in the same house. Another part couldn't possibly believe Caroline and he could ever be anything less than happy together. A third part had to admit that Caroline wasn't interested in getting married. She'd said several times she wanted to restart her career before anything else.

He reached the front door and frowned at the peeling paint on the doorframe. He would have to strip it down and repaint. He didn't mind the little projects. He sort of enjoyed the break from working on articles. But it was a never-ending list lately. Old houses were time suckers.

As he came through the door, he saw his father sitting in a wing chair in the entryway, legs crossed, hands folded over his chest, as if deep in thought. "One of your friends stopped by while you were out."

Brooks closed the front door behind him. "Which friend?"

"Marshall somebody. Said he'd heard we were ready to part with some antiques."

Brooks froze midstep. "Antiques?"

His father nodded, eyes locked on his. "That's what he'd said."

"Unbelievable." Brooks felt his jaw go tight. "He conned Caroline's mother out of all their china and silver. Their attic is cleared out of anything older than fifty years. He replaced the essentials with retail junk. Caroline was crushed, and there's nothing she can do to get it all back."

"I figured he was no friend of yours." His father heaved himself out of the chair. "That's all I wanted to tell you."

Brooks watched his father walk back down the hallway, shocked at how fragile he looked. The man was beaten, broken, lost. All over a marriage he wasn't happy to be part of in the first place. The illogic of it made Brooks's head ache.

And now Marshall was poking his nose around Badewood. Well, perhaps it was time he paid his "friend" a little visit.

"Your dog is breathing down my neck. Shoo, Absalom!" Blanche waved a hand over her shoulder. "He needs a visit to the doggy dentist."

Brooks checked the GPS and turned left. "You're hurting his feelings. He just wants to share the love." Still, Brooks cracked the window. Kids didn't use *dog breath* as an insult for nothing.

"I should have worn my sun hat. I feel exposed. If I'm undercover, I should have a disguise. I have a lot of friends in Oxford and somebody might spot me."

"Grandma, we're not undercover. We're just visiting."

She shot him a look. "You're visiting a friend forty-five minutes away without calling and you don't know the address but you won't ask them for directions?"

"Okay, we might be visiting unannounced." He paused to look at street numbers. "And uninvited."

"Should I be prepared for a fight? Is it over a woman?" She sat up straight and clutched her giant, lime-green tote to her chest. Her expression was one of sheer delight.

"No, nothing like that. This guy convinced Caroline's mother to hand over all the American primitives in the whole place. She even gave up the china and silver."

Blanche gasped. "The Stubbs? I loved those pieces." She frowned. "Funny. After that party where I added the rum to the punch by accident, I didn't get invited back."

Brooks pulled into a parking spot and left the engine running. "I still don't see how you can empty a whole liter of dark rum into the punch bowl by accident."

She rolled her eyes. "Of course I knew what I was doin'. I just didn't realize they'd already added it. I didn't taste a thing. It must have been real light and lots of syrup. When I saw that bottle in the kitchen, I just thought I would help out."

"I see how they might have been irritated when the guests started passing out all over the living room."

She snorted. "Passing out woulda been an improvement. Charlie Connelly tried to kiss Dr. Sunderlin's wife, and she thought he was a bit forward."

"She slapped him silly." Brooks could still hear the sound in his head. Kathleen Sunderlin had a good forehand from all those Thursday-morning doubles matches with the ladies.

"And then Elaine Connelly joined in faster than green grass through a goose. Those two girls went a-hair-pullin' and a-toe-stompin' like they were protecting their men's honor."

Brooks sighed. Maybe bringing Blanche with him today was tempting fate. He just wanted to look around. Maybe talk to Marshall a little bit. Not with his fists, although that sounded real nice. "Well, there won't be any hair pulling inside, so let's go in real quiet like."

"It's your visit." She shrugged. "But when it's over a woman, anything can happen."

He started to remind her it was over old buckets and rag rugs, but he just shook his head.

The shop was in a tourist-friendly part of town and he was soon standing in front of a window display of the Ashleys' best china. American primitives were hung from pegs around the large glass windows. GRANDPA'S ATTIC was written in gold letters. The irony of the title made anger expand in his chest. Marshall should have titled it Everybody's Attic. He was clearing out the best houses in the state.

"I don't think Absalom will be welcome in here." He hooked the dog's leash to the pole in front of the store. "Stay."

A charming little string of brass bells announced their arrival, and a young woman stepped from behind the counter. She couldn't have been more than eighteen, with rosy cheeks and long, straight hair. Her pressed shirt and slacks were professional looking even if her eyes flitted from Brooks to Blanche with a bit of anxiety.

"Welcome to Grandpa's Attic. Is there anything special you're looking for?"

"No, no, just peekin' around." Blanche waved a hand. "Maybe primitives, if you've got 'em."

"Oh, we have a wonderful selection. Come on back here." The young woman led them to a large room packed with ones wooden and iron and tin. "Let me know if you need anything more."

Brooks gazed around. He recognized the old skittles board on which he and Caroline used to play a counting game with marbles. He touched the tiny tag hanging from a string: $800. The multi-colored-striped wooden toys they always thought were some kind of bowling pins were marked Indian clubs, $500. The small wooden skis they used to strap on and use on the back stairs, $300. The head form for wigs, the painted child's toy hoop, the old weather vane, the iron shovel for the fire, the washboard they'd rubbed with spoons to make terrible music, it was all here.

A wave of anger washed over him so fast it made him dizzy. Caroline's whole attic seemed crammed in this room. Caroline's family had touched these items for hundreds of years, and now they were for sale in a crooked antiques shop. His gaze roved upward, and at first he didn't believe what he was seeing. On the wall, near the top, was a long strip of painted letters and numbers. His heart stopped in his chest.

Stepping closer, he squinted, looking for the telltale mark. There it was, right on *C.* A tiny scrape through the curve of the letter, a scrape Caroline had made one day when she was pretending to teach him the letters to her name.

"Well, isn't this adorable? It's a glove turner!" Blanche was working two ends of a gizmo that looked like a giant clapper. "You sewed the gloves, tucked them on, and then this turned them inside out. How smart is that?"

He nodded, not trusting himself to speak. The tag dangled near enough for him to read: $1,800. He was so angry he felt lightheaded. Manning had told him someone had broken into the old schoolhouse. He'd thought it was kids, looking for something to steal. Apparently, it had been adults, looking for something to steal. At first glance, he hadn't noticed anything missing, since the expensive copper pipes were still there and the large teacher's desk.

"Look at this one." Blanche waved a cleaver around. The end was shaped like a horse head, with a hole for the eye completing the picture. "This is a great piece. I bet I could cook real well with this sort of chopper."

She glanced up at him, as if realizing they weren't on a shopping trip. She whispered loudly enough to carry clear out the door, "Did you find anything?"

He nodded. "A few things." Such as the entire room. The memories twisted in his heart, almost painful in their clarity. The worst part, there wasn't anything they could do. Caroline's mother had given up the pieces willingly. And he couldn't prove the teaching stick was from Badewood. "We should go. I just came to check it out."

Blanche set down the cleaver and nodded. "Up to you. I could always try to sweet-talk the truth out of him."

Brooks choked back a laugh. His grandma had high regard for her sweet-talking abilities. It worked on him, sure. On a crooked antiques dealer, maybe not so much.

As they passed through the hallway, he heard voices raised in anger. He held up a hand to Blanche and tried to listen.

"I'm tired of being your errand girl. I don't want to do this anymore." The high voice was near tears, cracking on the final word.

"Too bad." Obviously a man, and Brooks would bet the farm that it was Marshall. "You signed up for this. You took money for the job. It's not finished."

"I'm finished. I've been to every mansion in three states. I can't go to one more party and recite those lies. Eventually someone will check it out."

"That's not my problem. Set up a fake website. Put out a news release. You thought it was a great plan four months ago and you've certainly made enough from it."

A door slammed. Brooks stepped to the side, trying to see down the hallway. A woman appeared, her long, dark hair swinging from side to side as she stomped out of the shop.

"Is that who we're looking for?" Blanche whispered behind him.

He shook his head. That wasn't whom he was looking for, but now that he'd seen her, it all made sense. "I'm done here. We should head out."

They exited the shop in a hurry, accepting the salesgirl's offer to take a card. Brooks unlooped Absalom's leash and quickly unlocked the car.

"We should stop for lunch. I need something to keep me going. Shoppin' can be such a drain on an elderly lady's reserves."

"Elderly?" He shot her a glance. "But you're right about the food. You choose. I'll take you wherever you want to go." He didn't have any appetite. Nothing was left for him to feel but anger. He was going to get those dishes back. And the silver and the attic treasures. He didn't care how much he had to pay, they were going right back to Caroline's place, where they belonged.

"I've a hankering for some pulled pork. Does that sound good to you?"

"Sure does." Pulled pork, pork chops, dog biscuits. It all sounded the same.

All he wanted right now was a few minutes with Marshall in a secluded area where they could have a little talk, man-to-man.

He moved a few steps nearer, and those few steps were enough to prove in how gentlemanlike a manner, with what natural grace, he must have danced, would he but take the trouble. Whenever she caught his eye, she forced him to smile; but in general he was looking grave.

—EMMA

Chapter Twenty

The old barn was open, both doors pulled wide. Caroline stepped out of her car, drawing a deep breath of what had to be freshly mown alfalfa. The frogs were calling to each other and a few crickets joined the chorus. It was a magical night, perfect in every way. The humidity had let up to a bearable level and she felt that she could inhale without drowning. The fine hairs on the back of her neck moved. Turning, she saw a man walking toward her across the gravel drive. His deep blue morning coat was perfectly cut and the breeches didn't show a single wrinkle, tapering into leather hunting boots. The vest and cravat glowed whitely in the dim light. Her eyes moved to his face and her mind worked to reconcile what she knew with what she was seeing. From the first glance, she'd known it was Brooks, simply by the familiar movements of his body. She knew his walk, his bearing, as well as she knew her own hand. And she knew that Mathematical knot.

But his expression was not that of the Brooks she knew. His mouth was a thin line, as if he were steadying himself for something painful. They locked eyes and he nodded at her, jaw tight.

"There you are." She waved enthusiastically and walked toward him, holding her long dress tucked in one hand. The curls from her elaborate hairdo blew into her eyes and she brushed them back with an impatient motion.

"Here I am." He held his arms out to the side and waited for a verdict.

"Where did you park?" She didn't see where he'd come from. It was as if he'd just popped out of the twilight.

He pointed to the edge of the field; his Brando-mobile leaned in the shadow of the barn. "Wouldn't we have made a pair, riding through the streets of Thorny Hollow on a vintage Triumph, in Regency gear?"

She giggled. "All the old people would have rushed to the doctor's for a checkup." Holding up the edge of her skirt, she said, "Poor dress wouldn't have survived that kind of treatment, forget about my hair."

He bent closer. A small smile touched his lips. "Forget-me-nots. Fitting for a girl who loves a mud pie from Bravard's."

"Right. The chili-slaw-dog-embroidered dresses were all sold-out."

He laughed out loud and she felt the breath catch in her throat. Nobody could possibly look better in this costume than Brooks. It wasn't humanly possible. His gaze locked on hers and for a moment she saw a debate rage inside. Then it was gone. He straightened up, away from her. The laughter was gone and in its place was this new, solemn Brooks.

"I know you didn't want to come. If it hadn't been for Debbie Mae—"

"I did. I did want to come," he interrupted. "I just didn't want to come as someone else."

"But you make a perfect Mr. Knightley." Caroline looked up at him, taking it all in once more. "Really. It's almost like you've walked right out of that PBS movie. I haven't seen it yet, don't tell our hostess. She might roast me for the guests instead of the pork shoulder the caterers brought. But, you're perfect. Definitely taller, but just as handsome."

Something in his face softened at her words. "As long you think so." He paused, shaking his head. "You see what terrible manners I have? My forebears are spinning in their graves. I haven't yet complimented you on your costume."

Caroline laughed, twirling in a circle. "It's not uncomfortable at all. When Debbie Mae hatched this plan, I thought we were going to be laced into corsets and be struggling with bustles." She ran her hands down the length of her bodice. "It's very soft. I think I might wear this all the time."

"You look beautiful." It was a pat answer, but something in his voice made her glance up in surprise. The tightness in his face was back and his expression was serious.

"You don't have to do this, you know." She moved forward, laying a hand on his arm. Maybe he had a phobia of costume parties. Maybe he was afraid of what Lauren would think of him.

His gaze fixed on her hand and he seemed to be choosing his words. "What can it hurt?"

She nodded, feeling a deep-down sureness that he was saying something quite the opposite. What was he dreading? Glancing back at the barn door, she could see the groups moving inside. She wondered if Frank was inside and if he was waiting for her. Bright costumes whirled by and laughter echoed out into the drive. An image flashed in her mind, of Lauren and Brooks sitting on the wrought-iron bench together in the botanical garden, admiring Badewood in all its beauty. Her heart squeezed in her chest. Had he asked her out and she refused him? But she seemed drawn to Brooks, just as much as every other woman in the universe.

"I'll protect you from all the pretty girls inside, okay?" She forced herself to laugh, but it came out sounding like a pale shadow.

"All of them? You promise?" He leaned toward her, eyes locked on hers.

"Promise." She smiled, hoping it looked genuine. Her heart was tight, wondering how any woman could refuse a man like Brooks. A light breeze sprang up, carrying the scent of jasmine and pushing curls into her eyes again.

He stepped closer. "There's only one I'm afraid of, honestly."

She nodded. She'd caught a glimpse of Lauren's bright white Regency dress through the open door. It was stunning in its simplicity, setting off her tan and her enormous gray eyes. She had looked like a nineteenth-century painting. "I'll do my best."

"If you said the word, everything would change." He took a deep breath. "Caroline—"

"But how?" She shook her head. "I don't have that much influence over anybody. I know you think I do, but I don't." And she certainly wouldn't tell Lauren to go out with him if she *did* have the power to change the girl's opinion.

He smiled, shrugging. "A man can always try."

The sound of footsteps reached them right before Manning's voice called out. "You two! Stop dillydallying around outside and come help me out. I've got more women than I can possibly partner."

"Oh, joy." Brooks sighed and threw a sharp look at Caroline as she laughed out loud.

"I thought you were resolved to dance tonight."

"I only had one partner in mind." He mumbled the words under his breath as he jammed the top hat on his head. Setting off for the door, looking grimly determined, he held out his arm.

She took it, holding the hem of her gown in one hand. They should have been wearing gloves, but it was so warm. She noticed the softness of his jacket, how the heavy material felt under her hands. No wonder he wasn't thrilled with this party. He must have been wearing a good five pounds of fabric compared to her loose and comfortable dress. The bodice was fitted, but it only came to the top of her rib cage. Nothing like the long coat he wore.

They could hear the party before they reached the wide-open front doors. The place was more than a hundred years old, but strong and true still. As they walked up the wide front steps, she glanced up at the rounded roof, so far above. This was nothing like the long, three-sided tobacco shed on Brooks's family property. This barn was built for a working farm and all the storage they needed. The farm was gone, but the barn still stood like a bright red sentry in the countryside.

The room was booming with sound, and she gasped in happiness as they stepped inside. The barn was decorated in long swags of evergreen boughs and dotted with sprays of white flowers. It would have seemed Christmassy except that the tables to the side were set with large displays of wildflowers. Two men stood at the entrance, dressed as foot servants, carefully taking bonnets and canes to a side area used as a coat check. The old wooden floor was freshly swept and hosed down, and the smell of the pine flooring added to the atmosphere of the party. White wooden folding chairs lined the long walls all the way to the stage at the front. The band was already playing a reel, and couples were marching up and down a long line. Brooks pulled her to one side and they stood, watching the swirl of dresses and tails.

"Word must have gotten out," he said into her ear. "This party is definitely bigger than Debbie Mae intended."

Caroline nodded, a huge smile spreading over her face. "I bet it was Blanche. She can really pull the folks together when we need it."

Tables draped in white held serving dishes piled with food, and several punch bowls filled with a deep-rose-colored drink.

Brooks leaned down again to say, "Manning hung the boughs. I swept the pigeon poop. I think I should get more points for tackling such a job."

She turned, laughing. His face was close to hers, and he looked happy, relaxed. "Gold star, definitely."

The band at the front moved in time to the music, and the three older African-American men let out an occasional hoot to go with the dancers' directions. A tiny woman, stooped with age, waved a hand and called out dance terms in a breathy whisper into the microphone. Her feet moved to the song, and Caroline grinned at the idea of this little woman's dancing her whole life to these ancient tunes.

The reel finally ended and the couples bowed to each other, then clapped for the musicians. Most were in costume but a few in T-shirts and shorts were mixed in. Caroline looked around for Frank, but didn't see him in the crowd.

Blanche appeared next to her. "Honey, you look perfect. Look at the stitchin'." She leaned down to examine Caroline's dress.

"Did you order your dress, Blanche? It's a beautiful color." The deep purple stood out in all the whites, creams and pinks.

"No, I made this myself. I'm Mrs. Bennet. Not my favorite character. She complains a lot. I'd rather be a cougar, but back then, there weren't a lot of attractive old ladies in literature. Probably not a lot of old ladies in general, with the mortality rate. Anyway, bein' Mrs. Bennet is better than bein' Lady Catherine. She was a real killjoy." Blanche held out an arm. "See that velvet trim? Hardest thing I ever did try."

Caroline's eyes went wide. "I had no idea you could sew. This must have taken ages."

"Not really. Brooks told me you all were havin' this party a month ago. I did work it all the way up to this afternoon, but I could have done it sooner if I hadn't been running all over the county with my grandson." Blanche winked at Brooks.

Caroline cocked her head. Running all over the county?

"Grandma, are they going to go another round? I think I see the—"

"Oh, you didn't tell her about going up to Oxford?" Blanche turned to Caroline. "He went lookin' for your Stubbs china. We found the place, all right. Packed full of good ol' family antiques."

Caroline turned to him, questions on her lips.

Brooks's cheeks had gone pink. "I didn't want to bring up a painful subject. I wanted to know . . . what he had done with them." Brooks gave his grandmother a look that was clearly meant to keep her quiet.

The fiddler played a bar of music and the guests clustered at the front. The tiny African-American lady held up a hand for attention. "This here's a favorite o' mine. I want my friend in the back to come up here. And bring the pretty gal with you."

Brooks opened his mouth and shut it again.

"Resistance is futile," Caroline said, laughing. She tugged him by the hand, all the way up to the front of the barn. Guests parted to let them through. Debbie Mae stood next to Manning, looking as beautiful as she had on her wedding day. Tiny rosebuds dotted her updo. She patted Caroline as she passed and whispered, "Good luck." Murmurs reached Caroline's ears as they passed.

". . . real sweet."

"Isn't that fine!"

"Just like a movie . . ."

Lexi wiggled her fingers at them from the side, and Caroline gasped. Lexi had transformed into a Regency girl, complete with white gloves and black, glossy ringlets framing her face.

Frank appeared to the right in full costume and Caroline waved, delighted to see him at last. His brown eyes were bright with laughter. He mouthed something to her that she didn't catch, but he flashed a thumbs-up to say he thought she looked beautiful.

Brooks quickly introduced Caroline to Jennie. The old woman looked her up and down. "Yup, I see how it is, son. I see how it is. There's no blamin' you."

Caroline shot him a glance and he shrugged, his face a little pinker. She spoke up, worried about ruining the dance. "Ma'am, I haven't had any practice. Maybe we should pair Brooks with another girl."

"No, you'll do. It's not hard to learn. You just follow your man, hear?" Jennie clapped her hands. "We're a-goin' to dance a little ditty called 'A Sure Thing.' Everybody try a few allemandes and a few turns." She winked at Brooks and walked to the front. The guests faced each other, moving in unison, laughter peppering the air.

"Brooks, I really don't think I can—"

"Here." He took her hand and moved her to the side. A short,

African-American man in a T-shirt that read SWINGERS DO IT BETTER under his Regency jacket nodded hello and grabbed her hand, swinging her back to face Brooks. "See, there's one move down."

She started to laugh. "But I can't just let you do all the work, passing me back and forth."

"You could." He smiled, his dimples deepening.

The couples started to line up and Jennie called partners to the right. The fiddler started, slow and sweet. Then the others jumped in after a few bars. The dancers were bobbing their heads and smiling across to the folks on the opposite line. Debbie Mae waved and grinned from her place two dancers down.

"Men, allemande half to the left," Jennie called to the beat, counting steps in between. "Left one-half and half a hey. Ladies chain and circle right. Do-si-do and make it right, back to your man and face each other."

Caroline was giggling by now, stumbling over her feet, desperately trying to keep track of Brooks. Other dancers moved in and out of her view, and hands grabbed hers and swung her around.

Brooks was back in front, his eyes bright. "Good to see you again," he said over the music.

Then he was gone, turning left, and a woman appeared. She had a beautiful dragonfly pin on the front of her pale violet gown, and she lifted a wrinkled hand to Caroline. All she could do was mirror the woman's movement, watching in fascination as they turned smoothly together, almost as if they were both trained dancers.

Brooks came back again, and all the men bowed to their partners. Jennie called out, "Gypsy turn," and Caroline saw his mouth go tight. It wasn't such a hard move after all, though. He held up his hands and she put her palms to his. They did a full turn on the spot, and she craned her neck to see what the other guests were doing.

"Look here, at me." His voice was soft, as if he wasn't sure whether to instruct her.

Jennie called out another gypsy turn and then went the other direction. Caroline locked eyes with Brooks, feeling the heat of his hands against hers. For just a moment, she felt the room shift and the guests faded away. It was only the two of them, and the music. But it wasn't Brooks and Caroline any longer but some other couple, from long ago and in another place. A couple that couldn't drag themselves away from the music and movement and heat of the dancing.

Then he was gone, and the short, African-American man was back. He gently guided her right hand to his, turning her toward his partner. The woman smiled broadly at Caroline and called out, "You're doin' a real fine job!"

Back they went, ladies chain and circle right. Brooks appeared, and her gaze sought his. She didn't want to look at her feet. She wanted to look into his eyes, to know the man beside her in a way only a dancer can know another.

Jennie called out, "Court'sy turn!"

Brooks took Caroline's left hand in his and put his right arm around her waist. "Give me your other hand," he said.

She reached for his right and they stood shoulder to shoulder, moving in a complete circle. He let her go and she went blindly to the next movement, the next dancer. Her heart was in her throat.

Jane Austen was a genius. A pretty turn, some handsome men, and Caroline didn't even know where she was anymore.

The song ended with a long formation of handoffs, until finally Brooks and Caroline were face-to-face once more. The last notes sounded in the barn, and Brooks bowed, his expression inscrutable.

"That was amazing!" Debbie Mae grabbed Caroline's arm, excitement in every line of her face. "Isn't this fun? Aren't you having a great time?"

Caroline nodded, feeling as if she were coming back to herself after a long time with a good book. "I'm a little . . . thirsty." She wasn't, but maybe a cold drink would help shake the fog from her brain. It was a good fog, but she felt off-kilter.

"I'll get you something." Brooks strode off toward the punch table.

"Having fun?" Manning stood behind Debbie Mae, glancing over Caroline's outfit. "You look real nice."

"Thank you. And you're the second person in two minutes to ask me if I'm having fun. Of course I am! You should be worrying about Brooks."

Manning nodded, his lips quirking up. "I do worry about Brooks, believe me." He turned to his wife and winked. "I'll be right back."

He walked away and Caroline let out an exasperated sound. "Those two are downright difficult to figure out."

Debbie Mae took Caroline's arm and walked her toward the food table. "Ignore him. He's mad there are no hush puppies. You've got to try the flummery. It's perfect!"

Caroline tried not to grimace at the sight of the quivering towers of multicolored jelly. She bent down and peered at one. "Is that . . . a boiled egg in there?"

"Sure is! They suspended all sorts of things in the middle. There's sweet flummery and salty flummery, and if you're really lucky, you might get one that has olives and plums together. I've heard it's really tasty."

Caroline had a vision of the pickle-and-raisin casserole and fought back a laugh.

Dr. Stroud walked over to survey the food and glanced up at Caroline, twice, in a perfect double take. "Why, Miss Ashley, I didn't recognize you at all."

"I would say the same, except . . ." She motioned as if stroking a beard.

He chuckled. "I'm willing to dress up in something a bit older than Civil War attire, but I can't possibly shave, not with Mobile Bay coming up in a month."

"I promised Debbie Mae I would go with her to watch her husband, Manning. I've never been to Fort Morgan." Caroline looped her arm through Debbie Mae's and grinned.

"You'll have a fine time. Not as fine as dancing the night away with Mr. Darcy, of course." Dr. Stroud nodded toward a group of well-dressed men. "But we Civil War enthusiasts have our own charms."

"Like cannons, you mean." Caroline knew all about the charms of the Civil War enthusiast and she was pretty sure they couldn't hold a candle to an Austen dance party.

Dr. Stroud blinked at her for a moment, then threw his head back and laughed. "We'll win you over yet, my girl. Give us time." He bowed low. "I'm going to find my wife. Debbie Mae, if I don't catch Manning, pass on my thanks for inviting us. This is the first party we have both enjoyed. Perhaps this will be the beginning of a local tradition."

The two women pretended to curtsy and watched him walk away.

"All right, who do you think is the best Darcy here?" Debbie Mae looked around.

"What about that tall guy by the door? He's got that same expression."

They peered around the milling crowd at a man sporting a

sour face. His arms were crossed, boots planted a foot apart, top hat jammed firmly on his head. "Oh, definitely. But don't get any ideas. I don't think you're enough to tempt him into dancing."

Caroline snickered at the *Pride and Prejudice* reference.

"There you are," a low voice said on her left. She looked up to see Frank smiling down at her. He was perfectly dressed in Regency attire, although his tie was a bit crooked.

"It's wonderful to see you," she said, offering her hand the way a Regency lady might.

He bent low over it, eyes locked on hers. His lips touched her skin, and she waited for some kind of emotion to zap through her system. But nothing came, just the warm press of his lips on the back of her hand.

"Frank." The tone in Brooks's voice was enough to make Caroline snatch back her hand. He stood behind them, holding a cup of punch. His face showed tightly controlled anger. "How is Lauren?"

Frank glanced at Caroline and rolled his eyes, laughing. "Fine, I guess. She's around here somewhere."

"You guess? I figure you'd know better than that."

Caroline glared at Brooks, willing him to stop with the hints. He was mistaken about the kissing in the car, she was sure of it. Debbie Mae was looking from one to the other as if she weren't quite sure what the conversation was about.

Frank didn't respond for a moment. His smile faded and he seemed to take stock of Brooks. "I saw her on the way in. She looked spectacular."

"You mean—you met her around the back before the dance." Brooks stepped forward, putting the cup of punch on the table. "See, Frank, I walked my bike around the corner so it would be out of the way. I saw you two back there."

Caroline looked from one to the other, bile rising in her throat. Why would Frank pretend not to know Lauren? Why try so hard to be unimpressed with her beauty, her talent?

Frank shrugged. "So, we had a little momentary diversion. It's the summer air. The costumes. No one can resist a man in breeches, you know. I'm sure—"

Frank broke off abruptly as Brooks stepped forward, hands clenched. He looked for all the world as if he were going to take a swing. Caroline put a hand on his arm, alarm coursing through her.

"Get away from her. I don't want to see you talking to her again. Don't call her. Don't invite her to lunch. Don't touch her. Ever. Again." Brooks's voice was deep and calm. He was more angry than Caroline had ever before heard him.

"Okay, back off, buddy. I'm going." Frank turned on his heel and walked away.

Caroline could feel the tension pulsing through Brooks's arm. "Hey," she whispered.

He turned and seemed to see her for the first time. "Sorry about that. You know I can't stand a liar."

She nodded. Lying set him off. But this was more than losing respect for a man who fudged the truth. This was about Lauren. He had warned Frank away from Lauren in a way that was completely proprietary, like a man would who found a creep touching the woman he loved.

The music started up behind them and Brooks tried to smile. "Ready for another round?"

She shook her head. "It's just a bit warm in there. I think I'll sit down for a moment. You go ahead."

He glanced at her, then dropped his eyes. "I'm sorry you had to hear that."

"I'm surprised. I suppose I should have known, but I'm not always the most observant." She felt her stomach tighten into a knot and she lowered herself into a chair. She'd seen how he acted that day she'd mentioned Lauren, the day he'd said he was staying for the summer. It was obvious. To anyone but her.

"Brooks, you can't hide over here." Manning jogged over. "There are way too many women here for you to stand in the corner."

Brooks opened his mouth to say something, then seemed to think better of it. Seconds later he was moving across the dance floor, taking up a position directly across from Lauren.

Caroline swallowed back the ache in her throat. He'd been trying to tell her for so long and she hadn't wanted to know. She never wanted anything to change, but the world didn't work that way. Everything changed. Even the deepest of friendships.

It is not every man's fate to marry

the woman who loves him best.

—MR. KNIGHTLEY

CHAPTER TWENTY-ONE

Brooks watched Frank hover by the exit until the dance was over. Lauren had smiled politely through her and Brooks's turn as partners, but as soon as the last notes sounded, she made her way to the doorway by Frank, slipping out into the night. He followed, glancing behind him.

Brooks was glad he hadn't actually punched the guy. Nothing worse than a good party devolving into an all-out brawl. He tried to force down the fury, but every time he saw Frank bending over Caroline's hand, and putting his mouth to her skin, he wanted to hit the man. He should have told her alone, should have broken the news some other way than by announcing it in midconversation. But what he'd seen behind the barn was not a momentary indiscretion. It was two seasoned lovers taking their chance at reacquainting themselves with the pleasures they had already sampled. Hands had roamed places hands didn't roam on a first date.

He glanced at Caroline's face and his chest went tight. She looked crushed. Frank had promised many things, spoken and unspoken. Brooks guessed that the job offer was really the least of her attraction to Frank. The guy was handsome, smooth, and a lot more fun than a journalism professor.

The next dance went on for what seemed an eternity. He tried his best to keep her attention, but she didn't seem able to focus. Their eyes would meet; she would look pained, then glance away. He cursed Frank and his slimebag, cheating ways.

"I feel weird." Caroline blinked a few times. "Do you feel weird?"

Brooks shrugged. "How weird? We're all dressed like people in a Jane Austen book. I think weird comes with the territory."

"My head feels woozy. Maybe it's the heat." She stood up and fell against him. "Ugh. Sorry. I wonder if I ate something bad."

"What did you have?" He looked at the table of wobbling structures and hoped she didn't have food poisoning.

Debbie Mae came up and her eyes opened wide. "Have you been drinking?"

"Me? Not a drop!" Caroline protested, but her words were slurring together.

Brooks sucked in a breath. "Oh, boy. I think I know what happened." He searched the barn until he found Blanche. He jogged over. "Someone's been messing with the punch again."

She laughed. "A little. I don't see how you can have a party with virgin punch."

He groaned. "Grandma, we've got people driving. You can't just dump a liter of rum into the punch bowls."

"It was only one bowl. The other one is fine. Nobody's complaining." She waved a hand. "See? Everybody's having a great time."

Not bothering to respond, he went to find Jennie Purdy. He explained as best he could and she nodded. Grabbing the microphone, she called out for quiet. "We have a little bit of news. Looks like there was a misunderstandin' at the punch table. Looks as if one bowl has got some liquor in it. We don't want any of y'all to be in danger driving back to town. If you had the rum, we ask that you find a ride home." The sound of murmurs and laughter filled the hall. "If you're in doubt, you come on up here and I'll smell ya. I can usually smell it real clear when a person's been drinkin'." With that, she turned off the microphone and stood at the ready to offer her services to the guests.

Brooks went back to Caroline and held out a hand. "Keys, please."

"No argument from me." She plopped them in his hand. "But this doesn't mean I'm riding home on the back of that old bike."

He grinned. "No, I'm not that mean. I'll drive you back."

He hated the thought of leaving the Triumph leaning up against the barn, but Debbie Mae and Manning were already smelling each other's breath. "Come on, you guys, let's head home. We'll come back and get the cars in the morning."

Brooks dropped Debbie Mae and Manning at Badewood. "I'll take Caroline home and walk back from there." She didn't offer an opinion, still feeling as if her head were full of fuzz. It made perfect sense to her. But then, probably any kind of plan would make sense right then.

"Why don't you go out the back?" she asked, when they pulled up. He agreed, probably more to make sure she was actually going to be able to make the stairs to the front porch.

She felt clearer as she stepped into the night air. She had no problem getting the key in the lock, but she tried to be quiet anyway, just in case her mother was awake. The living room was dark except for the small stained-glass lamp glowing in the far corner. Caroline dropped her handbag on the low table. She'd never been so glad to be home, and all she wanted to do was sprawl out on the couch.

"I think that was the longest party on record."

Brooks closed the door softly, following her across the room, toward the kitchen back door. "It only felt that way. Heartbreak will do that to you."

"Heartbreak?" Caroline stopped where she was, midway to throwing herself onto the cushions, and shot him a look.

"Did you want some water? It'll help with the hangover tomorrow."

"Wait a minute. What heartbreak?" Caroline stepped into his way and put out a hand.

"Forget I said anything about it." He rubbed a hand over his face.

"I can't. You just implied someone had their heart broken and as far as I can tell"—she patted her chest as if she'd lost something—"mine is still intact."

"Well, I'm glad. I just assumed that you'd be feeling a tiny bit of pain and betrayal since you and Frank were so chummy this summer."

Caroline felt her jaw drop. "Chummy?"

"Just an impression; don't ask me to define the term exactly. I don't always know what's going on with you, anyway."

"I said we were friends. I told you we might be working together."

"That's all? Really?" His eyes were narrowed. "It sure didn't look that way when you were driving to Spartainville for lunch."

Caroline rolled her eyes. "For heaven's sake. I don't understand why you're being so jealous." It was about Lauren, of course, but she couldn't bring herself to say it.

"Right. And I still don't understand how Frank managed to weasel his way into everyone's good graces when he didn't have anything other than a handsome face and some flashy clothes." Brooks stepped closer, features half-revealed in the dim light. "But I can tell you one thing. If Frank hadn't suddenly decided there was a better place to be tonight, he and I were headed to no good end. He was all over you."

"All over me?" Caroline put her fists on her hips and tried to make sense of the conversation. "Did you get into the punch, too?"

"I've never been more sober." He stepped closer still. The air seemed to vibrate with tension.

Maybe Brooks wasn't angry about Lauren after all. The implications of that thought sent the world tilting under Caroline's feet. She swallowed hard. "He's a player. You were right. The first day we met him, you said he was a snake-oil salesman. It was all true. Are you happy?"

"No." He was near enough that she could feel a buffer of heat between them. His next words were so soft she strained to hear. "I'm not happy and I don't know what to do about it."

She shook her head, his words bumping up against her heart like ripples in a pond. "But why?"

He didn't answer. The next moment he'd reached out, slipping his hand behind her head and placing the softest kiss on her lips. For an infinite pulse of time neither of them moved. He leaned back and she met his eyes, stunned.

"Finley." His voice was rough. "Now is when you tell me to get on home."

Of course she should. It was late. They were tired. Rum punch had addled her brain. Something strange and incomprehensible was happening. The best thing would be to put a firm hand to his chest and get some space.

Instead she wrapped her arms around his neck and kissed him as if she were drowning, as if he were her lifeline in a stormy sea. He let out a sound that was part groan, part sigh. His tongue touched hers for a fraction of a second and her knees went weak.

Her head was spinning and she shifted, catching her heel on the edge of the carpet. Losing her balance, but not willing or able to let go, she brought them both tumbling down to the couch. For the barest moment, she hesitated, and then all thought was gone. Pulling him close, she matched him kiss for kiss, breath for breath. Her universe narrowed to the fire that was building in her, to the desperate need that made her grip his shoulders. The rough shadow of his beard rasped against her cheek, her chin, and she ran her hands up through his hair.

Brooks, she was kissing Brooks. Her *friend*. It made no sense, but nothing had ever felt so right. His hands skimmed up her rib cage, making her gasp. His weight should have felt like a burden, as if she were being crushed, but she welcomed it with an aching need. Time ceased to have meaning and all she knew was the heat they created, as if they'd been soaked with fuel and someone had tossed them a lit match.

He kissed a trail down her neck and she wanted to weep. The familiar scent of him, the warmth of his skin, was like a drug, and she was helpless to refuse, to push away.

"Finley," he whispered, and brought his lips back to hers with a gentleness that squeezed hot tears from her eyes.

"Caroline?" her mother's voice sounded down the stairwell.

They froze for just a moment. Brooks rolled off the couch onto his feet and tugged his jacket back over his shoulders. She didn't remember pulling it off. He glanced over at her and his eyes traveled down her gown, to the hem. He pulled it from where it had crept near her calves down to her ankles.

"Caroline, are you home?"

She swallowed, trying to find her voice. "Yes, Mama." It came out weak and shaking.

"Did you have a good time?" She didn't sound like she was coming any nearer.

Caroline sat up, a pulse pounding in her head. "Yes, I did. I'll be right up. I'm just going to get some . . . water."

"Okay." The sound came of her mother's slippers' shuffling down the hallway.

Brooks met Caroline's eyes and his face was a mixture of shock and dismay. "Caroline," he whispered, "I'm sorry. I didn't meant to—"

She shook her head. Of course he was sorry. She'd practically attacked him and thrown him on the couch. She held a finger to her lips and stood. Walking quietly through the house, she made her way in the dark to the back door. He was right behind her, footsteps echoing her own.

She opened it and stood aside. Her face was burning and she was glad it was dark in the kitchen.

"Finley, I just don't know what to say. I'm sorry—"

She squeezed her eyes shut, willing herself not to cry. If only he would quit apologizing. "Can we talk about this later? Maybe when the punch has worn off?"

He stood for a moment silently. Then he nodded, walking through the door. "I'll see you tomorrow."

She didn't bother to respond, only closed the door softly and leaned her head against the cool wood. Her life had just turned upside down. Or right side up. For the first time, she understood herself. What had happened had nothing to do with the punch and everything to do with her being absolutely and unequivocally in love with her best friend.

And he was in love with someone else.

If I loved you less,

I might be able to talk about it more.

—MR. KNIGHTLEY

CHAPTER TWENTY-TWO

Brooks slapped a hand against his desk, making the old wood creak. Absalom lifted his head, looking at him in surprise.

He'd known it. He'd felt it as soon as he'd laid eyes on the man. A simple Google search would have turned up a lot of interesting items. Franklin Keene embroiled in a dispute with a publisher over copyright. Franklin Keene denies file sharing without permissions from international publishers. Franklin Keene changing the name of his company again and again, changing states, cities and Internet sites.

It was all pretty solid evidence, but when Brooks added Lauren's name to the search, he sat back in his chair in shock. Frank and Lauren not only knew each other, they were business partners.

Brooks gritted his teeth. He'd been pretty sure when he'd overheard her at Marshall's that there was no contract for any kind of book. He searched *Publishers Weekly* and there was no deal naming Lauren Fairfield for a coffee-table book on Southern mansions. She had some projects, but most were from a year ago. When he searched her publisher, she wasn't on the list of editors anymore. . . . But why would she join forces with someone like Frank? What could make her risk her job and her friends for someone like that? There was something more, some link Brooks couldn't quite find.

He stared up at the ceiling and tried to lay it out, step by step. Lauren was telling the residents that she was working on a book on plantation homes so she could scope out antiques. Frank and Lauren were in a relationship, but pretending not to know each other. Marshall was following behind Lauren, conning confused older people out of their antiques. What did Frank have on Lauren? Something was missing, and Brooks wasn't going to get the truth until he confronted one of them.

The whole situation made him furious. Most of all, the idea that Frank had bothered to woo Caroline on the side was almost more than he could take. . . .

He took a deep breath, but he was no better. He had kept his feelings hidden when he should have spoken out. He had let Caroline assume that all he felt was friendship when he should have declared himself like a gentleman. Images of last night flashed through his mind. He should never have kissed her when she'd been drinking. She'd looked fine but her judgment wasn't clear.

He swallowed hard. Things like that happened when alcohol was involved. His feelings were true and he'd known exactly what he'd been doing when he let himself be pulled down on the couch, but she'd had a little too much of Grandma's punch. Apparently enough to make him seem like a pretty attractive man. She'd never touched him like that before. Sure, she'd been friendly, warm. Last night wasn't friendly. It was . . . He pushed his chair back. He couldn't sit here and go over and over it in his head. It was a torture, especially since he was fairly sure that she would regret ever having kissed him.

He paced the small room, willing himself not to look out the window, at the clump of trees that hid Caroline's house from view. Grandma was always going on about ferreting out God's will. But he didn't even know where to start looking.

All he knew, all he was sure of, was that he hadn't made the right move last night. It had hurt their friendship and had maybe hurt Caroline. A man knew what he had to do, what he should do.

Sitting up slowly, he looked at the Homer painting, thinking of loss and grief and what can't be changed. The only one thing to do was to talk it over like adults. He let out a long breath and headed out the door. *Lord, there's so much to lose. But whatever happens, don't let me hurt her any more than I have.*

Debbie Mae slipped the apron over her head. "Manning has been hankering for some biscuits."

"Manning is always hankering for biscuits. And hush puppies. And collard greens and boiled peanuts and fried okra," Caroline said. She wished that she hadn't made plans with Debbie Mae for the day after the dance. She hadn't slept a wink and was barely functioning.

"I know, but it's such a small thing and I love to make him happy. If I can, why not? Life is hard enough with all the things we can't have. . . ."

Caroline reached out a hand and touched Debbie Mae's shoulder. She didn't know what to say to make the hurt any less.

Debbie Mae looked up, and Caroline was surprised to see that her eyes weren't full of tears. She was smiling shyly. "I didn't want to say anything because we've been down this road so many times before. But a few months ago, my doctor tested my hormone levels. He thinks the miscarriages were related to low progesterone."

"And, if you took some . . ." Caroline couldn't help sharing the smile that spread on Debbie Mae's face.

"I already have been. For about two months. And we just decided"—by now her smile was so big she could hardly talk without laughing—"we're ready to try for a baby again."

"Oh, wow," Caroline breathed, and she hugged Debbie Mae tighter than she ever had before. "Wow." She knew she was repeating herself but couldn't think of anything better to say. The absolute bravery it must have taken, to hold on to the hope it might work this time—it made her heart stutter in awe.

"We must look crazy," Debbie Mae said, pulling back and wiping her eyes. "But I love him so much and he loves me and we just can't seem to let go of this dream of having a baby of our own."

"You don't look crazy at all. I understand."

"Maybe someday you'll be telling me the same thing, right in this kitchen." Debbie Mae grinned.

Caroline didn't mind Debbie Mae's teasing. It was more of a sweet wish than the usual old women's nagging at her at parties. "I never thought I would consider . . . not right now . . . but things have changed." Caroline couldn't deny it. Last night had shown her just how oblivious she had been of what was happening in her life.

Her cousin's eyes went wide. "Are you talking about Brooks?"

Caroline nodded.

Debbie Mae let out a whoop that echoed around the kitchen and grinned. "I knew it."

"What? How?" Caroline hadn't even known it would happen, so she wasn't sure how her cousin could have called it before the fact.

"Well, I can't take total credit. Manning said it about six months ago. I thought he was nuts, but then I started watching you two together. You just needed a little shove, a little nudge. And the Emma party did the trick!"

"Thanks for the shove but . . . it was weird."

"First kisses are weird, for sure." Debbie Mae pressed the biscuit cutter into the dough.

Caroline followed the movements, saying nothing as the heat rose to her face.

"What? That wasn't your first kiss with Brooks? Am I slow on the uptake here?" Debbie Mae paused, hands covered in flour.

"No, no, it was our first kiss." Caroline chewed her lip. She carefully deposited one floppy, raw disk onto the greased baking sheet. "But it wasn't one of those first kisses like you get at the end of the date, at the front door, under the porch light."

"No?" Debbie Mae scooted a few biscuits to the edge of the sheet and dusted the cutting board again.

"It was like our first and our hundredth kiss, at once." It was the only way Caroline could describe it, and even as she said the words, she knew it didn't make much sense.

Debbie Mae's expression was a mirror of the confusion Caroline felt. "What does that mean?"

Caroline swallowed and focused on the biscuits. Her face felt hot, and the more she tried to focus on the facts, the more she remembered that evening. His hands, his breath against her neck, the length of his body pressing her into the couch in a way that made her want to weep with desperate happiness.

"Wow, I don't think I've ever seen you quite that color."

Debbie Mae's tone was teasing but her eyes had gone wide. "Was it the punch? Are you trying to tell me that you two went past the first kiss and on into the land of no return?"

"No, not at all!" Caroline twisted the cutter into the dough a little more forcefully than she meant to. "I was stone-cold sober by then. It was just more than a kiss."

Debbie Mae hadn't moved, eyes still fixed on Caroline's face. "Like how much more?"

"Not as much as you're thinking." Another flabby biscuit joined its sisters on the sheet.

"Then why the blushing? You're freaking me out, here."

Caroline paused, rubbing her forehead with floury hands and not even caring. "I've had boyfriends before."

"Sure. There was that guy, David, who took you to every alien-invasion/slasher flick that ever came to the theaters. Oh, and then there was the guy who tried to jump the picket garden gate and landed right on his—"

"Right, I remember all of them." Ugh, maybe she hadn't dated the smartest guys on the planet. "But no matter how cute I thought they were, during that first kiss, my brain was still functioning. I was still thinking about how my hair looked or if I was going to be tired the next day because it was so late or if I'd picked up the mail."

"Brain function is always good." Debbie Mae plopped the last biscuit on the sheet.

"Boy, that's the truth." Caroline couldn't help the tone of her voice, bordering on downright regret. "With Brooks, it was like I'd been stun-gunned. But I was still conscious."

Debbie Mae's eyebrows had gone way up. "Awake but nobody home?"

"Well, maybe awake but somebody home with really, really bad judgment."

"Uh-oh." Debbie Mae took the sheet and slid it into the oven, setting the timer. "What has he said about it?"

"We haven't talked about it at all. Just sort of pretended like it didn't happen."

Debbie Mae whirled around. "He didn't call yet?" She folded her arms across her chest. She looked like an angry mama bear, ready to take on the man that had dared mess with her cousin.

"You can stop being angry right now because I don't expect anything from him. I'm not some wronged, young girl who's had her innocence taken from her." Caroline stared at the counter, trying to gather her thoughts. And there was the problem of Lauren. Caroline had gone over and over that scene and all she remembered was Brooks on the verge of hitting Frank. "I don't even know what to think, honestly."

Debbie Mae was quiet for a moment. "I suppose you're right. It's true that not every kiss is the same, and we can't hold anybody to the emotions of the moment." She took a breath, her blue eyes shadowed with concern. "This is what I know. Brooks is a good guy. He always has been. He's not going to be kissing you if he didn't mean it."

Caroline felt a weight begin to lift from her heart. "I know he is. Whatever happened, we both should take responsibility for it and act like adults."

"But at the same time . . ." Debbie Mae paused again, as if not wanting to speak the words. "At the same time, humans are complicated creatures with physical needs. As much as we think we have control over every action in our lives, there are moments where we act on our baser instincts."

Caroline nodded, the weight coming back to settle with a vengeance. Physical needs. It made sense, really. Two healthy adults could have a passing, momentary loss of sanity brought on by natural desires. "The thing that I keep coming back to is my own response. I mean, if some guy just grabbed me, I'd give him a righteous kick. But Brooks . . . I just . . ." She blinked and shook her head. She had flung herself into his arms, practically dragging him down onto the couch. A vague memory of her hands running up the long muscles of his back, under his suit coat, made her catch her breath. He'd been so warm, so solid. All she'd wanted to do was be as close to him as humanly possible.

Debbie Mae was grinning. "And I always thought you two were such intellectuals, living the cerebral life, with no temptation to distract you. Little did we know, you're all just as—"

"There you are." A deep voice cut into the conversation, and Caroline felt shock travel up her spine, all the way to the base of her skull. She knew who it was before she even turned around to see Brooks standing in the kitchen doorway, eyes shadowed with some unnamed emotion. He didn't look as if he'd slept well, but he was showered and shaved. A button-up shirt and khakis had replaced the Regency clothes, but when she looked at him, she still saw the tails and the cravat.

Her face went hot and she stared at the biscuits as if they held the words she needed to say so they could all go back to being comfortable around each other.

He gave Debbie Mae a hug and then shifted, as if not sure whether to cross the kitchen to Caroline.

"Hey," she choked out. "What are you up to?" She wanted to bite the words back. Obviously he was standing in her kitchen, visiting her.

He glanced at Debbie Mae, who began studiously scrubbing the biscuit dough from a bowl. "I thought maybe we could talk, if you had time."

"Sure." Caroline wiped her hands on her apron and gestured to the living room.

He followed behind her, silent except for his footfalls. She realized Absalom was at home and her stomach went tight. She'd feel so much better about this talk if Absalom were there to push his heavy body against her legs, like a shield against heartache.

They stood in the living room, facing each other but not meeting each other's eyes. He cleared his throat. "I'm sorry for last night."

She let out a breath. "I know." He'd already said that twice before.

"I should not have kissed you. I needed to tell you something far, far earlier than that moment." He straightened his shoulders. "When I saw Frank with Lauren, it made me crazy. I couldn't imagine how he could be flirting with you while he was in a relationship with her, even if it was secret."

She nodded, staring at the floor. He cared about Lauren, that had always been clear. "You sure told him where to get off that train."

His lips tugged up for a moment. "I was mad. Totally inappropriate timing, but I didn't want to see him—"

"I know." Touching her, kissing her, calling her. Lauren was a lucky girl. Caroline didn't want a caveman, but something about Brooks's standing over Frank and threatening him made her wish for a little bit of that, too. "He'll probably ignore you."

Brooks was silent for a moment, his eyes narrowed. "I need to tell you something I found out about Frank."

Caroline listened, shock filling her from head to toe. "I can't believe it."

"It's true. And Lauren is involved."

Caroline covered her mouth with her hand. How horrible for Brooks. He cared for Lauren and she was throwing it all away for that shyster Frank.

"I know you must be angry with me for—"

"I'm not. I'm really not." She couldn't bear that Brooks be in any more pain than he was already. She took a breath, willing herself to be strong. "I understand needs and urges. We're both adults. These things happen."

There was a pulse of silence. She looked up to see his eyes widen in disbelief. Sure, she was being pretty understanding, but she was partly to blame. Okay, maybe a lot to blame.

"I see." His voice had gone tight and hard.

"We both probably should just move on." Her throat closed over the words. She didn't want to move on, she wanted to step forward and let him hold her again. She wanted to feel his mouth on her and the weight of him against her and the heat of his hands. She blinked back hot tears. God give her strength, she was going against every fiber of her being. She fought for control, swallowing back the ache in her throat. "Let's not make this harder than it has to be."

Those words were like flicking a switch inside him. He nodded, eyes impossibly sad. "You're a good friend, Caroline."

She nodded, not trusting herself to speak. She wanted so much more than friendship. But that wasn't her right and she wouldn't make him feel guilty for something they both had done.

"Are you coming in for lunch? We have a chicken roasting and the biscuits should be almost ready." Her voice shook but she held her chin high.

"No, no." He patted his stomach. "I'm . . . okay. Still full from breakfast." He glanced at the door and her heart squeezed in her chest. He was desperate to get away, now that they'd had their "talk."

"Okay, well, see you later. You're coming to Mobile Bay, right?"

He turned, frowning. "Mobile Bay?"

"Debbie Mae has roped me into going down to Alabama with them for the reenactment. She said you and Manning would be at Fort Morgan."

He nodded slowly, brows drawn together. "I'll be there."

"Then . . . See you in a couple weeks." She almost flinched. She was trying to give him space, freedom. But all she felt was a vicious ache in her chest.

"Right." He turned to the door, giving her one last glance, then he was gone.

Caroline sank onto the couch and let hot tears flow down her cheeks. She didn't bother to wipe them away or calm herself. Her heart was breaking and it was the worst pain she'd ever experienced in her life.

It was over and nothing could be done to fix it. The image of Lauren flashed through her mind. Of course he'd fight for her. Of course she'd forget Frank and learn to love Brooks. As much as Caroline wished otherwise, she couldn't imagine Lauren doing anything else.

It had been a horrible week. Caroline had gotten two rejections on articles she'd submitted, no calls on her recent job applications, and Lexi *still* hadn't managed to catalog all her art even though the website had been up and running since last Thursday. Hovering over and humming under all of these things was the knowledge that Brooks was gone. Not physically, since he lived just a mile away, but emotionally. Her best friend, who had turned into so much more, was gone. She felt empty, hollow, grieving. Numbness would be a blessing because at night Caroline could have sworn it hurt just to keep breathing. It had been a miserable, wretched, never-ending week and now it sounded as if it was going to get a lot worse. Caroline, shaking her head, at a loss for words, stood before her mama as she sat on a stool in the bright yellow kitchen, It wasn't enough that Caroline was dealing with a broken heart and the implosion of her deepest friendship. Now her mama was talking about inviting Marshall back into the house.

"He's coming over this afternoon? Hasn't he done enough damage here? There's hardly anything left for him to steal." Caroline was so angry her voice came out choked and shaking.

"Steal? That man has done me a favor by taking a lot of this old stuff off my hands. Don't worry about your inheritance. There are plenty of leftover knickknacks to go around. I don't see why anyone should tell me what to do with my things." Her mother shrugged and stared off into the corner of the kitchen, as if she were too tired to talk about it any longer.

Caroline felt the fury rise up faster than she could track it, faster than she could gain a hold on it, and it burst from her in a torrent of angry words. "I'm not worried about my inheritance. I'm not concerned about whether there will be any antiques to put on a shelf in my kitchen." She hesitated, seeing her mother's frown. "And I don't mean your kitchen. I mean the kitchen I'll have when I leave here. I'm not living here forever."

Her mama waved a hand. "I think we had this conversation several times already. Once when you were twelve. You've always been telling me about the home you'll make far away from here."

Was she? Caroline grimaced at the double-sided insult. That she never did what she said she'd do, and that she sounded like a petulant teen. "I'm trying to say I don't care what you do with your family's antiques. I'm not laying claim to them." Even though those same antiques were from her ancestors, Caroline didn't argue the point. "What I'm saying is that when you give this stuff away, I feel like I'm losing Daddy all over again."

Caroline paused to regain control of her voice. She didn't expect her mother to understand. She'd already mocked how Caroline's daddy had loved the antique silver, saying it shouldn't have been important to him since he'd married into the history of it all.

Something in her mama's expression stole the next words out of Caroline's mouth. Her mama's eyes were filled with tears, but she looked angry, so angry. "Caroline, it may hurt you a little bit to not see the silverware here, but it kills me to use it. Every item he loved, every piece of my family's history that he cleaned and stored, kills me. Everywhere I look, I see your daddy teaching me things I didn't know about my own history. I grew up with it all. I liked it because it was mine. But I didn't really appreciate it. He changed that."

Her mama stood up, fists clenched. "The first time I brought him home to visit, he picked up a piece of crockery and explained how he knew it was stoneware from Maryland. History was his hobby, and the very first thing that brought us together. Can you imagine what's it like to live here, without him, after being together for thirty years? Can you even understand what it feels like to walk into any room in this house?" She pointed to an old tin lamp high on a shelf. "I remember him holding that out and showing me how the little windows were made from shaved sheep's horn. And that windup toy baker that stirs the little bowl? He loved it more than you ever did when you were a baby, and I can't look at it." She pointed out one item after another. "He loved that cupboard because it has a barrel for a back, but the pie safe was his favorite. He taught me how they punched the tin in those patterns, holding them up against the light to make sure the holes were clear. . . ." Her voice was lost in sobs. She hauled in a breath, tears streaming down her face.

Caroline stood frozen, her own eyes filling with hot tears. She had thought her mama was selling the antiques because she was too drunk to see the memories attached. But her mama had more memories of Caroline's daddy than she did, and they were deeply entwined in every item in that house. The grief that had swallowed her whole was not the grief that comes from not having anything else to do. A part-time job wouldn't have kept her mama from loving her daddy as much as she did or saved her from the moment he died. Her grief came from being surrounded, day after day, by thousands of reminders of the person she loved the most, but couldn't touch ever again. Caroline had wanted to keep it all so the memories of her daddy wouldn't fade. But it was her mama's worst torture.

Caroline moved forward, folding her mama in her arms. Caroline knew that even if she retrieved ever single item Marshall had stolen, it wouldn't change the past. Everyone grieved in his or her own way, people said. Caroline and her mama were living proof. Caroline didn't know what to do, but she knew that refilling her home with all the old treasures and forcing her mama to face all those happy memories again was not the answer.

Her mama's thin shoulders shook with sobs and Caroline cried with her. Cried for the person they both had lost, the compass of their family, the laughing man who taught them so much. And she cried for the kind of love that lasted a lifetime, whether it made you happy anymore or not. She knew what that was like because she loved Brooks that way, even though there was no chance of his wanting her. It made her miserable, and she loved him anyway.

Caroline lay flat on her back, staring up at her bedroom ceiling. She should be working. She should be researching, writing and scouring the job sites for any openings. But she was drained, emotionally spent and absolutely uninspired. What did it matter if she left this area or not? Everything she wanted was here.

Her cell phone trilled and she reached for it without thinking. Her heart was pounding before she even registered the unknown number on the display. Not Brooks. Of course it wasn't. Hating how quickly hope sprang up in her—hope that he might call and everything would be okay again—Caroline touched the screen.

"Hello," she said, not bothering to hide the flatness in her tone.

"Caroline Ashley? This is Lewis Browning, of the *Washington Post*."

She popped to a sitting position. She had reapplied for her old job, but the managing editor of her former department said that they didn't have any openings. Caroline knew you didn't walk away from that kind of job, then turn around and ask for it back. It had been a few years, but newspaper editors had long memories. She searched her memory for anything about Lewis. He'd been her boss's boss. Maybe even higher, she couldn't quite remember. "Hi, Mr. Browning. Good to hear from you again."

"Call me Lewis," he said, sounding just as Caroline remembered. Cheery and a bit distracted, as if he were working while they talked. "We weren't able to fit you into the politics and policies area, but I was wondering if you'd be interested in doing something different."

"I'd certainly like to hear more." Something different. She quickly wondered how low she would go to regain a position there. In truth, she would go pretty low. Not mail-room low, but definitely local-entertainment-section low.

"Things have changed since you were here last. We've started expanding into local news areas."

Caroline closed her eyes. She would be writing up small pieces on the local charity drives for canned food and donated toys at Christmas, probably be calling spokespersons to get an official statement when they didn't send one out. A desk job, probably working from home a few hours a week. She made another internal check, and she was still pretty okay with that. The only thing she didn't quite understand was why Lewis Browning was making the call. Maybe he'd been demoted.

He went on, "The world is getting smaller, as they say. People love a human interest story even more than they did five years ago. We want to cheer for people, sometimes in small towns, doing important things." He paused, but Caroline just waited. "I was wondering if you would be interested in being our Southern correspondent for these types of stories. There might be quite a bit of travel, sometimes several weeks a month, but you could be based where you are now."

Caroline opened her eyes. "Wait, these stories . . . Are they like the schoolkids having a bake sale to replace their play equipment? That sort of thing?"

Lewis laughed, a sharp bark in her ear. "No, not that. I mean the stories that go viral and capture the imagination of the country. We've been building a team of journalists who manage certain areas, but work for the *Post*. When a story like that hits, we send them out first."

"Isn't that how it usually works?"

"Yes and no. We had people flying all over the country. My idea was to have a team in place, in every region. It's worked really well. Most of the time, they hear the story before I do. They get better quotes and are accepted so much easier because they're a little more local."

"So, sort of the way foreign reporters work overseas."

"Exactly. And this way, everybody's a little happier. Not as much travel for our DC folks who don't want to, and I get the very best reporters in every region on my team. This isn't a part-time job, though. There's a lot to go around. I don't want to make it sound like a hassle, but I also want to be honest. It's a big-time commitment. So what do you think?"

Caroline could have hesitated, told him she needed a few days to think, but she knew, at that moment, this job was an answer to her prayer. Her mother wasn't well enough to be alone full–time, and Caroline cringed at the idea of jumping back into a city the size of DC when she'd become so happy in Thorny Hollow. And even though she couldn't have Brooks—as a friend or as something more—she didn't want to move too far away from this place. She needed to be close to him, even if she couldn't be with him.

"I think it's perfect." She could hear the smile in her own voice. "When do I start?"

"Excellent." Another sharp laugh. "Human resources will get ahold of you. And, Caroline?"

"Yes?" She couldn't stop grinning.

"Welcome back."

Where the wound had been given,

there must the cure be found, if anywhere.

—EMMA

CHAPTER TWENTY-THREE

Caroline parked in the gravel area beside Gas n Go and shut off the car. She sat, staring out the window at the squat, cement-block building and watching the Hispanic man pumping gas into an old Ford pickup. The building was painted a garish Pepto-Bismol pink, and the faded sign attached to the flat roof was leaning to one side. Lexi Martinez's father wore grease-stained coveralls and a tattered ball cap as he moved from the truck to a small sports car. He smiled and shared a few words with the driver and scrubbed at the windshield with a squeegee he dipped into a dirty blue bucket. Caroline could feel the summer heat leaking into her car even though the air-conditioning had been off for mere minutes. She couldn't imagine how it felt to wear heavy coveralls and stand on the blacktop in work boots for hours every day.

Mr. Martinez looked up and caught sight of her. He nodded once and turned back to finish with his current customer. A woman with a bright blond beehive hairdo handed him a check and he tipped the brim of his baseball cap as she put the car in gear. Caroline opened her door and angled out. She shouldn't be nervous. She was here to advocate for Lexi and her art. This man had no authority over her. But Caroline knew that Mr. Martinez worked harder in one day than she had most of her entire life, and as a father, he had a say over his child's future.

"Miss Ashley, I'm glad you made it." His voice was an odd mix of Southern drawl and traces of a Spanish accent. "Come on in and sit down for a moment."

Caroline followed him inside, feeling her light blue T-shirt start to stick to her back. Inside wasn't any cooler, but a large oscillating fan moved the damp air from one end of the tiny room to the other. Mr. Martinez went behind the counter and sat on a stool. He motioned to the one across from him and Caroline sat. He brought out two Cokes from a small fridge and set one in front of her. She wrapped her hands around it, glad for the cold.

"I want you to know, before we start, that I respect your job very much." Caroline shifted on the stool. She felt uncomfortable here, in this tiny, sweltering space, and it wasn't just the heat. He was a workingman who could only dream of the financial security she had.

His brows went up. "Do you now?"

"Well, yes." Caroline swallowed.

"Then you're a fool, Miss Ashley. There's nothing great about this job. I wouldn't wish it on anybody. But it's what I have and it's kept Alexis in school."

She grimaced. "Okay, I don't think I said that very well. I meant that your job isn't any worse or any better than any other."

He leaned across the counter, brown eyes sharp. "Are you crazy? Do you want to take a day out there in the heat, pumping gas for your friends? Maybe they're stopping by on their way out to their place on the river, or maybe they're heading down to Biloxi for a week at the beach. You get to fill up their car and hear about their plans, then you hurry on to the next car and try not to think about how you haven't had no vacation in years."

She paused. She could see Lexi out there, year after year, summer after summer. She didn't want that for her any more than Lexi's dad did. "Can we start over? I shouldn't have said that."

He leaned back and took a long drink from his Coke. "Sure, we can start over."

"I called you because I wanted to see if we could reach some kind of understanding about Lexi's future. I know she'll be the first person in your family to go to college, but I think it's a mistake to put all that pressure on her." Caroline glanced up, then rushed on. "Lexi has an amazing gift. I don't want her to give up everything to study accounting, just because it's respectable or it's the safe option."

He nodded slowly. "I hear you. But you've got it all wrong."

Caroline looked down at her Coke, willing herself to stay quiet. She knew he was going to talk about how a good job would give Lexi the security she needed so she could get ahead in the world.

"You've got it wrong because this place is the safe option." He waved a hand around the tiny gas station. His nails were dark with accumulated grease. "She's got a home here. A little room in the back, a steady job, her friends nearby, everybody knows her. This place is the easiest place for her to be, and she's being the brave girl I raised her to be when she packs that suitcase and gets out of town."

It felt as if the air were knocked from Caroline's lungs in one big whoosh. To think that this awful little place was where Lexi felt most at home, most loved, most secure. Caroline looked around with new eyes. How did a girl such as Lexi, raised by a single dad who ran a gas station in a tiny town, have the courage even to apply for college?

He went on, "I've been telling her since she was just a little girl that she could do anything. I worked every day except Sunday and saved every penny. It wasn't near enough, but then she got that scholarship, and she was going to have her chance to live a better life than this. She was scared, but I told her every night, when we said our prayers before bed, that she was made for great things."

Caroline stared at her hands, her eyes filling with tears. She'd been coming at this situation from the wrong direction. Just as Brooks had said, she was thinking of Lexi as if she were raised in a nice house, with everything she ever needed, with people who had been to college and expected her to do the same. It wasn't the same, not nearly the same, as a girl who was going to be the first in her whole family to get a degree.

"Mr. Martinez, I hope you know I was only trying to help." Caroline cleared her throat. "I thought she was taking the easy way out because she didn't have enough confidence." She shrugged, knowing how silly it sounded now.

He pushed up the bill of his cap and wiped his forehead. "You seem like real nice folks, but Lexi was all set to go before she met you at that party. Then she started making noises about putting it off for a year, spending some time painting."

Caroline repressed a groan. As Brooks said, if Lexi didn't go now, she might never get another chance. "Let me talk to her again, Mr. Martinez. I see where you're coming from now." She glanced around. She saw where they were both coming from.

"I'd appreciate that." He looked out the window at a dusty van that was pulling up beside a pump. "And I'd better get back to work. Lexi's over at the senior center today, helping Mr. Anderson with a special class, but she'll be back in a few hours."

"Maybe I'll go try and catch her there." Caroline stood up. "Thank you for . . ." She didn't know what to say. For not being angry at how she'd interfered? For not telling her how painfully misguided her advice had been?

He nodded and pulled his cap lower over his eyes. "Alexis is a special girl. We *all* want her to be happy." With that he walked out the door, into the hot sun, the tinkling of the brass bell over the door like punctuation to his sentence.

Brooks had been right. Caroline put a hand to her chest, as if to ward off the pain to her heart. Even thinking his name was hard to do. He had tried to tell her, tried to explain that she was seeing Lexi's situation through the lens of her own too-brief career. She straightened her shoulders. She'd been wrong, but she didn't have to leave it that way. She'd go over and see if Lexi could be convinced to give college another shot. It was too late to go back and change the mistakes she'd made with Brooks, but she might still have a chance to fix the mess she'd made with Lexi.

Caroline parked at the corner and walked toward the senior center. The air was muggy and hot, and she could feel her hair frizzing around her face. Out of the corner of her eye, she caught a flash of dark hair, a tall, slim figure exiting a little coffeehouse on Main Street, and knew exactly who it was. She stopped midstep and stared as Lauren came down the sidewalk, her gaze fixed somewhere above and behind Caroline. Lauren was only feet away when she noticed Caroline for the first time. The emotions that flitted across her face spoke volumes.

Lauren slowed, then stopped. "Well, hello, Caroline." Her voice was wary.

"Hi." Caroline wasn't sure what she was going to say. She'd gone over this moment many times in the past month, and now that it was here, she still didn't quite know how to say what was in her heart. All Lauren's lies had come undone, and Caroline was no closer to the truth of it than when they'd first met, back at the Werlins' party. It seemed ages ago. Back when she and Brooks were still friends, back before she'd realized what he meant to her, back before their friendship had been broken into pieces, along with her heart.

Lauren brushed back her dark hair and smiled brightly. "It was thrilling to hear you'd gone back to journalism. At least, that's the rumor."

News of Caroline's new job had made it through the grapevine, it seemed. "I'll be working from home and traveling around the area. I'm relieved I don't have to move back to DC."

Lauren's gaze darted at a passing car. "Right. Well, I'm much more at home in New York City than I am down here in this little place. I'm scouting out a lot of new possibilities myself, right now."

Caroline said nothing. Lauren was scouting out new jobs since she'd been fired the minute her bosses had learned that she'd been stringing along a whole lot of people, making promises she couldn't keep, all in the name of a reputable company. "Well, great news and congratulations." Lauren was easing herself away, as if to keep walking, when Caroline put out a hand.

"Can you answer me one thing?" Caroline had to know. She might not ever get another chance to ask her.

Lauren's eyes went wide. She looked as if she wanted to run. "Depends on what it is. I'm sure you . . . understand what happened. I don't need to give all the details."

"I don't," Caroline protested, "I really don't. How can a woman who has everything, a woman as beautiful and smart and ambitious as you, end up involved in a scam like that?"

Lauren's cheeks went pink and she lifted her chin. "It didn't start out like that. I didn't know what was going on at first."

"And when you figured it out?" Caroline couldn't believe the whole idea of a fake coffee-table book just came out of nowhere.

"You don't understand."

"That's what I'm telling you. I don't understand and I want to, Lauren." This was the woman that Brooks was in love with, the woman he was pining for, and if there was any way to figure out why she had lied to so many people, maybe Caroline could learn to live with it.

Lauren dropped her gaze to the pavement, and for the first time Caroline saw how young she was. She looked so tired. "I love him."

"Who?" Even saying the word was painful. Caroline didn't know if she could handle hearing Lauren talk about Brooks.

"Frank. I've loved him since we met in college. He was always a little dangerous." Lauren glanced up. "I mean, he always had plans that sort of skirted the edge of the rules. And I loved that about him. He was smart and knew how to get people to do what he wanted."

"So, he came up with the plan?"

She nodded. "Right. And I thought that his uncle would take all the information and use it to contact them, asking if they wanted to sell."

"His uncle . . . Marshall?" Of course, there had to be a reason a guy such as Frank would work with a creepy geezer like that.

"But Marshall was visiting to check if they were too old to know if their stuff went missing. He'd fast-talk the men and sort of romance the women." Lauren sighed. "I hope your mom wasn't too hurt. I don't know what women found in him that was so attractive. But then, I don't have the best taste, either. Frank dumped me as soon as we got found out."

Caroline was thankful her mother had never fallen for any of Marshall's "romance." "I'm sorry. And my mama is okay. She's taking a cruise right now. Getting out of the house will be good for her." Her mama was also thinking of moving to a condominium in town just to give herself a break from the memories in that old house.

Caroline took a breath and tried to seem at ease. "She's taking that cruise with Blanche Elliot, Brooks's grandma."

Lauren nodded. Nothing changed in her expression. No interest or concern. Caroline couldn't believe that Brooks's offering his heart to Lauren had made that little of an impression. "I hope she has a good time. And I'm sorry. For what it's worth." Lauren put her hand over Caroline's, tentatively, as if unsure whether Caroline would shake it off.

"Thank you. Brooks helped me get a lot of it back. But some things were sold before we could retrieve them." Sadness rose up in Caroline's throat. Not for the antiques, but at the memory of the awkwardness that had passed between them when Brooks had come. Their easy friendship was gone, and in its place was something she didn't even recognize.

"I should go." Lauren stepped away, straightening her shoulders. "I'm just here to pick up a few things from my aunt's house and then I'm headed back to the city."

"Take care of yourself." Caroline couldn't think of anything else to say. She watched Lauren walk down the sidewalk and sighed. Caroline knew what it was like to have a broken heart. What a mess it was, with three people who loved someone they couldn't have. Frank was the only one who had come out of it with his heart in one piece. Sometimes, the world just didn't seem fair.

"But . . . I don't understand." Lexi's dark brown eyes were wide. She stood stock-still, her hands full of wet paintbrushes. A stained painting smock hung about her neck, and her glossy dark hair was swept up in a careless ponytail. The senior center was still filled with the remnants of Mr. Anderson's painting class.

"I'm sorry. I was wrong." Caroline stated it as plainly as she could. She reached out and took the paintbrushes from Lexi's hands and dried them on a paper towel. "I thought it would be awful to give up your painting to study accounting. But you manage to paint on the side now, while you work at the gas station, and before, when you went to high school. It wouldn't be any different if you painted in your free time at Ole Miss."

Lexi grabbed another pile of brushes and held them under the tap. "I suppose. But I was really getting into the idea of staying at home. I like it here. A lot of my friends are staying here, too. My friend Joan is taking a few classes online. I thought maybe I'd do that, too."

"I suppose if someone has to, online courses can be a blessing, but it could take you forever to get a degree that way. And you'd miss out on all the experiences of living in a dorm and meeting new people."

Lexi laughed, shaking her head. "I'm fine with my friends. Why would I want to make more? I'm not one of those people that think you need a thousand Facebook friends."

Caroline set some brushes in the canister to dry. "I'm talking about real friends. Friends that last a lifetime. Friends that come to your wedding and celebrate the birth of your kids and visit you in the summer when everyone is out of school." She took a deep breath. "Just think about it. You have a while before summer is over. You were accepted, and as far as the college knows, you're still going. So, just take some time and think about it."

Lexi nodded. "Okay. That website is really hard to figure out anyway. Maybe if I brought my art supplies when I went to Ole Miss, I could find a group down there. We could sell our stuff on the weekends at the farmers' market or something."

"Exactly. And you could be building both your careers. You know"—Caroline hesitated, cautious not to plant any more ideas—"if you have a degree in accounting, that could really help you when you run your own business. If you own a gallery or teach painting, or sell your own work, you wouldn't have to hire anyone else to keep your records."

"Good point." Lexi beamed at her and handed over a new batch of brushes. "Do you want to come back to my house for lunch? I cooked some really great chicken potpie yesterday and it's even better the next day." Lexi smiled brightly.

"Thank you, but I better get back home." Caroline wiped off the brushes with a paper towel and stowed them in the container, hiding the relief that flooded through her. Maybe she hadn't destroyed Lexi's future after all. Maybe everything would work out in the end.

Well, everything except . . . Brooks's face rose unbidden in her mind. There was no chance that everything was going to work out between them. Even if that punch-fueled kiss hadn't happened, he was in love with Lauren, who was in love with Frank, who was running a countywide scam.

Caroline fought back a groan. This mess couldn't be sorted out with a conversation, no matter how her heart ached for it to be true. In a few weeks she'd be in one of the most beautiful places in the country and would probably be face-to-face with Brooks for the first time since the day after the party. She had no idea how she was going to pretend everything was all right. She hardly slept, had no appetite, and felt as if she had no reason to keep on living. It was so ironic. She'd thought if her mother had kept a job during her marriage, it would have kept her safe from an emotional breakdown.

But yet again, Brooks had been right. If you loved someone the way he or she was meant to be loved, loved the person all the way without reservation, then no day job would save you. It was ridiculous to even wish that it could.

Mr. Knightley, if I have not spoken, it is because I am afraid I will awaken myself from this dream.

—EMMA

Chapter Twenty-Four

The sparkling blue water spread before her like a glass quilt, rippling and shimmering. Caroline let out a long sigh and lifted her face to the warm sun. There wasn't a more beautiful spot in the world, she was sure of it. Crossing Mobile Bay on a slow-moving steamboat, cold iced tea in her hand, was about as good as it got. And she couldn't enjoy a moment of it. The reproductions of ironclad Civil War ships sailed lazily in the distance. A few smaller ships were gathering near the shore, but most were taking up their positions in the bay. In an hour or two, the battle reenactment would begin, and Caroline would be wearing a heavy dress and plugging her ears. Brooks would be somewhere in the group of soldiers. Caroline simultaneously dreaded and yearned to see him. She missed him so much it was as if she carried a physical wound. She let out a long sigh.

"Still moping? You need to get some guts, girl." Debbie Mae adjusted the strap on her sundress and squinted across the bay. Manning was already on the mainland, gathering with the other men who would defend the besieged fort against the attacking Union forces. In one of the most decisive battles of the war, the death toll was small, but once the bay was sealed, the Southern cities were at a terrible disadvantage. Caroline thought she knew just how the soldiers felt as they surrendered under heavy cannon fire.

"How does one go about procuring guts, Debbie Mae?" Caroline knew she was being irritable but it wasn't a question of getting guts. It was about Brooks's being in love with another woman. It wasn't an attraction she understood, but she knew love didn't follow the rules. She'd learned that lesson well.

"Just tell him how you feel. Manning says Brooks has been wandering around like some kind of resident ghost from the war, never speaking, hardly eating."

"It wouldn't matter if I told him how I feel because it's not about me. I know what I heard and I know what I saw. He's attracted to Lauren in a way that he's not attracted to me." Caroline sat up on the lounge chair, not wanting to talk about her broken heart anymore.

Debbie Mae snorted softly. "He was attracted enough to you to get a little kissing done."

"Yeah, that happened once in ten years and was preceded by some spiked punch, so I think I'm right." Caroline rubbed her eyes. "What are we doing when we get there?"

"Dr. Stroud has some costumes for us. I think we're local women." Debbie Mae leaned over, lowering her voice. "I'm not real sure there were women at that fort, but I won't complain. I love watching the ships and hearing the cannons."

Caroline smiled. "You're sounding just like the boys, now."

"A bona fide diehard," Debbie Mae agreed, nodding. "How's your friend Lexi? Did she ever get her business up and running?"

Caroline shook her head. "It just wasn't working. We both tried really hard but it was more than I knew how to do. I talked to her dad and he made me realize that for Lexi, leaving Thorny Hollow was a very brave thing to do. She's not taking the easy route." Caroline looked up into the bright white-blue sky. She'd been so arrogant to think so. "The good news is that she'll be taking her art supplies to school. She won't give up on her gift just because she has to split time between her studies and her art."

"And the bad news?"

"The bad news is that she's still determined to study accounting." Caroline grinned. "But, hey, the world needs accountants, right?"

"It sure does. Especially artist accountants." Debbie Mae leaned back in her chair. "I guess Brooks was right."

"Thanks for bringing it up, but, yes. Brooks was right." It hurt to even say his name. Caroline felt a lump lodge in her throat and she blinked hard. Maybe in another year or so, she could talk about him and not feel as if her world were falling to pieces. . . . She could always hope.

An hour later they docked and walked down the log pier to the fort. The enormous star-shaped, stone structure stretched across the horizon, blocking the view of the green surrounding countryside. Four stories tall, with tiny gaps in the masonry for windows, it had a grass-covered rooftop that blended into the hills beyond. The main entrance was crowded with visitors. Caroline hoped that inside the building, out of the sun, it would be cool. She wouldn't dare hope the almost-two-hundred-year-old structure had any air-conditioning anywhere. It had been used in four wars, and it showed. Most of the fort was closed to visitors, due to cracks in the walls and general disrepair, but men milled around, holding muskets and wiping sweat from under their hats.

"There's a ceremony to commemorate the bricklayers at two in the afternoon." Debbie Mae was looking at the schedule as they walked down the crowded path. "Most of them were enslaved African-Americans, and they've got some descendants on hand to reveal the new area of the living-history museum that talks about it."

"Okay, but I think Dr. Stroud said to head through the sally port to pick up our costumes. We should do that before we get sidetracked." Caroline wasn't looking forward to putting on a heavy dress in this heat. They headed through the arched tunnel to the main courtyard. Children chased each other around on the grass, and tourists snapped photos of each other against the stone walls. Caroline couldn't help searching for Brooks and within seconds had spotted him. His back was to her, but she knew the slope of his shoulders, the angle of his jaw.

He turned as if he felt her gaze and his eyes widened just a bit. She lifted her hand in a mute greeting. He smoothed the front of his jacket and nodded to her, then turned back to the group. She swallowed back the disappointment. Of course, he was playing a role. He wasn't going to break ranks and rush to greet her.

"Miss Caroline! Miss Debbie Mae!" Dr. Stroud stood before them in full Confederate costume, his white mustache looking particularly bushy. "Come on inside and I'll have you outfitted to match the group."

"With a musket and pair of hobnail boots?" Debbie Mae giggled. "I tried Manning's and thought they were the most uncomfortable shoes I ever put on my feet."

"That's because they're not made for left and right. Just for a foot. Saved on shoes, when you think of it. No need to search for a lost right boot when you can grab any boot."

Caroline nodded. It made sense. She looked down at her strappy, blue sandals and was glad she was a modern woman.

They were led into a room where several dresses hung. "How do they know these will fit?" Caroline eyed the yards and yards of material. The Regency dress had been sewn to her exact measurements.

"I think everything is fairly big, and then they bring out the corsets." Debbie Mae wrinkled her nose. "As if it's not hot enough out there."

They helped each other change, lacing up the back of the corsets and gathering their hair into tight buns. When they were satisfied, they emerged into the main area of the fort. The battle had already started and the boom of the ship cannons could be heard in the distance. A man called out the movements of the battle, and people stood with binoculars at the edge of the railing.

"Shelby!" Caroline saw her old friend and called out without thinking. She clapped a hand over her mouth and hoped she hadn't ruined the entire scene. A professor of Civil War history teaching at Millsaps, Shelby was a regular on the reenactment circuit, especially now that she was married to Ransom Fielding, the famous historian. Enemies turned friends turned so much more, those two were more in love than anyone Caroline had ever seen. They'd had a rough start, but now the first year of their marriage looked as if it was definitely agreeing with Shelby.

Gorgeous auburn hair and hazel eyes were all Shelby, but the outfit was not. She was head-to-toe Civil War womanhood. She grabbed Caroline and squeezed the breath out of her. "Look at you! How did you get sucked into all of this craziness?"

"Watch it." Ransom stood a bit behind Shelby, darkly handsome and with a grin that made Caroline feel as if they could be instant friends. "We're called historians, technically."

"Are you staying long? We can have dinner." Shelby patted her pockets. "Shoot. I had to surrender all my technology."

Ransom handed over a small notebook and a pencil that looked as if it had been sharpened with a pocketknife.

"Thanks, sweetie." Shelby stood on her tiptoes and gave him a kiss. He reached out and snagged the notebook and pencil back.

"What now? No pencils allowed?" Shelby put her fists on her hips and looked dangerously irritated.

"No, I just liked that reward and thought we should repeat the process." He held out the notebook and pencil. She giggled and took it, planting another, louder, kiss on his mouth.

Caroline rolled her eyes. "Sickeningly cute."

She and Shelby exchanged information, and the next moment Caroline felt a touch at her elbow. She turned, sucking in a sharp breath. Brooks stood there as tall and as handsome as she remembered him. It had been only a month, but she missed him so much that tears sprang to her eyes. She glanced out at the bay, feeling her cheeks go hot. *Get a grip, he's trying to say hi. Nothing more, nothing less.*

"Captain Owen Hartford, at your service." He tipped his hat.

Oh, so it was going to be like this, was it? She searched her memory for a good name. "Patience Corntower. Of Thorny Hollow way."

His grin went wide. "We are well acquainted. You may not recollect me."

"But I do, sir. Quite clearly."

Something flickered in his gaze. "Would the miss be available for a short walk on the pier?"

"In the middle of a battle?" Her eyes went wide and she tried not to laugh. "Aren't you supposed to be getting something amputated?"

"Shhh." He held up a finger, eyes crinkled at the corners. "Don't break character."

"Sorry," she whispered.

He offered his arm and they strolled out onto the pier. People snapped photos of them as they walked.

"Miss Corntower, I am happy to find you here." His voice was tight, as if it weren't quite true.

She threw him a look and tried to smile.

"I've been wanting to address you for some time."

She frowned, trying to translate the old-fashioned terms into something that made sense.

He paused near a secluded spot and turned to her. "You once said you knew me, Miss Corntower."

"So I did." She searched his face, trying to understand what he was doing.

"I don't believe you were correct." He looked over her shoulder and took a breath. "I don't believe you know everything about me. And I would like very much if I could bare my soul to you, in a way I have not yet been able."

Her eyes went wide. Who was going to bare his soul? Brooks or Owen Hartford?

He reached into his pocket and pulled out a white handkerchief. It was tied in a knot and he worked to loosen it, muttering a few words under his breath. It came undone and he pulled a small, gold ring from the fabric. He knelt down, holding it out. His hand was shaking but his voice was clear.

"I am asking you to be my wife. I want to grow old with you, to raise children with you, to spend every moment of my life being the best of friends with you."

She stared at the ring, speechless. It was her worst nightmare. She was being proposed to by Brooks, and she had to answer as Miss Corntower. She opened her mouth to respond but no words came out.

Panic flared in his eyes. "The ring is etched with forget-me-nots. They're a special flower for you, are they not?"

She nodded, confusion flooding through her. Brooks had gone to the trouble of having a ring made for this playacting scene?

"If you can't give me your answer now, please say I can have some chance to win your heart."

She wanted to say yes but her eyes filled with tears. "I don't understand you people." The cannons boomed behind her. "Battles and amputation and dressing up as people long dead, fine. But this? Isn't this going a bit too far?"

He shot to his feet. "Caroline, I didn't mean it like that."

He reached out for her and she pushed him away. "You never mean it like that, Brooks. Don't you think I have feelings? Don't you think I might take this proposal seriously?"

He put his hands on her face, palms hot against her cheeks, ring still held between a thumb and forefinger. "Caroline, I love you. I've loved you for so long I don't even know when it started. I'm not kidding around." He dragged in a breath. "I proposed like this because I thought it would be easier if we stepped out of our shoes and pretended to be someone else. I never meant that I wasn't serious."

Her lips parted but she couldn't speak. With all the noise behind them, maybe she'd misunderstood, maybe he was still playing some Civil War role in a story she'd never heard.

"Please, Caroline. Tell me I have a chance with you."

She tried not to weep but the tears squeezed out from under her lids. A cannon boomed in the distance. The ships were in position and the main battle had begun. "Brooks, if I haven't said anything, it's because I'm afraid this is all just a big misunderstanding. What about Lauren? Are you Owen Hartfield? Are you proposing to me or to Patience Cornstock?"

He gripped her hands and laughed. "I thought your name was Corntower."

She laughed but it came out in a sob.

"Lauren? I wasn't interested in Lauren. I've known for a long time that she was with Frank, even when you wouldn't believe it." He paused, steadying himself. "Caroline, I've never loved anyone but you. I didn't go about any of this in the right way, so can we pretend this is the first time we've ever tried to talk? Every time I tried to tell you, it got shoved aside by my fears of losing you. Then Frank showed up and I thought I was going to lose my mind over him flirting with you. That kiss was all wrong, but I meant every second of it. Do you think we could try to start over?"

She took a shaky breath. "Oh, boy. This isn't really good timing, is it? I've got a new job, my mom is moving into a condo, and your dad . . ."

He nodded. "I know your mom isn't well, but she's doing better. My dad hasn't had a great year and we have a lot of work to do to take care of both of them. But you're family to me. You're everything I've ever wanted and you were right in front of me all along. I can't give you up, I *won't* give you up."

She walked into his arms, sobbing into his shirt. She gasped for breath. She'd always hated those girls who cried all over their boyfriends but sometimes it just happened that way.

He smothered her with kisses, kissing her eyes and her hair and her cheeks. "Is that a yes, Finley? Will you marry me? I promise to bring you chili-slaw dogs and taste all your terrible cakes and never worry about Absalom being poisoned by your cooking."

She laughed, pure happiness spilling out of her. "Yes to the slaw dogs, but it's okay to keep Absalom from my cake disasters." She gazed up at him, loving every wrinkle, every feature. "I thought I knew you, Professor Elliot. I thought I knew everything about you, and you still surprised me."

He leaned down and kissed her nose. "It happens sometimes."

She closed her eyes, not really hearing the rest of what he murmured against her ear. All she knew was that it echoed everything that was in her heart. He was a surprise. *Love* was a surprise. And a surprise love between friends was the best kind of all.

Dear Reader,

Thank you for reading the second book in this series, Jane Austen Takes the South! *Emma* has always been my favorite of Austen's novels and I couldn't wait to see where our Southern characters went with the story.

As romance novels go, the friends-turned-more story is one of the hardest. There is no lightning-bolt moment, except perhaps at the end. If you can get the reader to that moment, it's all good, right? Austen was brilliant at keeping us entertained until Mr. Knightley got up the guts to profess his love and Emma woke up enough to see he was the only man she ever loved.

Midlands College and Spartainville are purely fictional places, but hold similarities with other small college towns.

I hope you enjoyed meeting Brooks and Caroline (and Absalom). And I hope you enjoy the recipes for Mississippi Mud Pie and Chili-Slaw Dog.

Mary Jane Hathaway

Recipes

Mississippi Mud Pie

Preheat oven to 350 degrees F.

Start with about 40 cookies (chocolate-sandwich type, such as Oreos) and 5 tablespoons of melted butter. Crush the cookies and add the butter, pressing into a pie shell. Put it into the freezer for a bit so it will set.

Combine in a pan and stir until melted:

4 tablespoons butter
6 ounces dark chocolate, chopped
1 tablespoon vanilla extract
2 tablespoons instant espresso powder
¼ cup coffee (brewed)
¼ teaspoon salt

Next:
Separate 6 eggs.

Blend the yolks with ½ cup sugar until foamy, about 4 minutes, then add to the melted chocolate mixture.

Mix the whites with ½ cup sugar, then fold in carefully to the melted chocolate until just combined. Add this to the cookie crust (from your freezer) and bake about 40 minutes. Take it out even if it moves a bit in the middle. That's normal. Let it cool.

Now add ½ cup unsweetened cocoa powder, such as Hershey's, to:

4 ounces dark chocolate
¾ cup sugar
¼ cup cornstarch
¼ teaspoon salt
4 large egg yolks
4 tablespoons butter

Whisk all of these together in a saucepan on a medium heat until it's a thick paste.

Gradually whisk in 2½ cups milk until it boils, stirring constantly. Transfer to a cool bowl and let sit for ten minutes.

Scoop into the cookie crust, refrigerate for 30 minutes and top with whipped topping.

Enjoy!

Chili-Slaw Dog

This is your basic hot dog . . . except it's got all sorts of good stuff piled on top.

Grill a great hot dog. Some people do a kielbasa sort of thing, but I like just a beef hot dog.

Add a good sourdough bun, steamed until hot, but not sloppy, with one side smeared with mustard. You can use stone-ground mustard or the bright yellow stuff.

Add spicy chili. (Homemade is best, but I know we can't have everything! Grab a can of Hormel's, put it in a bowl and stick it in the microwave. There. Chili.)

Top with creamy, sweet coleslaw. Some people (such as my husband) add chopped onion, but I prefer mine traditional.

Enjoy!

Acknowledgments

When I wrote this book, I had the strange feeling of being simultaneously a lonely writer and a member of a wildly enthusiastic Jane Austen Takes the South fan club. Thank you to everyone who commented or messaged me through the Facebook page, offering ideas, support and encouragement. You made every step of the process more fun than it had any right to be. Special thanks to Susan Spears, Julie Hilton Steele (no seersucker!), Christalee Scott May (bless your heart) and many others who offered their time and talents as beta readers. Thank you to the amazing team at Howard Books, specifically my editor Beth Adams, who made this book a million times better by simply asking the right questions. Thank you to assistant editor Katie Sandell, who keeps track of the little details so I can look like I have it all together. Thank you to the Howard Books team members for helping in the publication of this book—all editors, copyeditors, proofreaders and interior and cover designers! Lastly, a huge thank-you to my oldest daughter, Isabel. Without her picture-book-reading expertise, mac-and-cheese-making talent and overall ability to keep little ones happily occupied, I would not have been able to run to my computer when inspiration struck, to insert one of a hundred small details that made this book what it is.

About the Author

Mary Jane Hathaway is the pen name of an award-nominated writer who spends the majority of her literary energy on subjects unrelated to Jane Austen. A homeschooling mother of six young children who rarely wear shoes, she's madly in love with a man who has never read a single Jane Austen novel. She holds degrees in religious studies and theoretical linguistics and has a Jane Austen quote on the back of her van. She can be reached on Facebook at Pride, Prejudice and Cheese Grits.

A Howard Reading Group Guide

Emma, Mr. Knightley and Chili-Slaw Dogs

Mary Jane Hathaway

Introduction

Life doesn't always turn out like you planned. Just ask Caroline Ashley. Convinced she will be a career woman and never marry, she never imagined leaving her dream job as a journalist in D.C. to return to Thorny Hollow to care for her grief-stricken mother after her father's death. Or ask Brooks Elliot. He never intended to see his lifelong friendship with Caroline change in ways that alarmed and confused him. Neither one of them could have planned the unexpected series of circumstances and relationships that set them up to be modern-day actors in Jane Austen's classic story of *Emma*. And no one was more surprised than they were at where the road led them.

Topics & Questions for Discussion

1. What did you enjoy most about *Emma, Mr. Knightley and Chili-Slaw Dogs*? Which character was your favorite? Which one annoyed you the most?

2. On page 8, the narrator of the story says: "Taking care of her [Caroline's] mom had turned into taking the easy way out." Describe what you think the narrator meant by this comment about Caroline. Based on what you learned about Caroline throughout the story, do you agree?

3. One of the themes of the novel is the indirect communication between some of the characters, more specifically between the men and women. What are some of the pros and cons of the indirect style of communication between the various charac-

ters in the novel? What impact does the indirect communication have on their relationships? Do you prefer indirect or direct communication? Why?

4. Compare and contrast Caroline Ashley with Emma Woodhouse in Jane Austen's *Emma.* How are the worlds they inhabit both similar and different?

5. On page 51, Caroline and Brooks argue over their opinions about how men and women view each other. In what ways do each of their actions throughout the story confirm or refute their expressed opinions?

6. Describe how each of their parents' marriage has shaped Caroline's and Brooks's beliefs about marriage. What do they each fear about marriage? In what ways have your beliefs about relationships been shaped by your family relationships?

7. On page 78, the narrator says: "He [Brooks] understood her [Caroline's] unspoken question." Describe the ways that Brooks and Caroline accurately interpret each others' unspoken words and actions as well as ways they misinterpret one another throughout the story. How does their familiarity with one another contribute to their misinterpretations?

8. Why do you think Caroline Ashley takes such an interest in Lexi Martinez and her career choice? On page 95, Caroline says: "You need to follow your heart. God's given you a gift and you shouldn't squander it in accounting classes," and, on page 94, Lexi says: "Finding your calling sounds like some-

thing rich people worry about." Which one do you agree with? What does Caroline's advice reveal about her assumptions about life? How would you have advised Lexi?

9. Compare Brooks Elliot to the character of Mr. Knightley in *Emma*. What do you appreciate the most about Brooks? Did anything annoy you about him?

10. What role does the relationship between Lauren Fairfield and Franklin Keene play in the story? What characters from *Emma* do Lauren and Franklin resemble?

11. What are the various perspectives of marriage presented throughout the story? Contrast these with the perspective of marriage presented in *Emma*. How are marriage and social status related in both stories?

12. How does Caroline's inherited social status inform her assumptions and biases about life and the future? What are some of the catalysts in the story that challenge her assumptions and biases?

13. In what ways does Caroline's relationship with her mother reflect one of Caroline's fatal flaws? Describe the flaw and how it is reflected in other relationships as well. Do you see any growth in Caroline throughout the story?

14. If you could spend an afternoon with one character from this story, who would you choose? Why?

Enhance Your Book Club

1. Watch the movie *Emma*. Compare and contrast the attitudes toward women, marriage and communication reflected in the time periods of the two stories, *Emma* and *Emma, Mr. Knightley and Chili-Slaw Dogs.*

2. Take a field trip and go antiquing. As you look at various items, imagine the stories that brought the item to its current place.

3. Throw a Jane Austen party, inviting people to come dressed up as their favorite Jane Austen character. Serve pink lemonade.

A Conversation with Mary Jane Hathaway

What inspired you to write this story?

Emma by Jane Austen, of course!

Do you have a favorite Jane Austen novel?

I thought it was *Pride and Prejudice*, but after reading and rereading *Emma* so many times for this book, I realized it was much funnier than I remembered. There are lines in the original *Emma* that make me laugh every single time I read them . . . and that is hard to do. I've heard some say that not much of anything happens in *Emma*, but I disagree. I love the heroine, in all her stages, not just the end where she learns to stop trying to make the world bend to her will. I love Mr. Knightley as the family friend, and as hero stuck firmly in the friend zone. I especially love him at the end, when he is brave enough to offer his heart to Emma, even though he doesn't think he has much of a chance.

Do you like chili-slaw dogs and pink lemonade? What inspired you to include them as part of the story?

Funny, I love pink lemonade! I have wonderful memories of pink lemonade at parties in my youth, but it's not a very sophisticated drink. I thought it would be fun to torture Caroline with pink lemonade everywhere she goes.

I've had a chili-slaw dog twice, and it was fine. I'm not a fan of coleslaw so I felt like I was ruining a really good hot dog, though. It's hard to find a food I won't eat, but I might have my slaw on the side next time.

As for why they're in the story, I have a friend who loves to stop at a little stand outside his town in Mississippi and have a chili-slaw dog. He was gracious enough to ask the owner for the exact ingredients, and then I made some here in Oregon. I know, the life of writer is so much work! Eating and talking and writing and eating some more.

Antiques played a central role in this story. Are you an antique collector?

Not at all. I think Austen said it best in *Persuasion*, when she had Mary Elliot Musgrove say, "A lady, without a family, was the very best preserver of furniture in the world." I can have a house full of kids (including four boys under ten) or I can have nice antiques.

But I do love giving new life to old or broken furniture. Every now and then someone will throw out or give away a very old dresser or table or trunk. I really enjoy spending time cleaning, sanding, repainting or staining it, then putting the piece to good use. My oldest kids and I have refurbished a hundred-year-old trunk, and that was a great family project. Lots of time and elbow grease involved, but we learned a lot. The Internet is a global community and we found many sites that offered direction on refurbishing. We found how-to advice, replacements parts and even hobbyists who would examine a photo of your item and tell you the make/year/style. We have another project waiting for good weather so we can do the work outside and not worry about the mess.

Who was your favorite character to develop in this story?

My favorite character was probably Blanche.

What endeared her to you?

I know it's a little cliché to have a crazy old lady/grandma figure, but I loved her spark and her curiosity about everything in the world. She's had her share of grief (losing her husband and her daughter), but she finds the good in every experience. When Brooks mentions the Austen dance, Blanche dives into the planning and puts her own spin on the party.

I think the most annoying character was Frank. I know he's the villain, but I wanted to reach through the page and give him a smack. It's easier to deal with an honest villain than the villain who pretends to be the hero. Frank is charming, funny, exciting and smart. But even when he's turning on the charm, Caroline sees small habits and attitudes that raise red flags. He acts in a way that Brooks never would, because Brooks is a gentleman and Frank is not.

What was the hardest part of writing a story that is patterned after a classic like *Emma*?

I thought I would really struggle with the "friends turn into more" story line but it was so much fun. I had to find little ways to show the reader that Brooks and Caroline were in love, without letting the characters realize it. It seems too obvious to those of us on the outside, but it really needed to take them both by surprise at some point. Of course, that point was different for both Caroline and Brooks, so that was another fun part of the story. Brooks realizes his feelings for Caroline first, while Caroline takes much longer, just like the original Emma.

The hardest part was not stealing every scene that Austen wrote. She had a wonderful eye for setting up a character's emotional state, and I had to work at finding my own places for Caroline and Brooks to interact. Every now and then I would find myself slipping back into the idea of Brooks visiting, the way a man in the Regency period would. Or I would want to write a big dinner scene with a long table filled with delicious food. There are always visits and dinners, but the Regency period included a lot more social entertaining and visiting than we do now in our modern, busy lives. It sounds odd, but I have a Post-it stuck to my laptop screen that says, USE CELL PHONES AND CARS. When I'm in the middle of an Austen story, I want everyone to send letters and walk everywhere!

Would you have enjoyed living during the time period of one of Jane Austen's novels?

I might get my "Austen fan girl" card taken away, but I would say no. Especially as a mom of six, I do like modern medical care. We've never had any real medical emergencies, but I'm grateful that if we do, I won't have to be calling the country doctor to set a bone or watching my kids suffer through diseases we've eradicated.

That said, I adore the dresses and the manners and the dancing! If I could spend half my time there (as a noblewoman, mind you) and half here, I would take that offer in a heartbeat.

What do you enjoy doing for leisure when you're not writing novels?

I like to run marathons. (All my real-life friends just fell over laughing. I actually despise running. I like to watch other people run, though.)

I have a billion projects going at once, it seems. I love to paint, and my laundry room has two eastern-facing windows that make it the perfect spot. I also like to refurbish furniture, although I'm not very good at it and it takes a lot of time. My kids are always interested in some new thing (owls, planes, geology, pirate treasure maps) so we like to take short trips around the area. I've learned a lot from their hobbies, since I was never really interested in birds, aviation or geology, but so far we haven't found any pirate treasure.

Who are some of your literary heroes, other than Jane Austen? What kind of books do you enjoy reading?

Oh, boy. I'm a reader at heart and I'll try to keep this answer short. Just looking at the bookshelf, I'll write down some authors I love (as in, top of the top, and there are many more I love but are for some reason out of sight and I'm too lazy to get up):

Stephen Crane, Louisa May Alcott, St. Teresa of Ávila, Bruce Catton, The Brontës, Franny Billingsley, Nancy Werlin, The Brothers Grimm, Markus Zusak, Willa Cather, Elizabeth Barrett Browning, Aimee Bender, Edna St. Vincent Millay, Erich Maria Remarque, Langston Hughes, Neil Gaiman, Lemony Snicket, Shannon Hale, Holly Black, Laini Taylor, Jonathon Stroud, C. S. Lewis, Scott Westerfeld, James Artemis Owen, Alan Bradley, George Eliot, Harriet Beecher Stowe, Helen Simonson, Lois Duncan.

And now you know that my shelves are completely disorganized.

As a writer, did you identify with Caroline's season of seeming disappearance from her career as a journalist?

Absolutely. After college I attended the Warsaw School of Economics. I had studied years of Eastern European languages (Polish, Russian, Ukrainian, Bulgarian, Old Church Slavonic). When I came back to Oregon, I thought it was a temporary stop on my way somewhere exotic. I met my husband, a Mexican immigrant working in a local factory, and decided to stay just a little longer in this small town. It's not quite the same as what happened to Caroline, since her decision to return home (and stay) was more about taking care of her family, but I know her journey.

Have you ever had a season when you let go of your writing in order to care for other priorities in your life?

> I started writing in 2009, so I suppose I could say this doesn't apply to me. But I could also say, "every single day." Like any working parent, I have to make choices about when and where I work, and how to balance my home life. It's easy to get caught up in e-mail or little projects or promotions or even jotting down ideas. But as it says in Ecclesiastes 3 (KJV), "To every thing there is a season, and a time to every purpose under the heaven." No matter if it's during one day or days of the week or times of the year, I have to let go of my writing and care for my family. And I'm happy to do so!

How have you gained so much knowledge about the design of Southern antebellum homes?

> Um . . . Google? Really, there is so much information available now that I could spend hours of writing time every day just reading about these old homes. I have two small books about antebellum and Civil War–era structures, but it's wonderful to be able to take virtual tours of some of these historic landmarks.

What can we expect from you next?

> I thought the next book would be based on *Sense and Sensibility*, but even though I have five chapters already written, I may just be heading toward *Northanger Abbey*! It seems Henry Tilney has quite a fan club, and I get messages every week hoping that Henry is the next "Austen Takes the South" hero. I had no idea that he was so high on the list of

favorite Austen heroes, but when I reread the book, I see why. Henry is witty, sensitive, wry, noble, and chooses the woman he loves over his fortune. There's a gripping love triangle, feuding friends, bad influences, money grubbers, lots of flirting and broken engagements. In the middle of it all are Catherine, a girl who expects life to mirror all her favorite novels, and our hero Henry.

Unless I get a sudden surge of requests for *Sense and Sensibility*, it looks like like *Northanger Abbey* will find a new home in Mississippi!

Keep reading for a sneak peek at Book 3 of
the Jane Austen Takes the South series:

Persuasion, Captain Wentworth and Cracklin' Cornbread

Coming soon in 2014!

No: the years which had destroyed her youth and bloom had only given him a more glowing, manly, open look, in no respect lessening his personal advantages. She had seen the same Frederick Wentworth.

—ANNE ELLIOTT

CHAPTER ONE

"This is an effort to collect a debt. Any information obtained will be used for that purpose."

Lucy Crawford leaned her forehead against the wall and closed her eyes. The mechanical voice droned on, rattling through an 800 number and requesting a call back. The time stamp was an hour ago. There was a brief pause, and the next message began:

"This call is for William Crawford. I am a debt collector and this is an effort to collect a debt. Any information—"

Lucy reached out and punched the skip button. The message machine flashed three more calls in the queue. She didn't know if she could listen to them all at one time. It was too depressing, like watching the recap of the Georgia Bulldogs falling to Alabama by thirty points, over and over again. Except that there was always next year for her favorite football team, and there wasn't any end in sight to her daddy's financial issues.

Skip. Skip. Skip. Maybe all the calls were from the same creditor, but probably not. Lucy heaved herself upright and trudged into the foyer. She might as well get the mail now while she was already feeling low. The black-and-white tile expanse of the entrance area gleamed dully in the summer light shining through the leaded panes of the double doors. In all of her thirty years, she had never seen them so scuffed. Old Zeke polished the floors of every room in the house once a week, and always spent extra time on the entrance. He was proud of his job and being part of keeping up the historic Crawford House. Or at least he had been, until Lucy had fired him.

She paused in front of the side table where a five-inch stack of bills waited. The conversation with Zeke flashed through her mind, and she felt the unfamiliar burn of tears. She wasn't a crier. When she sat Zeke down, she had done well, speaking clearly and confidently until he had bowed his head in defeat. The defeat in his posture was like a stab of hot iron in her heart. Zeke had always seemed larger than his five-foot-five frame, probably because Lucy remembered being very little, pulling on his pant leg and looking far, far up to the Crawford House handyman. He was like family, and she was telling him he wasn't going to be part of their daily lives any longer.

And then he had glanced up, black eyes still bright despite his seventy-five years. "Miss Lucy, I know'd this time be coming. I's not as strong as I once was."

She wanted to drop to her knees, wrap her arms around his fragile shoulders and cry like a little girl. She wanted to cry like the time she'd lost her dolly down the irrigation pipe in the back pasture, before Zeke had retrieved it for her. Like the time her own heart had broken into tiny pieces and he sat beside her, patting her shoulder and whispering, "There, there" until she fell asleep, soggy and exhausted.

But she didn't do that. Instead Lucy had explained, again, about the debts and the reverse mortgage and the repairs they couldn't afford. Only, no matter what she'd said about bills and bankruptcy and foreclosure, old Zeke hadn't quite seemed convinced. The memory of it was so strong, she felt chilled, even standing in the stifling air of the foyer. Lucy reached out and grabbed up the pile of envelopes, not even bothering to glance at the addresses. They wouldn't be able to pay them, or any new ones that would have come in.

"Honey, is that you?" Her daddy's rich baritone echoed through the large entrance hall. Seconds later he appeared around the corner, dressed in a perfectly pressed pair of yellow-and-green plaid golf pants, Ralph Lauren polo shirt casually unbuttoned at the neck. Willy Crawford's close-cropped hair was still black but for a bit of gray at each temple, and for a man of sixty, he was still lean and fit. "I'm headed to the club for quick round with Theon James."

Lucy winced inside. Theon James excelled in three things: golf, business and goading her daddy into spending money to keep up his reputation as the richest man in town. She suspected Theon was playing a game, enjoying how easy it was to convince Will Crawford that it was time to get a newer car or take a month-long vacation to St. Simon's Island.

"Will you be home for lunch? I have a casserole in the oven I think you'd really like, Daddy."

He cocked an eyebrow. "Does it have any meat in it?"

She was tempted to lie. Really, he acted as if vegetarian cooking was poison. "No, but the eggplant tastes just like—"

"Nah." He pulled on a matching green-and-yellow plaid golfer's cap and shouldered his bag. "You know I don't like that sort of thing. Put some ham in it next time. And don't say I always want meat, because I eat some of that vegetarian food, too. Your mama was a great cook. Her beignets were so light and fluffy, fried just right, a good bit of powdered sugar on top . . ." He paused, a small smile on his face. Lucy knew just what he felt. Sweet memories were all they had left of her mama.

"Before you go," she started to say, holding out the mail, but he cut her off.

"No time now, sugar. Theon's already there." Her daddy leaned in and gave her a quick kiss on the head, leaving a whiff of Old Spice and cigars.

"It's just I thought you were going to sort through some of these on Sunday after church, but you went out to lunch. We need to see if there were a few we could pay off right away. It would save a lot on interest in the long run and . . ." He wasn't listening to her.

"Don't be disrespectful." His face was stiff with anger. "I didn't raise you like that."

Lucy dropped her gaze to the floor. When she was little, her daddy had heard her mouth off to her mama. He hadn't used the switch on her, like she'd thought he would. He sat her on his knee and explained he could forgive a lot of sins, but he could never love a stubborn, strong-willed girl. She'd apologized to her mama and tried her very best to be a good girl ever since. She was a grown woman now, but Lucy still couldn't seem balance on that fence between gentle coaxing and shrewish nagging.

"I didn't mean to offend, Daddy."

Bending over his golf bag, he rummaged inside. "Anyway, when I get back, I'll take care of it. And there's no *we* about payin' these bills. I've got the money, just need to cash out a few old savings accounts and I'll be settled up with those people."

Lucy almost sighed out loud. *Those people*. Her daddy always drew a thick black line between their family and the rest of the world. If she tried to suggest that they were close to bankruptcy, he would point out how the Crawfords had owned the finest home in Brice's Crossroads, Mississippi, since right after the Civil War had ended, or how his great-granddaddy had founded the area's first African American business league, or how the Crawfords had attended Harvard before the Roosevelts. The Crawfords were good stock. They were on the boards of hospitals, joined exclusive clubs, were admired by everyone. They didn't have financial issues, and they certainly didn't worry out loud about it if they did.

"Some of these are probably Paulette's," Lucy said. "You've got to get those credit cards from her. She's got closets full of designer clothes and she just buys more."

"Your sister is a fine lookin' woman in search of a husband. I won't be interferin' with that." He winked at her.

"But Janessa managed to get a husband without spending sprees in Atlanta." She crossed her arms over her chest. Her oldest sister had many faults, but being a fashionista wasn't one of them.

"You leave Paulette be. She's not like you. She's still young and hasn't given up on men. I don't mind her spending a bit to make herself look presentable. It's part of keeping up appearances. She certainly doesn't want to live in her daddy's house the rest of her days." His voice was light, but there was a warning in his eyes.

Did he think she'd given up on men? She swallowed past the hurt of his words and said, "Alrighty, as soon as you get back, let's go over these bills together. Mama's not here, and you need to keep track of these things."

The door was already closing on the end of her sentence, and

Lucy listened to him cross the wide wooden porch, his footfalls fading with each step toward his shiny red Miata. She sagged against the side table and resisted the urge to throw the whole stack of letters against the door. He wasn't listening. She had done everything possible to keep the bank from foreclosing on the house, but it was only a matter of time before they lost everything. Her mama had been so good at managing the household finances. Maybe too good. Her daddy had been happy to turn it all over to her and focus on his golf game. He was the face of Crawford Investments, but her mama had been the brains. And when she passed, her daddy just pretended like nothing had changed, creating chaos at home and disaster for the business.

Just the thought of Mama gave Lucy a sharp pain, even though it had been close to nine years now she'd been gone. One early morning she'd collapsed in the kitchen, and Lucy's life had changed forever.

Lucy breathed a prayer of thanksgiving for the time they'd had together, all the way through her teens. She used to love sitting in the bright blue kitchen and watching her Mama cook. Their housekeeper, Mrs. Lawry, made perfectly fine meals, but her Mama wasn't happy if she didn't mix up a batch of gumbo or hush puppies once in a while. Straight from Cane River, she spoke with the lyrical accent of a native Creole speaker and had eyes the color of Kentucky bluegrass. She liked to sing, all the time, and it was like having a radio you could never turn off. Gospel hymns, blues, low country ballads. The house was so quiet without her. Lucy had the dark eyes and skin of her daddy, but her curves and throaty laugh were all her mama's doing.

She still had the curves, but it had been months since she'd heard herself laugh.

A rap at the door sounded like a gunshot in the quiet foyer.

Lucy hesitated, wondering if bill collectors ever came to the door in their "attempts to collect a debt." Peeking through the beveled glass, she let out a breath. When trouble comes, family arrives close behind, for better or for worse.

"Auntie," she said, swinging the door wide.

Aunt Olympia held out both hands and stuck out her lower lip. "Oh, honey, come here." She gripped Lucy's hands and hauled herself over the threshold like a shipwreck victim grabbing hold of a life raft.

"You got my message," Lucy said into her aunt's elaborately braided updo. She was being squeezed and rocked from side to side, and her words sounded like she was running.

"Yes, bless your heart. And I've been busy solving your problems," she said. Letting go of Lucy, she shut the door behind her and started toward the kitchen. "Come, let me tell you all about it over a little sweet tea."

She knew better than to laugh. There was no way Aunt Olympia could have solved anything in the hours since Lucy had called, giving the dire news of impending foreclosure. Instead, Lucy trailed along behind her, wondering how such a tiny woman could exude such force. Where Olympia went, everyone followed.

"Aren't you supposed to be at the museum today?" her aunt called over one shoulder as she swept past the staircase. Of course she would have noticed her jeans and T-shirt ensemble right away. Her aunt didn't believe in casual clothes. Her neon-green tracksuit said JUICY on the rear, and her earrings bounced with every movement. She was all fancy, all the time.

"They closed for maintenance. And it's an interpretive center, not a museum." She didn't want to talk about her job. Aunt Olympia would say she should have a better position, maybe something with a fancy title and a yearly bonus.

"Which means what? Cleaning?" Aunt Olympia moved around the cheery kitchen, reaching into the fridge for the pitcher of tea.

Lucy dropped into a chair. "Yes. Cleaning." Maintenance made it sound as if the center might get a new roof or any of the other desperately needed items on her list. But upgrading access to a Civil War battlefield site wasn't high on the list of popular causes in Tupelo.

"I don't know why you work over there. You probably are only gettin' the people who wander through from the Elvis museum."

She said nothing. It was a sad fact that if Elvis had been born in Brice's Crossroads, they'd have an event center with a full kitchen, green rooms and a theater—not to mention a chapel and a gift shop with its own apparel line.

"Hun, you need to find yourself a better job. Iola is working on the top floor of a smoked glass high-rise in Atlanta. She wears the prettiest outfits and has a whole closet for her shoes. She says—"

"I know," Lucy interrupted, unable to stand one more rendition of Iola's happiness at being a secretary for a group of slick lawyers in pinstripe suits.

"I know," she said more slowly. "But working at the center is perfect for me, Auntie. I love this area, these people. If I could have majored in the history of Tupelo, Mississippi, I would have. Being curator doesn't come with fame or glory, but it makes me happy."

Aunt Olympia's frown softened into a sigh. "You deserve a little happiness, that's for sure."

Lucy wondered for a moment if she meant because of the way Lucy's Mama had passed away so suddenly, or if she was talking about another time, long before. An image of a laughing, blond-haired boy flashed through her mind, and she shoved it away. Her present was bad enough without wallowing in the past.

Her aunt glanced in the oven, frowning. "Is that lasagna? You know your daddy doesn't like ethnic dishes."

"It's baked ziti, and he's already taken a pass."

"Oh, honey, you need to learn how to cook. You're never going to catch a man with that kind of food." Aunt Olympia shook her head, as if knowing the perfect fried chicken recipe would resolve Lucy's single status.

She didn't want the conversation to veer off into marriage talk. "What sort of plan did you come up with for the house?"

"I've got a sure-fire idea to get you all out of this mess," Aunt Olympia said, taking a sip of tea. A bright smear of orange lipstick decorated the rim of her glass.

Sure-fire. That couldn't be good. Aunt Olympia had flair, beauty, style and one of the finest Southern mansions in the state, but she had about the same amount of business sense as Lucy's daddy. She knew how to spend money, not make it.

She leaned forward, resting her hand on Lucy's. Her long nails were sunset orange with tiny black palm trees. "I called my friend Pearly Mae and she—"

Letting out a groan, Lucy slumped in the chair. "Oh, boy."

Aunt Olympia paused, lips a thin line. "You can make all the fun you want, but Pearly Mae knows everything about everyone."

"Now she knows everything about us, too."

"Yes, well, that's part of the bargain, isn't it? You tell her what you need, and she tries to help out."

"While calling every friend of hers on the way." Lucy had just enough pride left to be horrified at the idea of her family troubles being spread around town.

Ignoring that last comment, she went on. "She heard that the Free Clinic of Tupelo needed a new space. They got a big grant from the state to upgrade all their equipment, but the place over on Yancey Avenue is too little for all their clientele. Crawford House has thirteen rooms and . . ."

Lucy held up a hand, eyes closed. "Wait, now. Wait just a minute here."

"I know you think they'll destroy the place," her aunt said. "But they won't make any significant changes, and you all can still live here, too."

She cracked an eye and stared at her. "Live here. With the Free Clinic of Tupelo." She wasn't sure which was worse: the idea of Crawford House being rented out as a medical facility or living in what would amount to a waiting room for sick people.

"You wouldn't have to interact with them at all, of course. You and Willy keep the front part of the house and the library, sitting room, kitchen and your bedrooms. The back part could be turned into a waiting area and consultation rooms."

Something about her aunt's wording rang a warning bell. "You've already been talking to someone about this? Someone other than Pearly Mae?"

"Lucy, it happened so fast, it must be God's will." She sat forward beaming. "And Dr. Stroud says he knows you. Last Christmas he was here with his wife at Crawford House's annual party, and you two stood by the punch bowl half the night, chatting about battlefield amputations."

Lucy remembered Dr. Stroud. Bushy white mustache, bow tie, seersucker suit. She'd figured he was retired and no longer practicing medicine because he seemed to spend all his time on Civil War collections and reenactments. He'd said that he was surprised the African American community wasn't more involved with Brice's Roads Crossing since half the Union dead were part of Bouton's Brigade of United States Colored Troops, and then he'd tried to recruit her for the next battle. She'd wavered under his charm, but the idea of battling mosquitos in five layers of Civil War dress made it easy to say no.

She chewed the inside of her lip. If Aunt Olympia had named any other person in the area, she would never think of agreeing, but Dr. Stroud understood the history of a place like Crawford House. He wouldn't be setting his coffee cup on the hundred-year-old white-oak fireplace mantel from Philadelphia, or hanging his coat from the cast-iron wall sconces.

"How much will they pay? And what are the terms of the lease?"

"See, I knew you would agree," Aunt Olympia said. "It's enough that you can pay off that mortgage in a few years. They'll be over in about fifteen minutes. I told him to give me a little time to get you comfy with the idea."

"I'm not agreeing to anything. Daddy's not even here to make a decision." Lucy stood up, glancing around the kitchen. Mrs. Lawry only came on Tuesdays and Thursdays now. There were dishes in the sink, the counters had crumbs and her daddy's coffee mugs dotted the drain board.

As if following her train of thought, Aunt Olympia wandered to the sink and stood in front of it, blocking the view of the mess. "Honey, I can convince Willy to do what's right. I'm more worried about getting you on board. This is the best thing that could have happened. You won't have to move, Willy can get out of debt and the house will be used for something other than gathering dust. Plus, I know Paulette is counting on having a big fancy wedding as soon as she finds her man."

Lucy leaned around her aunt and held a dishrag under the

faucet, saying nothing. She wasn't agreeing to this so that Paulette could have the wedding of the year when she finally chose between all her boyfriends.

"There is one small detail I should mention." The tone of forced cheerfulness in her aunt's voice made Lucy pause.

She turned, wet rag in one hand. "What? Will they put a sign on the front of the house? Install bars on the windows?"

"I'm not sure about any of that." Aunt Olympia's cheeks turned darker and the sight filled her with dread. Her aunt was never embarrassed. It was practically impossible to shame the woman. She firmly believed she was in the right at all times.

When Lucy didn't respond, her aunt hurried on. "They're bringing in a new doctor. He's part of The Rural Physician's Scholarship Program, and now that he's graduated, he's coming back to practice in a rural community so he can erase his school debt."

Lucy reached out for the back of the kitchen chair. She could hardly feel the smooth wooden top rail under her hand. *Please, Lord. Not him.* The kitchen had turned small, her aunt's voice fading away. A flash of a crooked smile, blond hair tousled from the wind, a gentle voice, the warmth of large hands against her back.

"Honestly, it's not a big deal." Aunt Olympia let out a sigh as if her niece was being difficult.

"Who is it?" Even as she asked the question, Lucy knew the answer. Her aunt wouldn't have saved this point for last if it wasn't important.

"Jeremiah Chevy." Her aunt reached out to pat her hand, changed her mind when she saw the wet rag clenched in one of Lucy's fists. "You'll be fine. It's been a long time. Ten years almost. It was the right thing to do and you know it. First of all, that name. Did you really want to be Mrs. Chevy?"

Lucy slid into a chair. *Mrs. Chevy.* She'd actually practiced that name on the inside cover of her school notebooks, over and over in her best handwriting. *Mrs. Lucy Crawford Chevy.*

Her aunt waved a hand, as if the concept had let off a terrible smell. "Can you imagine? It was insanity, being engaged at eighteen to a boy like that."

"Like what, Auntie?" Lucy could hear the trembling in her voice. She didn't know if it was from shock or fury or both. "White? Poor? Or was it that Jem has a teen dropout for a mama?"

"Well, sure, all of those things." She wasn't embarrassed now. "It never would have worked. He didn't even know if he could get into college. I don't know how he got through medical school, and he must have mountains of debt. Probably in the hundreds of thousands."

Lucy stared at her aunt, wondering if the woman honestly believed medical school debt was any worse than what her daddy had accrued with bad investments and lavish vacations.

"He had nothing but his daddy's name, which he couldn't trade for beans. And if you thought your mama would have been happy with you marrying a white boy, you're wrong," her aunt said.

Lucy felt her throat close up. Had her mama been a racist? She hadn't said much at the time, not about his color. "Mama had green eyes. Someone somewhere didn't care about color," she whispered.

"Oh, don't start with that. You know better." Her aunt's face was stony. "There's no chance those pretty eyes came from a mixed couple in love a hundred years ago. Somebody knew the story but didn't want to pass it down, and that tells us enough right there."

Lucy dropped her chin to her chest. The news had sucked every logical thought from her head. Oh, the irony was laughable. She'd been persuaded to break it off with him because she was wealthy, black, and guaranteed a good job after being accepted to Harvard. Only one of those things was still true.

The doorbell sounded dimly in the distance.

"Oh, there they are," her aunt said, jumping to her feet.

Lucy's stomach turned to ice. "They?"

"Dr. Stroud and Jem. I can show them around if you want. I know you didn't get a chance to put on anything nice." She paused, cocking her head. "And you haven't been to the hair dressers in too long. You need one of those coconut oil treatments under the hair dryer and maybe some extensions. You're hardly fit to entertain guests. You just stay in the kitchen, hear?"

She sat frozen to the spot as Aunt Olympia swayed out the doorway. She would have given anything in the world to rewind the last ten minutes and keep this from happening. She would have called them, told them it wouldn't work, made some excuse, any excuse.

Deep voices carried faintly to her, and she wanted to clap her hands over her ears. She hadn't heard anything from Jem in ten years. Not an e-mail, not a text. Completely understandable, really. Once they had been the best of friends, finishing each other's sentences and talking for hours into the night. And love, there had always been love. She never let herself think of it, but now, in a flash, she remembered clearly the overwhelming need to be near him, to touch him. He was like air to her then, and she couldn't live without him.

And yet, she had. When her aunt convinced her it would never work out, she had stood on his rickety front porch and told him she had decided it was better if they saw other people. It was such a stupid thing to say, something she copied from a TV show about teenagers who swapped boyfriends like shoes. There were no other people to see, no one else she wanted, then or after. The memory of the shock and hurt on Jem's face haunted her dreams, stole her appetite, gnawed away at her peace of mind. By the time she reached her breaking point months later, he was gone. There was nothing for her to do but sleep in the proverbial bed she had made.

The kitchen was silent except for the sound of her own breathing. Time seemed suspended, as if the world was waiting on her next move.

Lucy ran a hand over her hair, feeling the slight frizz at her hairline, the dryness at the ends. She wasn't wearing much makeup, had only a pair of simple pearl studs in her ears. She glanced down, taking in her battered running shoes, straight-leg jeans, last year's marathon T-shirt that had a tiny hole at the hem. When she'd known Jem, she'd put in about the same amount of time on her appearance as any wealthy teenage girl. But after he'd gone, there wasn't any reason to get her nails done or a facial at her favorite spa. She'd thrown herself into her studies and done her best to keep her mind off her heartache. This was who she was now. Putting off this meeting until she made it to the hairdresser's implied that anything could be changed. She heaved herself to her feet. There was no choice except to walk in there like the grown woman she was, and welcome them into her home. *Please give me strength*, she whispered. And it would be nice if she didn't trip, stutter or blush.

The hallway seemed to take hours, but finally she reached the end, emerging into the foyer. Her gaze landed on Dr. Stroud first, as he swept an arm out toward the seating in the entryway. He was saying something about the Civil War–era sewing bench and square nails.

Lucy tried to focus on Dr. Stroud, but her attention was pulled, against her will, to Jem. He was half turned away, looking out the large windows onto the rose garden. At first glance, it was surreal to see him standing there in her house, as if ten years hadn't passed. But a closer look gave a hint to the years in between. Wearing a charcoal gray suit that fit him well, his hands were at his sides. He was taller than she remembered. Bulkier around the shoulders, more heft and muscle. As a teen he had always managed to get his feet tied up in chair legs or trip over wrinkles in the carpet or bump his head on a low doorframe. He had changed, but was still the same, so much the same that she could have recognized him from the back. The muscles under his jacket tensed, and she knew that he would turn and see her. The moment before their eyes met, Lucy felt as if she were dangling off this side of a cliff, holding on to one slim branch as it bent toward the ground. If he let on, in any way, with a smirk or a glint of laughter, what a humorous reversal of fortune this was, she didn't think she would survive.

He met her gaze steadily. There was no emotion on his face. It was as if they didn't know each other at all. His blond hair still stick straight, brows two shades darker, the long nose he inherited from his mom's side, the blue eyes from his dad's Irish grandparents. She looked at him, not able to think of a word to say. She wanted to catalog his features, to spend hours noting every tiny difference from ten years ago. But he wasn't hers and hadn't been for a long time. He might even be married and have kids.

"Oh, here you are. Miss Lucy Crawford, let me introduce my colleague, Dr. Jeremiah Chevy. He's just completed his residency at Boston General, focusing on pediatrics." Dr. Stroud beckoned her forward, bushy mustache twitching with excitement. "He's also quite a fan of our local history. You might have crossed paths, with being the curator over at Brice's Crossroads."

"We've met before," he said casually. "Nice to see you again."

She nodded. "And you." He'd already looked away, gazing up at the high ceiling and the brass chandelier, probably noticing how shabby the ornate ceiling medallion looked, small bits of paint flaking off at the curves of the motif. Her chance was long gone, and he was only a stranger now. Worse than a stranger. They could never be friends.

"Excellent. Then we're all introduced and we can talk about the future of the Free Clinic." Dr. Stroud clapped his hands together. "Miss Lucy, will you lead the way?"

She tried to look as if her pulse wasn't pounding in her ears. "My aunt said you'd like to look at the back of the house, near the former servant's quarters?"

"Let's start there. If the rooms are big enough, we can make the examination rooms." Dr. Stroud glanced around. "What a magnificent old place. Your family must be incredibly proud."

Proud. She cringed at the word. If they had been proud, her daddy would have made sure that their home was safe, instead of adding reverse mortgage after reverse mortgage on the old place. There was no bank in the state that would forgive that kind of debt just because it was a Civil War–era home. They didn't care that Great Granddaddy Whittaker had brought that pie safe all the way from Philadelphia or that Grandmama Honor had hand-picked the wallpaper. Family history didn't matter to a big bank, and if her daddy had been truly proud, then he would have been more careful.

"Follow me back, then." She turned and crossed the foyer, knowing she would do whatever it took to save her home, but wishing with all her heart that this day had never come.